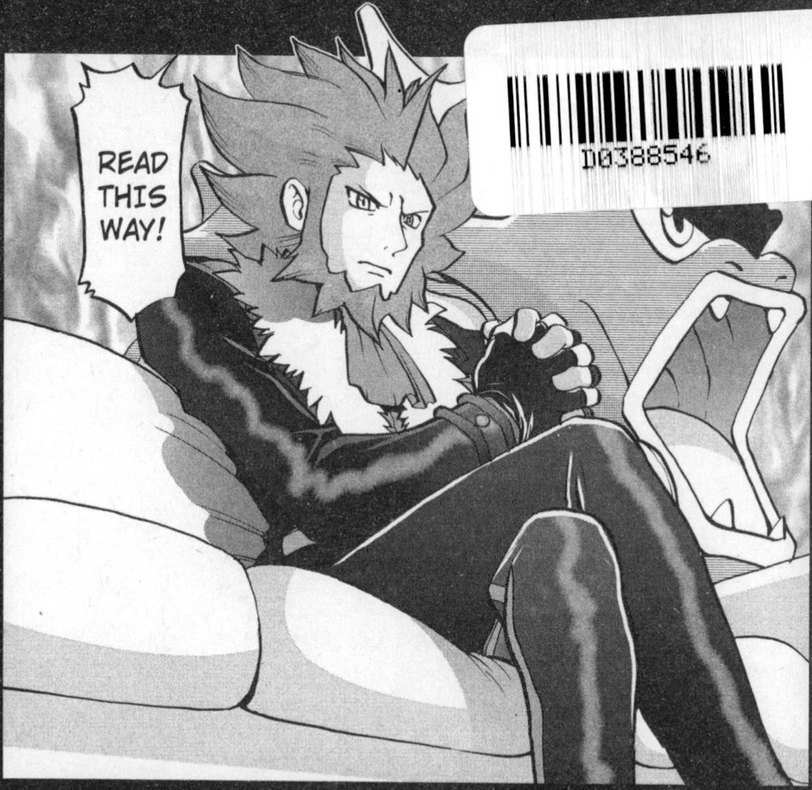
READ THIS WAY!



## THIS IS THE END OF THIS GRAPHIC NOVEL!

To properly enjoy this VIZ Media graphic novel, please turn it around and begin reading from right to left.

This book has been printed in the original Japanese format in order to preserve the orientation of the original artwork.

Have fun with it!

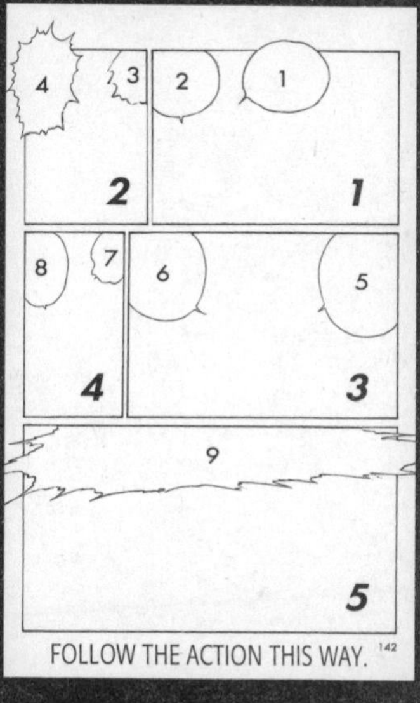
1
2
3
4
5
FOLLOW THE ACTION THIS WAY.

# POKÉMON™

## SWORD & SHIELD

Story by
Hidenori Kusaka

Art by
Satoshi Yamamoto

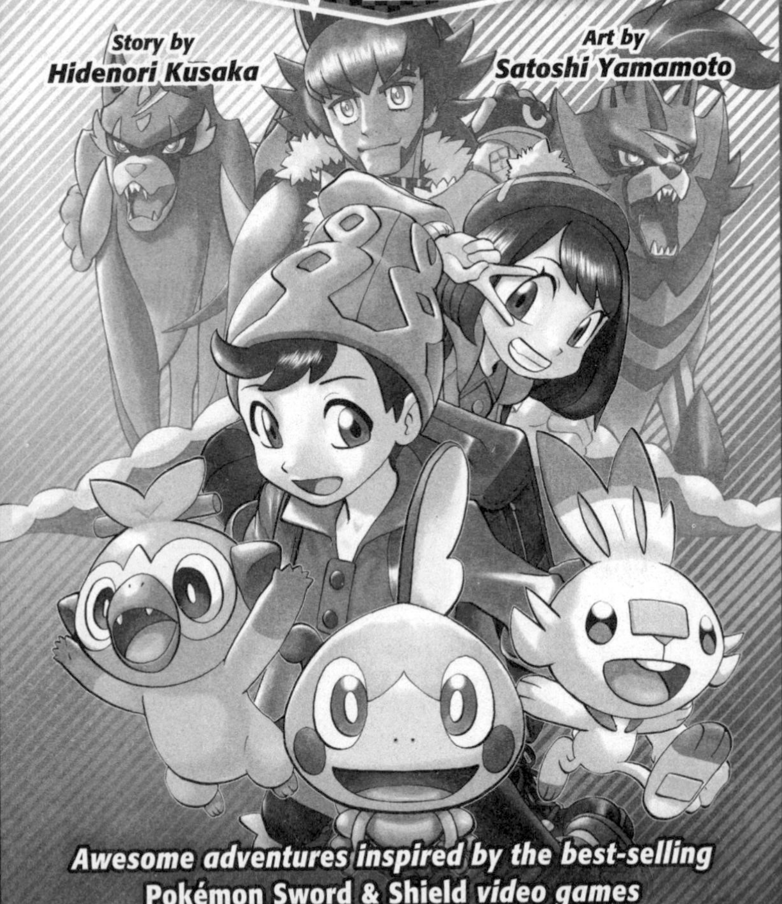

**Awesome adventures inspired by the best-selling Pokémon Sword & Shield video games set in the Galar region!**

POKÉMON™

ADVENTURES

X·Y

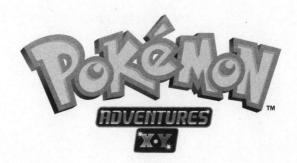

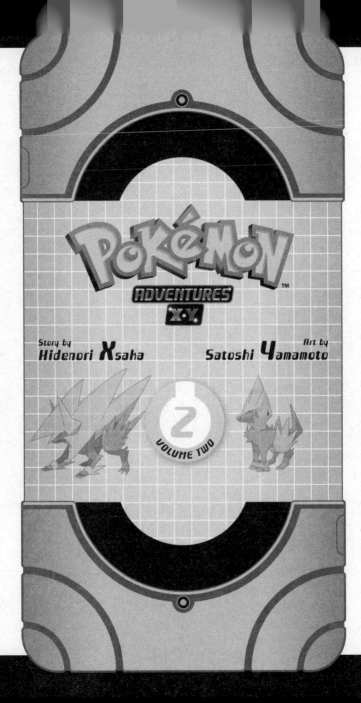

# Pokémon™ Adventures X·Y

Story by
Hidenori Xsaka

Art by
Satoshi Yamamoto

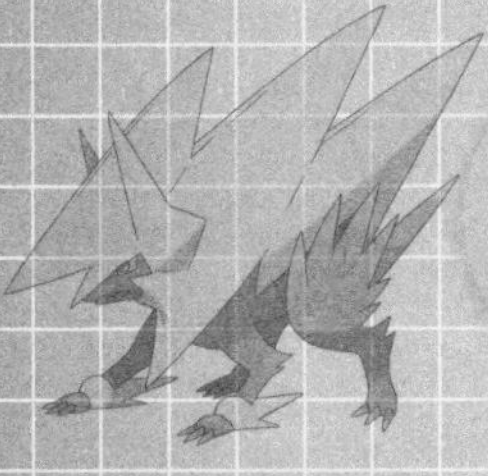

2
VOLUME TWO

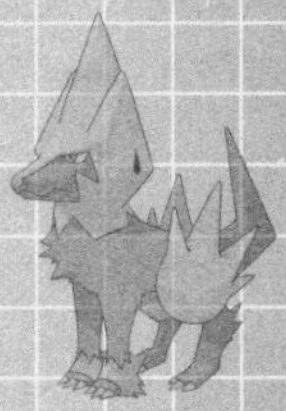

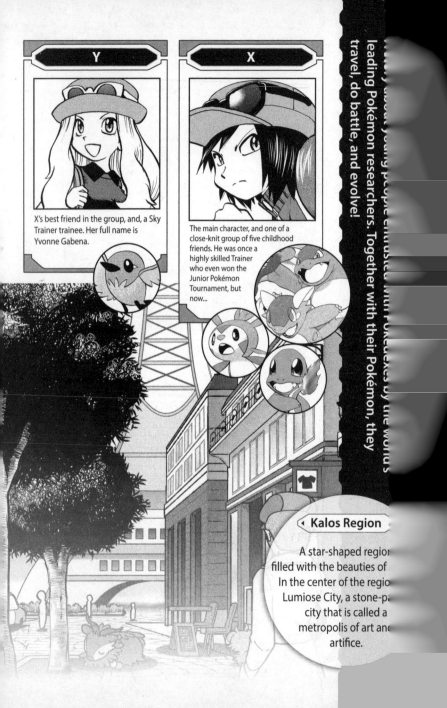

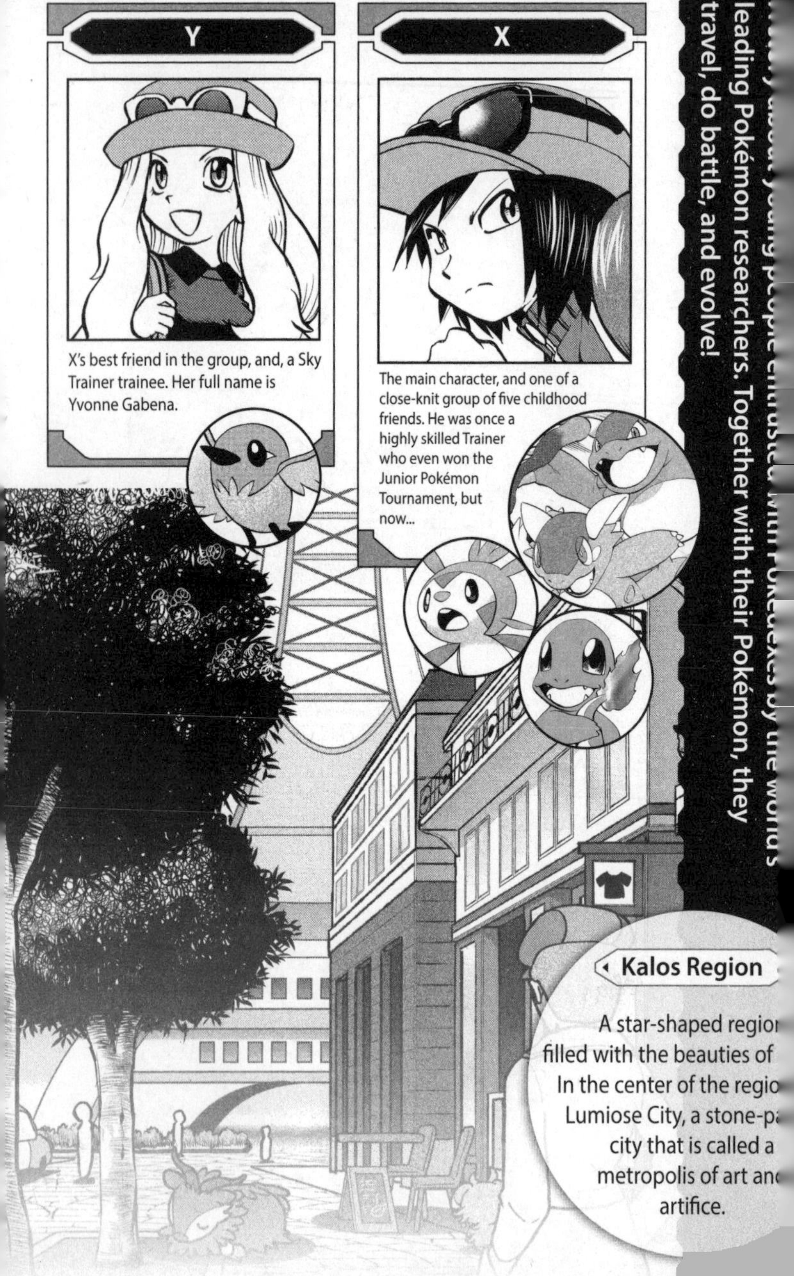
leading Pokémon researchers. Together with their Pokémon, they
travel, do battle, and evolve!
X
The main character, and one of a close-knit group of five childhood friends. He was once a highly skilled Trainer who even won the Junior Pokémon Tournament, but now...
Y
X's best friend in the group, and, a Sky Trainer trainee. Her full name is Yvonne Gabena.
Kalos Region
A star-shaped regio
filled with the beauties of
In the center of the regio
Lumiose City, a stone-pa
city that is called a
metropolis of art anc
artifice.

## THE STORY THUS FAR

The Kalos region, Vaniville Town—four close childhood friends are trying to get the reclusive X out of his room when the legendary Pokémon Yveltal and Xerneas suddenly appear. Then they are all attacked by a mysterious group wearing red suits who try to steal the Mega Ring that X wears on his arm like a bracelet. After escaping, the five friends embark on a journey and discover that the name of the red-suited organization is Team Flare. One of the friends, Shauna, gets mind controlled by a Team Flare scientist, Celosia, but they manage to stop Shauna when she attacks, saving her from Celosia's control. The five friends then move on to Lumiose City, where Professor Sycamore's lab is located. There, they meet Lysandre, a mystery man with a secret agenda!

### Shauna

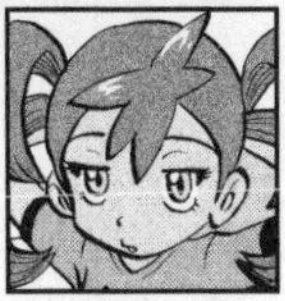

One of the five childhood friends. Her dream is to become a Furfrou Groomer. She is quick to speak her mind.

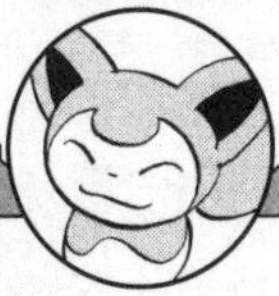

### Tierno

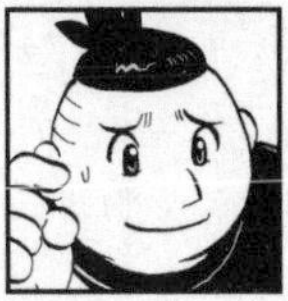

One of the five childhood friends. A big boy with an even bigger heart. He is currently training to become a dancer.

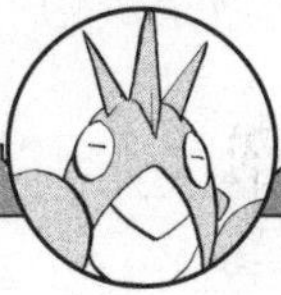

### Trevor

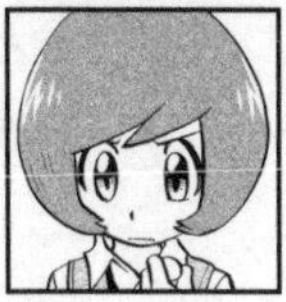

One of the five childhood friends. A quiet boy who hopes to become a Pokémon Researcher one day.

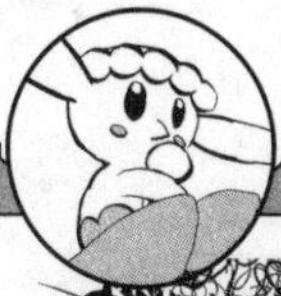

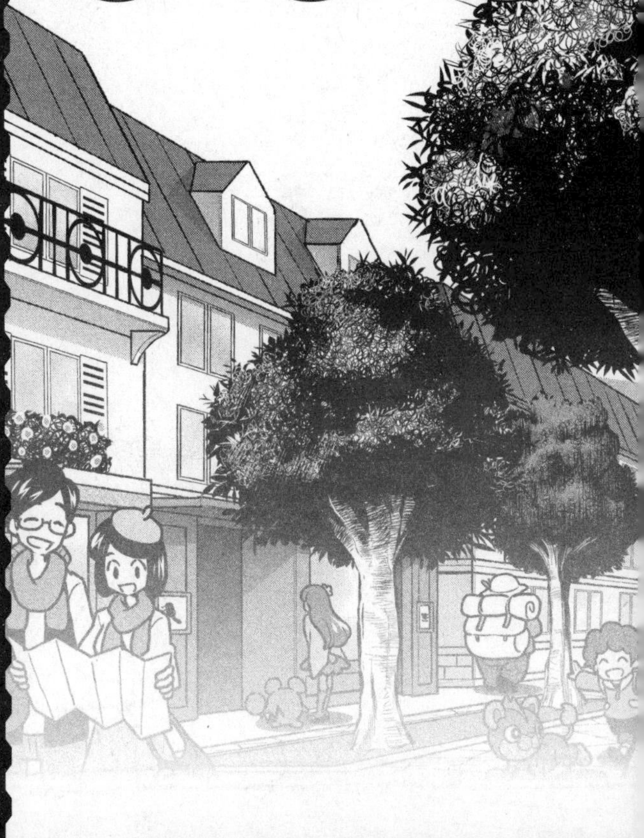

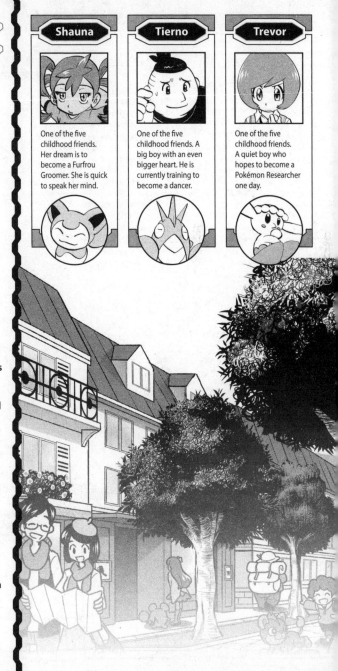

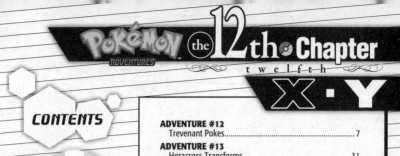

# Pokémon ADVENTURES · the 12th Chapter · twelfth · X·Y

## CONTENTS

### VOLUME TWO

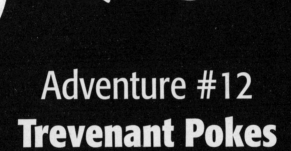

# Adventure #12
# Trevenant Pokes

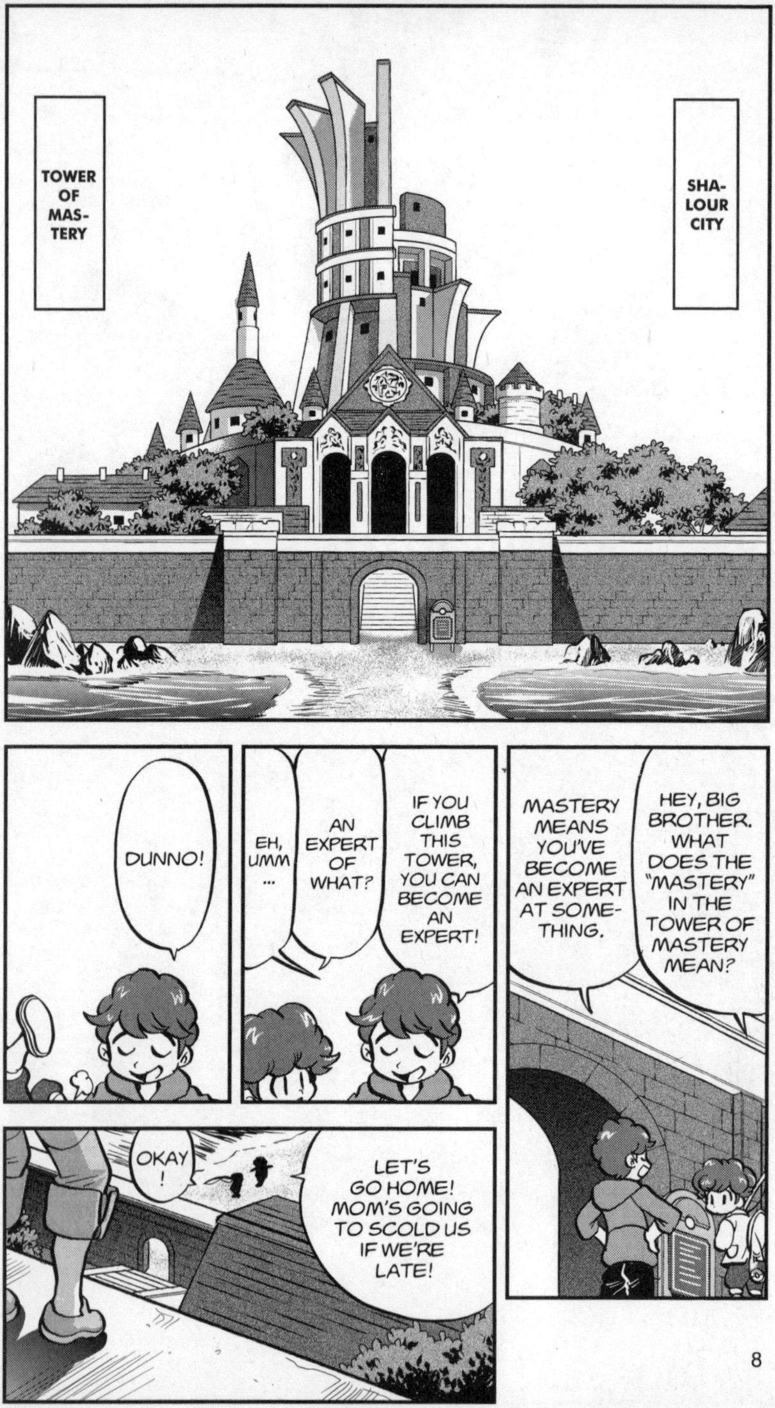
SHA-LOUR CITY
TOWER OF MAS-TERY
HEY, BIG BROTHER. WHAT DOES THE "MASTERY" IN THE TOWER OF MASTERY MEAN?
MASTERY MEANS YOU'VE BECOME AN EXPERT AT SOME-THING.
IF YOU CLIMB THIS TOWER, YOU CAN BECOME AN EXPERT!
AN EXPERT OF WHAT?
EH, UMM ...
DUNNO!
LET'S GO HOME! MOM'S GOING TO SCOLD US IF WE'RE LATE!
OKAY!

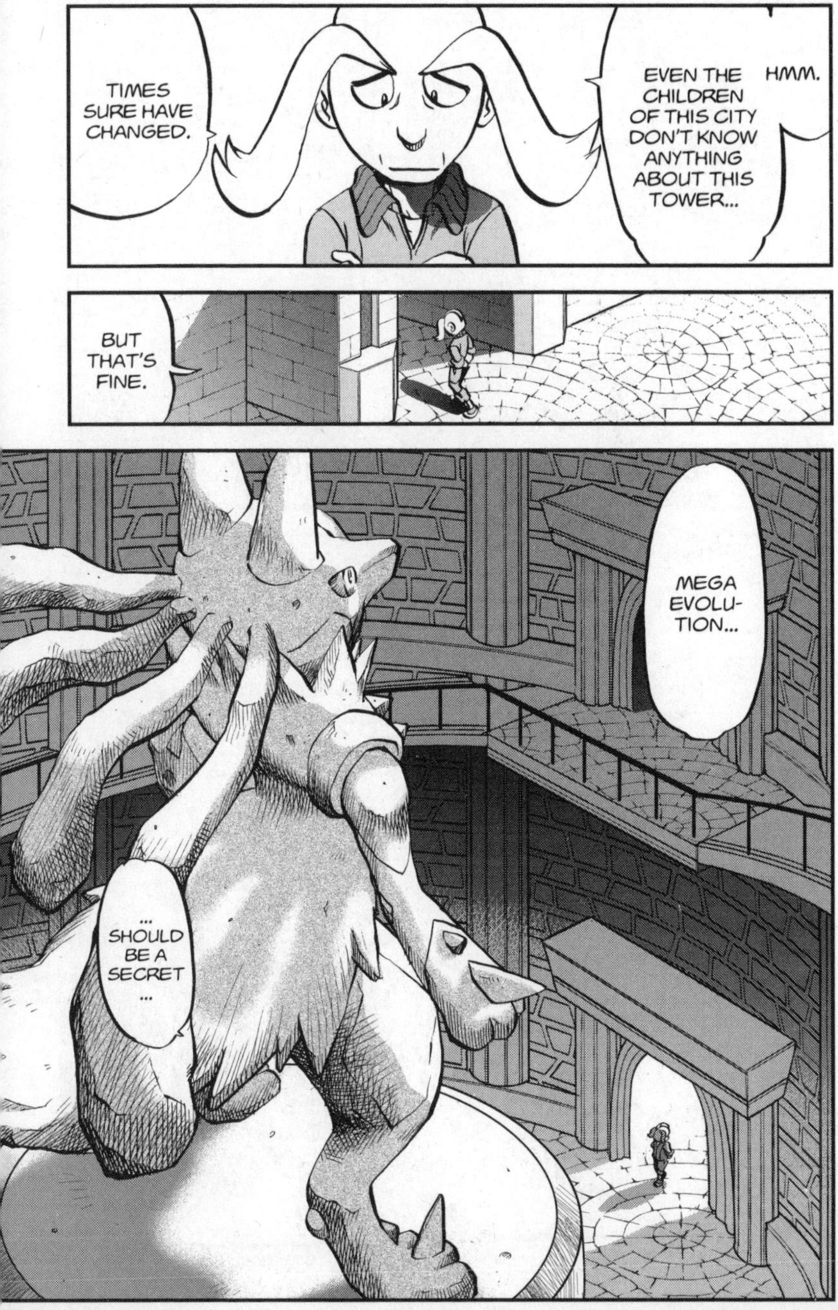
HMM.
EVEN THE CHILDREN OF THIS CITY DON'T KNOW ANYTHING ABOUT THIS TOWER...
TIMES SURE HAVE CHANGED.
BUT THAT'S FINE.
MEGA EVOLUTION...
...SHOULD BE A SECRET...

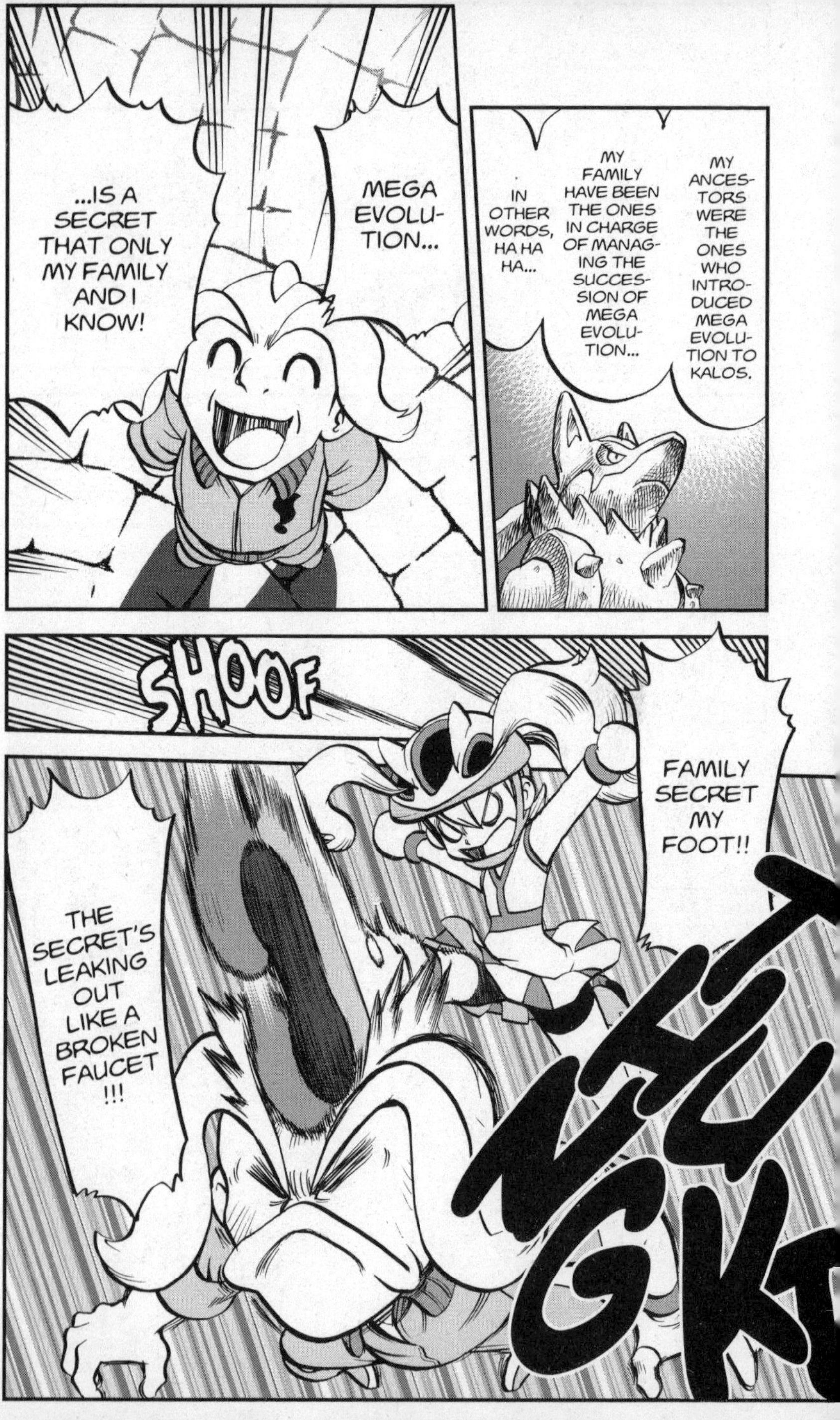
MY ANCESTORS WERE THE ONES WHO INTRODUCED MEGA EVOLUTION TO KALOS.
MY FAMILY HAVE BEEN THE ONES IN CHARGE OF MANAGING THE SUCCESSION OF MEGA EVOLUTION...
IN OTHER WORDS, HA HA HA...
MEGA EVOLUTION...
...IS A SECRET THAT ONLY MY FAMILY AND I KNOW!
SHOOF
FAMILY SECRET MY FOOT!!
THE SECRET'S LEAKING OUT LIKE A BROKEN FAUCET!!!

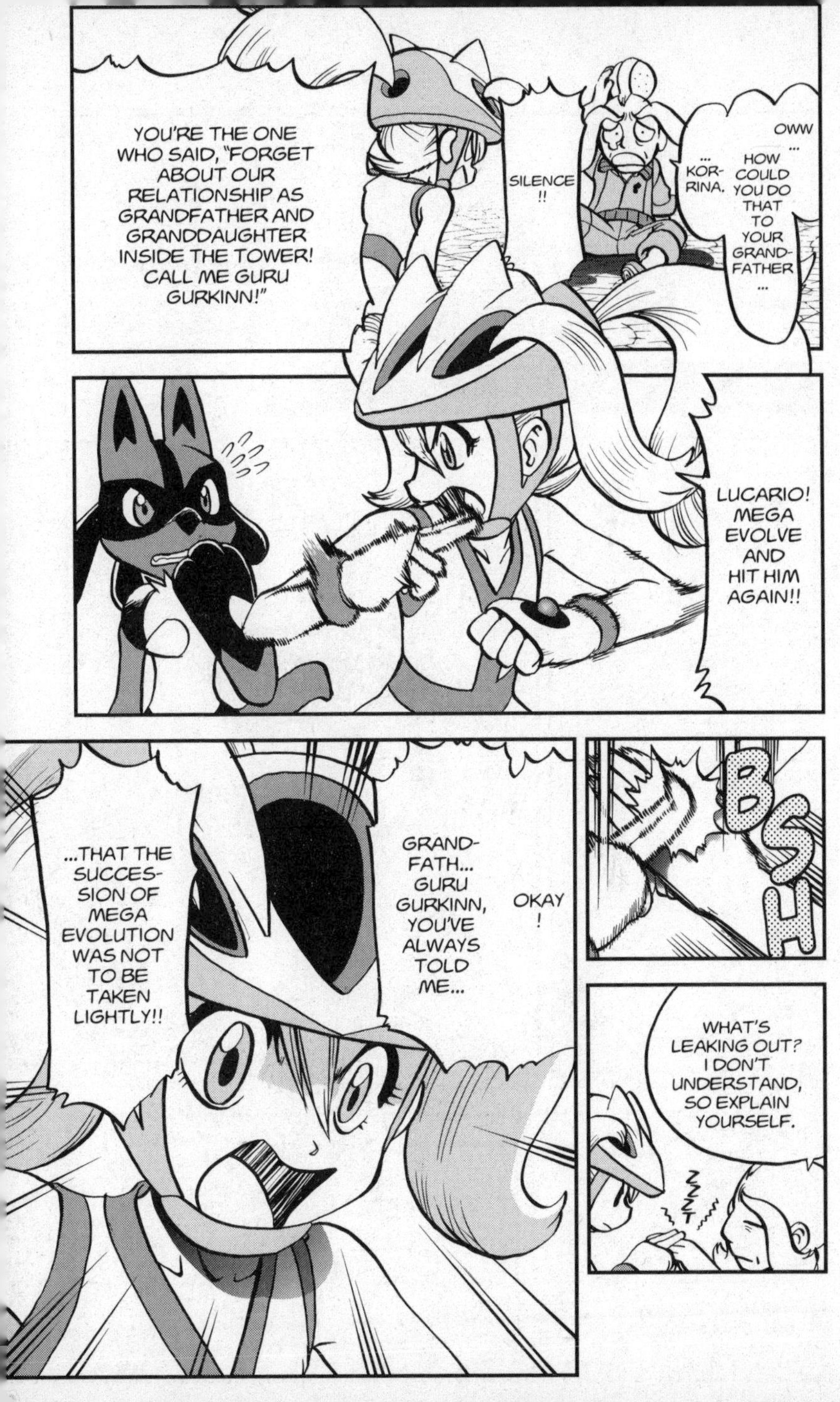
OWW... HOW COULD YOU DO THAT TO YOUR GRANDFATHER...
...KORRINA.
SILENCE!!
YOU'RE THE ONE WHO SAID, "FORGET ABOUT OUR RELATIONSHIP AS GRANDFATHER AND GRANDDAUGHTER INSIDE THE TOWER! CALL ME GURU GURKINN!"
LUCARIO! MEGA EVOLVE AND HIT HIM AGAIN!!
BSH
WHAT'S LEAKING OUT? I DON'T UNDERSTAND, SO EXPLAIN YOURSELF.
ZZZT
OKAY!
GRANDFATH... GURU GURKINN, YOU'VE ALWAYS TOLD ME...
...THAT THE SUCCESSION OF MEGA EVOLUTION WAS NOT TO BE TAKEN LIGHTLY!!

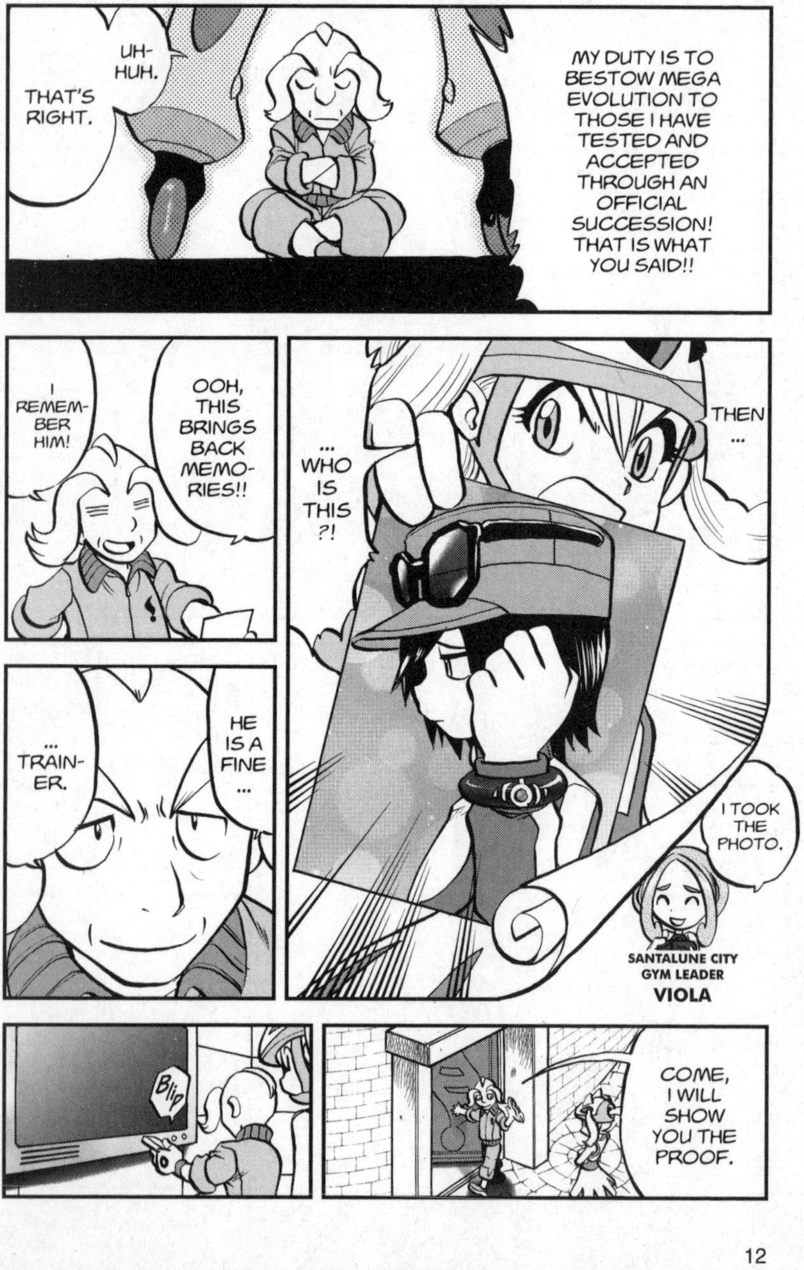
MY DUTY IS TO BESTOW MEGA EVOLUTION TO THOSE I HAVE TESTED AND ACCEPTED THROUGH AN OFFICIAL SUCCESSION! THAT IS WHAT YOU SAID!!
UH-HUH.
THAT'S RIGHT.
THEN ...
... WHO IS THIS ?!
I TOOK THE PHOTO.
SANTALUNE CITY GYM LEADER
VIOLA
OOH, THIS BRINGS BACK MEMORIES!!
I REMEMBER HIM!
HE IS A FINE ...
... TRAINER.
COME, I WILL SHOW YOU THE PROOF.
Blip

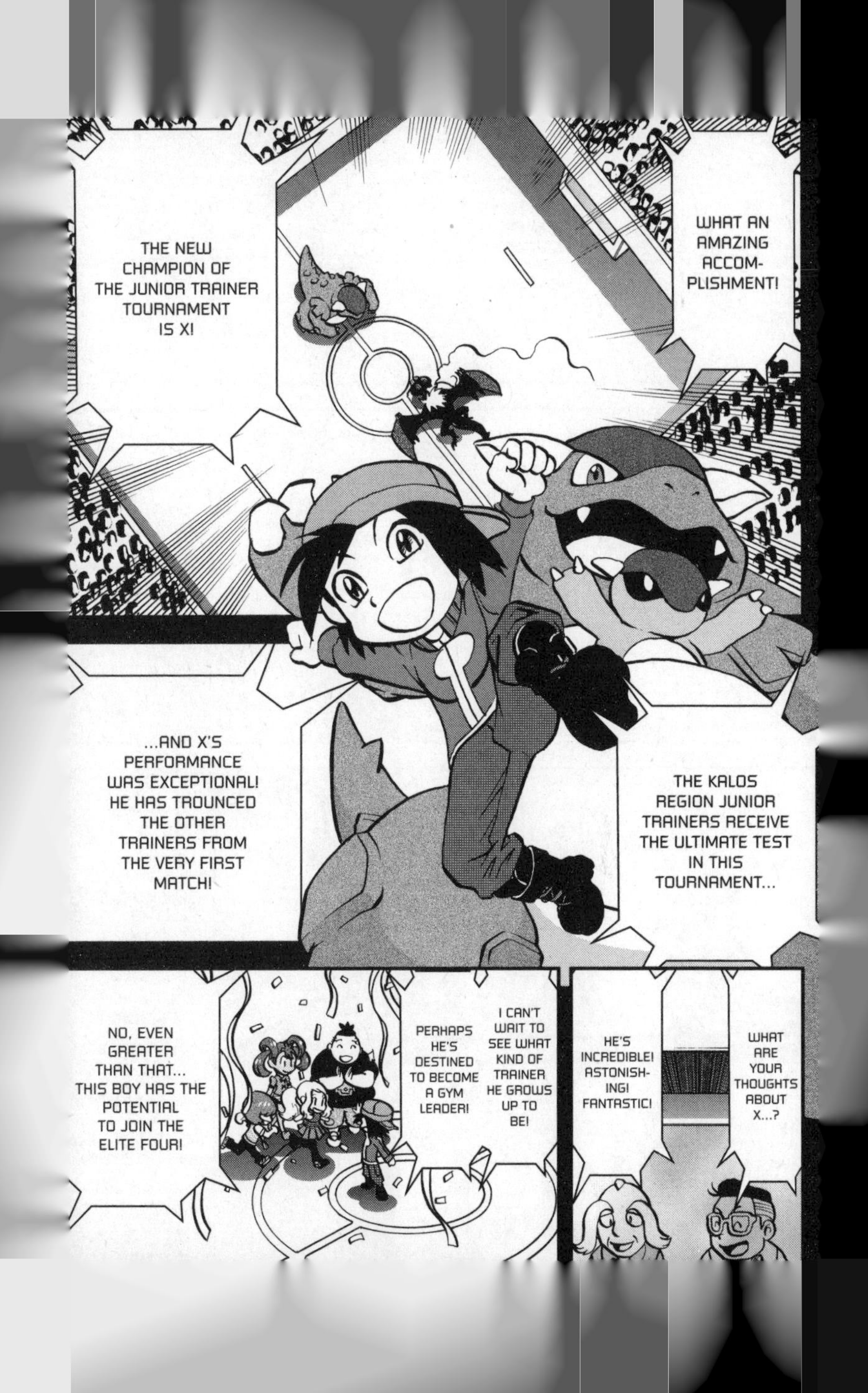
WHAT AN AMAZING ACCOM-PLISHMENT!
THE NEW CHAMPION OF THE JUNIOR TRAINER TOURNAMENT IS X!
THE KALOS REGION JUNIOR TRAINERS RECEIVE THE ULTIMATE TEST IN THIS TOURNAMENT...
...AND X'S PERFORMANCE WAS EXCEPTIONAL! HE HAS TROUNCED THE OTHER TRAINERS FROM THE VERY FIRST MATCH!
WHAT ARE YOUR THOUGHTS ABOUT X...?
HE'S INCREDIBLE! ASTONISH-ING! FANTASTIC!
I CAN'T WAIT TO SEE WHAT KIND OF TRAINER HE GROWS UP TO BE!
PERHAPS HE'S DESTINED TO BECOME A GYM LEADER!
NO, EVEN GREATER THAN THAT... THIS BOY HAS THE POTENTIAL TO JOIN THE ELITE FOUR!

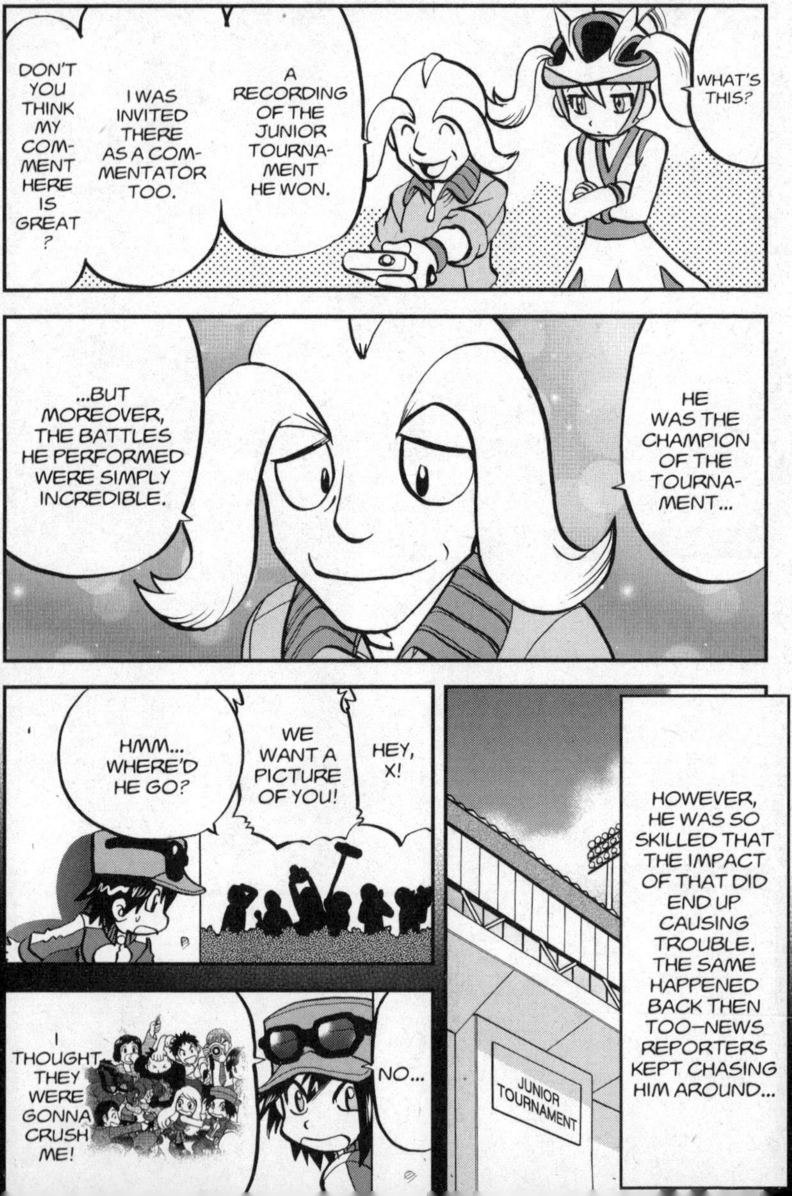
WHAT'S THIS?
A RECORDING OF THE JUNIOR TOURNAMENT HE WON.
I WAS INVITED THERE AS A COMMENTATOR TOO.
DON'T YOU THINK MY COMMENT HERE IS GREAT?
HE WAS THE CHAMPION OF THE TOURNAMENT...
...BUT MOREOVER, THE BATTLES HE PERFORMED WERE SIMPLY INCREDIBLE.
HOWEVER, HE WAS SO SKILLED THAT THE IMPACT OF THAT DID END UP CAUSING TROUBLE. THE SAME HAPPENED BACK THEN TOO—NEWS REPORTERS KEPT CHASING HIM AROUND...
JUNIOR TOURNAMENT
HEY, X!
WE WANT A PICTURE OF YOU!
HMM... WHERE'D HE GO?
NO...
I THOUGHT THEY WERE GONNA CRUSH ME!

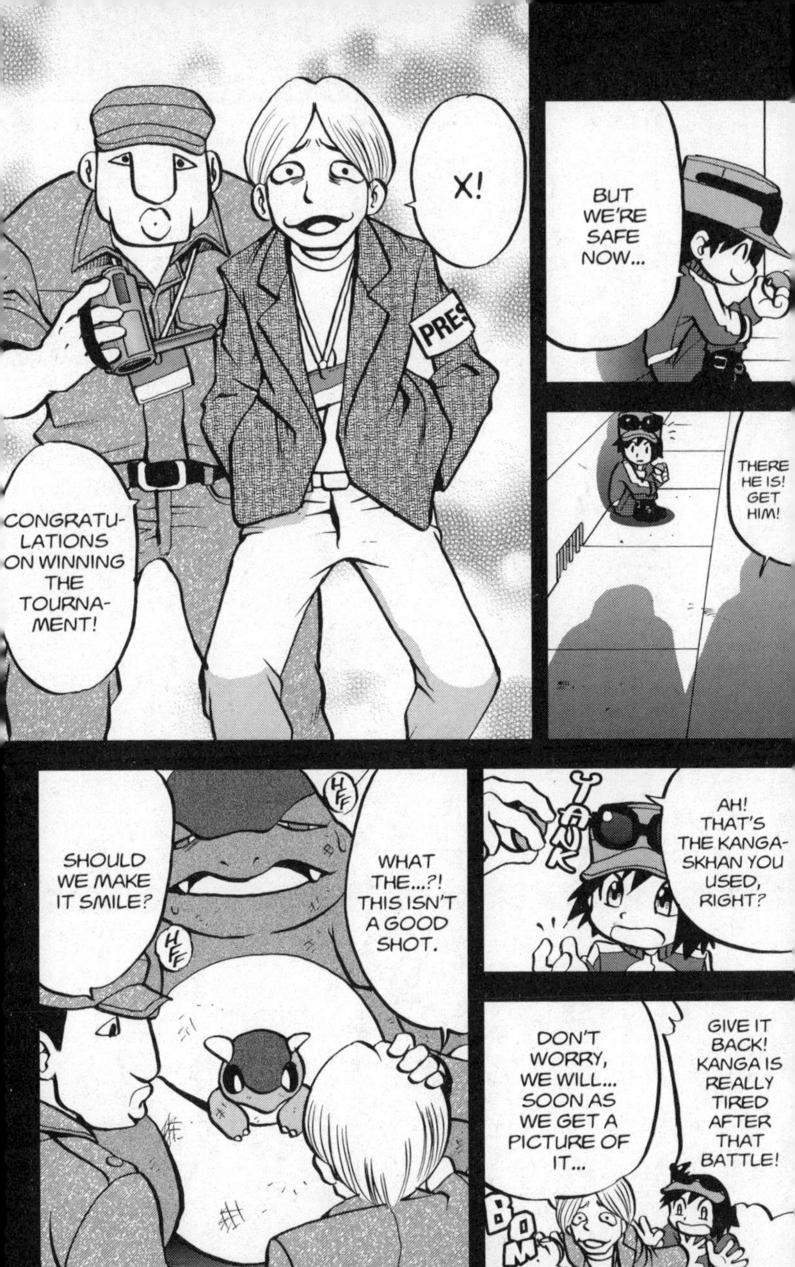

BUT WE'RE SAFE NOW...
THERE HE IS! GET HIM!
X!
CONGRATULATIONS ON WINNING THE TOURNAMENT!
YANK
AH! THAT'S THE KANGASKHAN YOU USED, RIGHT?
GIVE IT BACK! KANGA IS REALLY TIRED AFTER THAT BATTLE!
DON'T WORRY, WE WILL... SOON AS WE GET A PICTURE OF IT...
BOM
HFF
WHAT THE...?! THIS ISN'T A GOOD SHOT.
SHOULD WE MAKE IT SMILE?
HFF

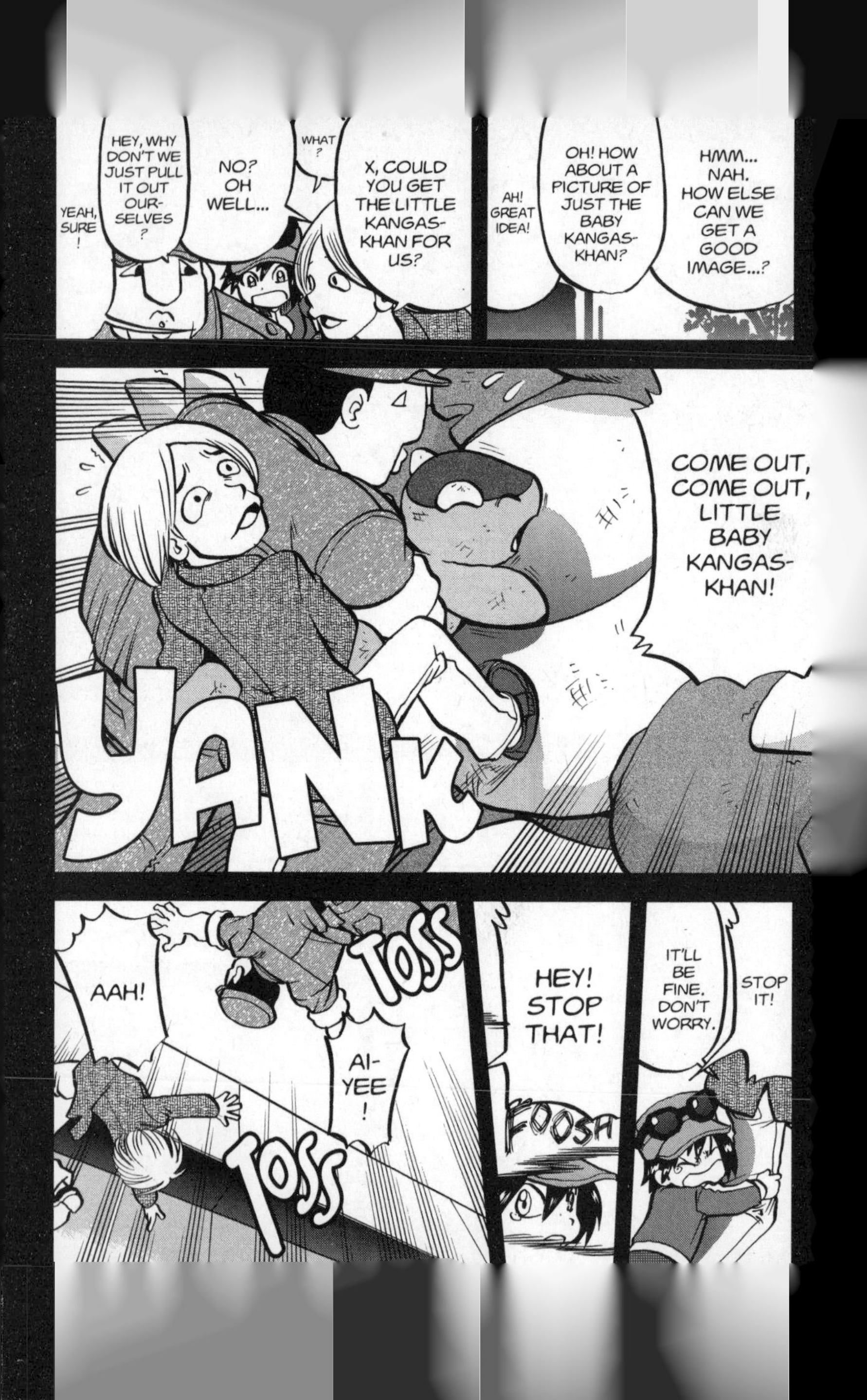

HMM... NAH. HOW ELSE CAN WE GET A GOOD IMAGE...?
OH! HOW ABOUT A PICTURE OF JUST THE BABY KANGAS-KHAN?
AH! GREAT IDEA!
X, COULD YOU GET THE LITTLE KANGAS-KHAN FOR US?
WHAT?
NO? OH WELL...
HEY, WHY DON'T WE JUST PULL IT OUT OUR-SELVES?
YEAH, SURE!
COME OUT, COME OUT, LITTLE BABY KANGAS-KHAN!
YANK
STOP IT!
IT'LL BE FINE. DON'T WORRY.
HEY! STOP THAT!
FOOSH
TOSS
AI-YEE!
AAH!
TOSS

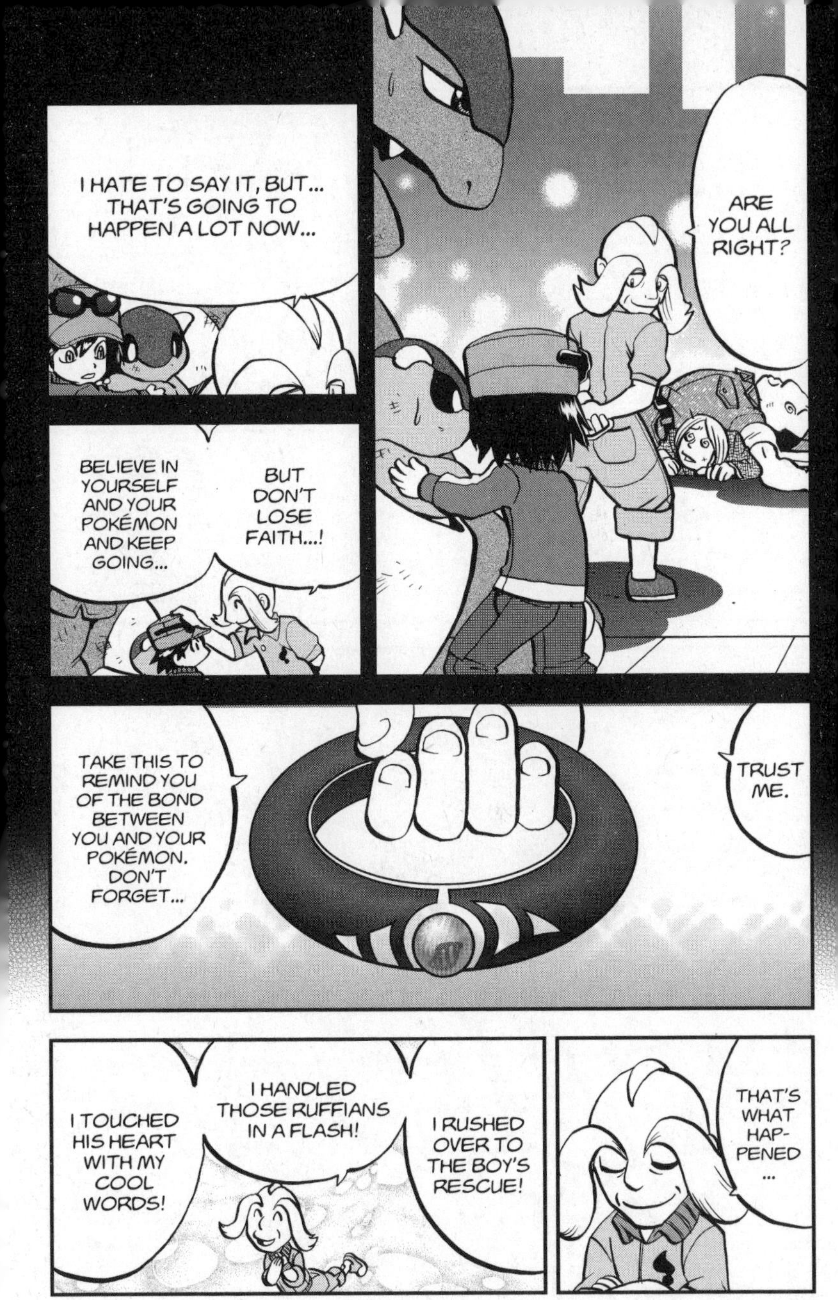
ARE YOU ALL RIGHT?
I HATE TO SAY IT, BUT... THAT'S GOING TO HAPPEN A LOT NOW...
BUT DON'T LOSE FAITH...!
BELIEVE IN YOURSELF AND YOUR POKÉMON AND KEEP GOING...
TRUST ME.
TAKE THIS TO REMIND YOU OF THE BOND BETWEEN YOU AND YOUR POKÉMON. DON'T FORGET...
THAT'S WHAT HAP-PENED ...
I RUSHED OVER TO THE BOY'S RESCUE!
I HANDLED THOSE RUFFIANS IN A FLASH!
I TOUCHED HIS HEART WITH MY COOL WORDS!

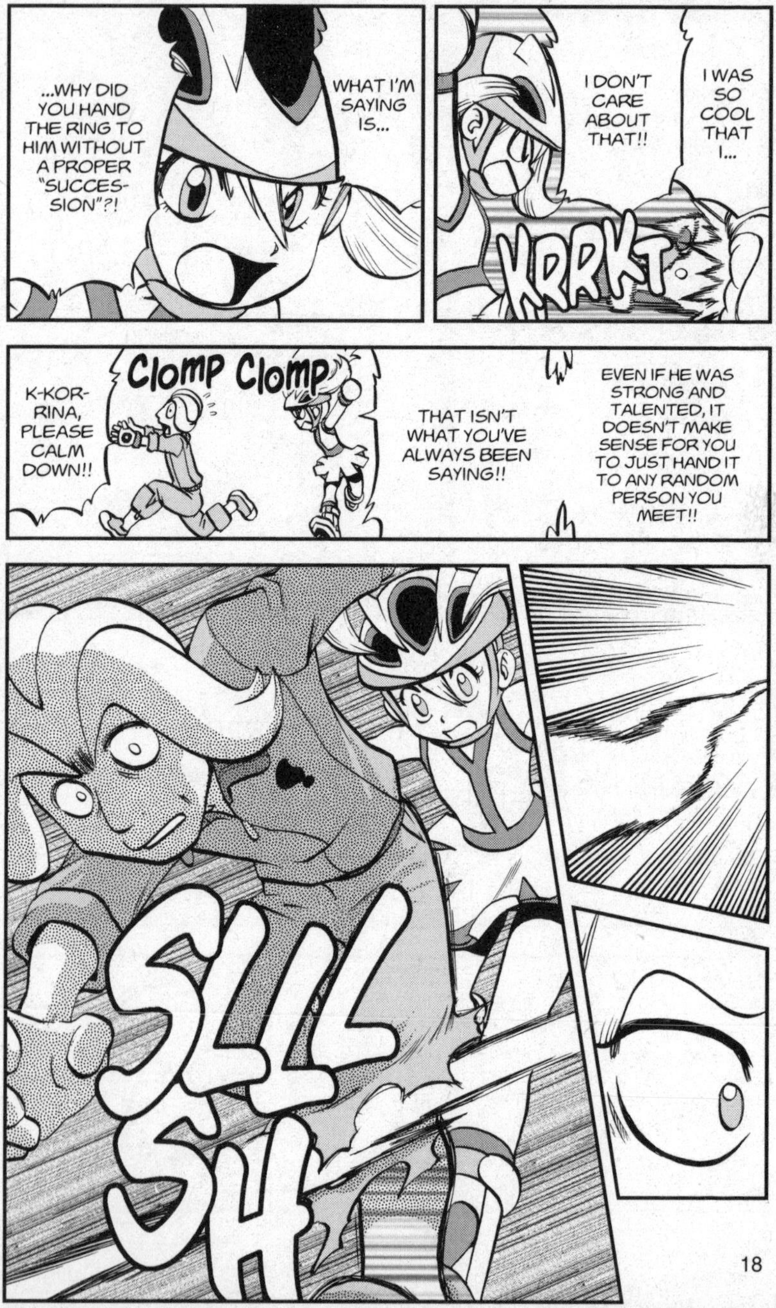
I WAS SO COOL THAT I...
I DON'T CARE ABOUT THAT!!
KRRKT
WHAT I'M SAYING IS...
...WHY DID YOU HAND THE RING TO HIM WITHOUT A PROPER "SUCCESSION"?!
EVEN IF HE WAS STRONG AND TALENTED, IT DOESN'T MAKE SENSE FOR YOU TO JUST HAND IT TO ANY RANDOM PERSON YOU MEET!!
THAT ISN'T WHAT YOU'VE ALWAYS BEEN SAYING!!
Clomp Clomp
K-KORRINA, PLEASE CALM DOWN!!
SLLSH

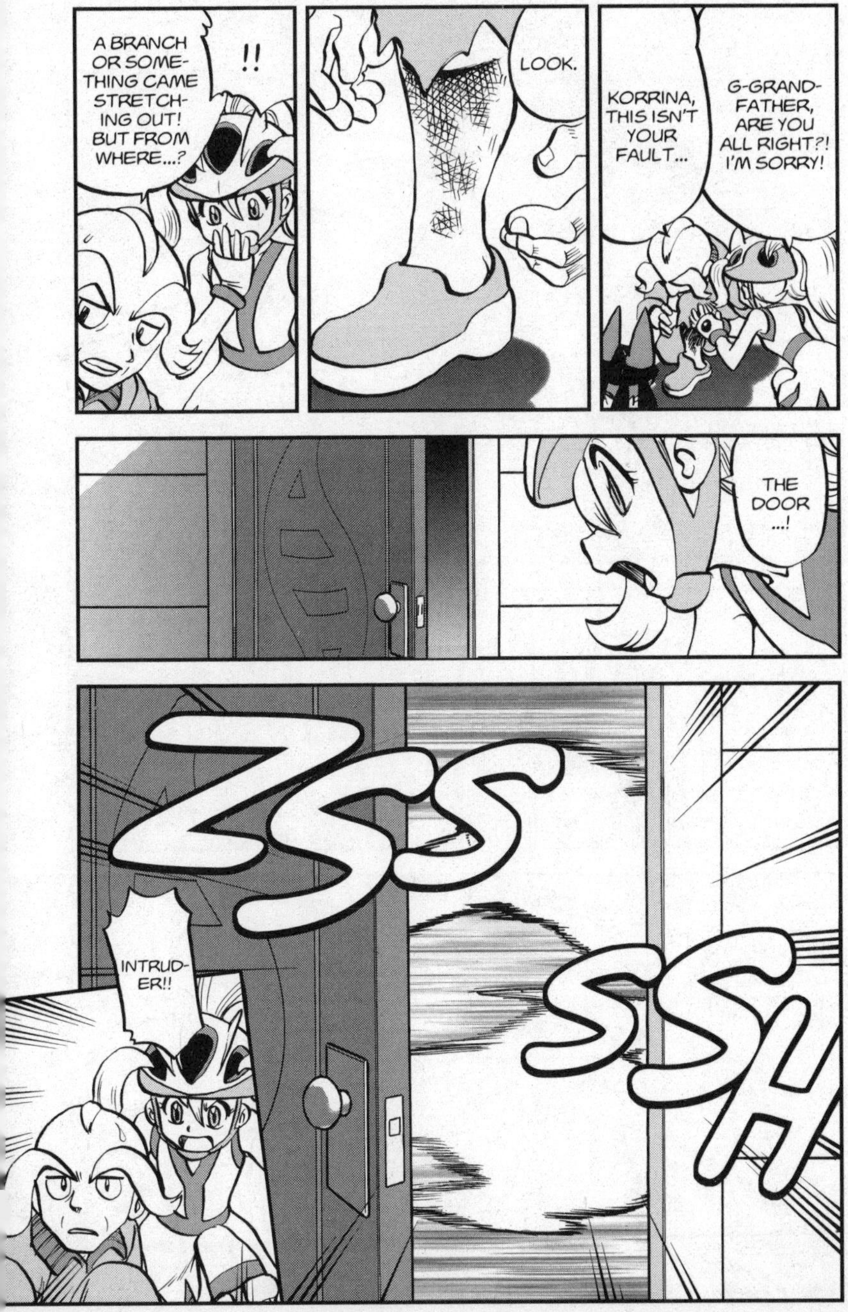
G-GRAND-FATHER, ARE YOU ALL RIGHT?! I'M SORRY!
KORRINA, THIS ISN'T YOUR FAULT...
LOOK.
!!
A BRANCH OR SOME-THING CAME STRETCH-ING OUT! BUT FROM WHERE...?
THE DOOR ...!
ZSS
SSH
INTRUD-ER!!

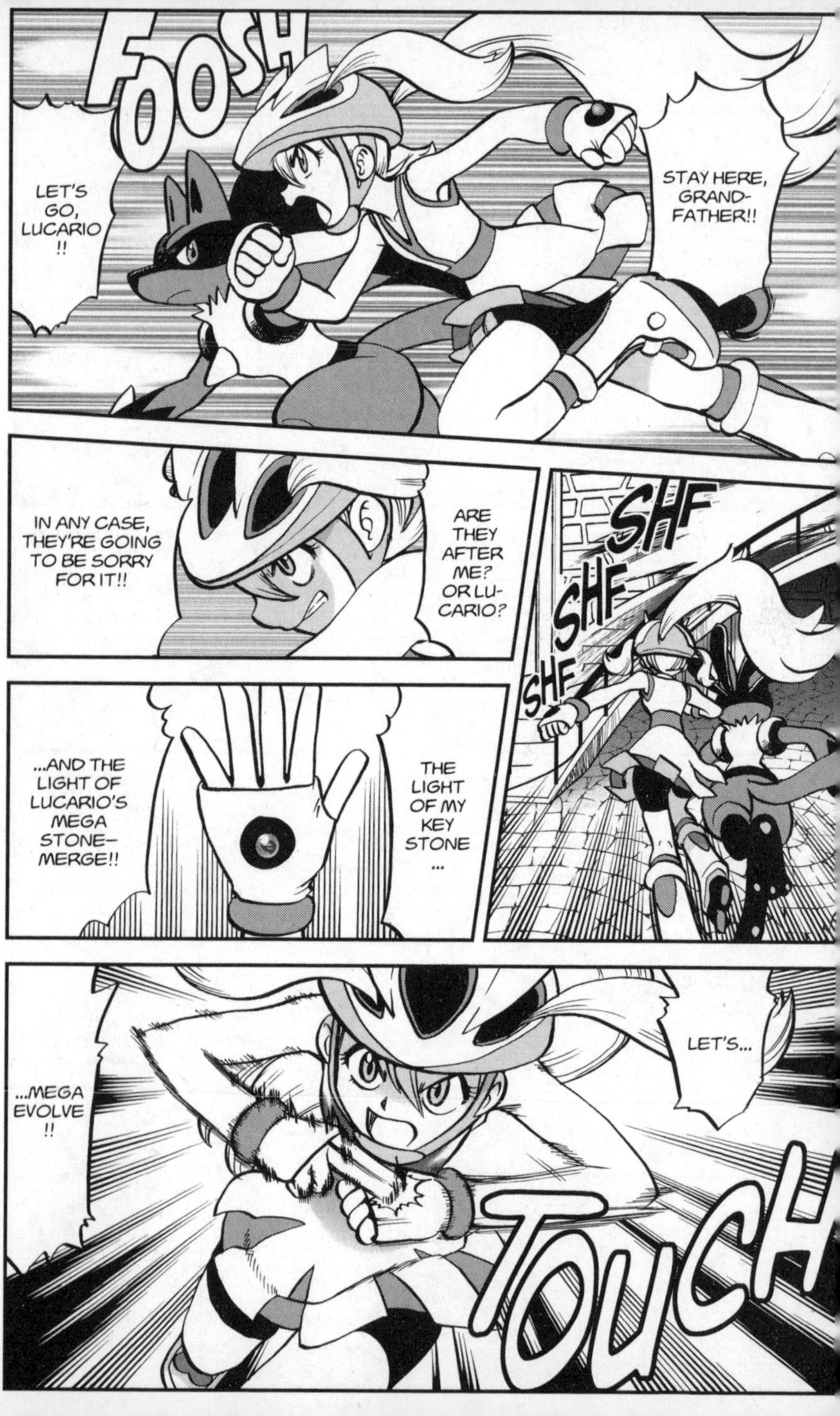
FOOSH
STAY HERE, GRAND-FATHER!!
LET'S GO, LUCARIO!!
SHF SHF SHF SHF
ARE THEY AFTER ME? OR LU-CARIO?
IN ANY CASE, THEY'RE GOING TO BE SORRY FOR IT!!
THE LIGHT OF MY KEY STONE...
...AND THE LIGHT OF LUCARIO'S MEGA STONE—MERGE!!
LET'S...
...MEGA EVOLVE!!
TOUCH

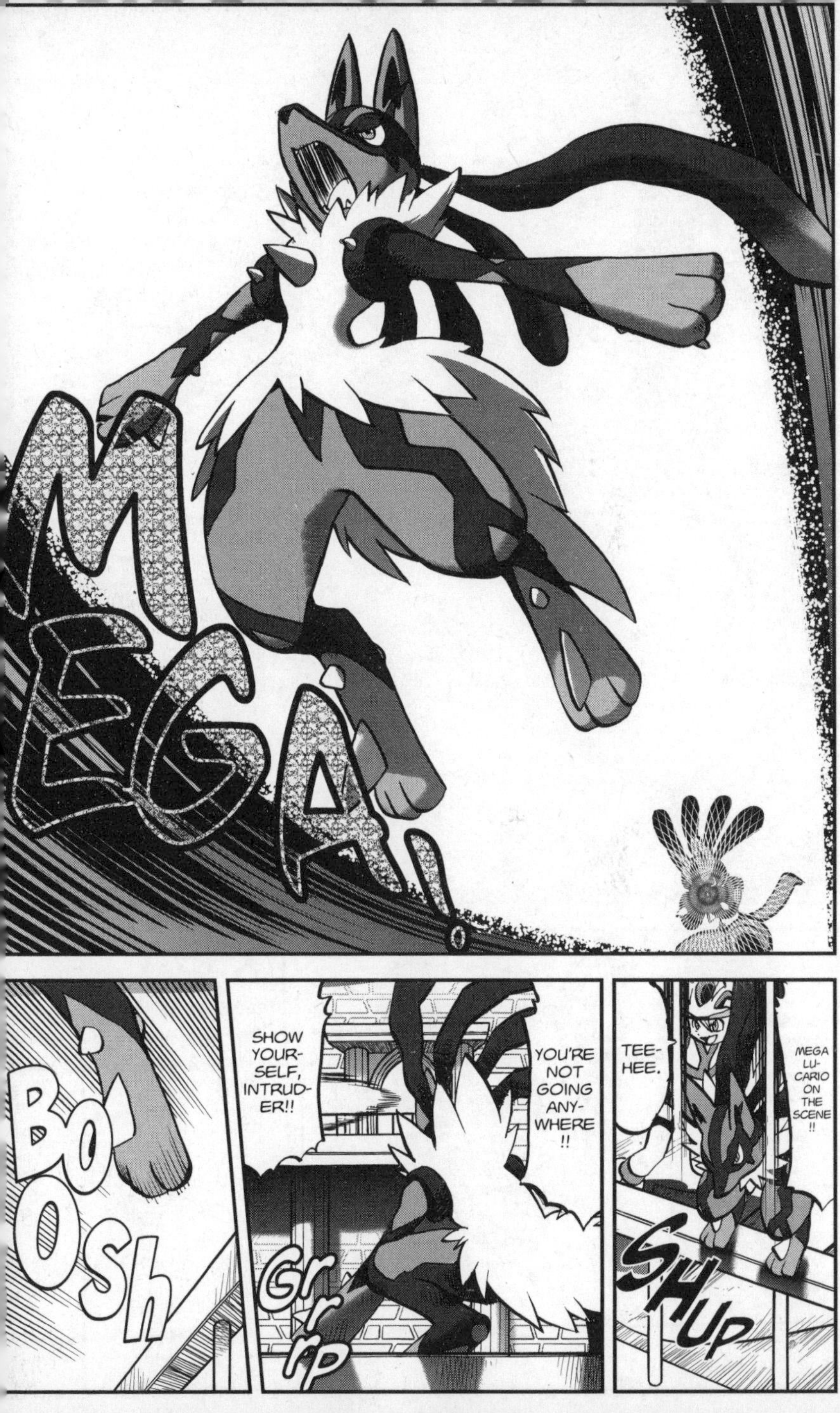
MEGA!!
MEGALUCARIO ON THE SCENE!!
TEE-HEE.
SHUP
YOU'RE NOT GOING ANYWHERE!!
SHOW YOURSELF, INTRUDER!!
Grrrp
BOOSh

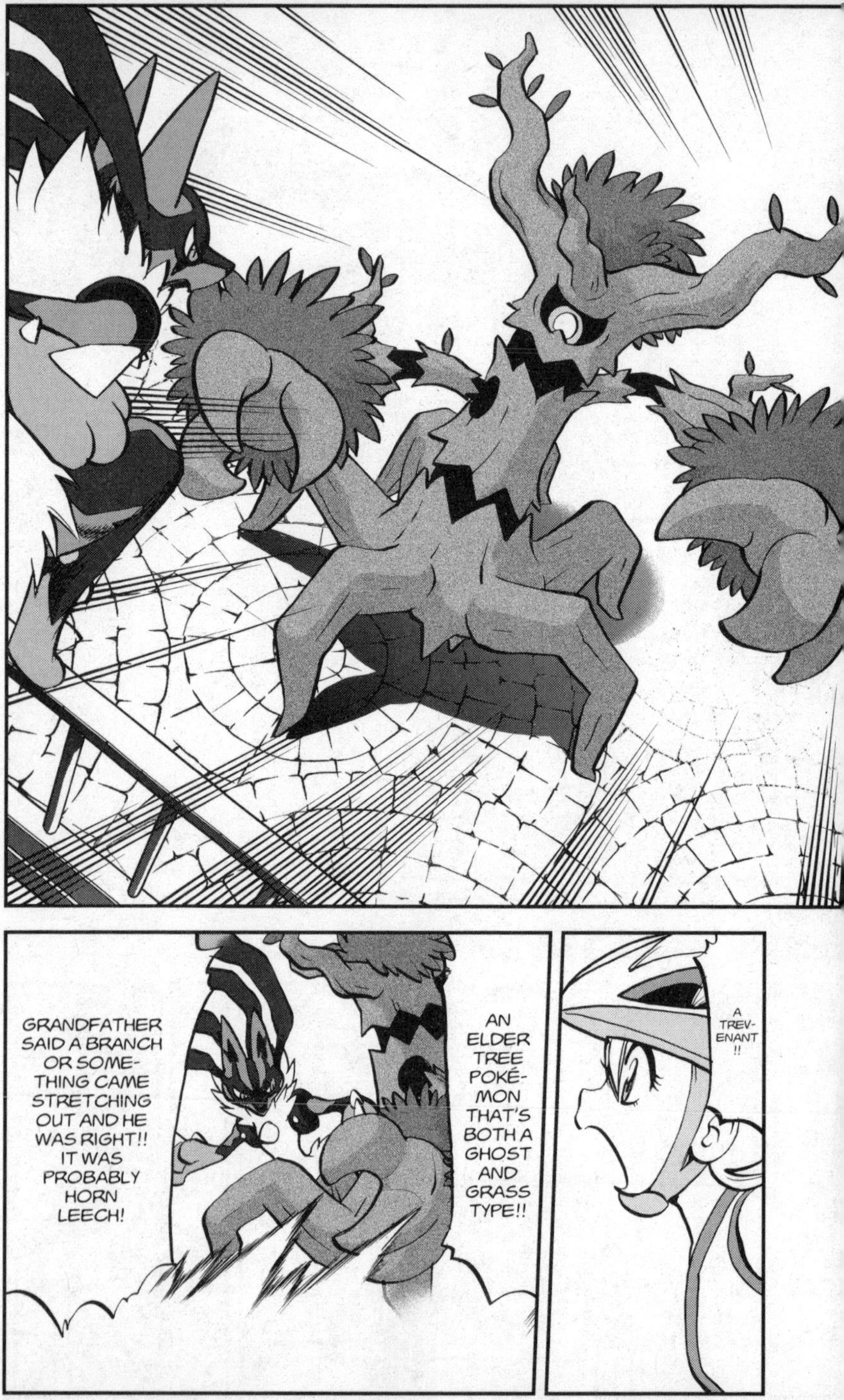
A TREV-ENANT!!
AN ELDER TREE POKÉMON THAT'S BOTH A GHOST AND GRASS TYPE!!
GRANDFATHER SAID A BRANCH OR SOME-THING CAME STRETCHING OUT AND HE WAS RIGHT!! IT WAS PROBABLY HORN LEECH!

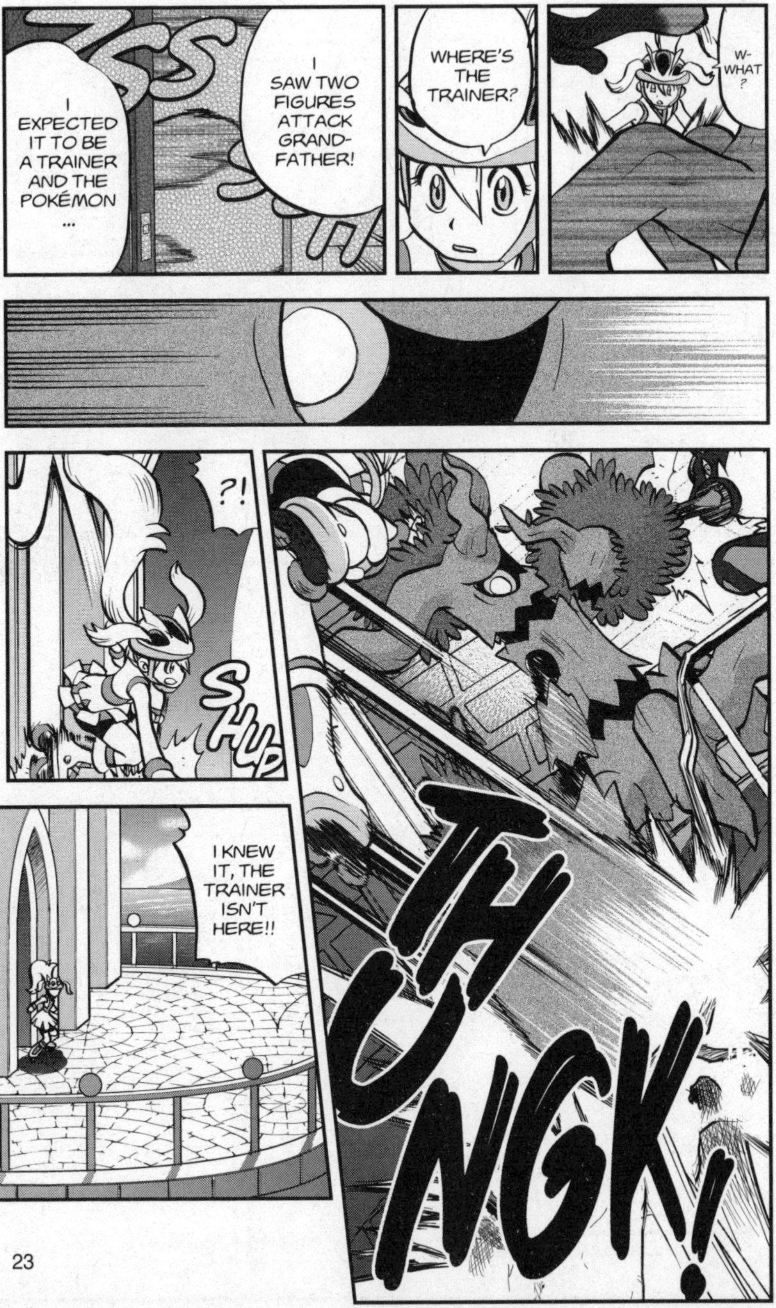
W-WHAT?
WHERE'S THE TRAINER?
I SAW TWO FIGURES ATTACK GRAND-FATHER!
I EXPECTED IT TO BE A TRAINER AND THE POKÉMON ...
THUNGK!
?!
SHUP
I KNEW IT, THE TRAINER ISN'T HERE!!

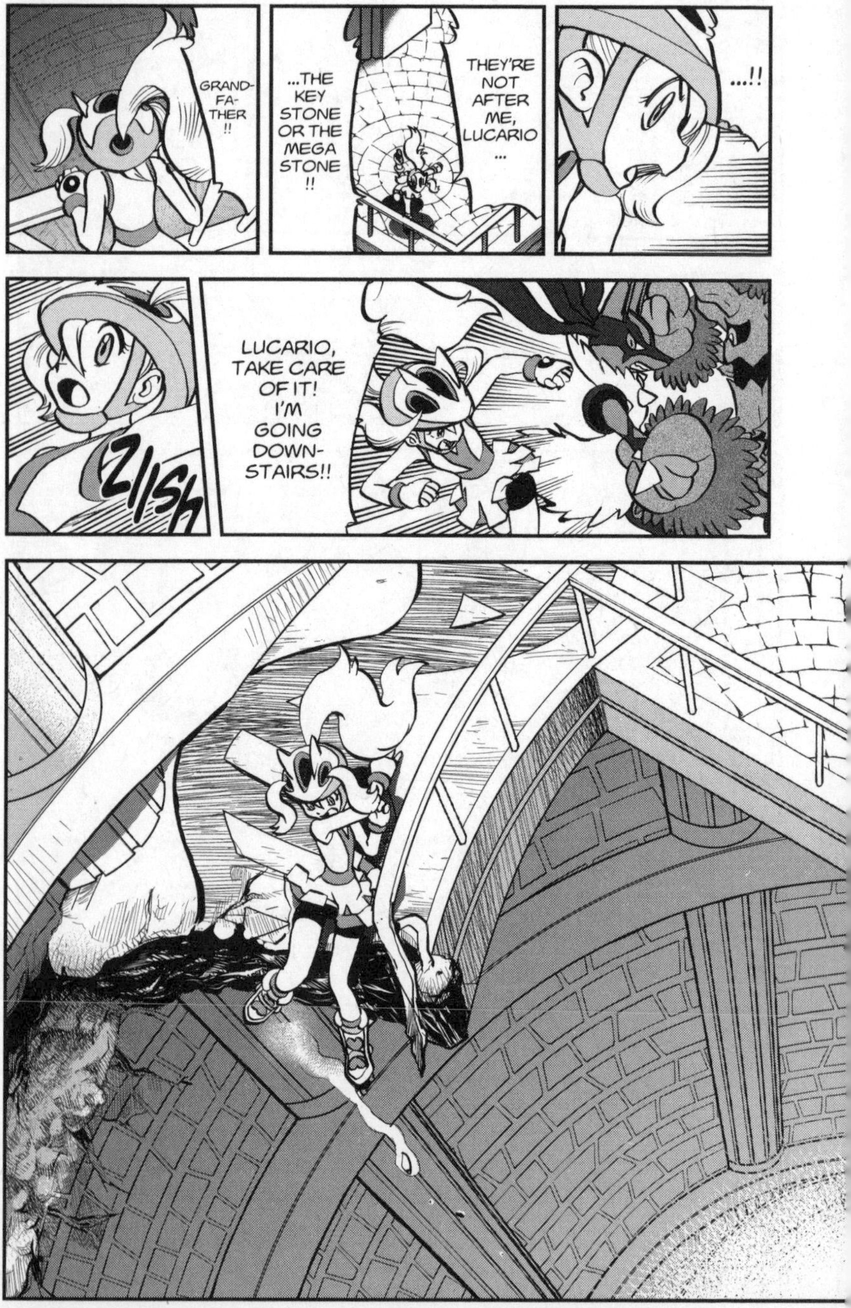
...!!
THEY'RE NOT AFTER ME, LUCARIO...
...THE KEY STONE OR THE MEGA STONE!!
GRANDFATHER!!
LUCARIO, TAKE CARE OF IT! I'M GOING DOWNSTAIRS!!
ZISH

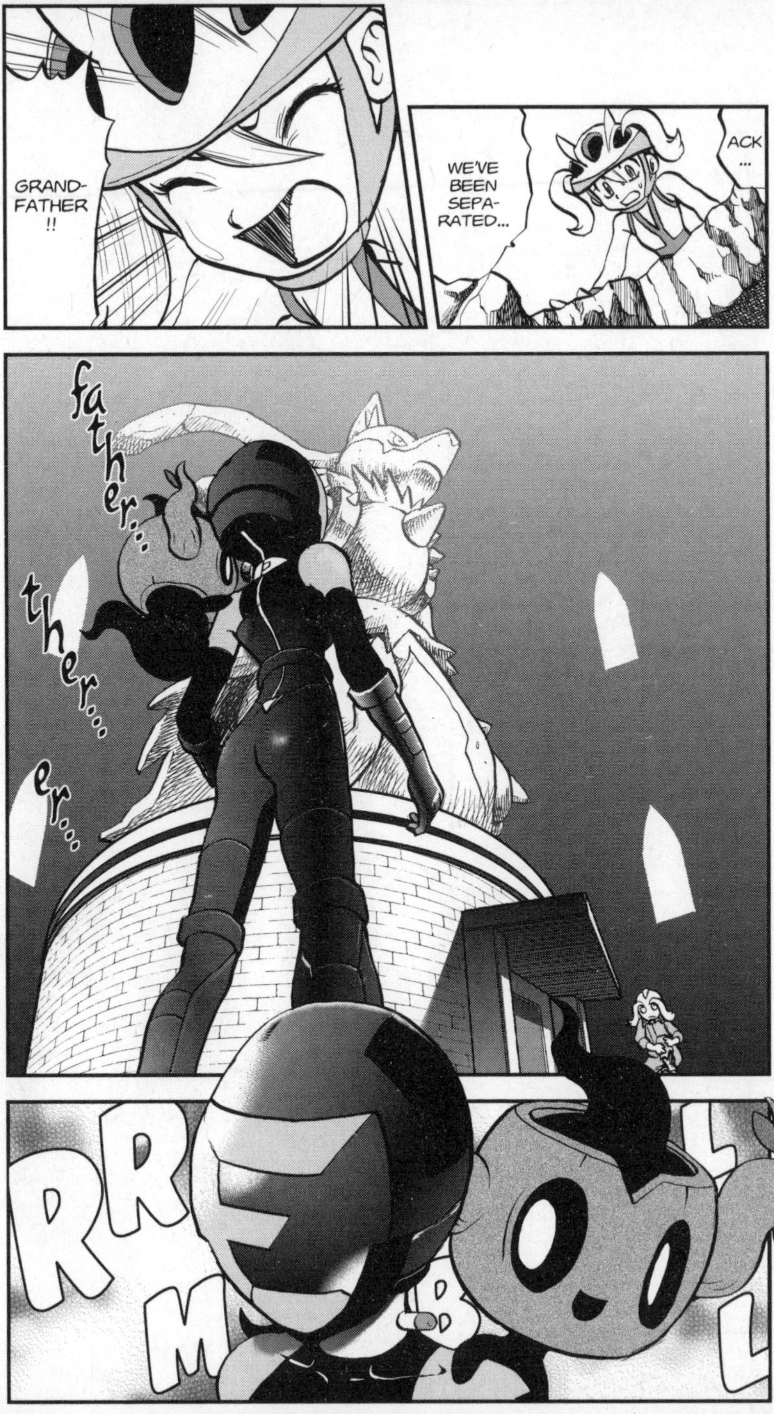
ACK ...
WE'VE BEEN SEPA-RATED...
GRAND-FATHER !!
father...
ther...
er...

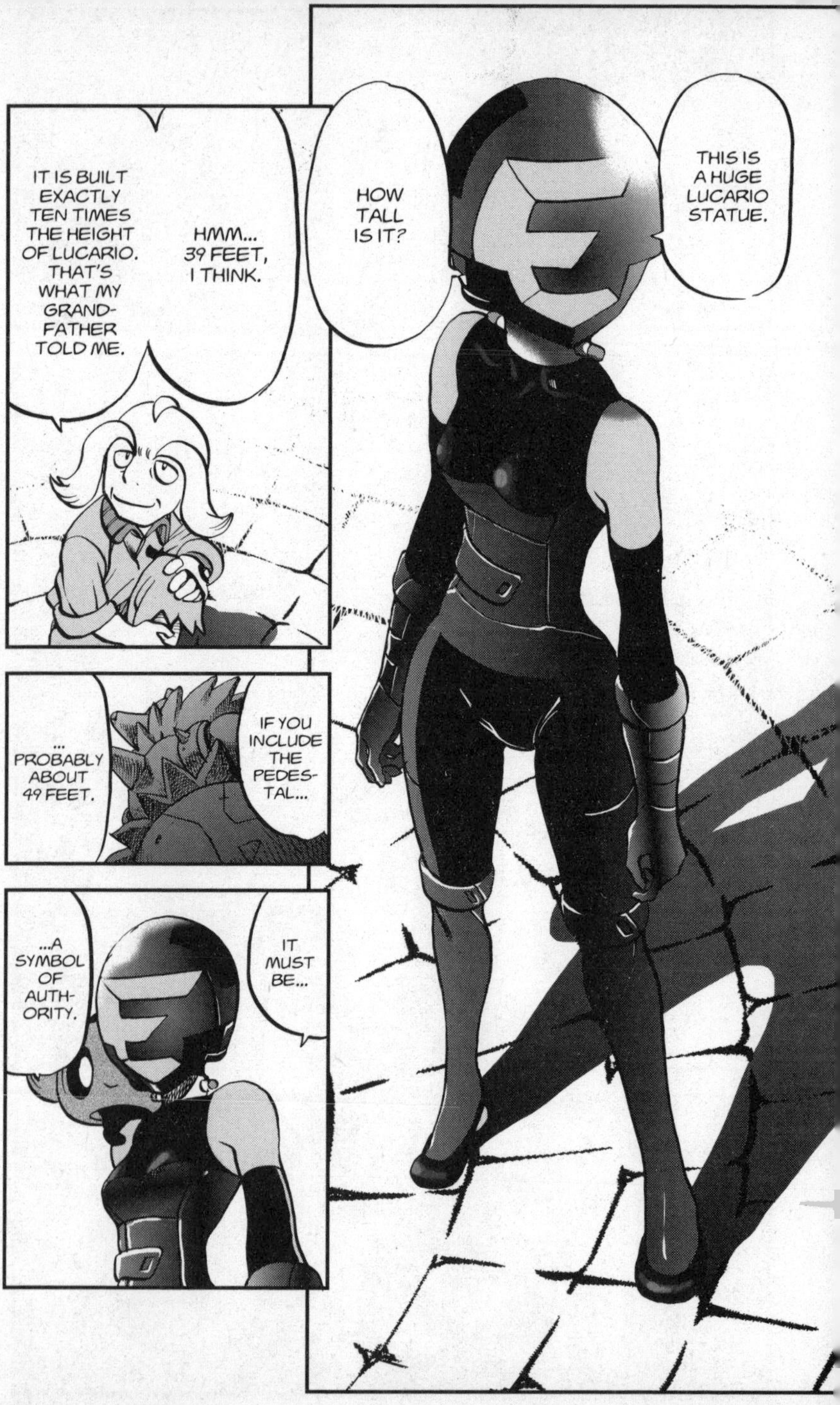
THIS IS A HUGE LUCARIO STATUE.
HOW TALL IS IT?
HMM... 39 FEET, I THINK.
IT IS BUILT EXACTLY TEN TIMES THE HEIGHT OF LUCARIO. THAT'S WHAT MY GRAND-FATHER TOLD ME.
IF YOU INCLUDE THE PEDES-TAL...
... PROBABLY ABOUT 49 FEET.
IT MUST BE...
...A SYMBOL OF AUTH-ORITY.

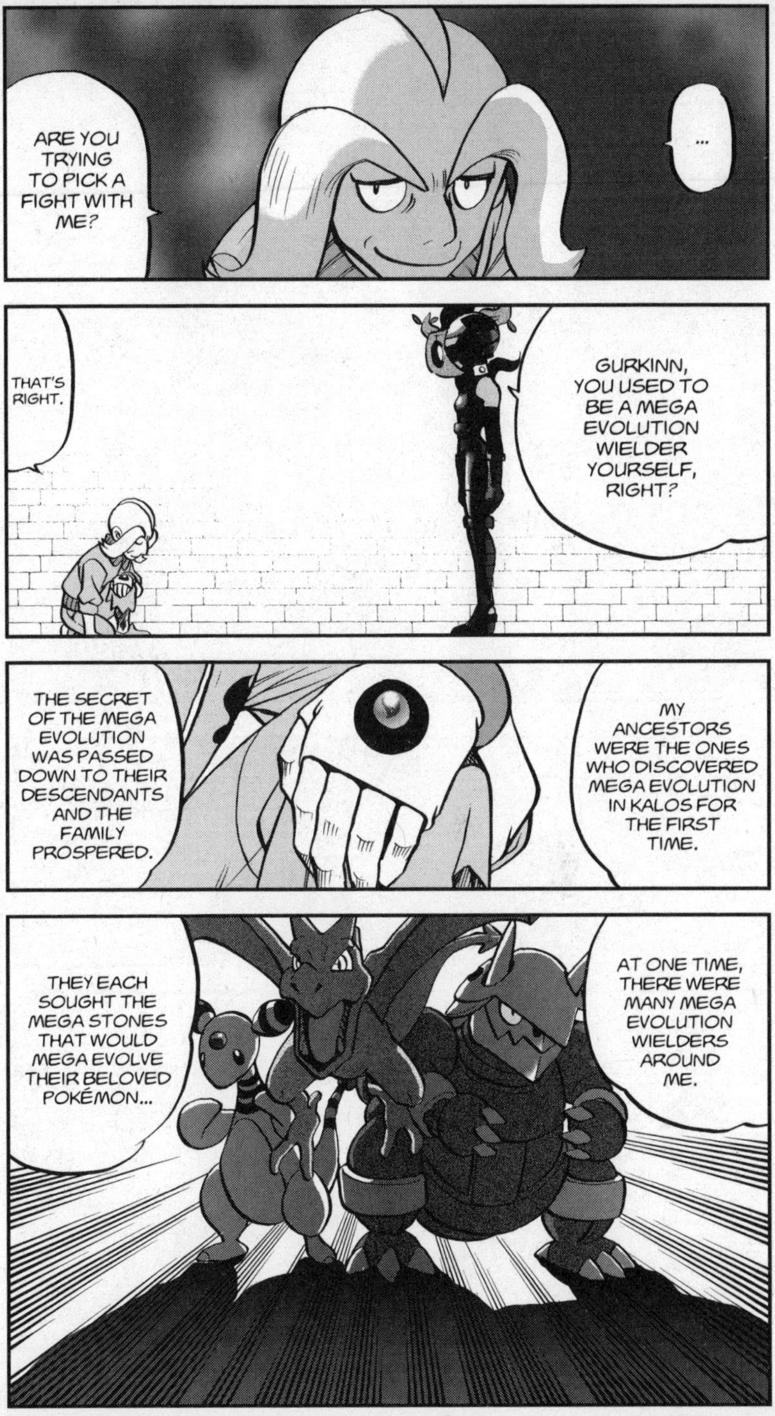
...
ARE YOU TRYING TO PICK A FIGHT WITH ME?
GURKINN, YOU USED TO BE A MEGA EVOLUTION WIELDER YOURSELF, RIGHT?
THAT'S RIGHT.
MY ANCESTORS WERE THE ONES WHO DISCOVERED MEGA EVOLUTION IN KALOS FOR THE FIRST TIME.
THE SECRET OF THE MEGA EVOLUTION WAS PASSED DOWN TO THEIR DESCENDANTS AND THE FAMILY PROSPERED.
AT ONE TIME, THERE WERE MANY MEGA EVOLUTION WIELDERS AROUND ME.
THEY EACH SOUGHT THE MEGA STONES THAT WOULD MEGA EVOLVE THEIR BELOVED POKÉMON...

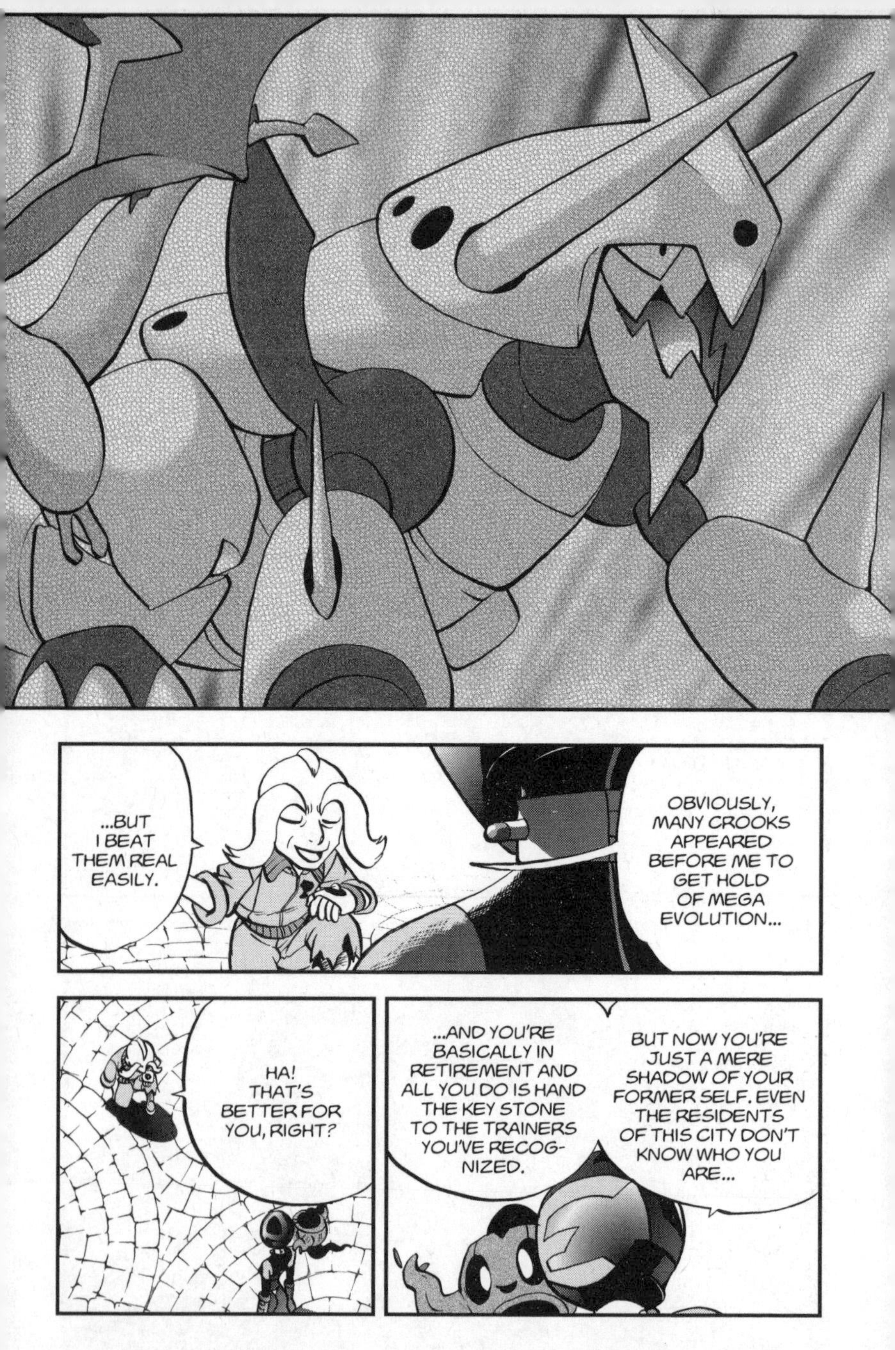
OBVIOUSLY, MANY CROOKS APPEARED BEFORE ME TO GET HOLD OF MEGA EVOLUTION...
...BUT I BEAT THEM REAL EASILY.
BUT NOW YOU'RE JUST A MERE SHADOW OF YOUR FORMER SELF. EVEN THE RESIDENTS OF THIS CITY DON'T KNOW WHO YOU ARE...
...AND YOU'RE BASICALLY IN RETIREMENT AND ALL YOU DO IS HAND THE KEY STONE TO THE TRAINERS YOU'VE RECOG-NIZED.
HA! THAT'S BETTER FOR YOU, RIGHT?

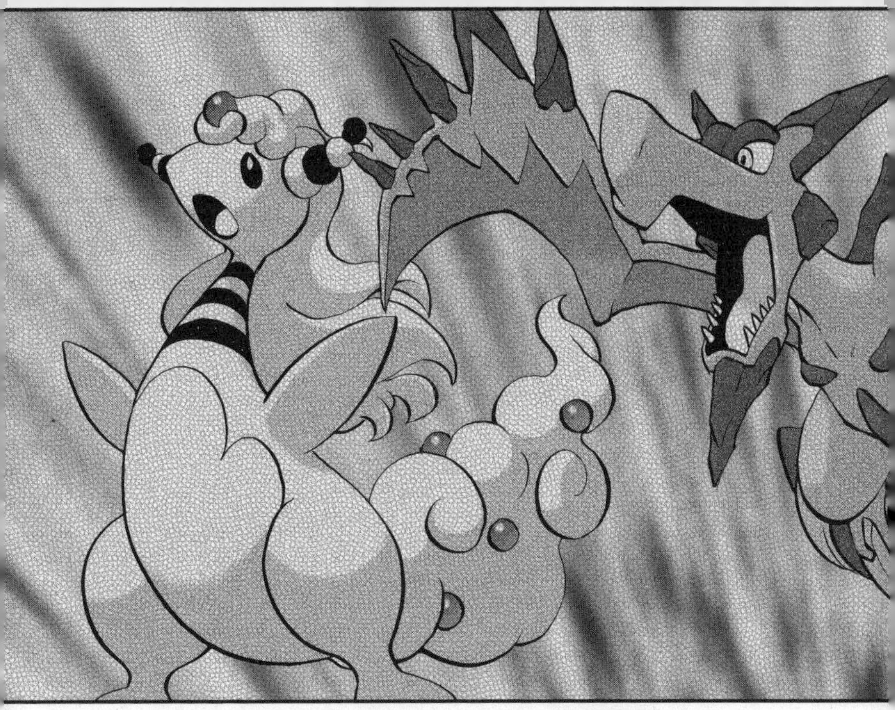

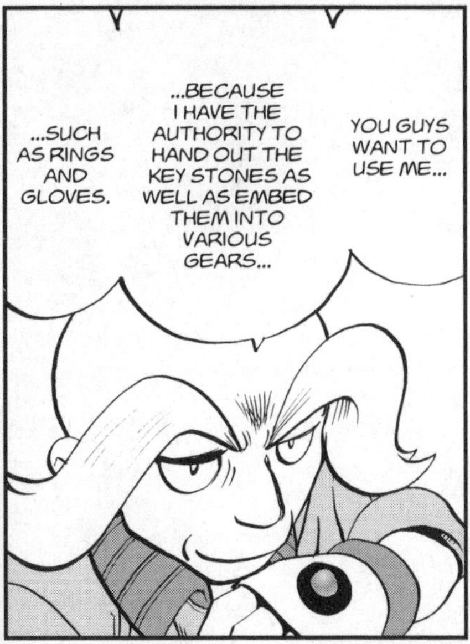
YOU GUYS WANT TO USE ME...
...BECAUSE I HAVE THE AUTHORITY TO HAND OUT THE KEY STONES AS WELL AS EMBED THEM INTO VARIOUS GEARS...
...SUCH AS RINGS AND GLOVES.

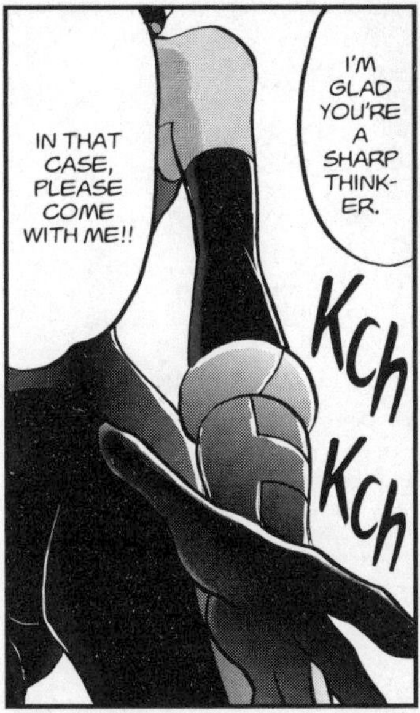
I'M GLAD YOU'RE A SHARP THINK-ER.
IN THAT CASE, PLEASE COME WITH ME!!
Kch Kch

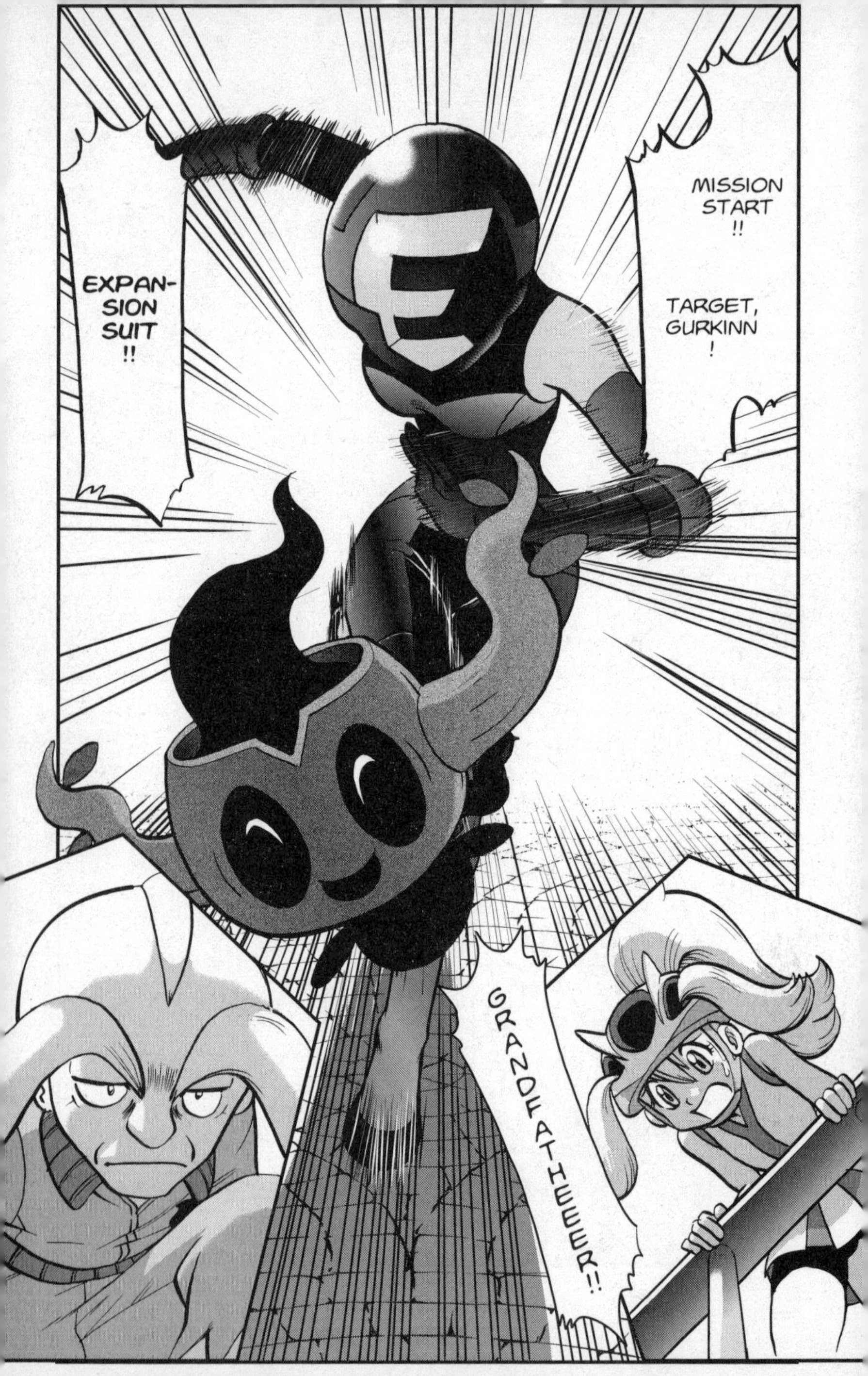
MISSION START !!
TARGET, GURKINN !
EXPAN-SION SUIT !!
GRANDFATHEEER!!

# Adventure #13
## Heracross Transforms

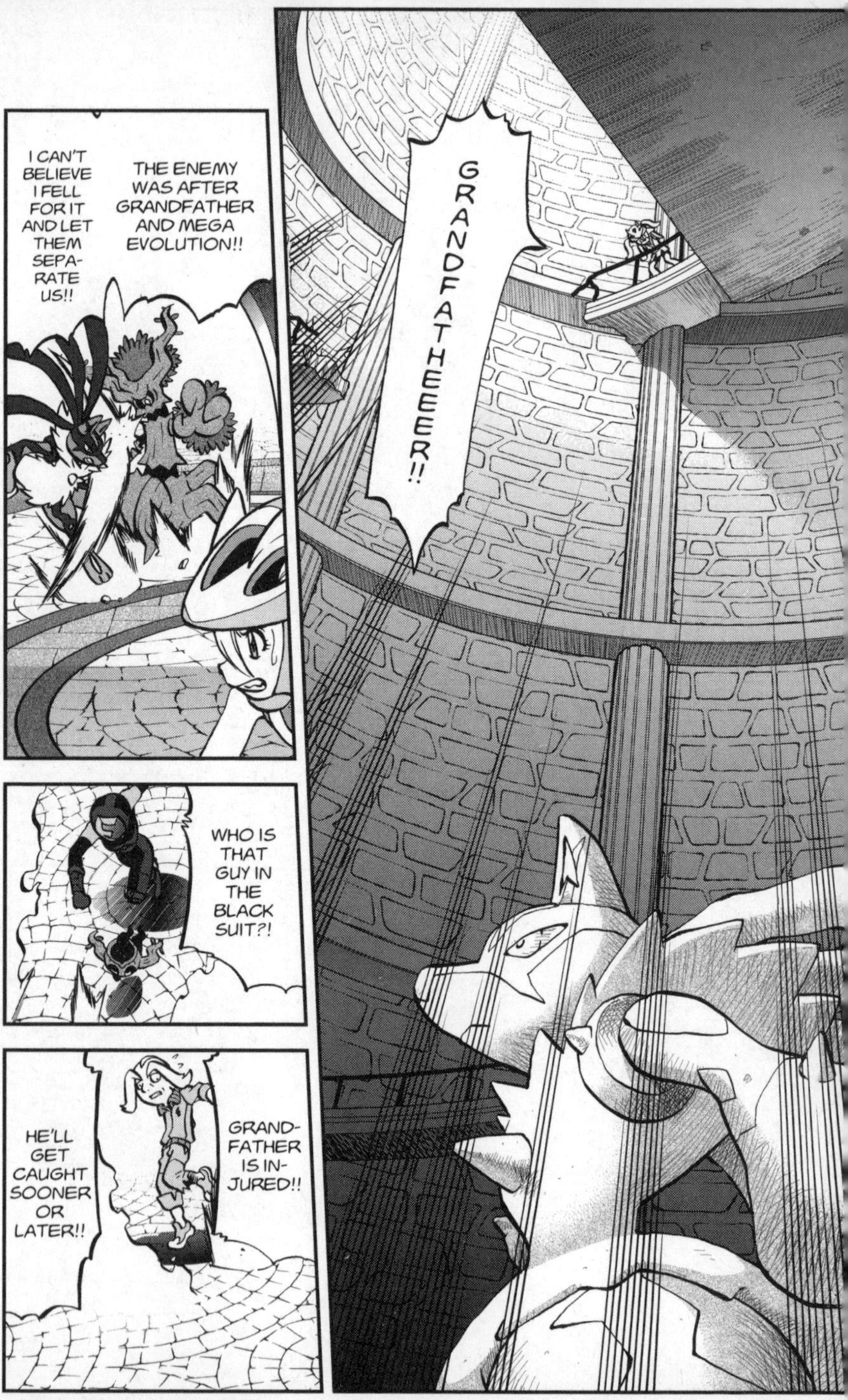
GRANDFATHEEER!!
THE ENEMY WAS AFTER GRANDFATHER AND MEGA EVOLUTION!!
I CAN'T BELIEVE I FELL FOR IT AND LET THEM SEPARATE US!!
WHO IS THAT GUY IN THE BLACK SUIT?!
GRANDFATHER IS INJURED!!
HE'LL GET CAUGHT SOONER OR LATER!!

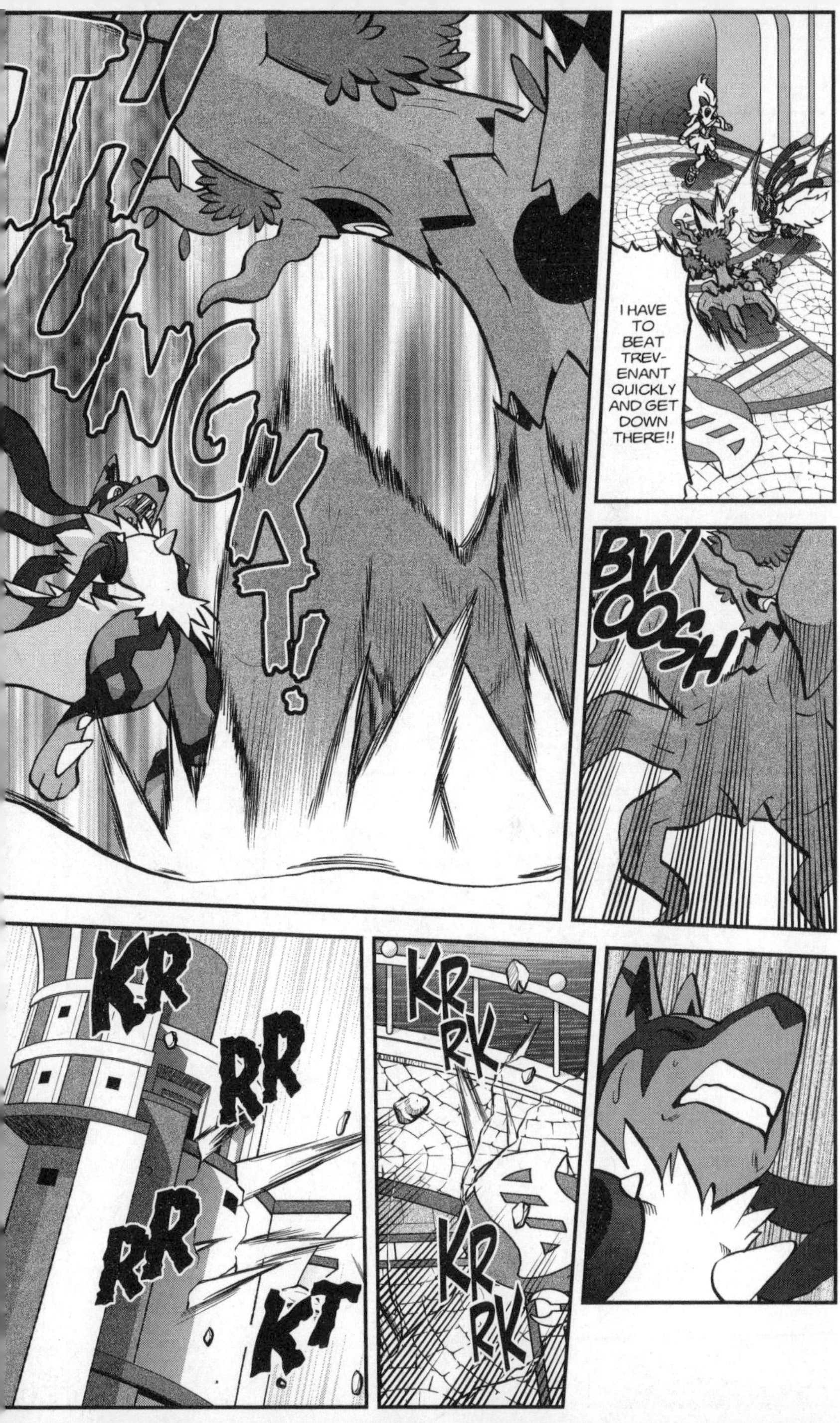
I HAVE TO BEAT TREV-ENANT QUICKLY AND GET DOWN THERE!!
BWOOSH
KR RK
KR RK
KR RR RR KT

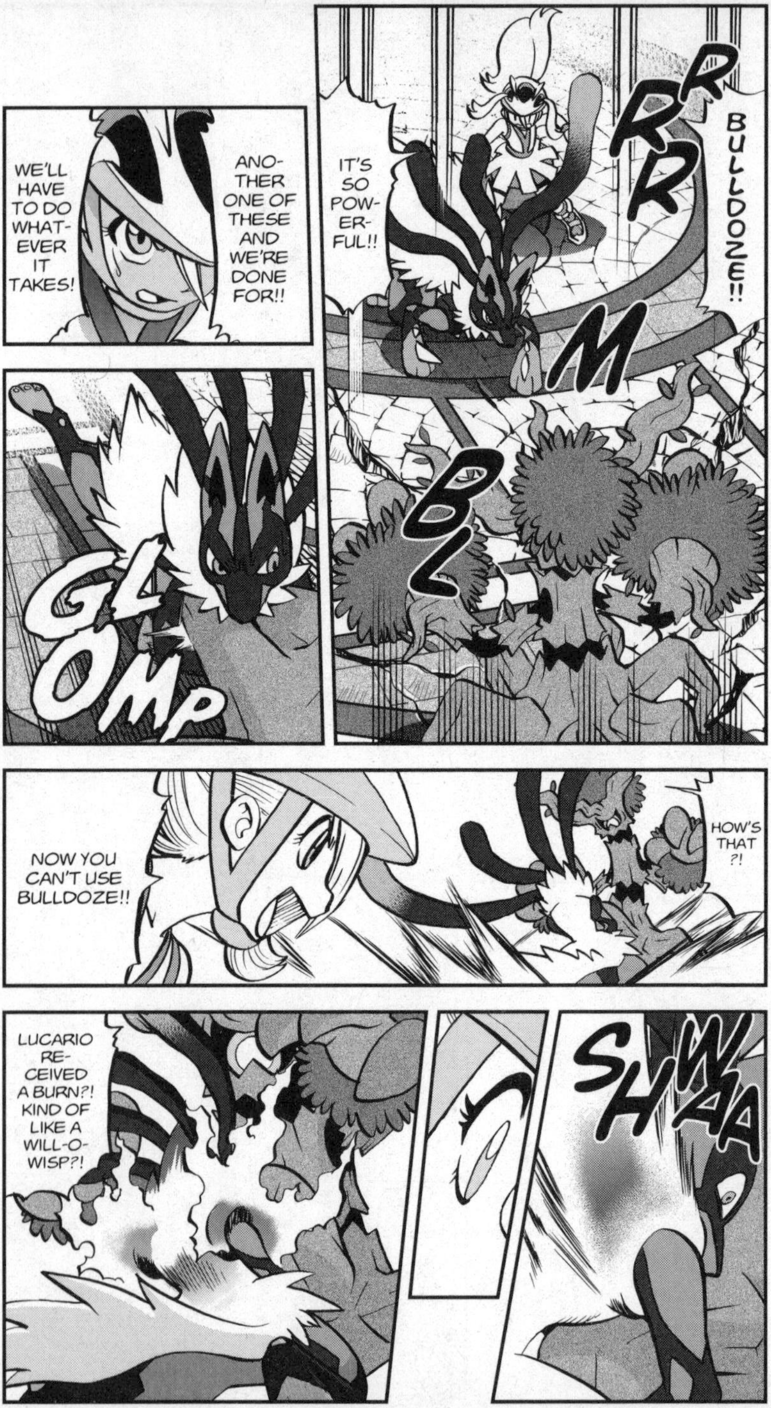
BULLDOZE!!
RRRR
IT'S SO POWERFUL!!
M
BL
ANOTHER ONE OF THESE AND WE'RE DONE FOR!!
WE'LL HAVE TO DO WHATEVER IT TAKES!
GLOMP
HOW'S THAT?!
NOW YOU CAN'T USE BULLDOZE!!
SHWAA
LUCARIO RECEIVED A BURN?! KIND OF LIKE A WILL-O-WISP?!

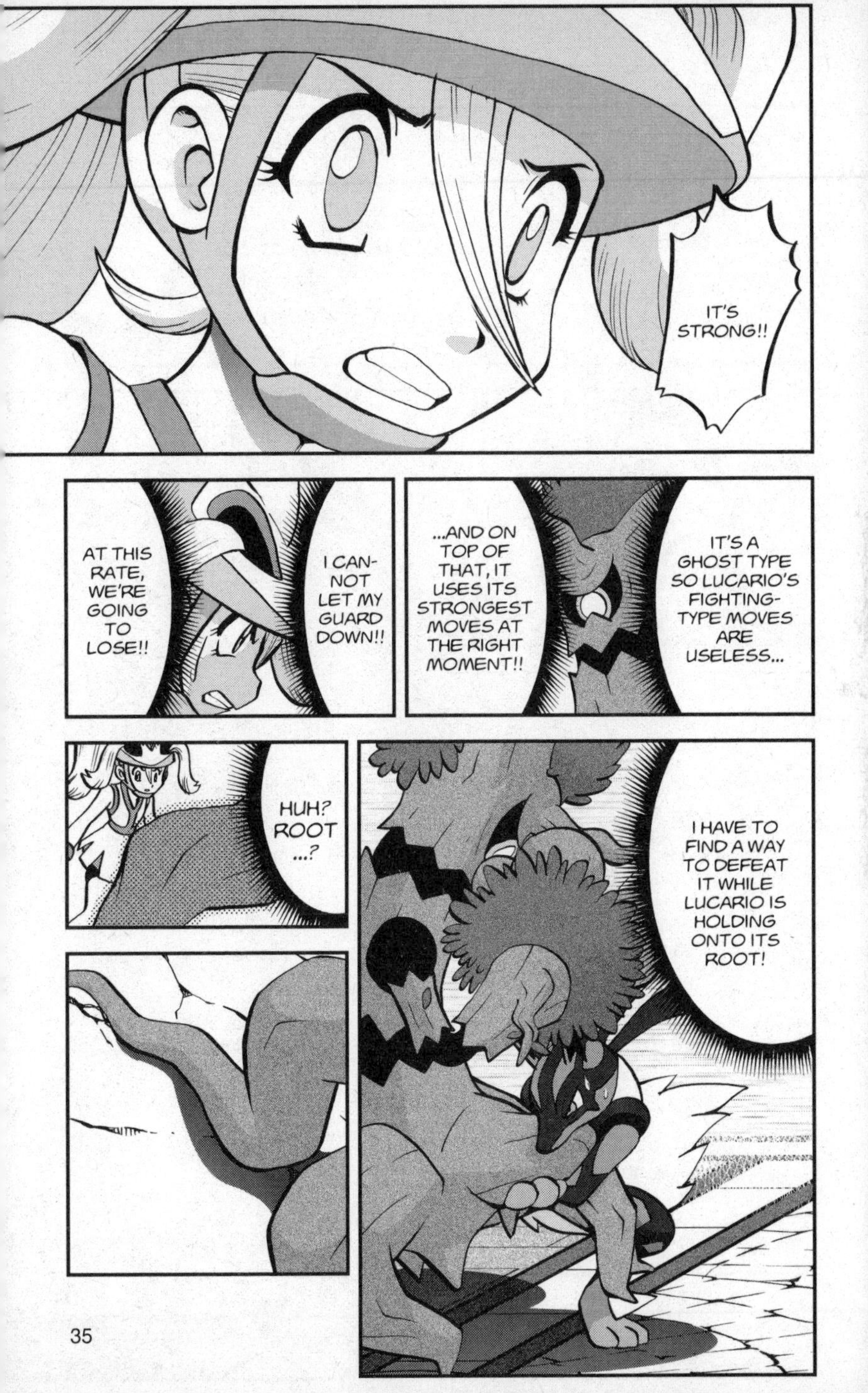

IT'S STRONG!!
IT'S A GHOST TYPE SO LUCARIO'S FIGHTING-TYPE MOVES ARE USELESS...
...AND ON TOP OF THAT, IT USES ITS STRONGEST MOVES AT THE RIGHT MOMENT!!
I CAN-NOT LET MY GUARD DOWN!!
AT THIS RATE, WE'RE GOING TO LOSE!!
I HAVE TO FIND A WAY TO DEFEAT IT WHILE LUCARIO IS HOLDING ONTO ITS ROOT!
HUH? ROOT ...?

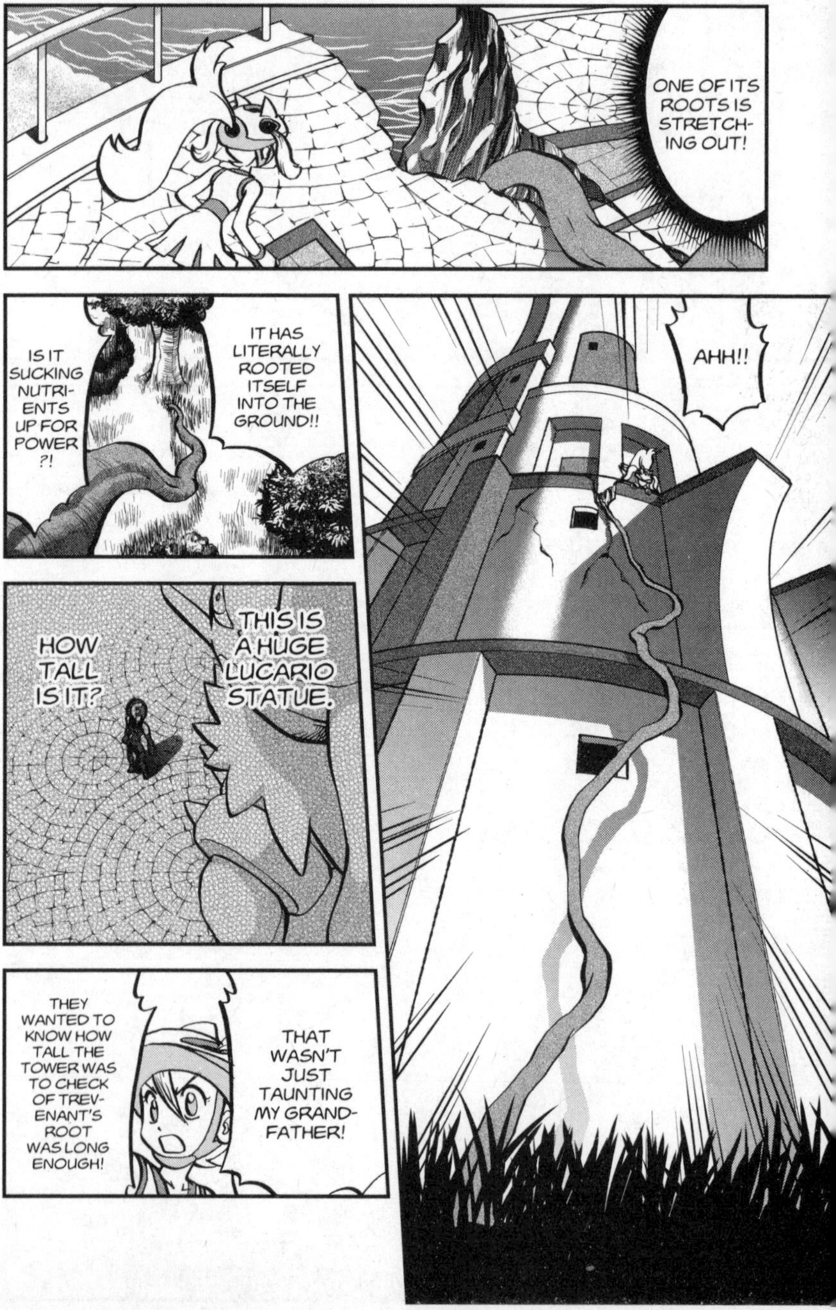
ONE OF ITS ROOTS IS STRETCHING OUT!
AHH!!
IT HAS LITERALLY ROOTED ITSELF INTO THE GROUND!!
IS IT SUCKING NUTRIENTS UP FOR POWER?!
THIS IS A HUGE LUCARIO STATUE.
HOW TALL IS IT?
THAT WASN'T JUST TAUNTING MY GRANDFATHER!
THEY WANTED TO KNOW HOW TALL THE TOWER WAS TO CHECK OF TREVENANT'S ROOT WAS LONG ENOUGH!

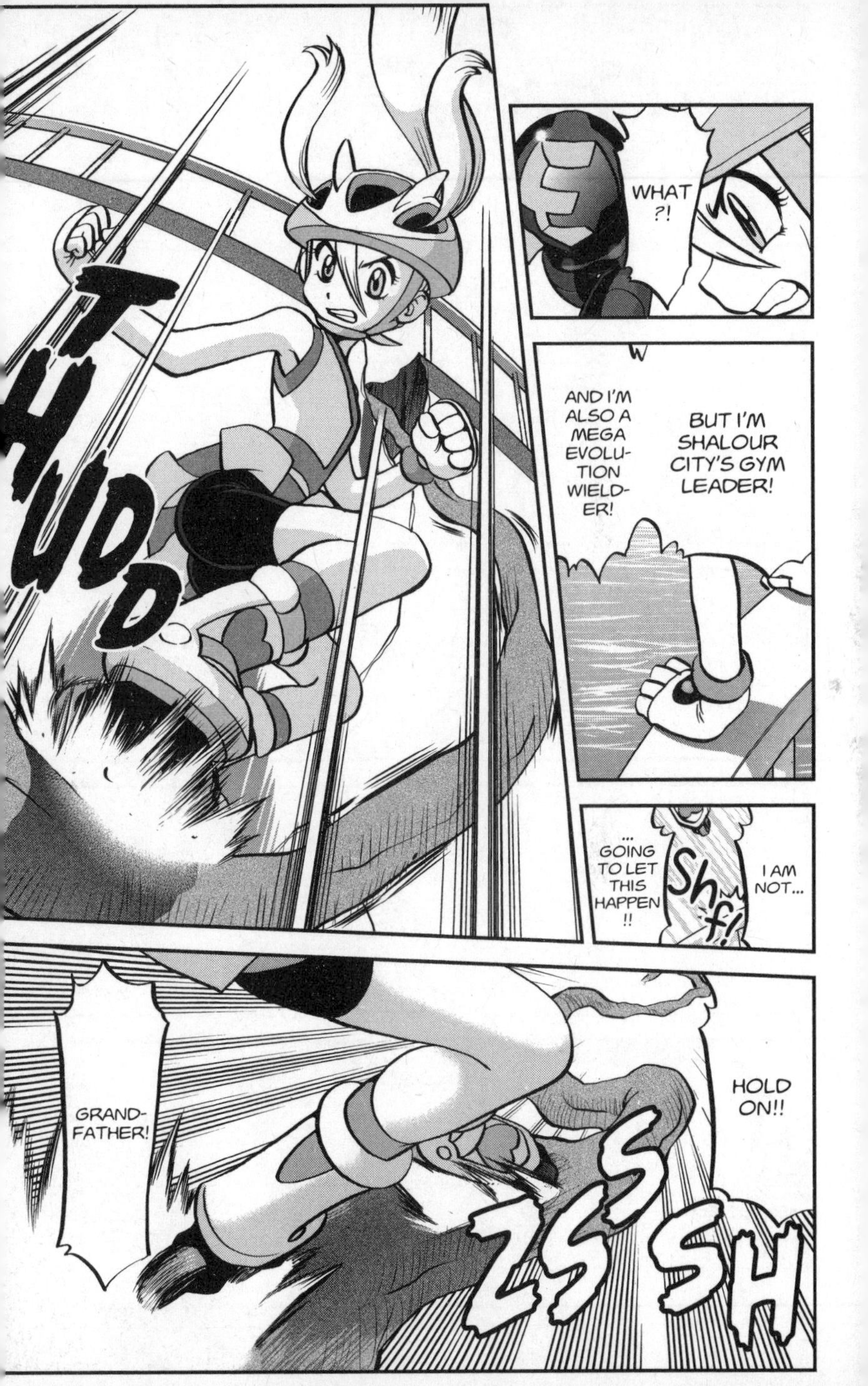
WHAT?!
BUT I'M SHALOUR CITY'S GYM LEADER!
AND I'M ALSO A MEGA EVOLUTION WIELDER!
I AM NOT...
Shf!
...GOING TO LET THIS HAPPEN!!
THUD
HOLD ON!!
ZSSSH
GRANDFATHER!

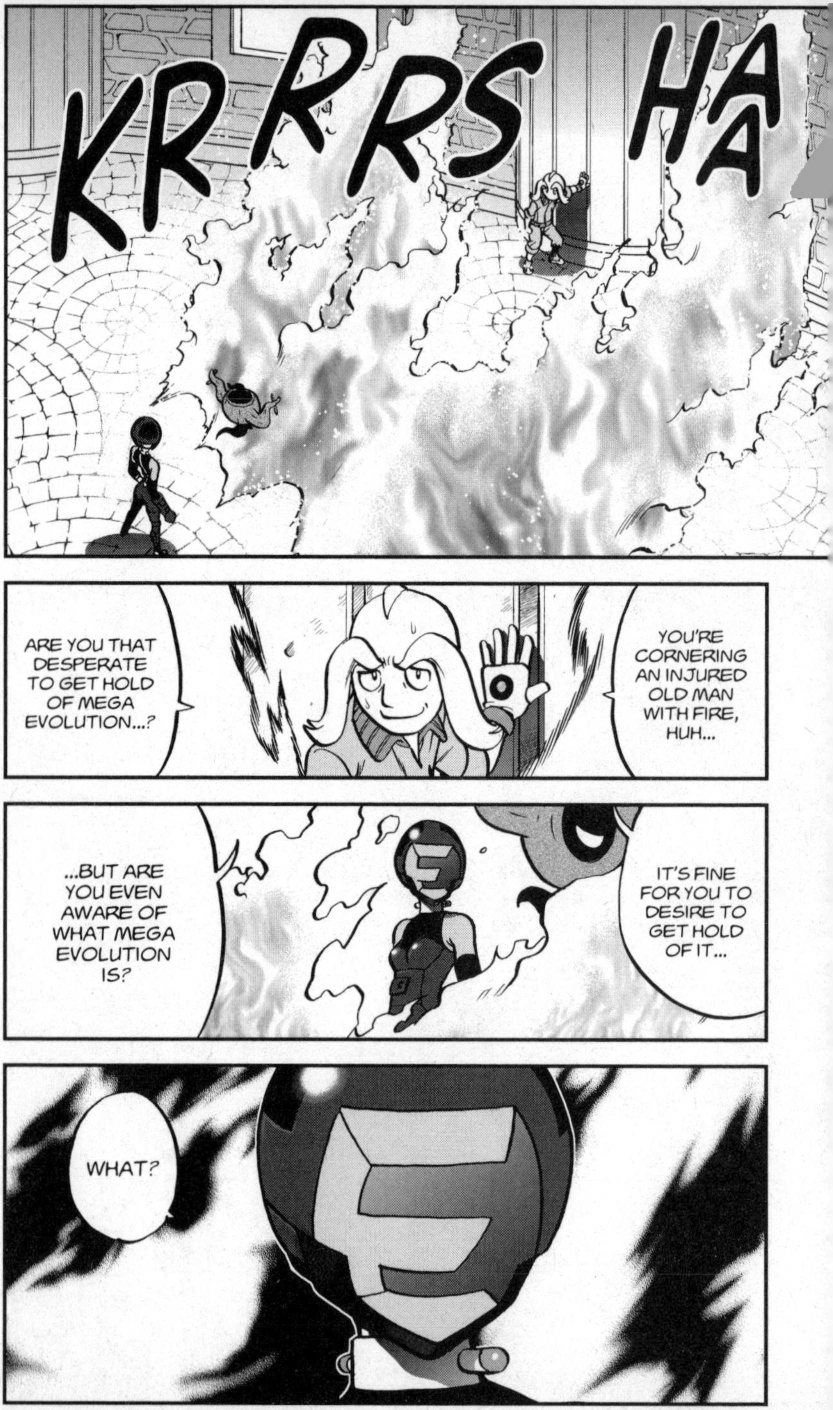
KRRRSHAA
YOU'RE CORNERING AN INJURED OLD MAN WITH FIRE, HUH...
ARE YOU THAT DESPERATE TO GET HOLD OF MEGA EVOLUTION...?
IT'S FINE FOR YOU TO DESIRE TO GET HOLD OF IT...
...BUT ARE YOU EVEN AWARE OF WHAT MEGA EVOLUTION IS?
WHAT?

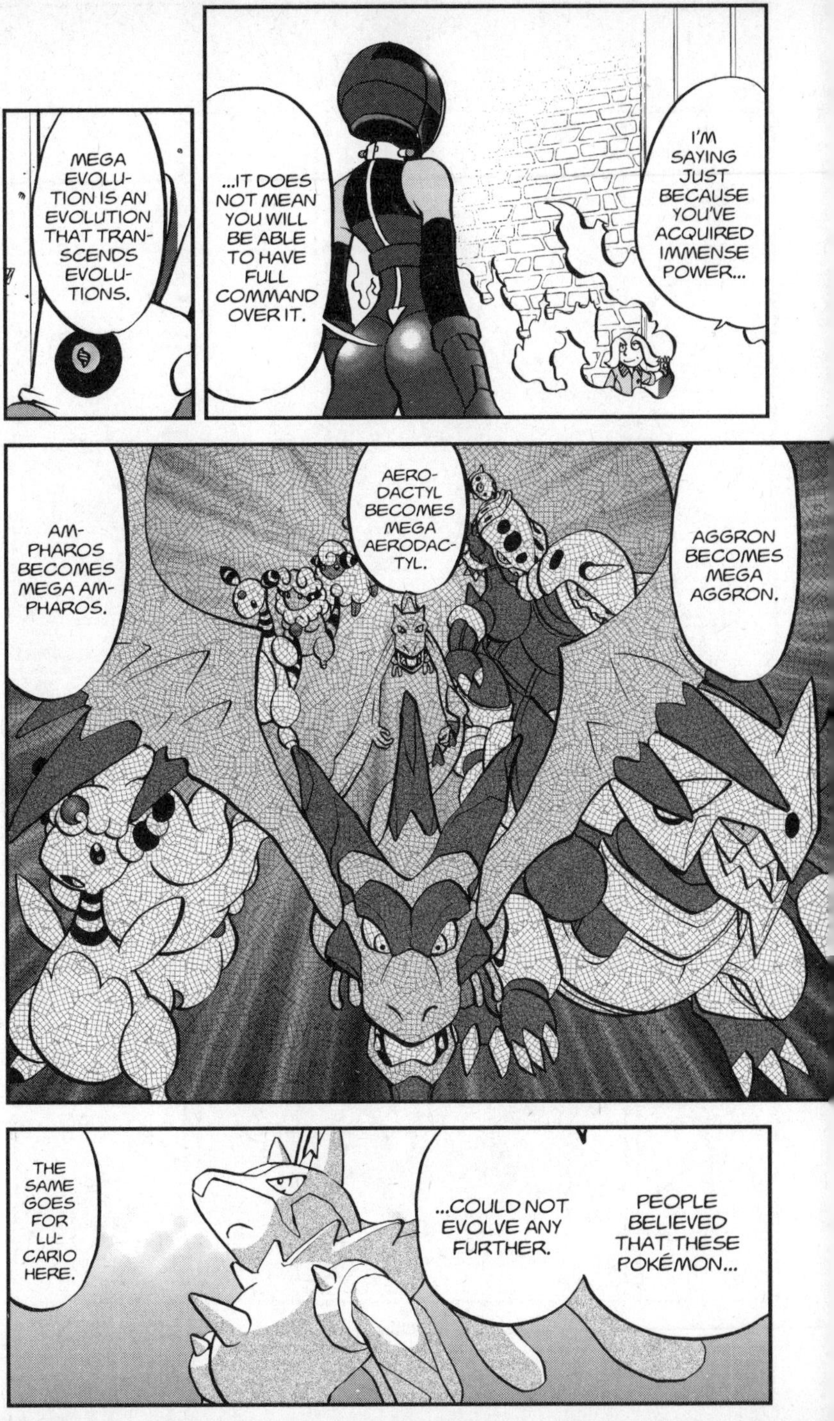
I'M SAYING JUST BECAUSE YOU'VE ACQUIRED IMMENSE POWER...
...IT DOES NOT MEAN YOU WILL BE ABLE TO HAVE FULL COMMAND OVER IT.
MEGA EVOLUTION IS AN EVOLUTION THAT TRANSCENDS EVOLUTIONS.
AGGRON BECOMES MEGA AGGRON.
AERODACTYL BECOMES MEGA AERODACTYL.
AMPHAROS BECOMES MEGA AMPHAROS.
PEOPLE BELIEVED THAT THESE POKÉMON...
...COULD NOT EVOLVE ANY FURTHER.
THE SAME GOES FOR LUCARIO HERE.

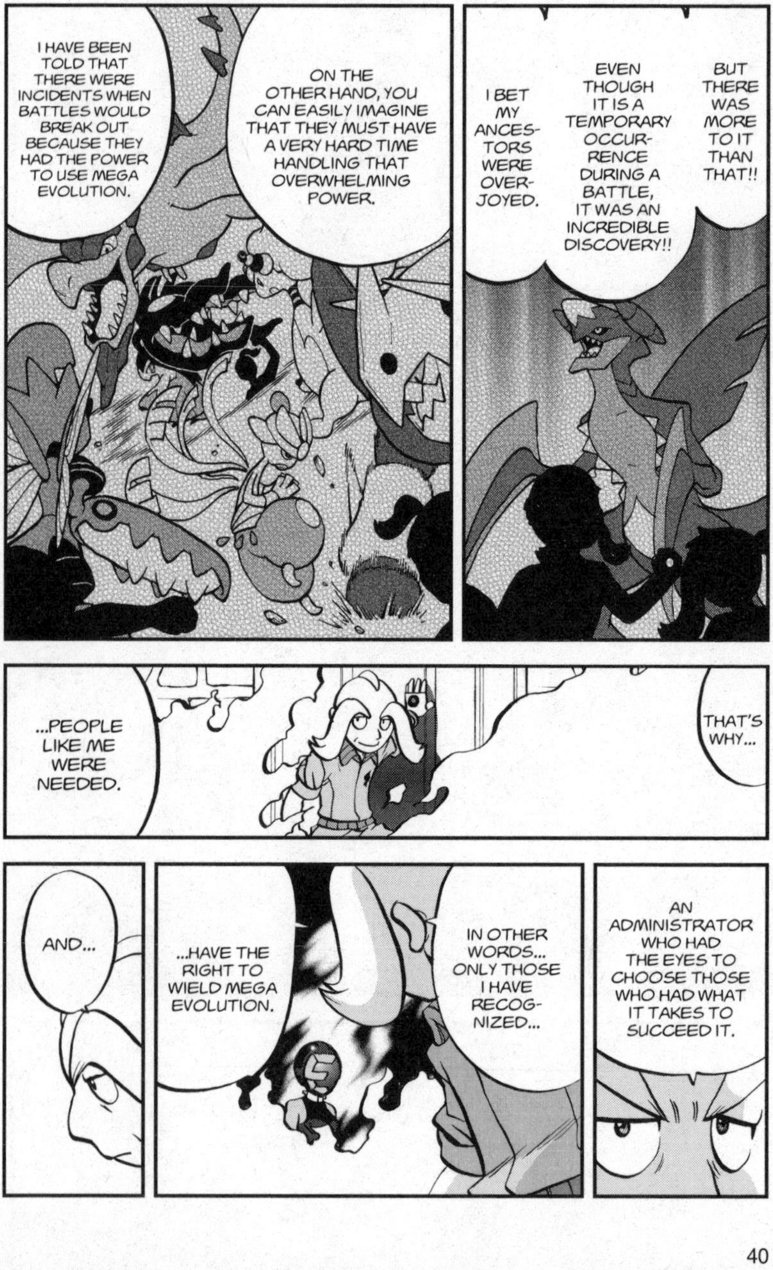
BUT THERE WAS MORE TO IT THAN THAT!!
EVEN THOUGH IT IS A TEMPORARY OCCURRENCE DURING A BATTLE, IT WAS AN INCREDIBLE DISCOVERY!!
I BET MY ANCESTORS WERE OVERJOYED.
ON THE OTHER HAND, YOU CAN EASILY IMAGINE THAT THEY MUST HAVE A VERY HARD TIME HANDLING THAT OVERWHELMING POWER.
I HAVE BEEN TOLD THAT THERE WERE INCIDENTS WHEN BATTLES WOULD BREAK OUT BECAUSE THEY HAD THE POWER TO USE MEGA EVOLUTION.
THAT'S WHY...
...PEOPLE LIKE ME WERE NEEDED.
AN ADMINISTRATOR WHO HAD THE EYES TO CHOOSE THOSE WHO HAD WHAT IT TAKES TO SUCCEED IT.
IN OTHER WORDS... ONLY THOSE I HAVE RECOGNIZED...
...HAVE THE RIGHT TO WIELD MEGA EVOLUTION.
AND...

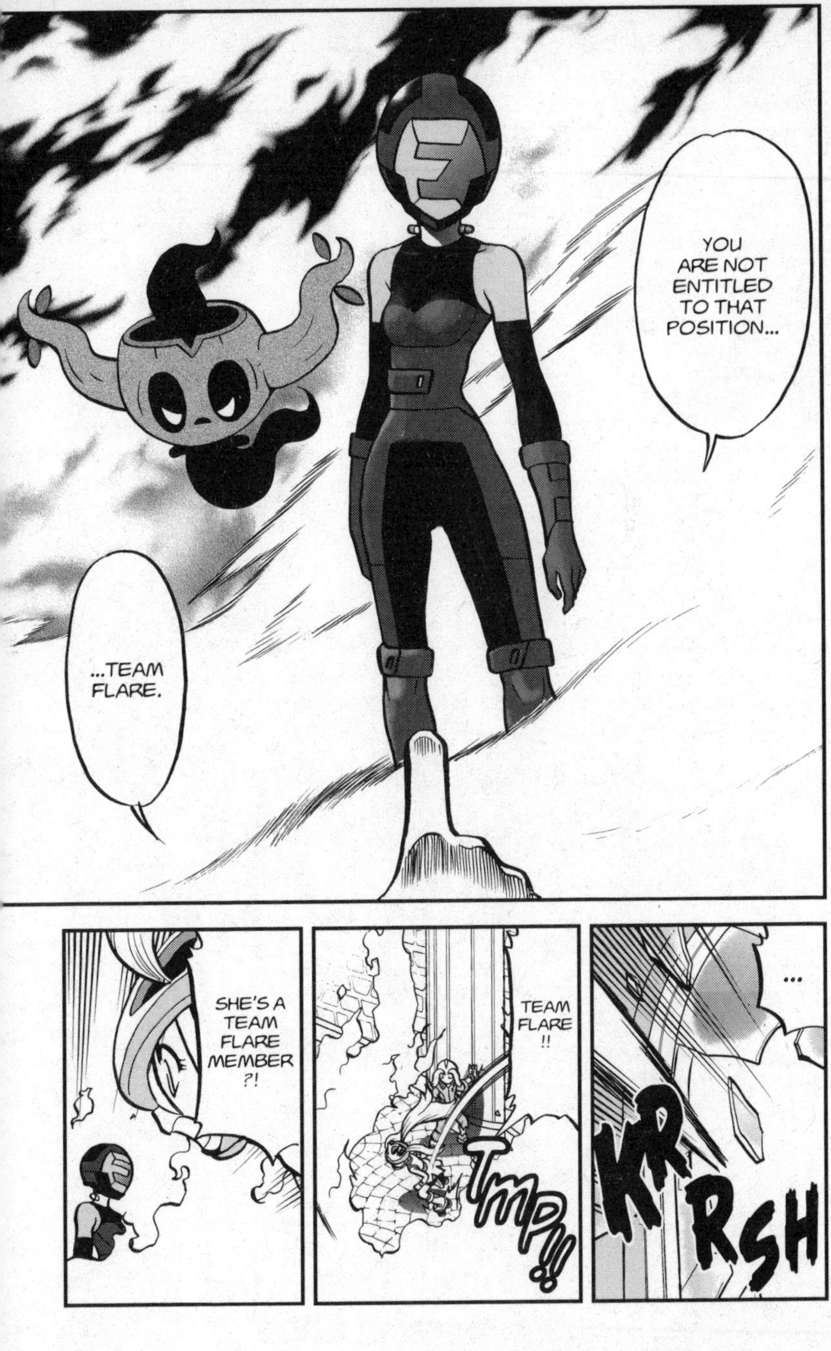
YOU ARE NOT ENTITLED TO THAT POSITION...
...TEAM FLARE.
...
KRRSH
TEAM FLARE !!
TMP!!
SHE'S A TEAM FLARE MEMBER ?!

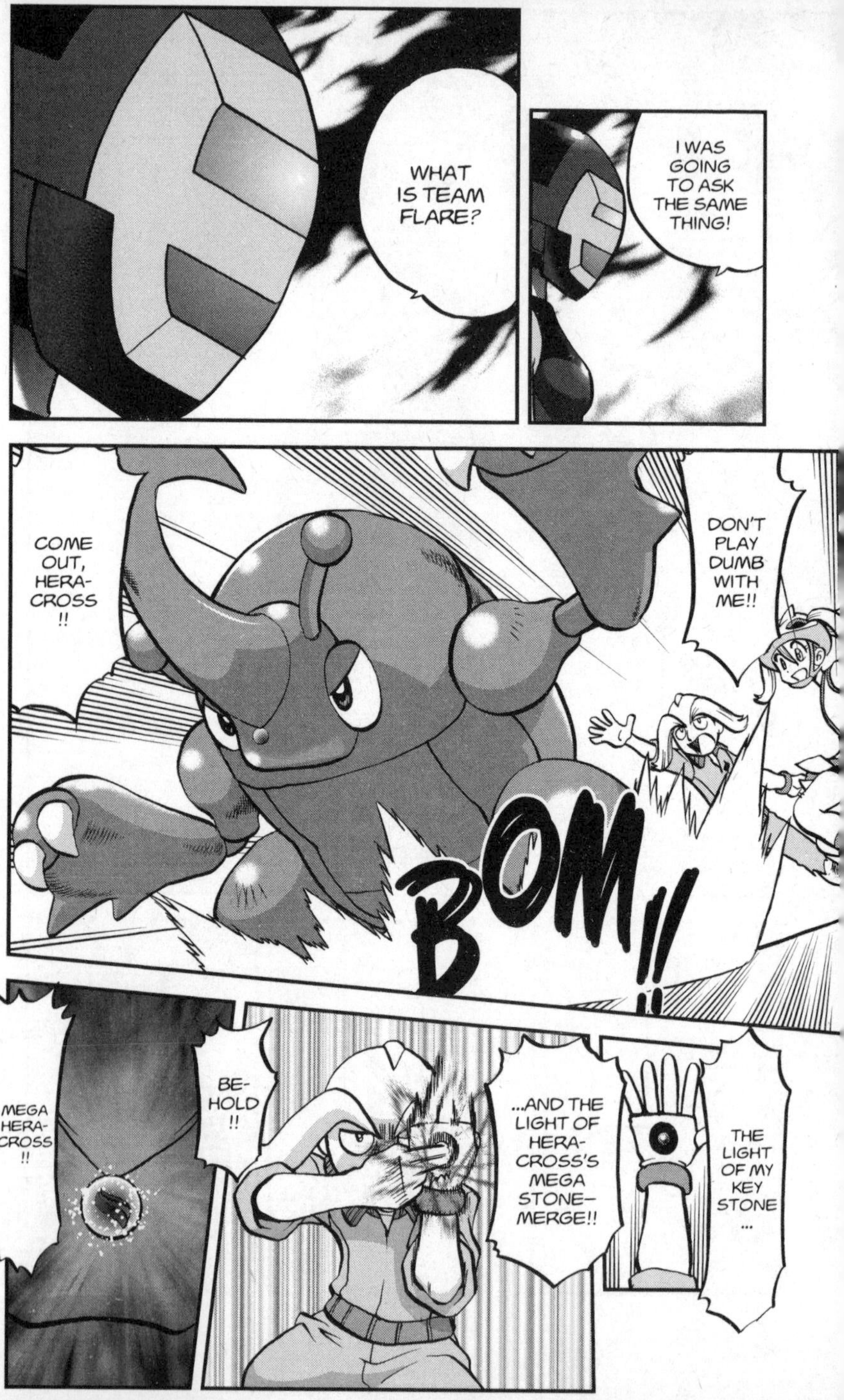
I WAS GOING TO ASK THE SAME THING!
WHAT IS TEAM FLARE?
DON'T PLAY DUMB WITH ME!!
COME OUT, HERA-CROSS!!
BOM!!
THE LIGHT OF MY KEY STONE...
...AND THE LIGHT OF HERA-CROSS'S MEGA STONE—MERGE!!
BE-HOLD!!
MEGA HERA-CROSS!!

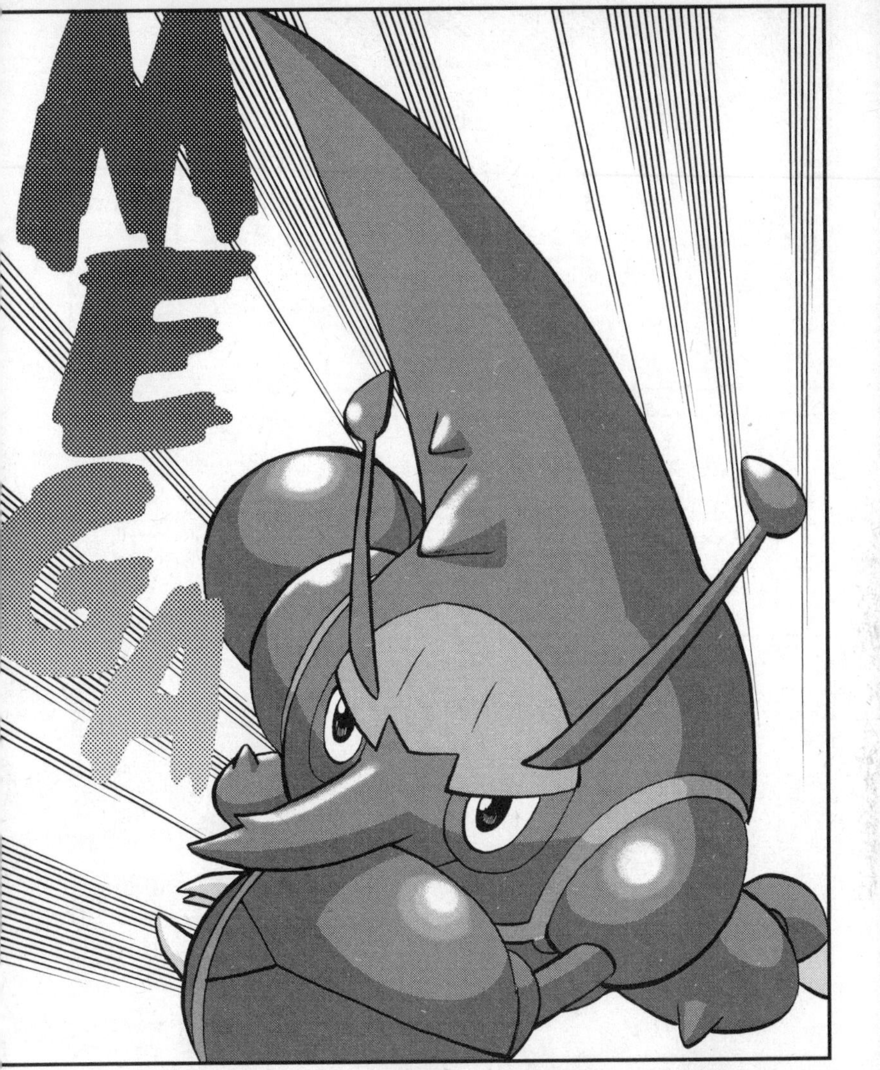
MEGA
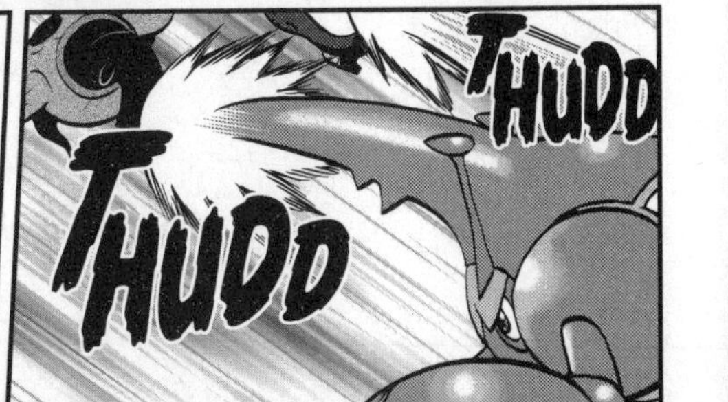
THUDD
THUDD
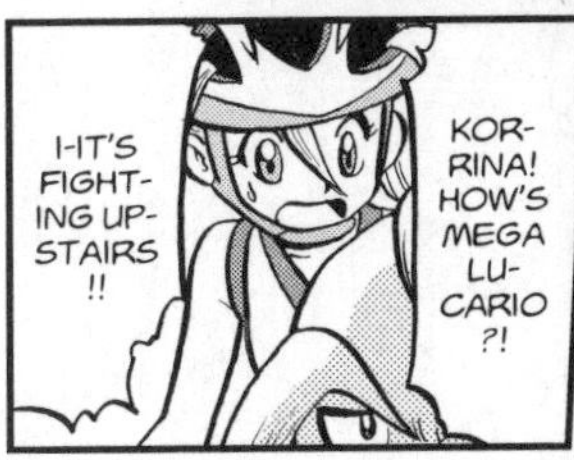
KORRINA! HOW'S MEGA LUCARIO?!
I-IT'S FIGHTING UPSTAIRS!!

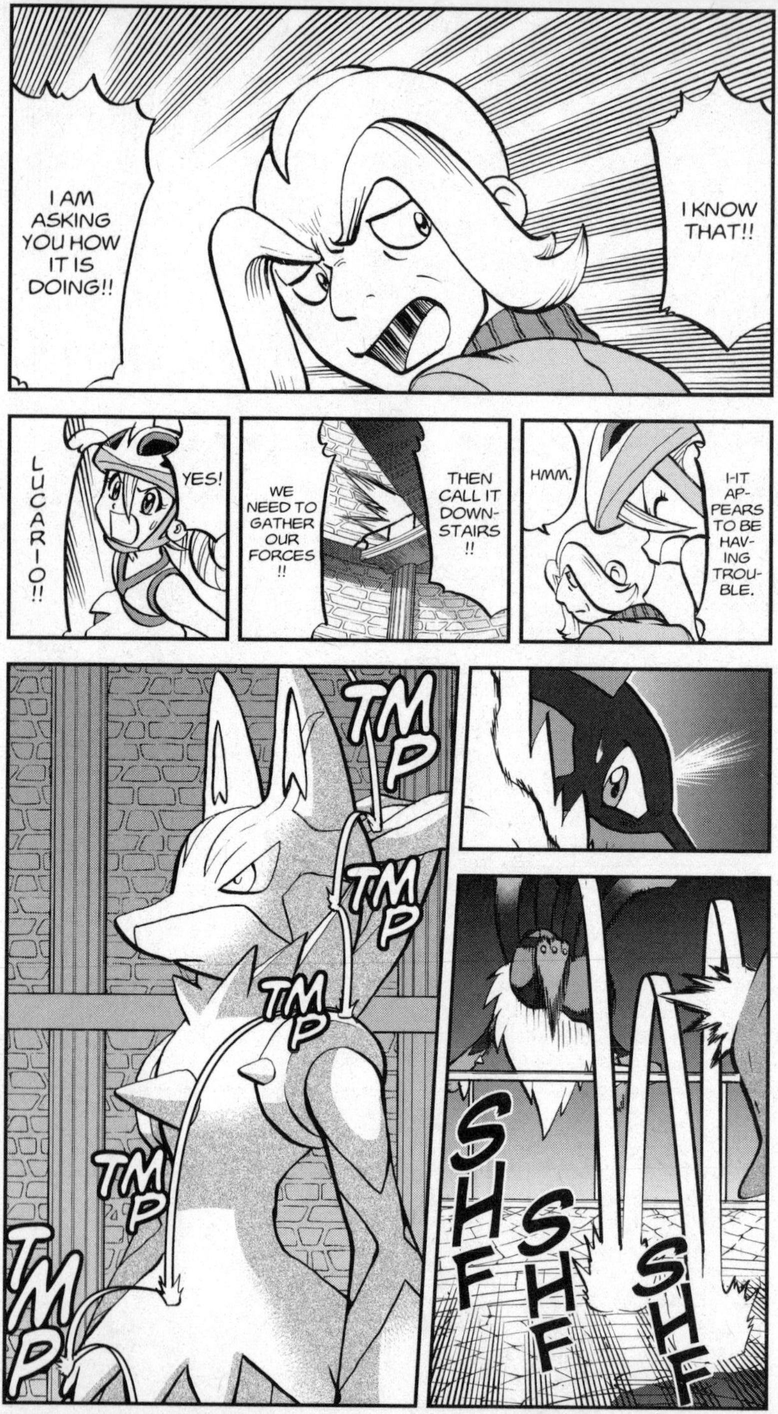
I KNOW THAT!!
I AM ASKING YOU HOW IT IS DOING!!
I-IT APPEARS TO BE HAVING TROUBLE.
HMM.
THEN CALL IT DOWNSTAIRS!!
WE NEED TO GATHER OUR FORCES!!
YES!
LUCARIO!!
SHF
SHF
SHF
TMP
TMP
TMP
TMP
TMP

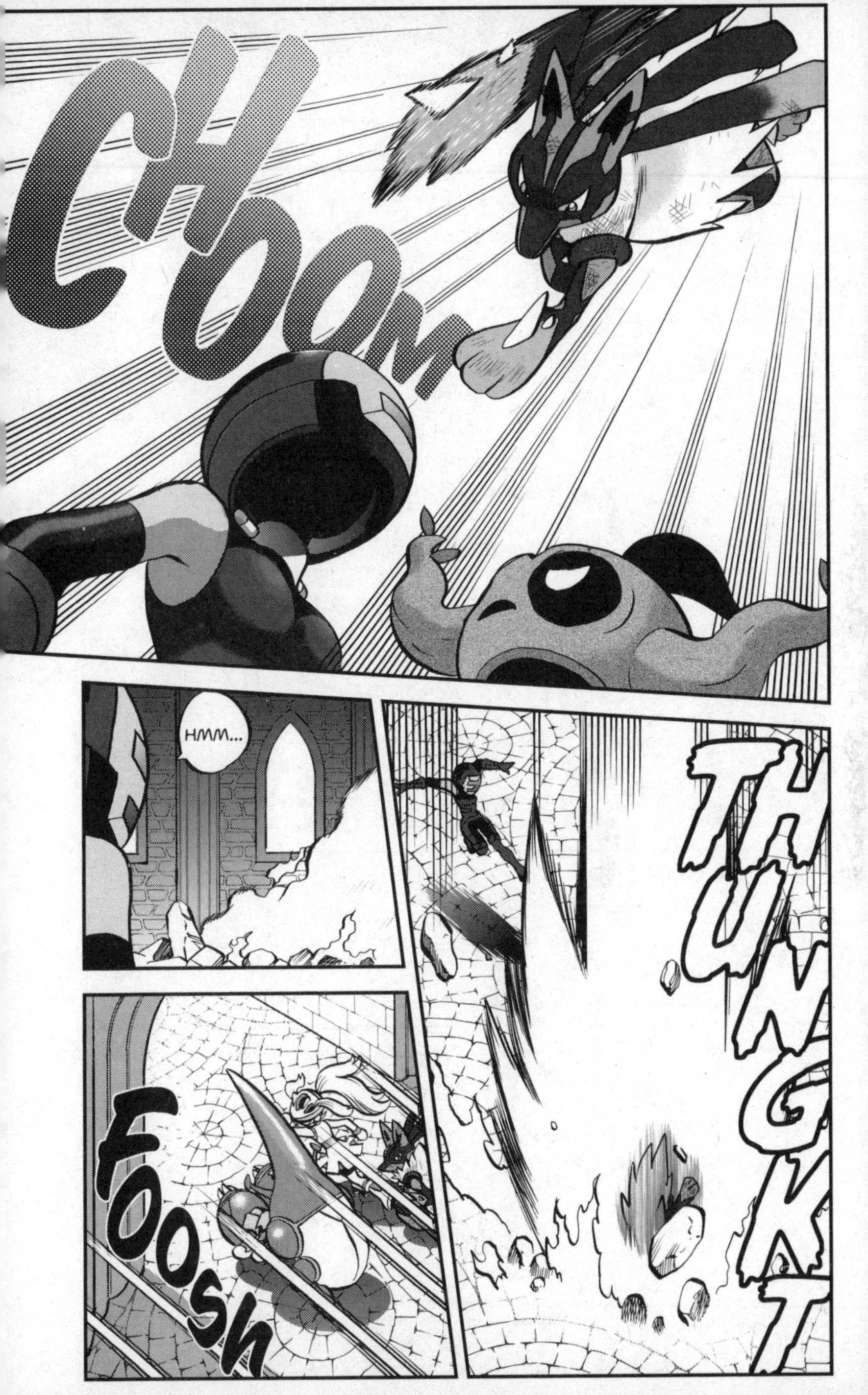
CHOOM
THUNGKAT
HMM...
FOOSH

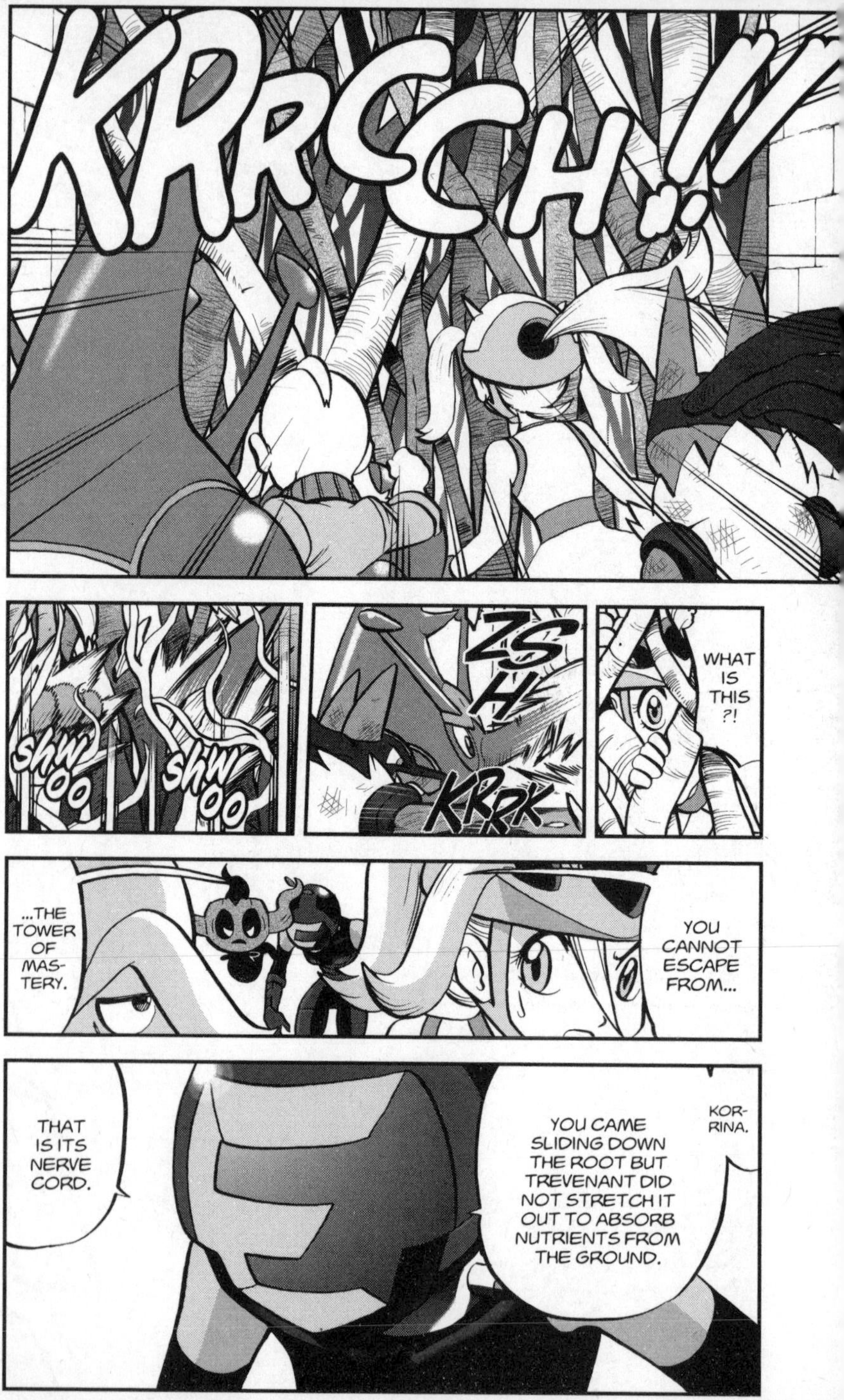
KRRCCH!!
WHAT IS THIS ?!
ZSH
KRRK
shwoo
shwoo
YOU CANNOT ESCAPE FROM...
...THE TOWER OF MAS-TERY.
KOR-RINA.
YOU CAME SLIDING DOWN THE ROOT BUT TREVENANT DID NOT STRETCH IT OUT TO ABSORB NUTRIENTS FROM THE GROUND.
THAT IS ITS NERVE CORD.

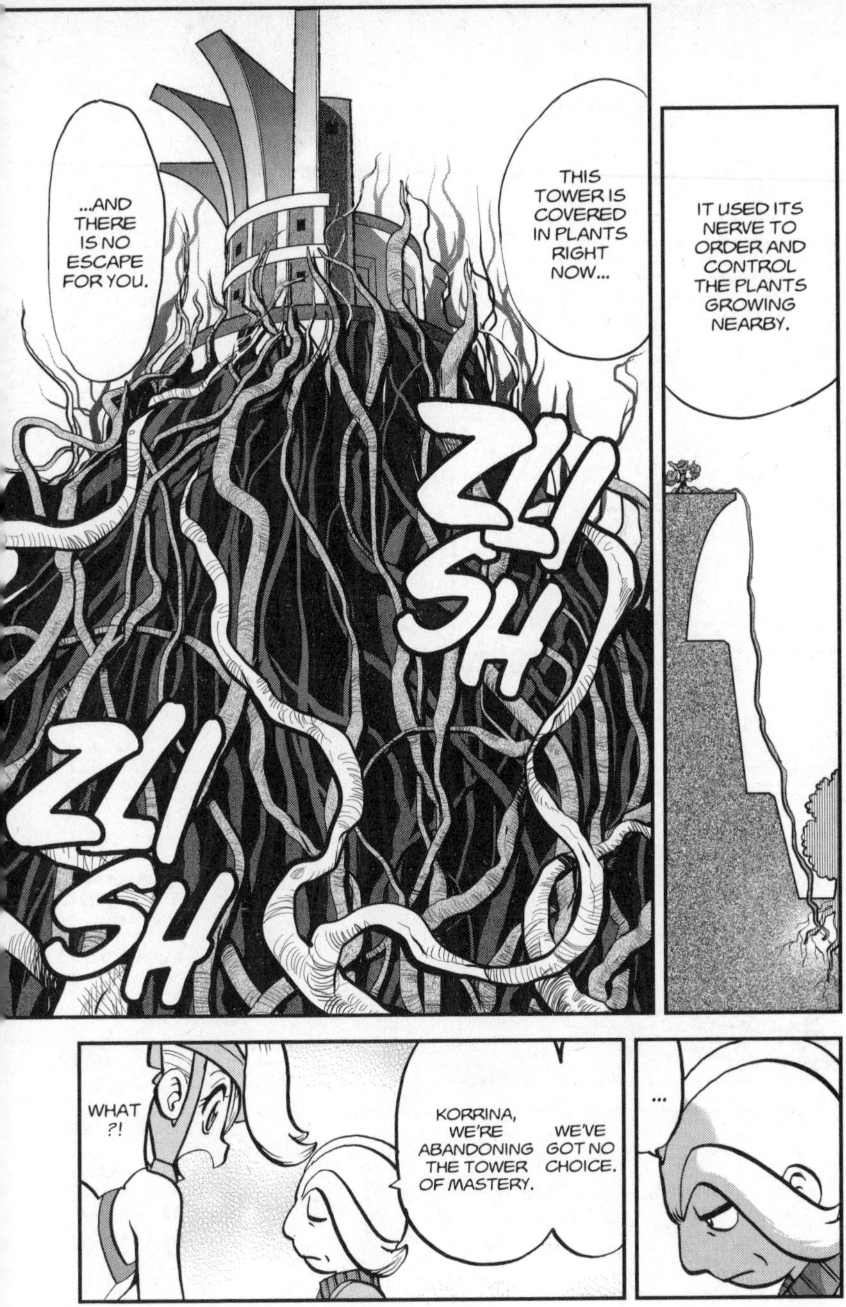
IT USED ITS NERVE TO ORDER AND CONTROL THE PLANTS GROWING NEARBY.
THIS TOWER IS COVERED IN PLANTS RIGHT NOW...
...AND THERE IS NO ESCAPE FOR YOU.
ZISH
ZISH
...
KORRINA, WE'RE ABANDONING THE TOWER OF MASTERY.
WE'VE GOT NO CHOICE.
WHAT ?!

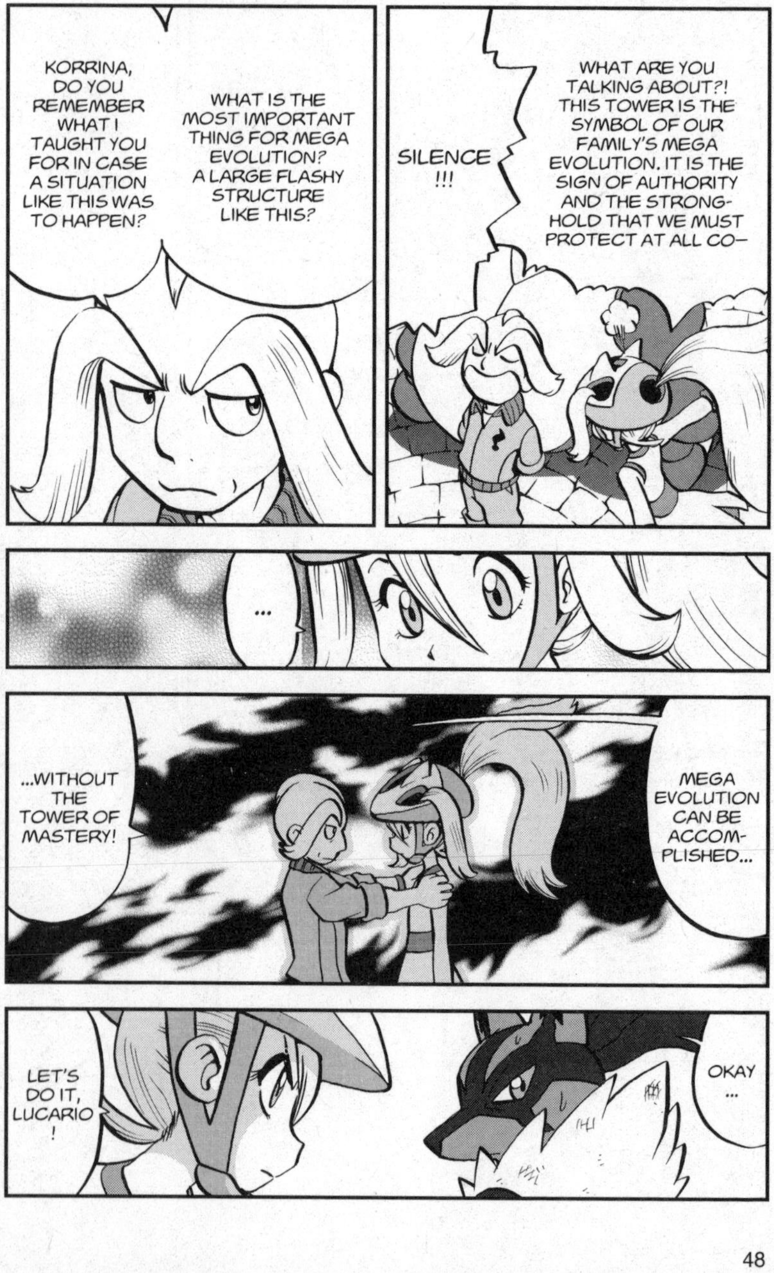

WHAT ARE YOU TALKING ABOUT?! THIS TOWER IS THE SYMBOL OF OUR FAMILY'S MEGA EVOLUTION. IT IS THE SIGN OF AUTHORITY AND THE STRONG-HOLD THAT WE MUST PROTECT AT ALL CO—
SILENCE!!!
KORRINA, DO YOU REMEMBER WHAT I TAUGHT YOU FOR IN CASE A SITUATION LIKE THIS WAS TO HAPPEN?
WHAT IS THE MOST IMPORTANT THING FOR MEGA EVOLUTION? A LARGE FLASHY STRUCTURE LIKE THIS?
...
MEGA EVOLUTION CAN BE ACCOM-PLISHED...
...WITHOUT THE TOWER OF MASTERY!
OKAY...
LET'S DO IT, LUCARIO!

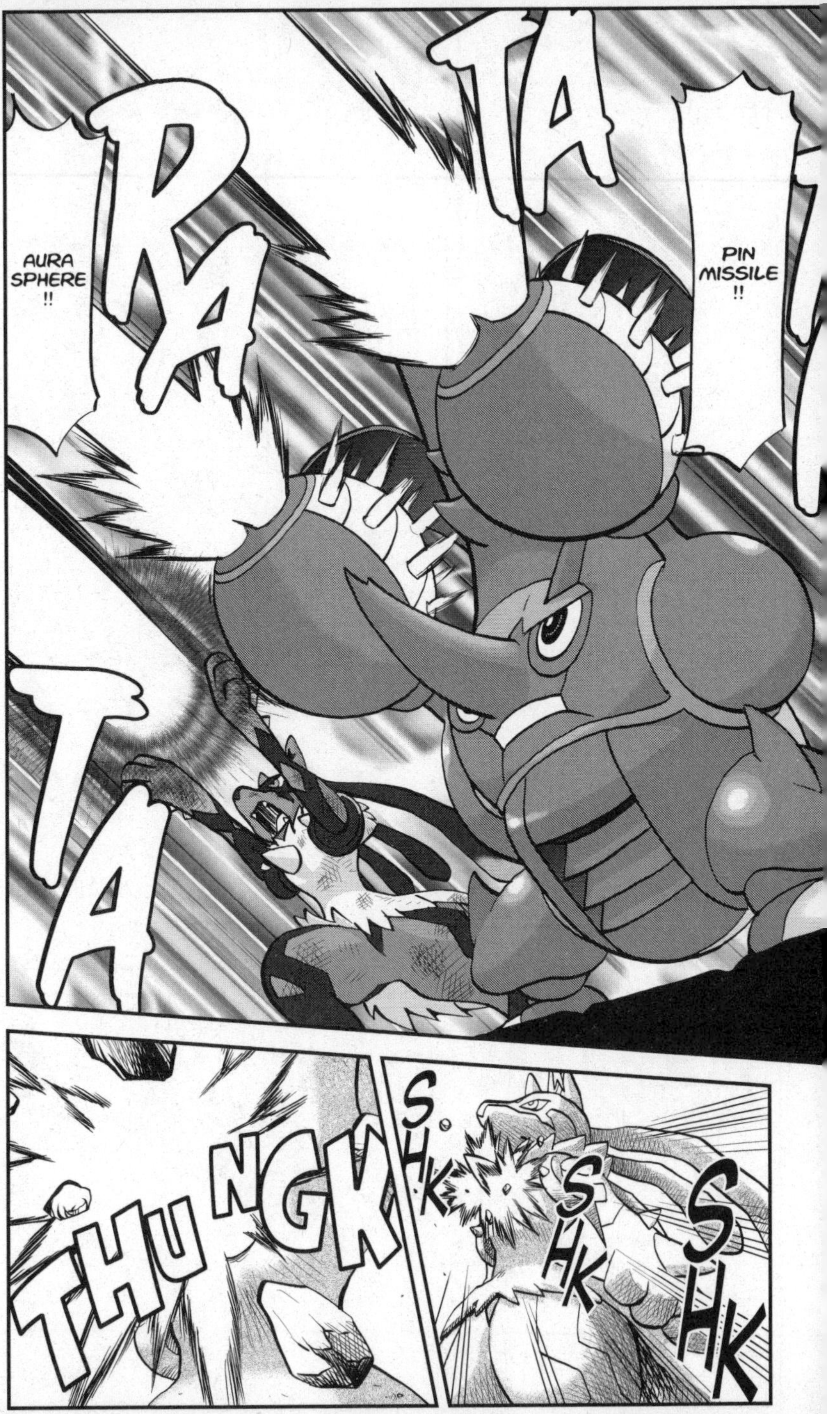
PIN MISSILE !!
AURA SPHERE !!
RA
TA
TA
SHK
SHK
SHK
THUNGK

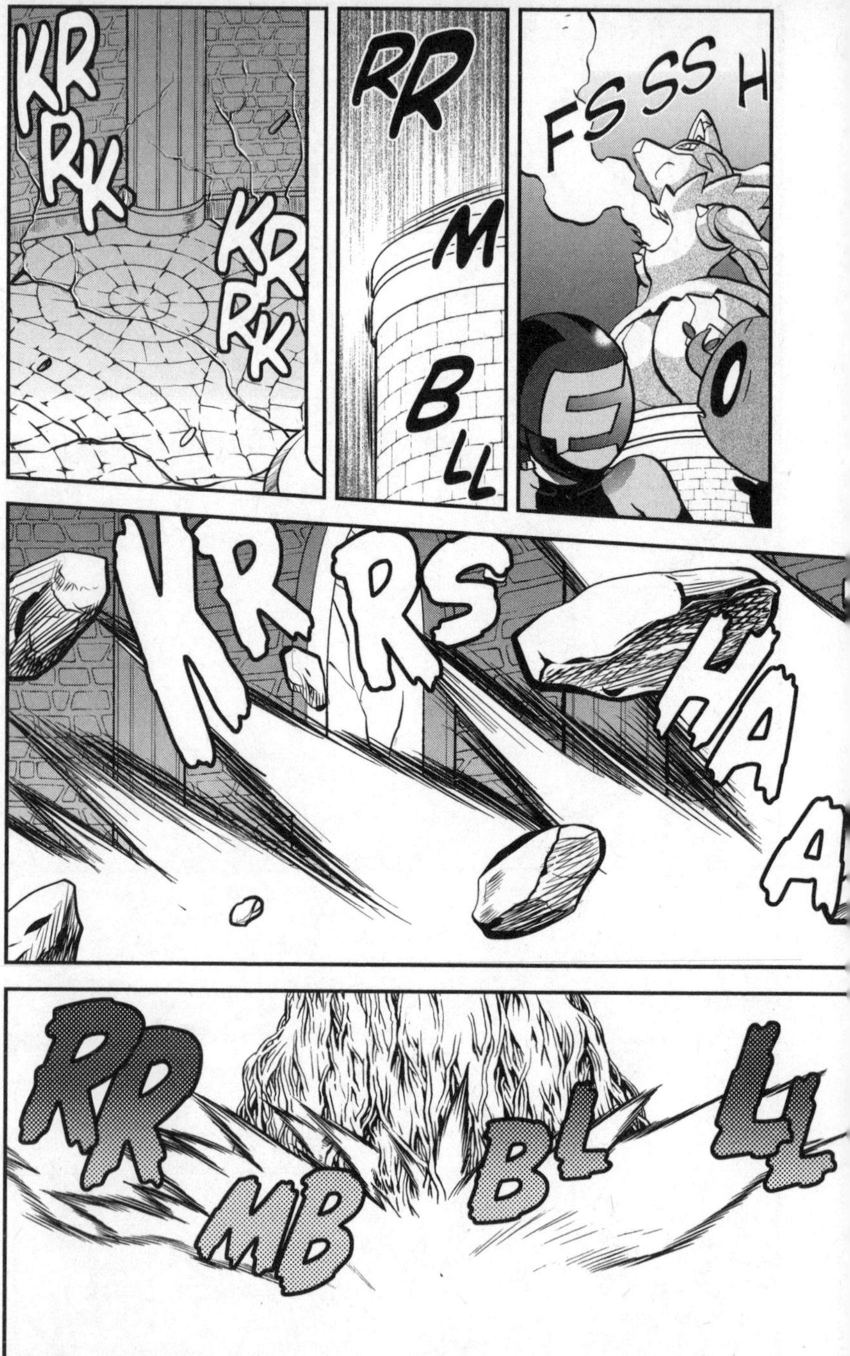
FSSSH
RR
M
B
LL
KR
RK
KR
RK
KRRS
HAA
RR
MB
BL
LL

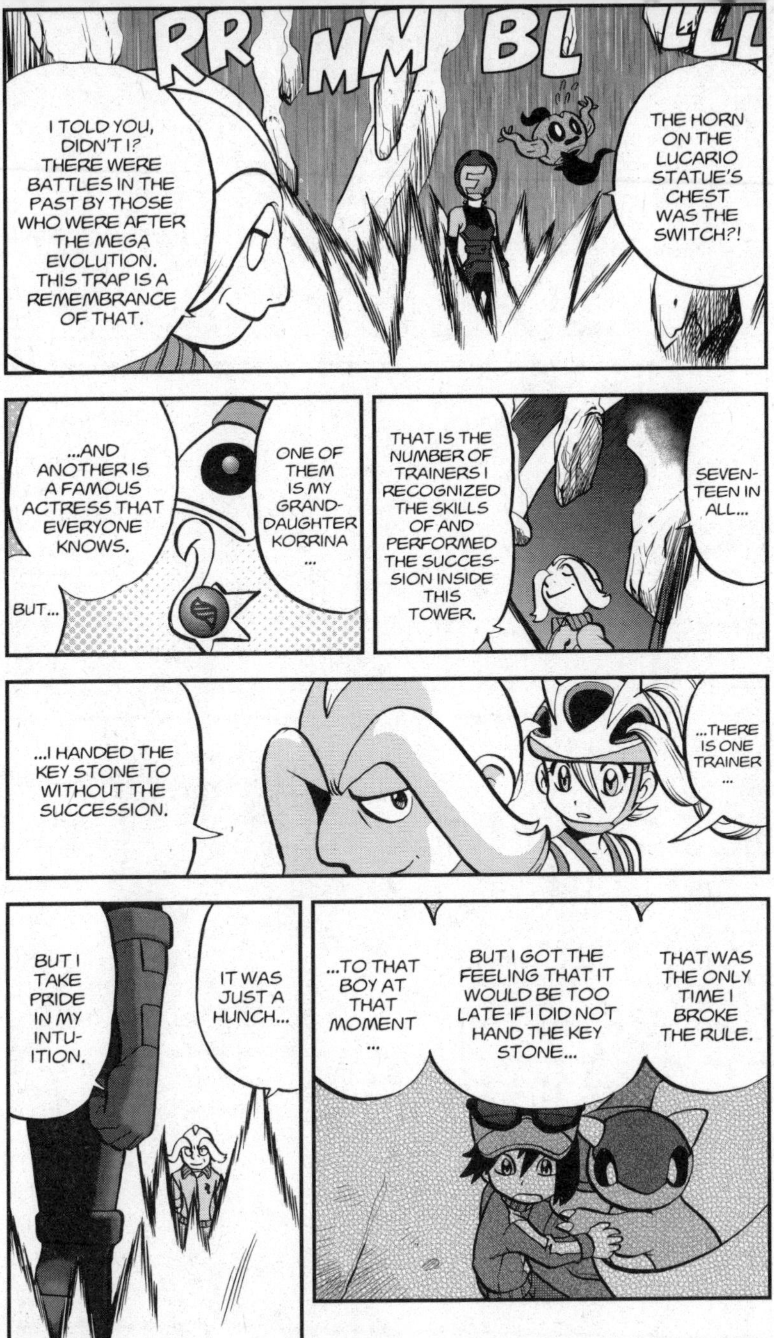
RR MM BL LLL
THE HORN ON THE LUCARIO STATUE'S CHEST WAS THE SWITCH?!
I TOLD YOU, DIDN'T I? THERE WERE BATTLES IN THE PAST BY THOSE WHO WERE AFTER THE MEGA EVOLUTION. THIS TRAP IS A REMEMBRANCE OF THAT.
SEVENTEEN IN ALL...
THAT IS THE NUMBER OF TRAINERS I RECOGNIZED THE SKILLS OF AND PERFORMED THE SUCCESSION INSIDE THIS TOWER.
ONE OF THEM IS MY GRANDDAUGHTER KORRINA ...
...AND ANOTHER IS A FAMOUS ACTRESS THAT EVERYONE KNOWS.
BUT...
...THERE IS ONE TRAINER ...
...I HANDED THE KEY STONE TO WITHOUT THE SUCCESSION.
THAT WAS THE ONLY TIME I BROKE THE RULE.
BUT I GOT THE FEELING THAT IT WOULD BE TOO LATE IF I DID NOT HAND THE KEY STONE...
...TO THAT BOY AT THAT MOMENT ...
IT WAS JUST A HUNCH...
BUT I TAKE PRIDE IN MY INTUITION.

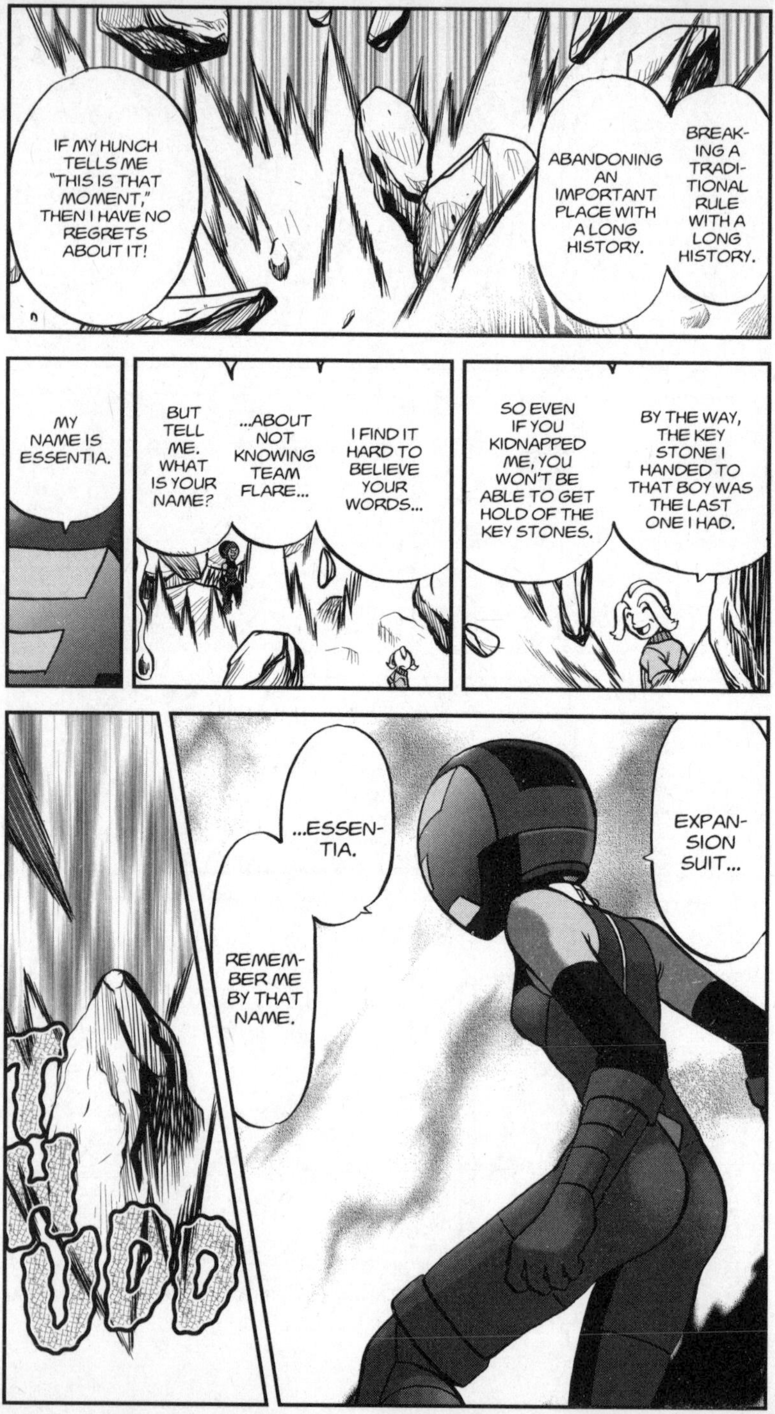
BREAKING A TRADITIONAL RULE WITH A LONG HISTORY.
ABANDONING AN IMPORTANT PLACE WITH A LONG HISTORY.
IF MY HUNCH TELLS ME "THIS IS THAT MOMENT," THEN I HAVE NO REGRETS ABOUT IT!
BY THE WAY, THE KEY STONE I HANDED TO THAT BOY WAS THE LAST ONE I HAD.
SO EVEN IF YOU KIDNAPPED ME, YOU WON'T BE ABLE TO GET HOLD OF THE KEY STONES.
I FIND IT HARD TO BELIEVE YOUR WORDS...
...ABOUT NOT KNOWING TEAM FLARE...
BUT TELL ME. WHAT IS YOUR NAME?
MY NAME IS ESSENTIA.
EXPANSION SUIT...
...ESSENTIA.
REMEMBER ME BY THAT NAME.

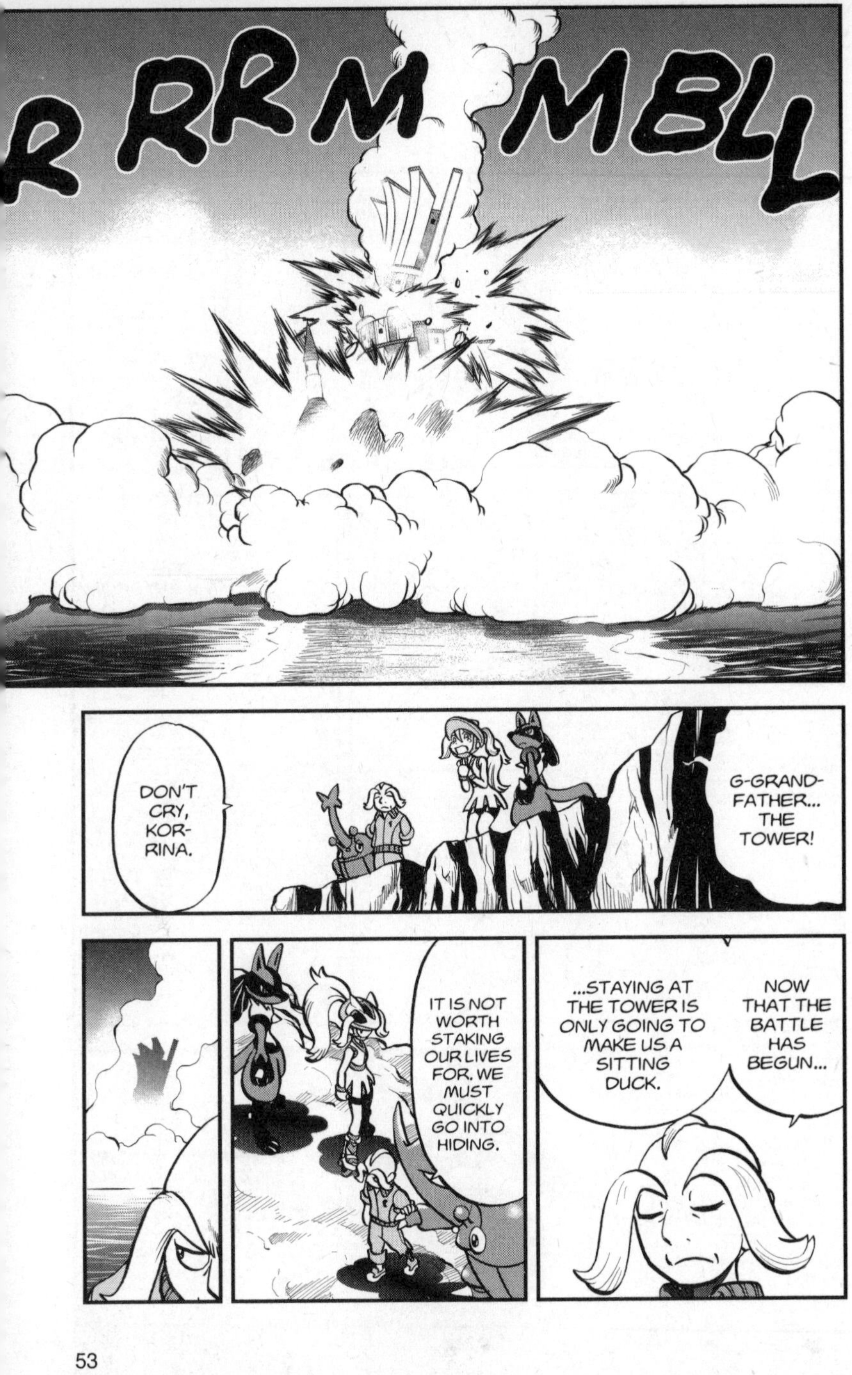
RRRMMBLL
G-GRAND-FATHER... THE TOWER!
DON'T CRY, KOR-RINA.
NOW THAT THE BATTLE HAS BEGUN...
...STAYING AT THE TOWER IS ONLY GOING TO MAKE US A SITTING DUCK.
IT IS NOT WORTH STAKING OUR LIVES FOR. WE MUST QUICKLY GO INTO HIDING.

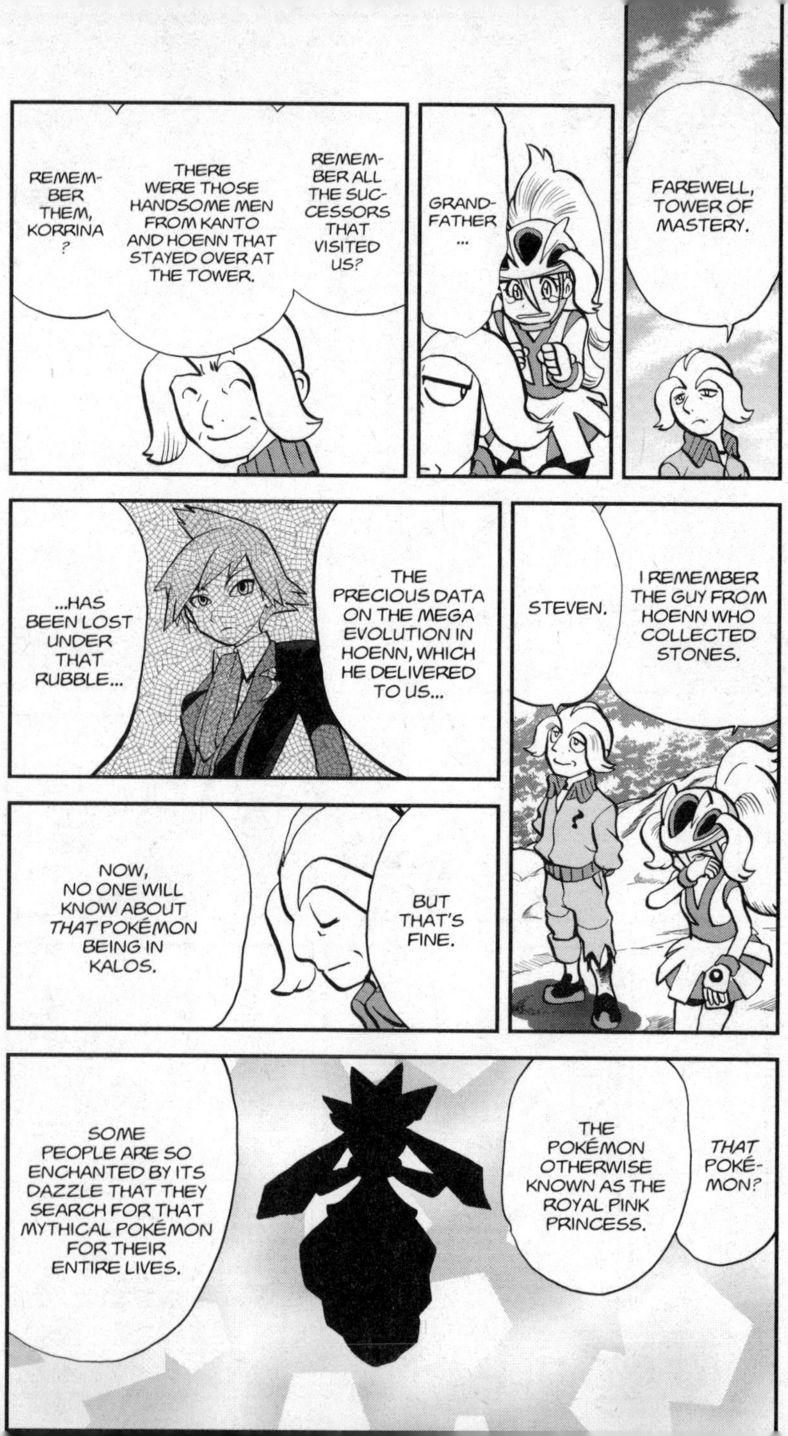
FAREWELL, TOWER OF MASTERY.
GRAND-FATHER ...
REMEM-BER ALL THE SUC-CESSORS THAT VISITED US?
THERE WERE THOSE HANDSOME MEN FROM KANTO AND HOENN THAT STAYED OVER AT THE TOWER.
REMEM-BER THEM, KORRINA?
I REMEMBER THE GUY FROM HOENN WHO COLLECTED STONES.
STEVEN.
THE PRECIOUS DATA ON THE MEGA EVOLUTION IN HOENN, WHICH HE DELIVERED TO US...
...HAS BEEN LOST UNDER THAT RUBBLE...
BUT THAT'S FINE.
NOW, NO ONE WILL KNOW ABOUT *THAT* POKÉMON BEING IN KALOS.
*THAT* POKÉ-MON?
THE POKÉMON OTHERWISE KNOWN AS THE ROYAL PINK PRINCESS.
SOME PEOPLE ARE SO ENCHANTED BY ITS DAZZLE THAT THEY SEARCH FOR THAT MYTHICAL POKÉMON FOR THEIR ENTIRE LIVES.

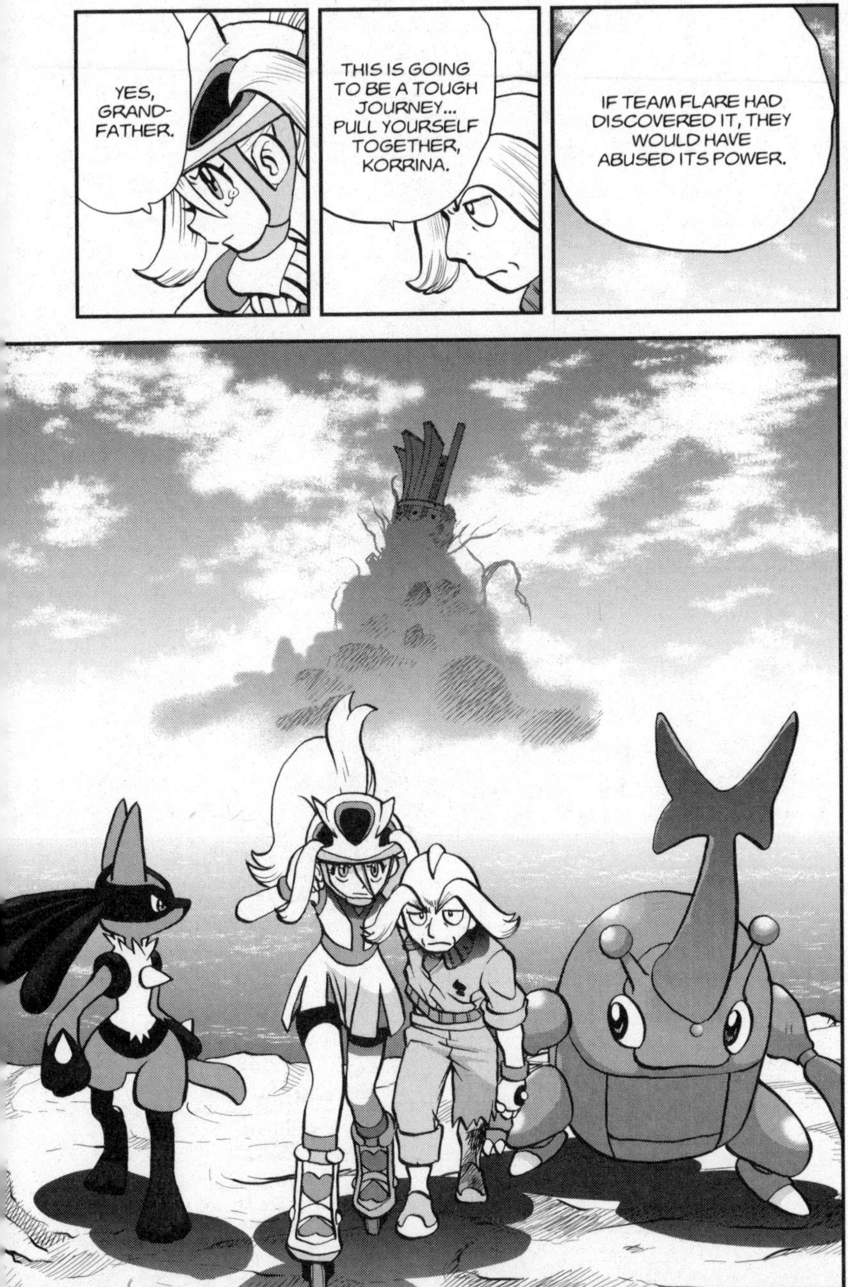
IF TEAM FLARE HAD DISCOVERED IT, THEY WOULD HAVE ABUSED ITS POWER.
THIS IS GOING TO BE A TOUGH JOURNEY... PULL YOURSELF TOGETHER, KORRINA.
YES, GRAND-FATHER.

## Current Location

**Lumiose City**

A dazzling metropolis of art and artifice, located in the very heart of the Kalos region.

# Adventure #14
## Pangoro Poses a Problem

X·Y

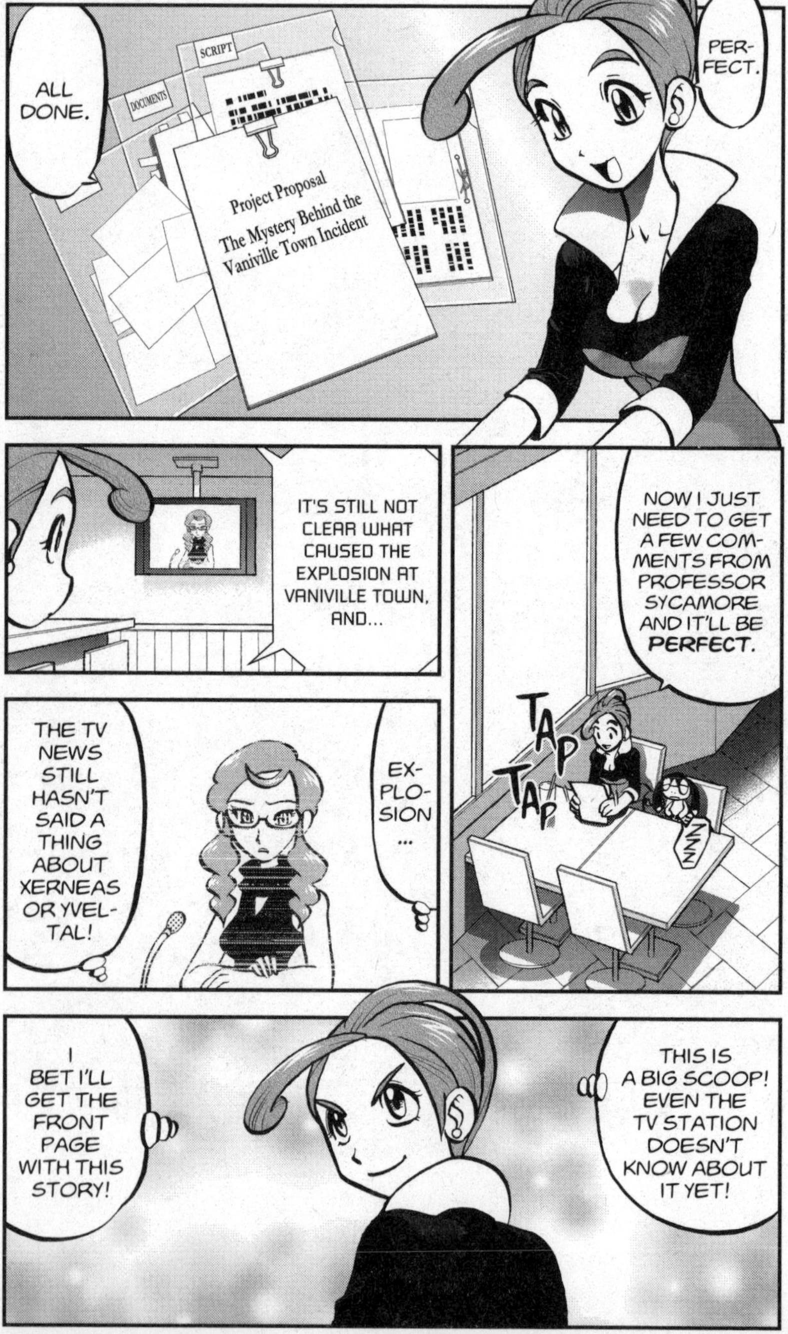
PER-FECT.
SCRIPT
DOCUMENTS
Project Proposal
The Mystery Behind the Vaniville Town Incident
ALL DONE.
NOW I JUST NEED TO GET A FEW COM-MENTS FROM PROFESSOR SYCAMORE AND IT'LL BE **PERFECT**.
TAP TAP
ZZZ
IT'S STILL NOT CLEAR WHAT CAUSED THE EXPLOSION AT VANIVILLE TOWN, AND...
EX-PLO-SION...
THE TV NEWS STILL HASN'T SAID A THING ABOUT XERNEAS OR YVEL-TAL!
THIS IS A BIG SCOOP! EVEN THE TV STATION DOESN'T KNOW ABOUT IT YET!
I BET I'LL GET THE FRONT PAGE WITH THIS STORY!

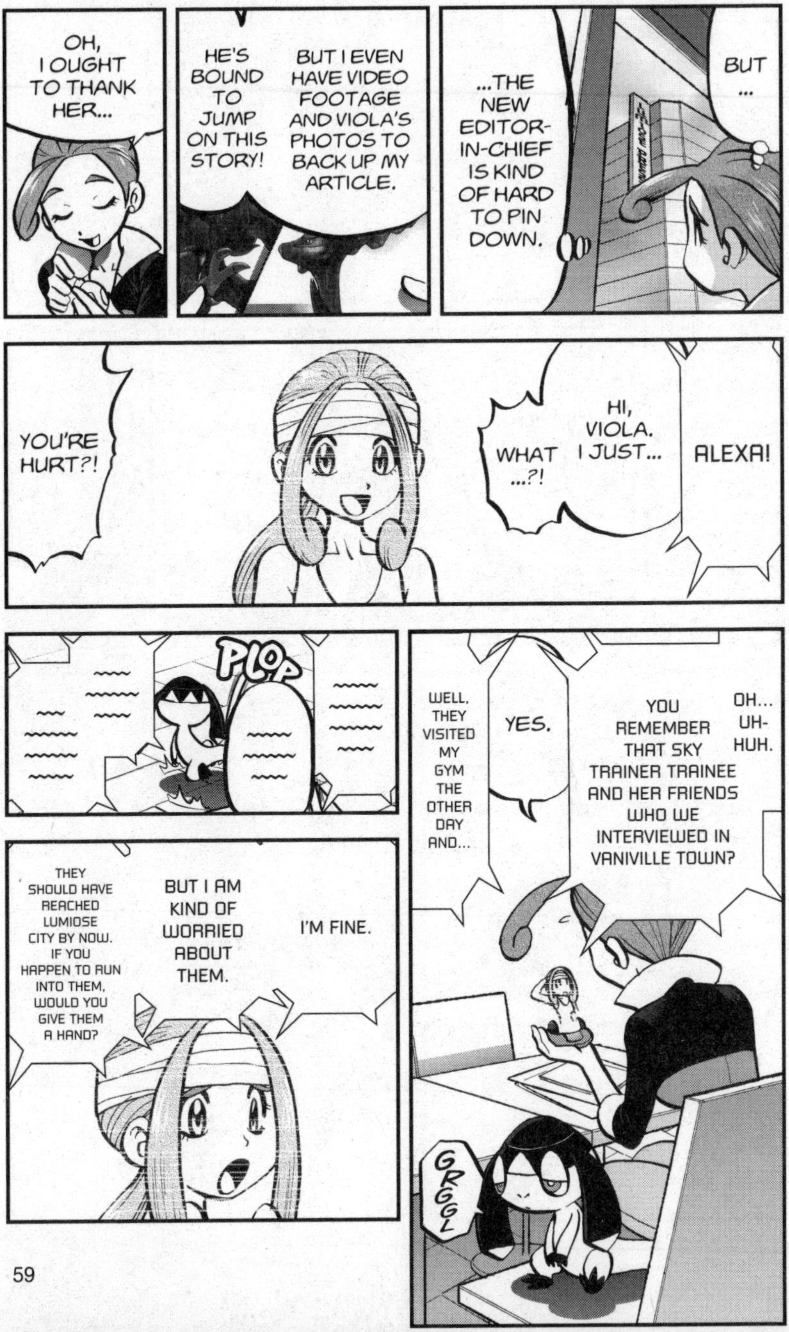
BUT ...
...THE NEW EDITOR-IN-CHIEF IS KIND OF HARD TO PIN DOWN.
BUT I EVEN HAVE VIDEO FOOTAGE AND VIOLA'S PHOTOS TO BACK UP MY ARTICLE.
HE'S BOUND TO JUMP ON THIS STORY!
OH, I OUGHT TO THANK HER...
ALEXA!
HI, VIOLA. I JUST...
WHAT ...?!
YOU'RE HURT?!
OH... UH-HUH.
YOU REMEMBER THAT SKY TRAINER TRAINEE AND HER FRIENDS WHO WE INTERVIEWED IN VANIVILLE TOWN?
YES.
WELL, THEY VISITED MY GYM THE OTHER DAY AND...
GRGGL
PLOP
I'M FINE.
BUT I AM KIND OF WORRIED ABOUT THEM.
THEY SHOULD HAVE REACHED LUMIOSE CITY BY NOW. IF YOU HAPPEN TO RUN INTO THEM, WOULD YOU GIVE THEM A HAND?

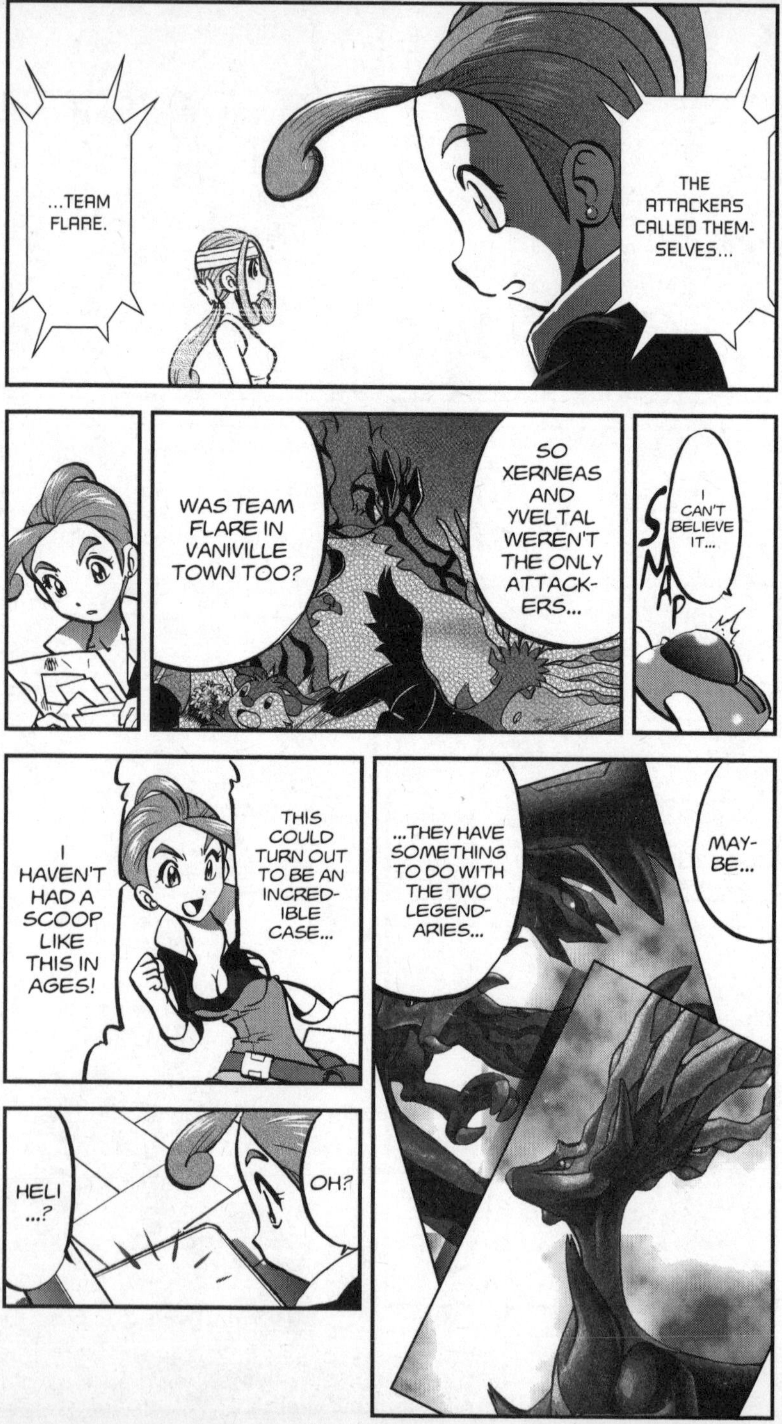
THE ATTACKERS CALLED THEMSELVES...
...TEAM FLARE.
I CAN'T BELIEVE IT...
SNAP
SO XERNEAS AND YVELTAL WEREN'T THE ONLY ATTACKERS...
WAS TEAM FLARE IN VANIVILLE TOWN TOO?
MAYBE...
...THEY HAVE SOMETHING TO DO WITH THE TWO LEGENDARIES...
THIS COULD TURN OUT TO BE AN INCREDIBLE CASE...
I HAVEN'T HAD A SCOOP LIKE THIS IN AGES!
OH?
HELI...?

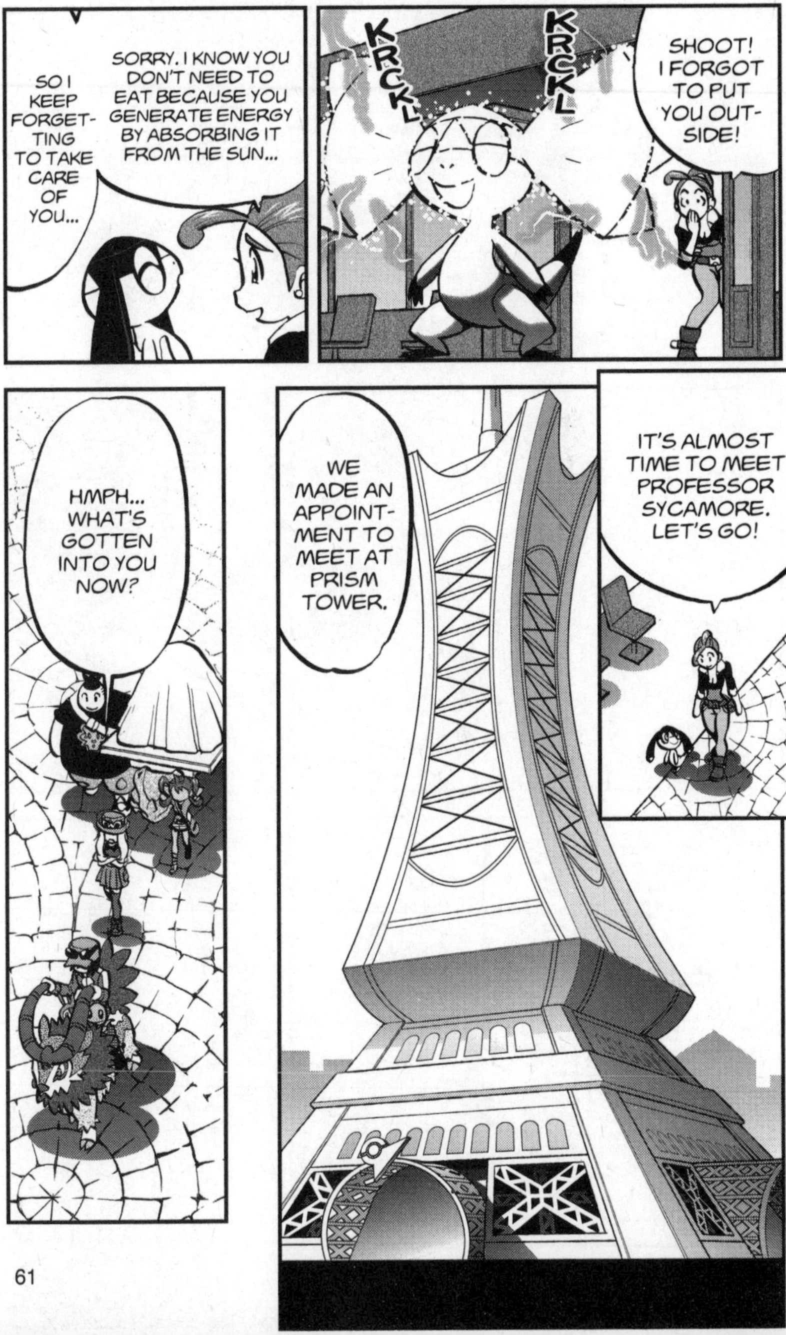
SHOOT! I FORGOT TO PUT YOU OUT-SIDE!
KRCKL
KRCKL
SORRY. I KNOW YOU DON'T NEED TO EAT BECAUSE YOU GENERATE ENERGY BY ABSORBING IT FROM THE SUN...
SO I KEEP FORGET-TING TO TAKE CARE OF YOU...
IT'S ALMOST TIME TO MEET PROFESSOR SYCAMORE. LET'S GO!
WE MADE AN APPOINT-MENT TO MEET AT PRISM TOWER.
HMPH... WHAT'S GOTTEN INTO YOU NOW?

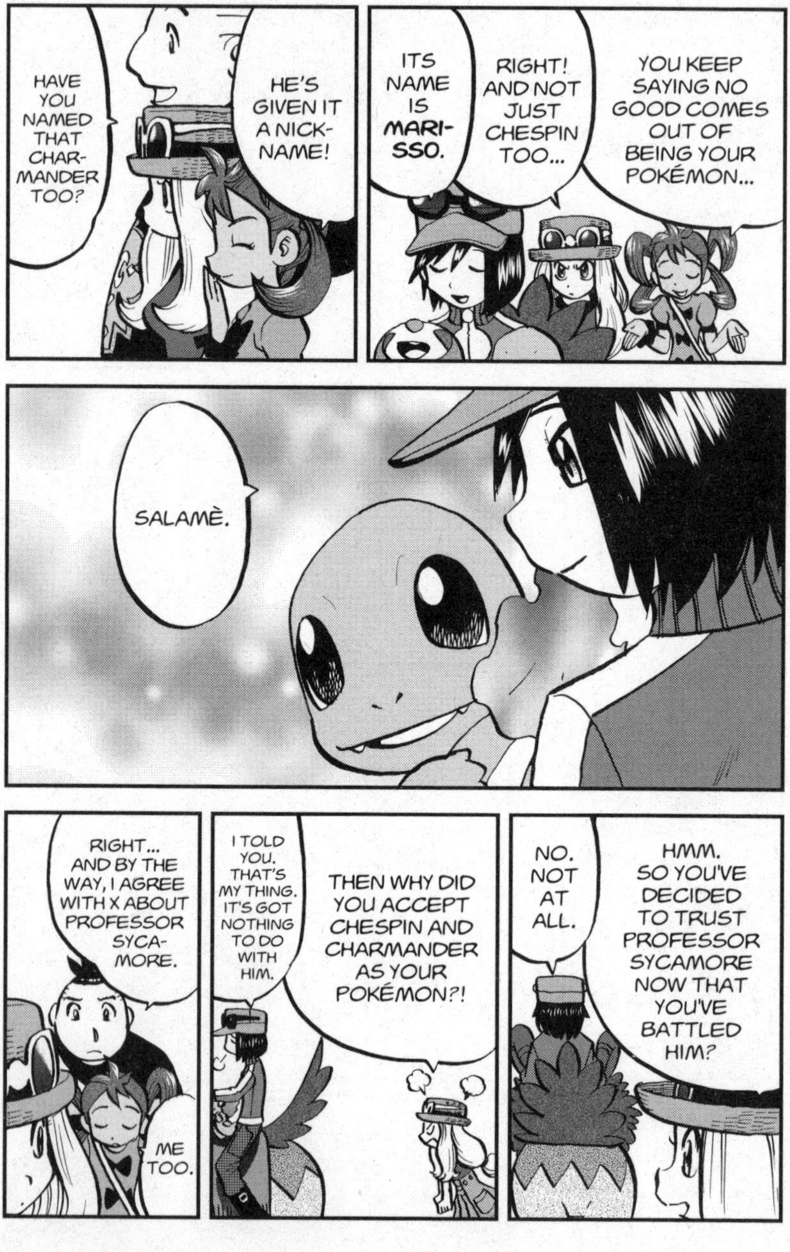
YOU KEEP SAYING NO GOOD COMES OUT OF BEING YOUR POKÉMON...
RIGHT! AND NOT JUST CHESPIN TOO...
ITS NAME IS **MARI-SSO.**
HE'S GIVEN IT A NICK-NAME!
HAVE YOU NAMED THAT CHAR-MANDER TOO?
SALAMÈ.
HMM. SO YOU'VE DECIDED TO TRUST PROFESSOR SYCAMORE NOW THAT YOU'VE BATTLED HIM?
NO. NOT AT ALL.
THEN WHY DID YOU ACCEPT CHESPIN AND CHARMANDER AS YOUR POKÉMON?!
I TOLD YOU. THAT'S MY THING. IT'S GOT NOTHING TO DO WITH HIM.
RIGHT... AND BY THE WAY, I AGREE WITH X ABOUT PROFESSOR SYCA-MORE.
ME TOO.

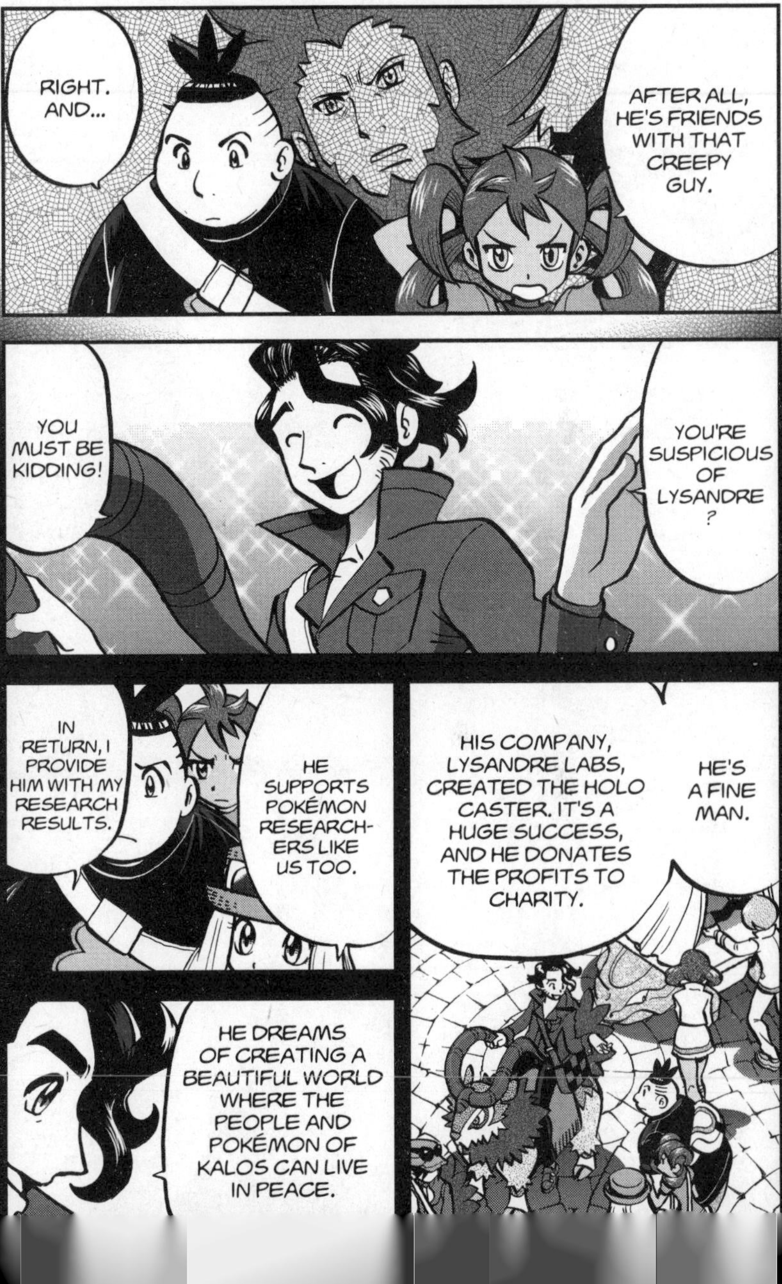
AFTER ALL, HE'S FRIENDS WITH THAT CREEPY GUY.
RIGHT. AND...
YOU'RE SUSPICIOUS OF LYSANDRE?
YOU MUST BE KIDDING!
HE'S A FINE MAN.
HIS COMPANY, LYSANDRE LABS, CREATED THE HOLO CASTER. IT'S A HUGE SUCCESS, AND HE DONATES THE PROFITS TO CHARITY.
HE SUPPORTS POKÉMON RESEARCH-ERS LIKE US TOO.
IN RETURN, I PROVIDE HIM WITH MY RESEARCH RESULTS.
HE DREAMS OF CREATING A BEAUTIFUL WORLD WHERE THE PEOPLE AND POKÉMON OF KALOS CAN LIVE IN PEACE.

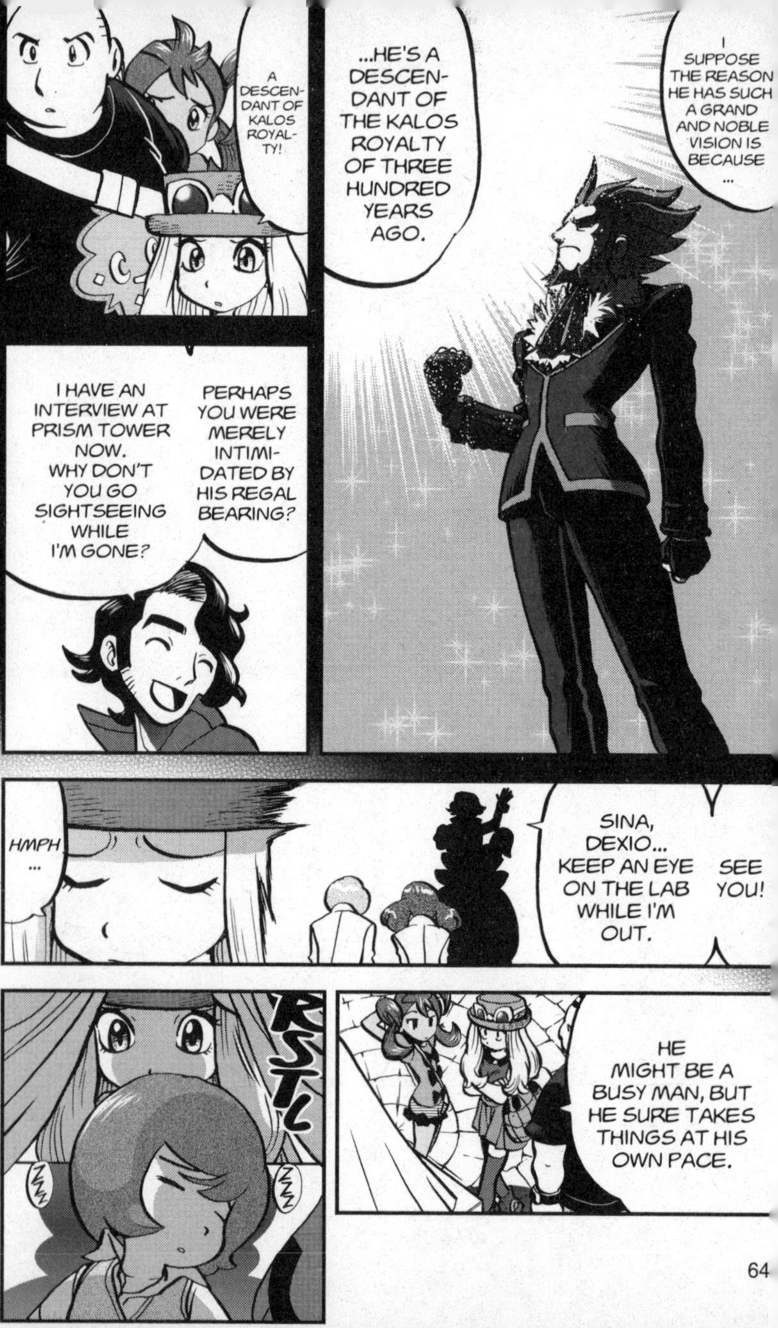
I SUPPOSE THE REASON HE HAS SUCH A GRAND AND NOBLE VISION IS BECAUSE...
...HE'S A DESCENDANT OF THE KALOS ROYALTY OF THREE HUNDRED YEARS AGO.
A DESCENDANT OF KALOS ROYALTY!
PERHAPS YOU WERE MERELY INTIMIDATED BY HIS REGAL BEARING?
I HAVE AN INTERVIEW AT PRISM TOWER NOW. WHY DON'T YOU GO SIGHTSEEING WHILE I'M GONE?
SEE YOU!
SINA, DEXIO... KEEP AN EYE ON THE LAB WHILE I'M OUT.
HMPH...
HE MIGHT BE A BUSY MAN, BUT HE SURE TAKES THINGS AT HIS OWN PACE.
RSTL
ZZZ
ZZZ

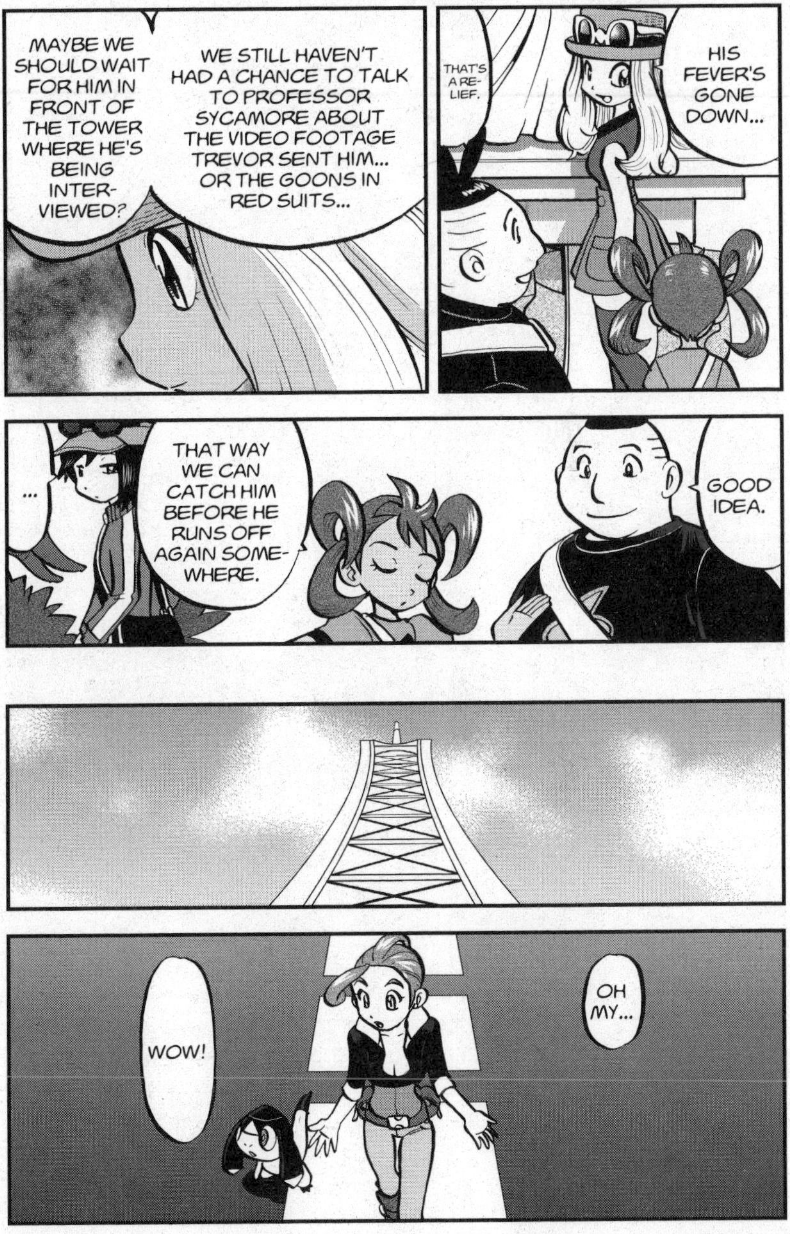
HIS FEVER'S GONE DOWN...
THAT'S A RE-LIEF.
WE STILL HAVEN'T HAD A CHANCE TO TALK TO PROFESSOR SYCAMORE ABOUT THE VIDEO FOOTAGE TREVOR SENT HIM... OR THE GOONS IN RED SUITS...
MAYBE WE SHOULD WAIT FOR HIM IN FRONT OF THE TOWER WHERE HE'S BEING INTER-VIEWED?
GOOD IDEA.
THAT WAY WE CAN CATCH HIM BEFORE HE RUNS OFF AGAIN SOME-WHERE.
...
OH MY...
WOW!

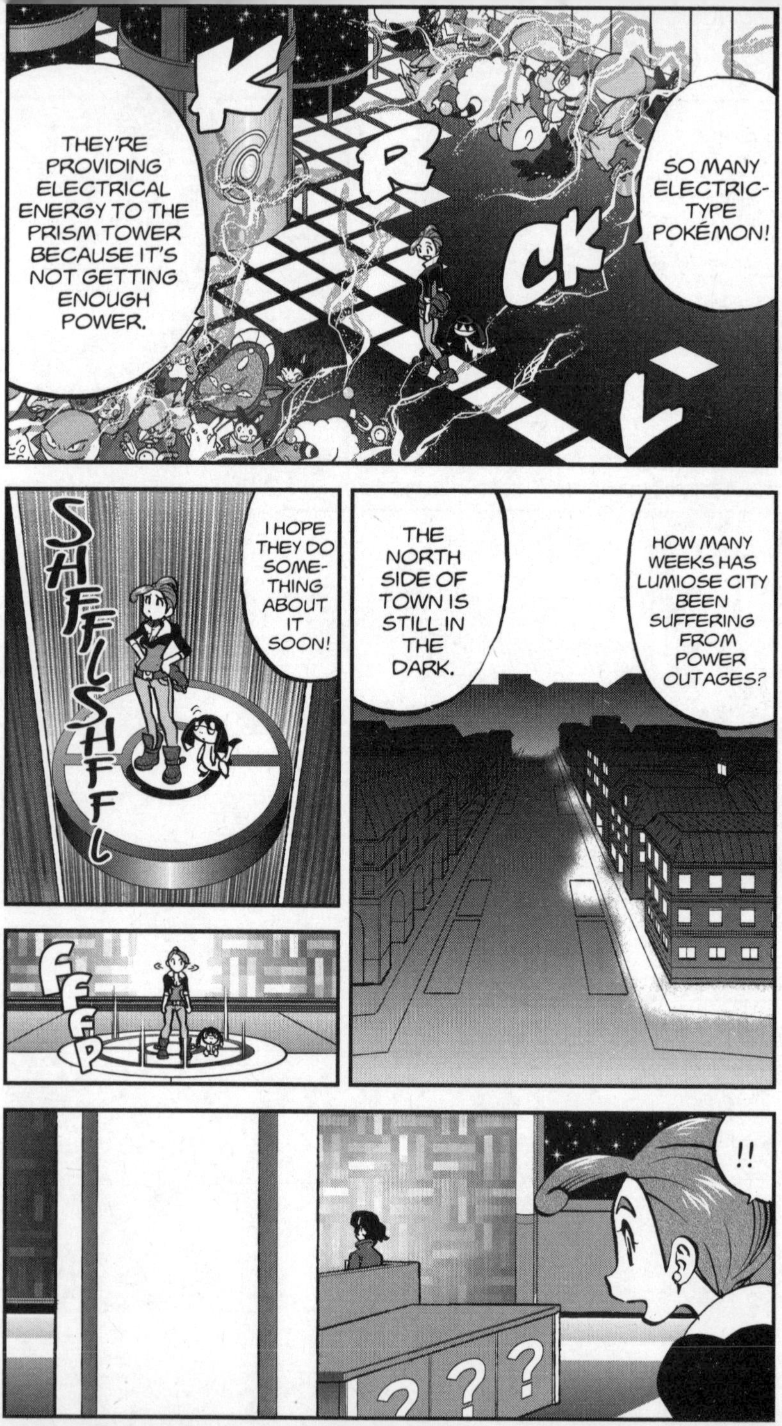
SO MANY ELECTRIC-TYPE POKÉMON!
THEY'RE PROVIDING ELECTRICAL ENERGY TO THE PRISM TOWER BECAUSE IT'S NOT GETTING ENOUGH POWER.
KRCKL
HOW MANY WEEKS HAS LUMIOSE CITY BEEN SUFFERING FROM POWER OUTAGES?
THE NORTH SIDE OF TOWN IS STILL IN THE DARK.
I HOPE THEY DO SOME-THING ABOUT IT SOON!
SHFFLSHFFL
FFFP
!!
???

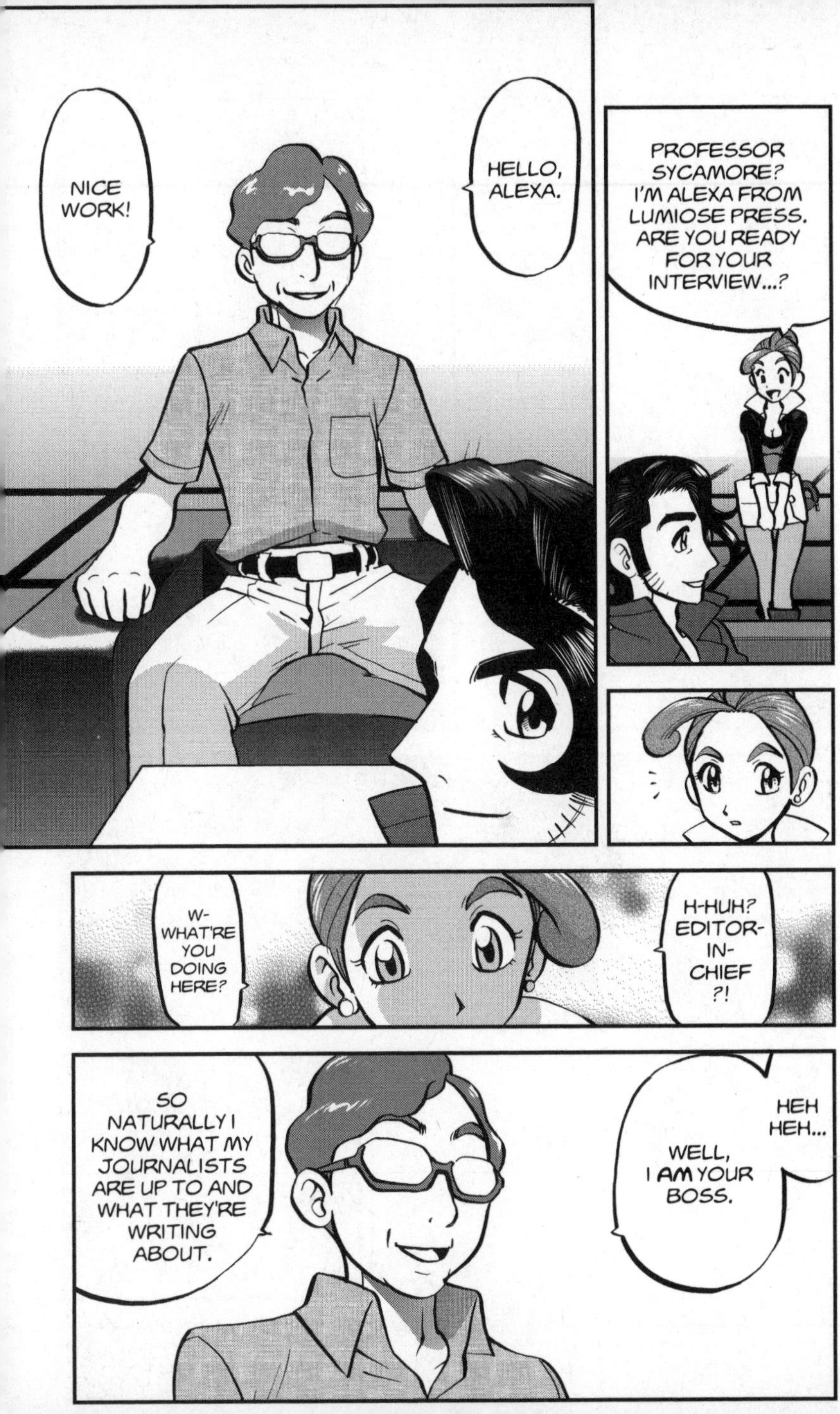
PROFESSOR SYCAMORE? I'M ALEXA FROM LUMIOSE PRESS. ARE YOU READY FOR YOUR INTERVIEW...?
HELLO, ALEXA.
NICE WORK!
H-HUH? EDITOR-IN-CHIEF?!
W-WHAT'RE YOU DOING HERE?
HEH HEH...
WELL, I **AM** YOUR BOSS.
SO NATURALLY I KNOW WHAT MY JOURNALISTS ARE UP TO AND WHAT THEY'RE WRITING ABOUT.

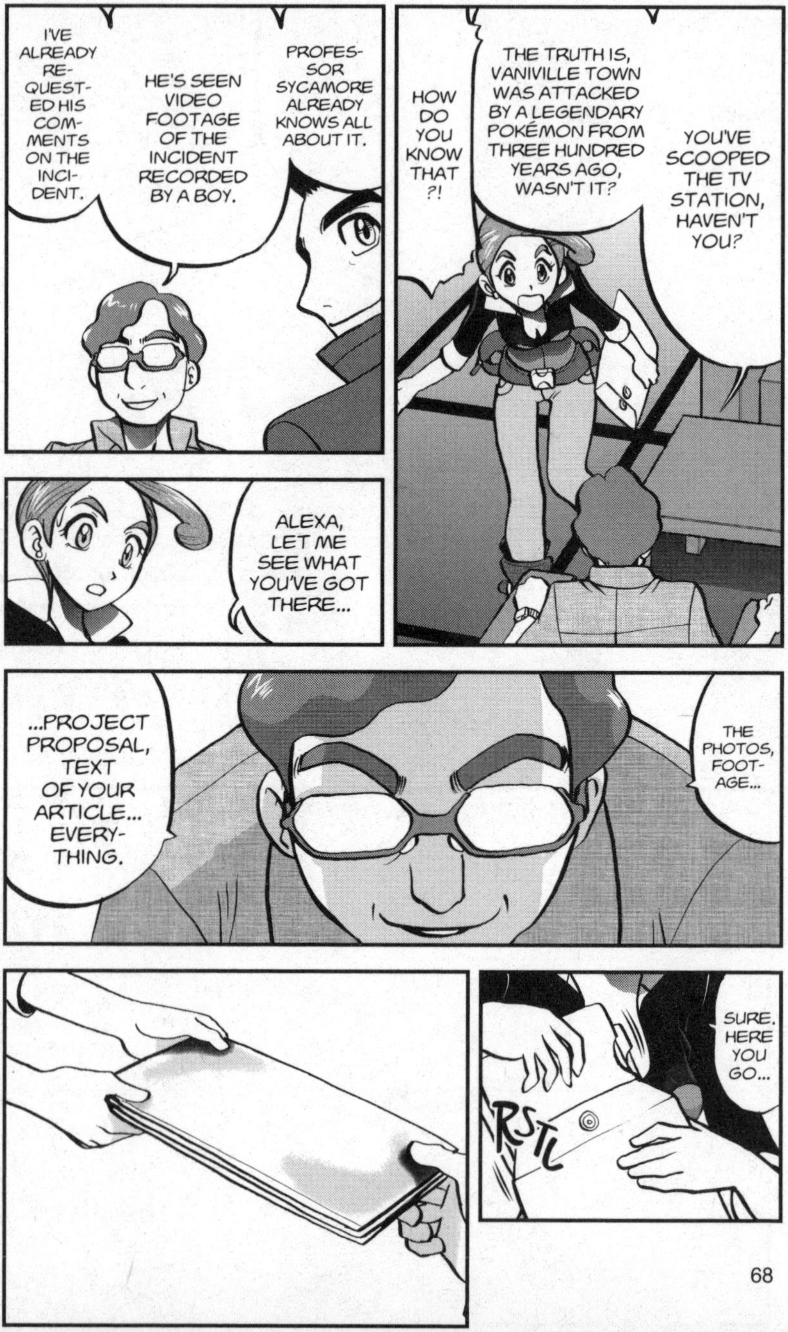
YOU'VE SCOOPED THE TV STATION, HAVEN'T YOU?
THE TRUTH IS, VANIVILLE TOWN WAS ATTACKED BY A LEGENDARY POKÉMON FROM THREE HUNDRED YEARS AGO, WASN'T IT?
HOW DO YOU KNOW THAT?!
PROFESSOR SYCAMORE ALREADY KNOWS ALL ABOUT IT.
HE'S SEEN VIDEO FOOTAGE OF THE INCIDENT RECORDED BY A BOY.
I'VE ALREADY REQUESTED HIS COMMENTS ON THE INCIDENT.
ALEXA, LET ME SEE WHAT YOU'VE GOT THERE...
THE PHOTOS, FOOTAGE...
...PROJECT PROPOSAL, TEXT OF YOUR ARTICLE... EVERYTHING.
SURE. HERE YOU GO...
RSTL

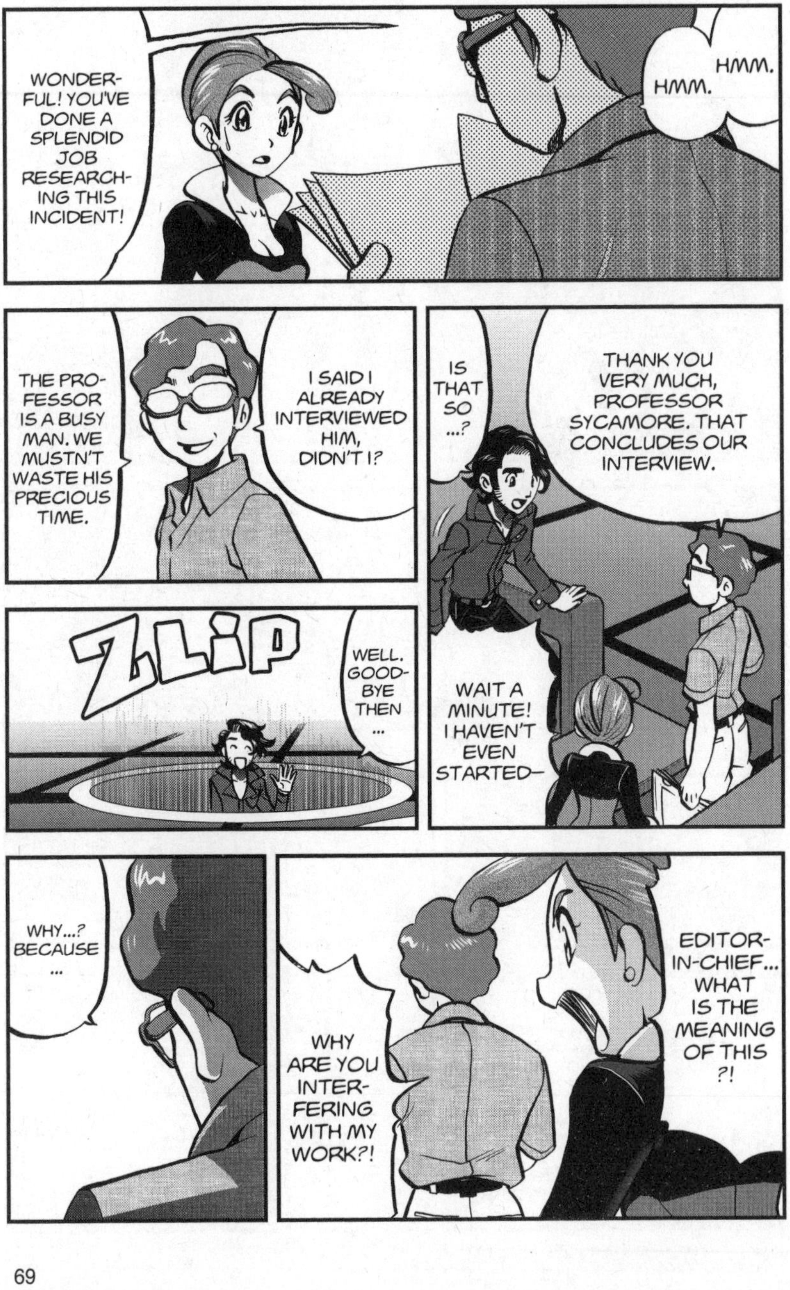
HMM. HMM.
WONDERFUL! YOU'VE DONE A SPLENDID JOB RESEARCHING THIS INCIDENT!
THANK YOU VERY MUCH, PROFESSOR SYCAMORE. THAT CONCLUDES OUR INTERVIEW.
IS THAT SO ...?
WAIT A MINUTE! I HAVEN'T EVEN STARTED—
I SAID I ALREADY INTERVIEWED HIM, DIDN'T I?
THE PROFESSOR IS A BUSY MAN. WE MUSTN'T WASTE HIS PRECIOUS TIME.
WELL. GOODBYE THEN ...
ZLIP
EDITOR-IN-CHIEF... WHAT IS THE MEANING OF THIS?!
WHY ARE YOU INTERFERING WITH MY WORK?!
WHY...? BECAUSE ...

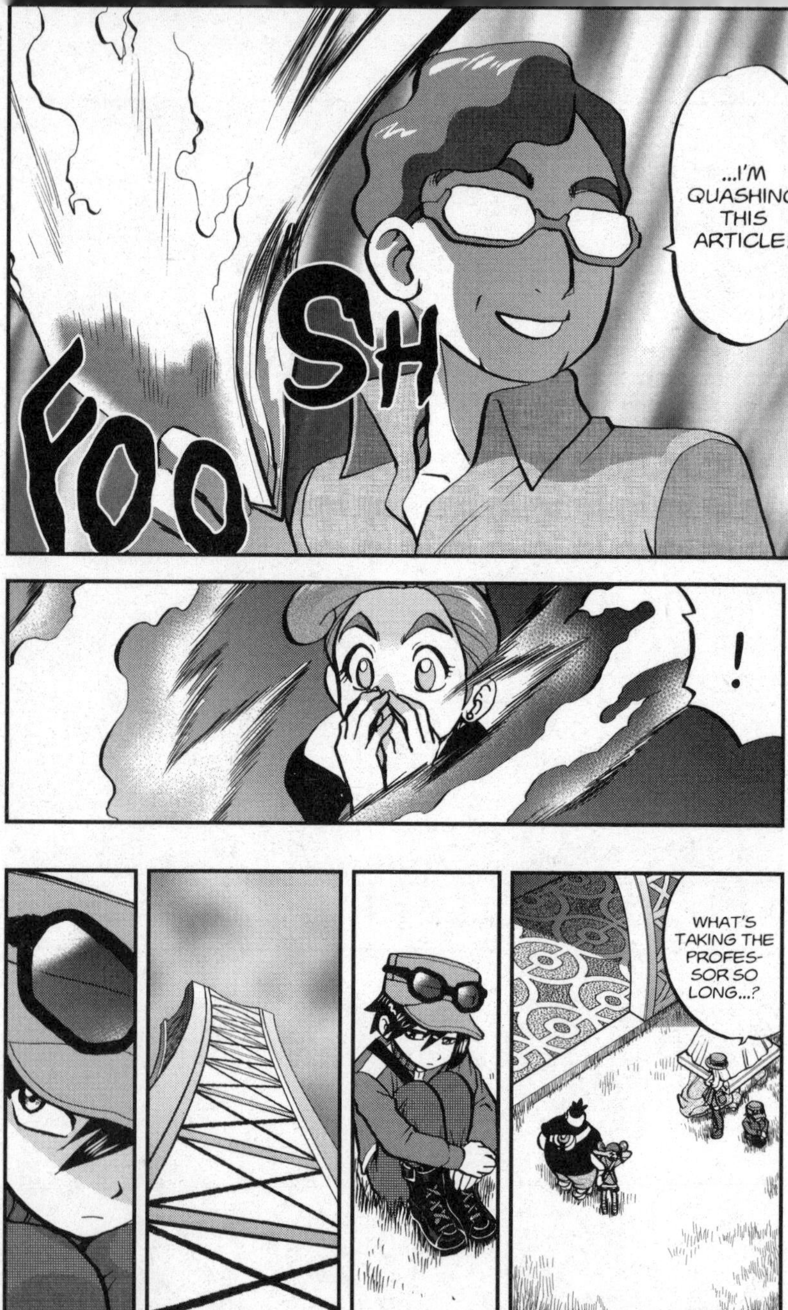
...I'M QUASHING THIS ARTICLE!
!
WHAT'S TAKING THE PROFES-SOR SO LONG...?

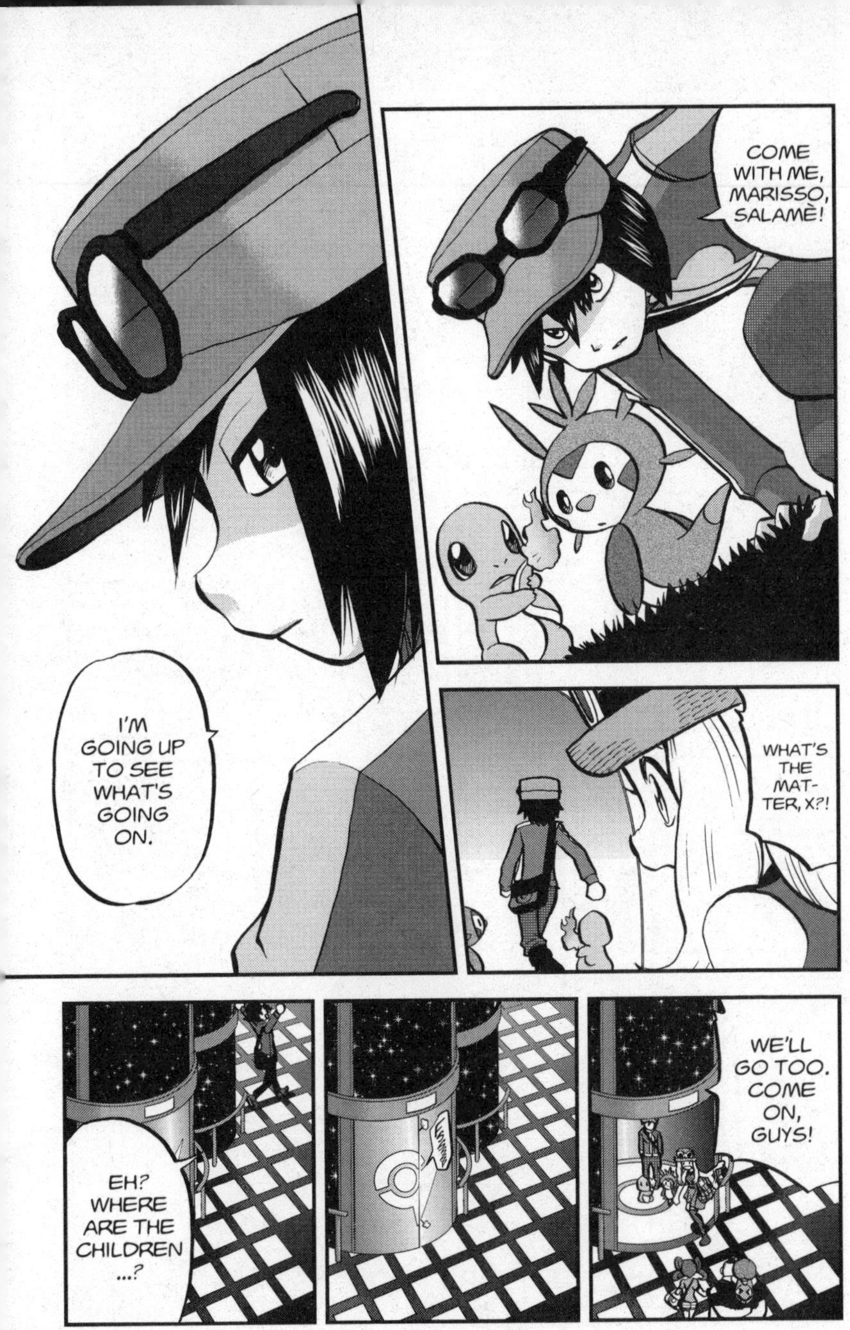
COME WITH ME, MARISSO, SALAMÈ!
WHAT'S THE MAT-TER, X?!
I'M GOING UP TO SEE WHAT'S GOING ON.
WE'LL GO TOO. COME ON, GUYS!
EH? WHERE ARE THE CHILDREN ...?

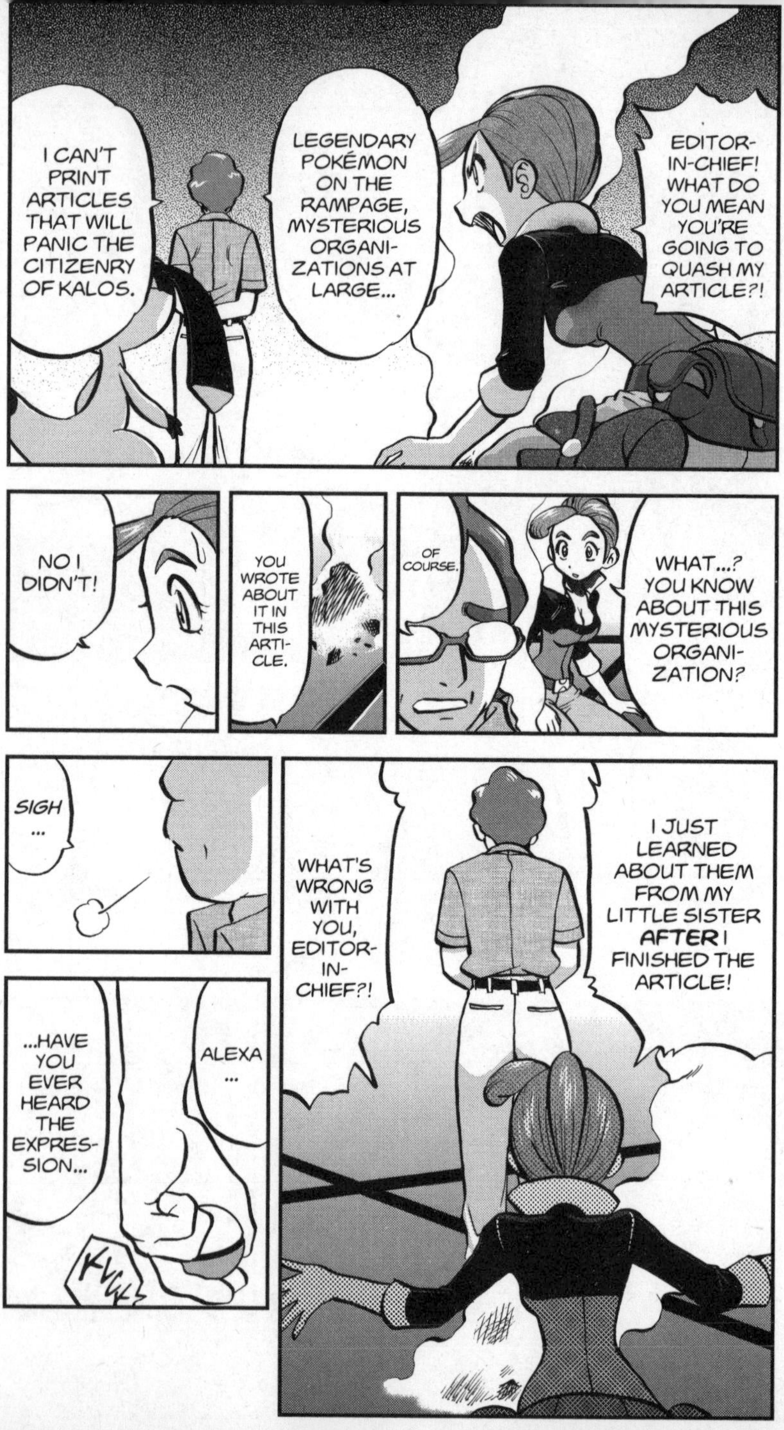
EDITOR-IN-CHIEF! WHAT DO YOU MEAN YOU'RE GOING TO QUASH MY ARTICLE?!
LEGENDARY POKÉMON ON THE RAMPAGE, MYSTERIOUS ORGANIZATIONS AT LARGE...
I CAN'T PRINT ARTICLES THAT WILL PANIC THE CITIZENRY OF KALOS.
WHAT...? YOU KNOW ABOUT THIS MYSTERIOUS ORGANIZATION?
OF COURSE.
YOU WROTE ABOUT IT IN THIS ARTICLE.
NO I DIDN'T!
I JUST LEARNED ABOUT THEM FROM MY LITTLE SISTER **AFTER** I FINISHED THE ARTICLE!
WHAT'S WRONG WITH YOU, EDITOR-IN-CHIEF?!
SIGH...
ALEXA...
...HAVE YOU EVER HEARD THE EXPRESSION...
KLICK

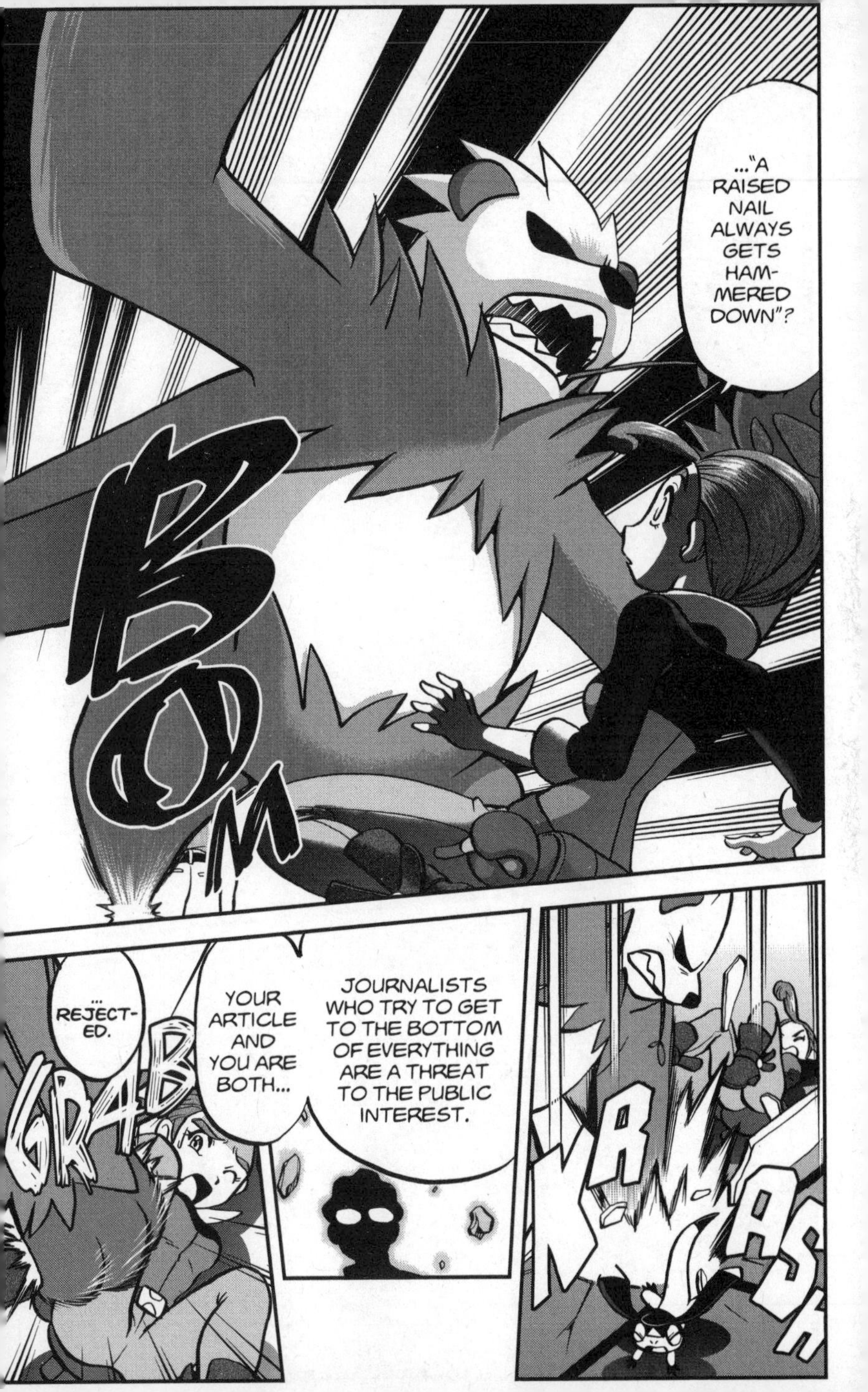
..."A RAISED NAIL ALWAYS GETS HAM-MERED DOWN"?
BOOM
KRASH
JOURNALISTS WHO TRY TO GET TO THE BOTTOM OF EVERYTHING ARE A THREAT TO THE PUBLIC INTEREST.
YOUR ARTICLE AND YOU ARE BOTH...
...REJECT-ED.
GRAB

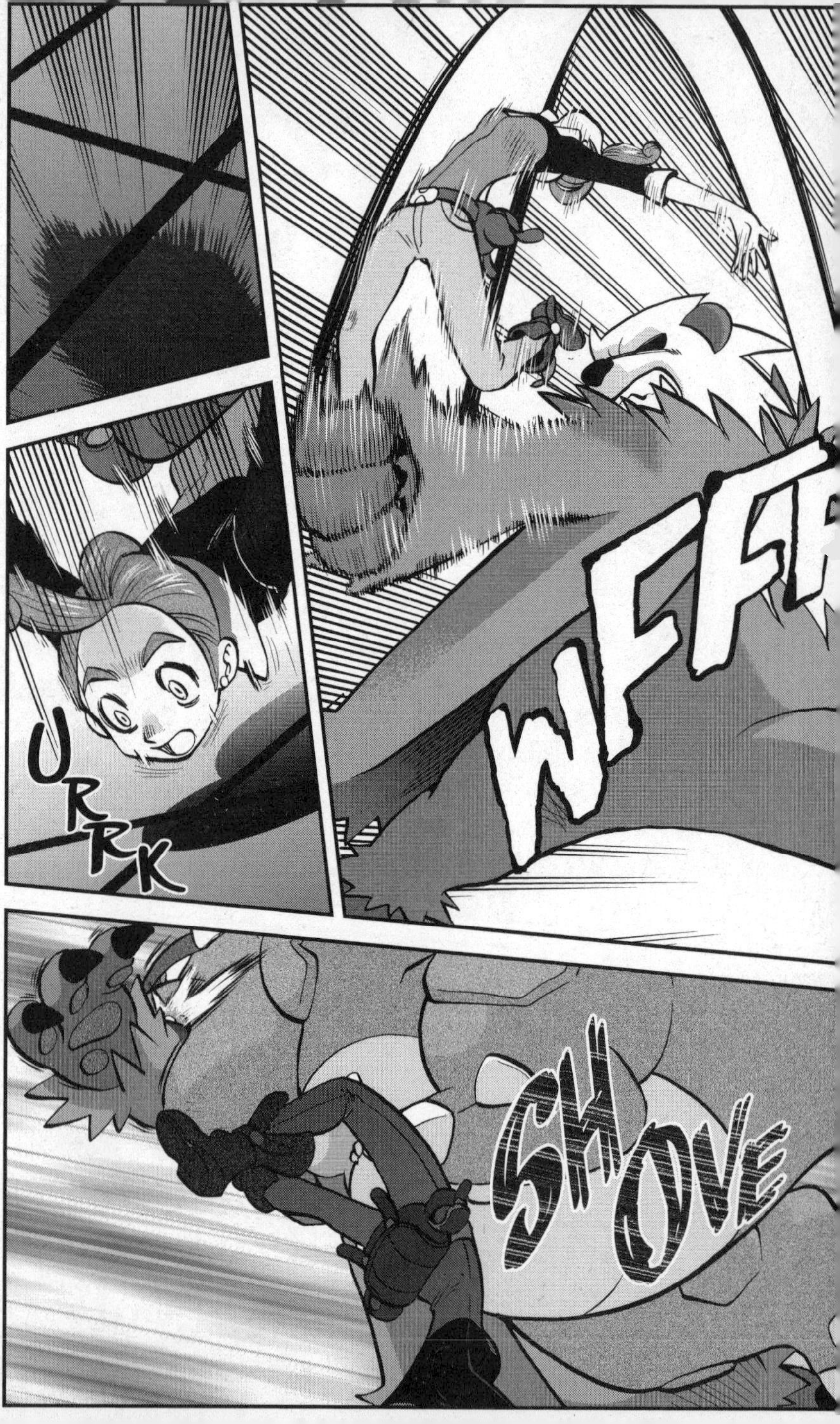
WFF
URRK
SHOVE

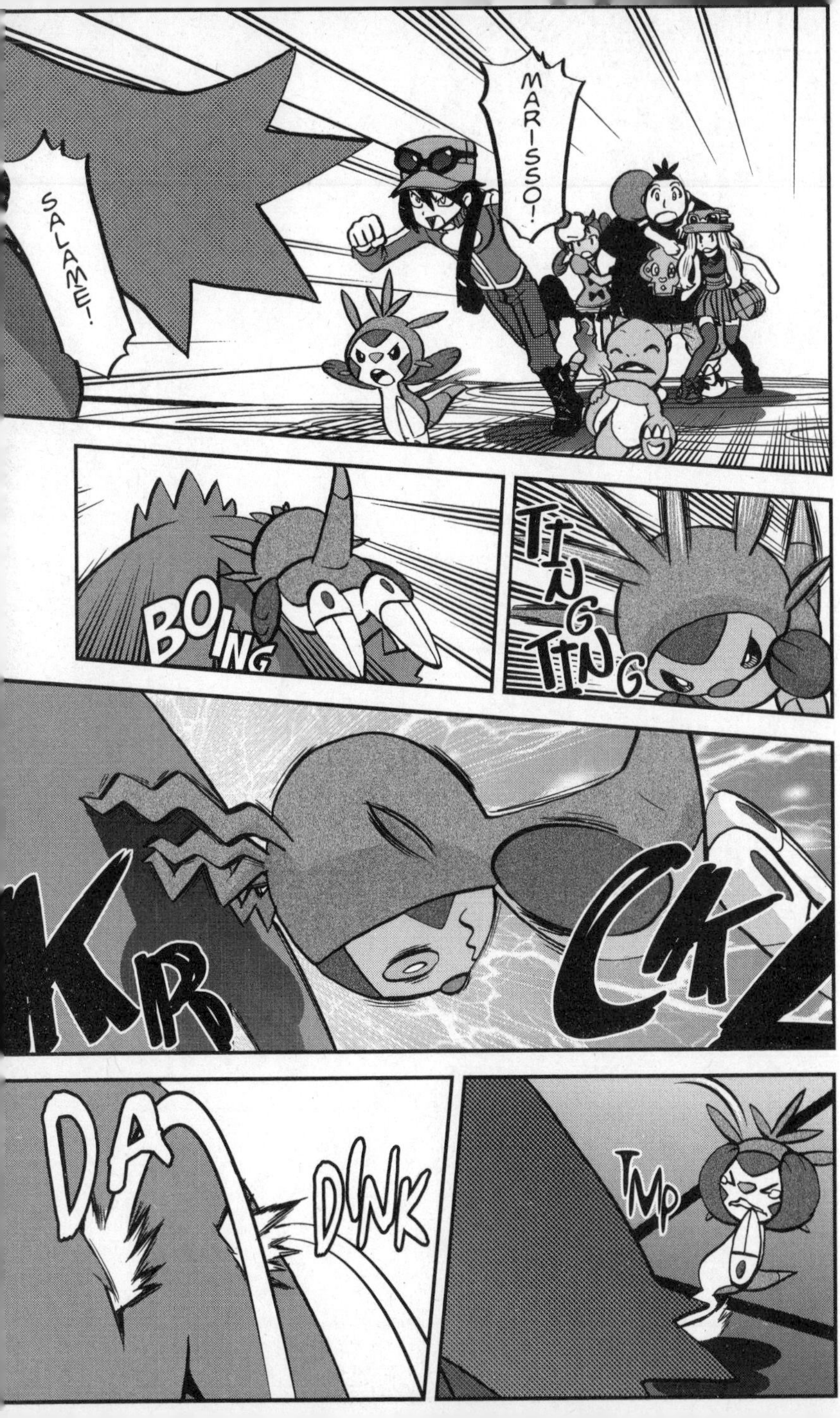
MARISSO!
SALAMÈ!
TING TING
BOING
KR
CK
TMP
DA
DINK

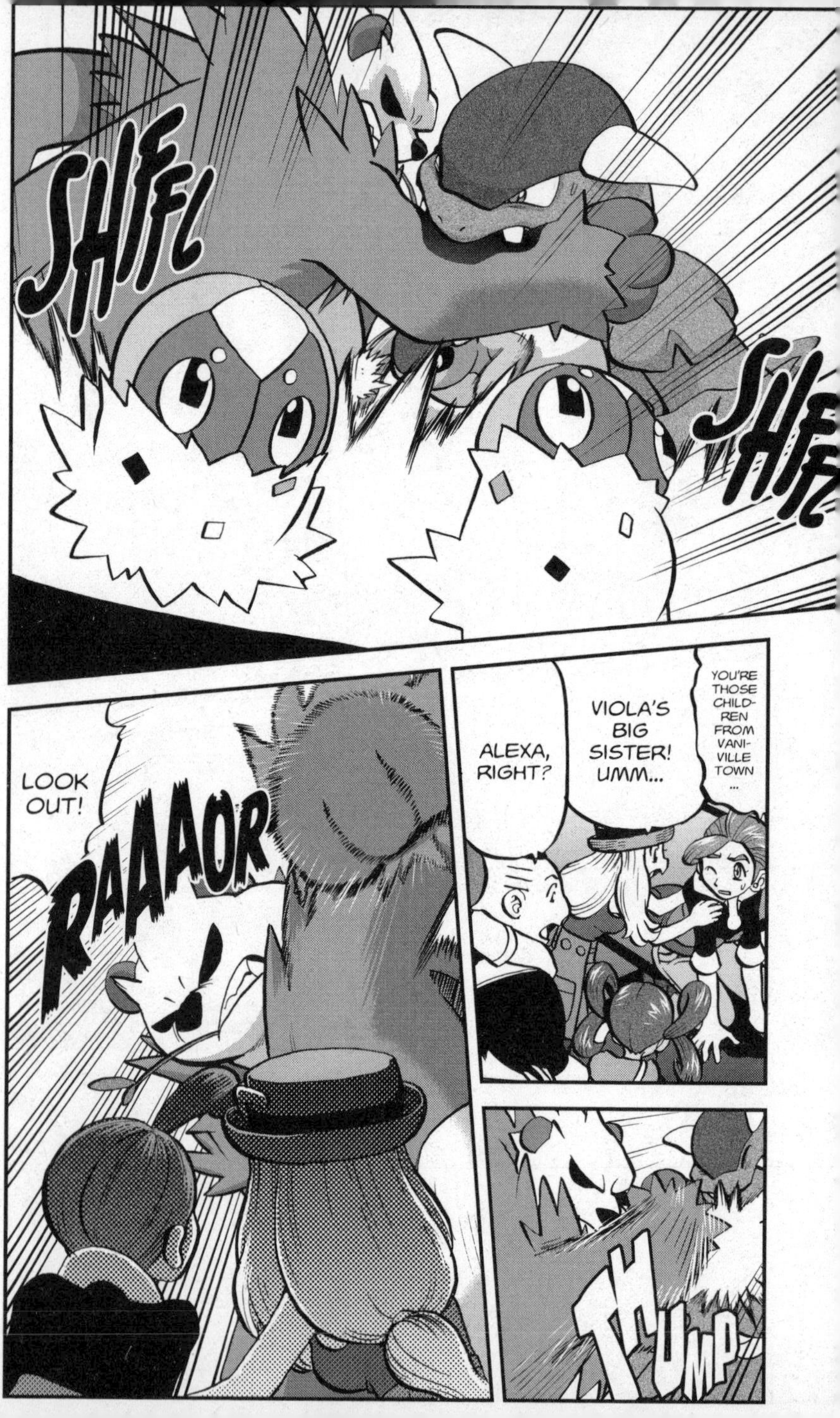
SHIFL
SHIFL
YOU'RE THOSE CHILDREN FROM VANIVILLE TOWN...
VIOLA'S BIG SISTER! UMM...
ALEXA, RIGHT?
THUMP
LOOK OUT!
RAAAOR

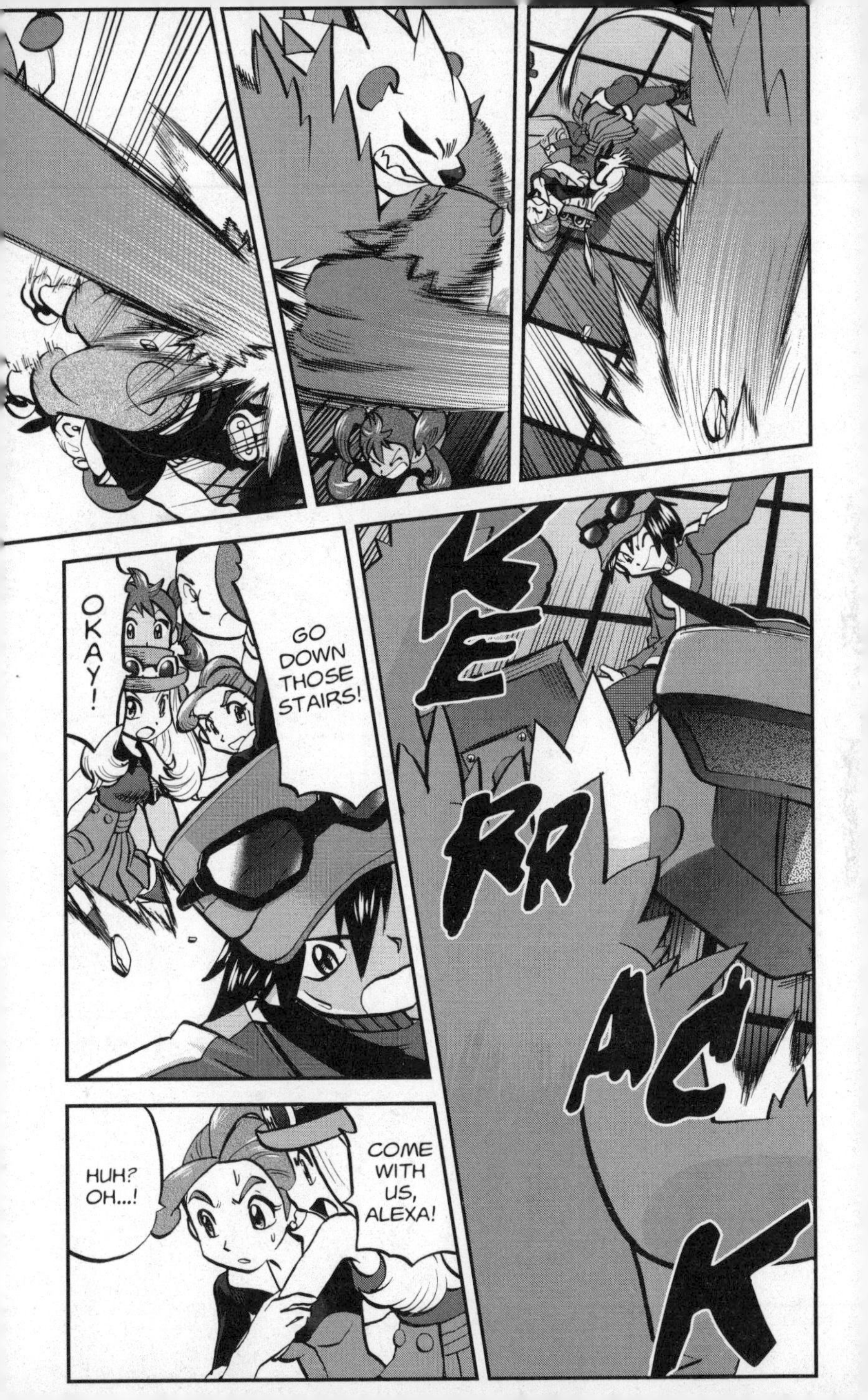
KERRACK
GO DOWN THOSE STAIRS!
OKAY!
COME WITH US, ALEXA!
HUH? OH...!

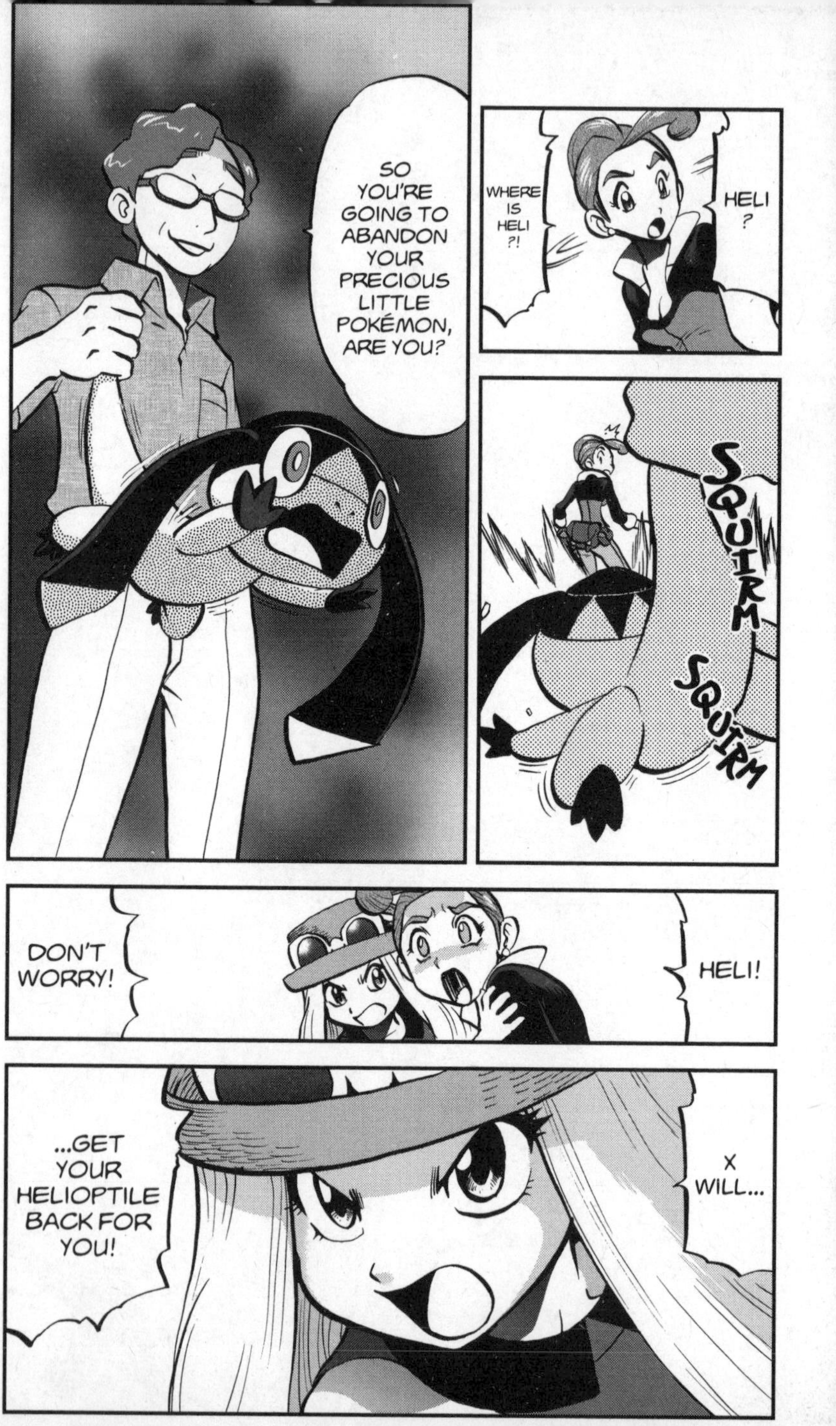
HELI ?
WHERE IS HELI ?!
SQUIRM
SQUIRM
SO YOU'RE GOING TO ABANDON YOUR PRECIOUS LITTLE POKÉMON, ARE YOU?
HELI!
DON'T WORRY!
X WILL...
...GET YOUR HELIOPTILE BACK FOR YOU!

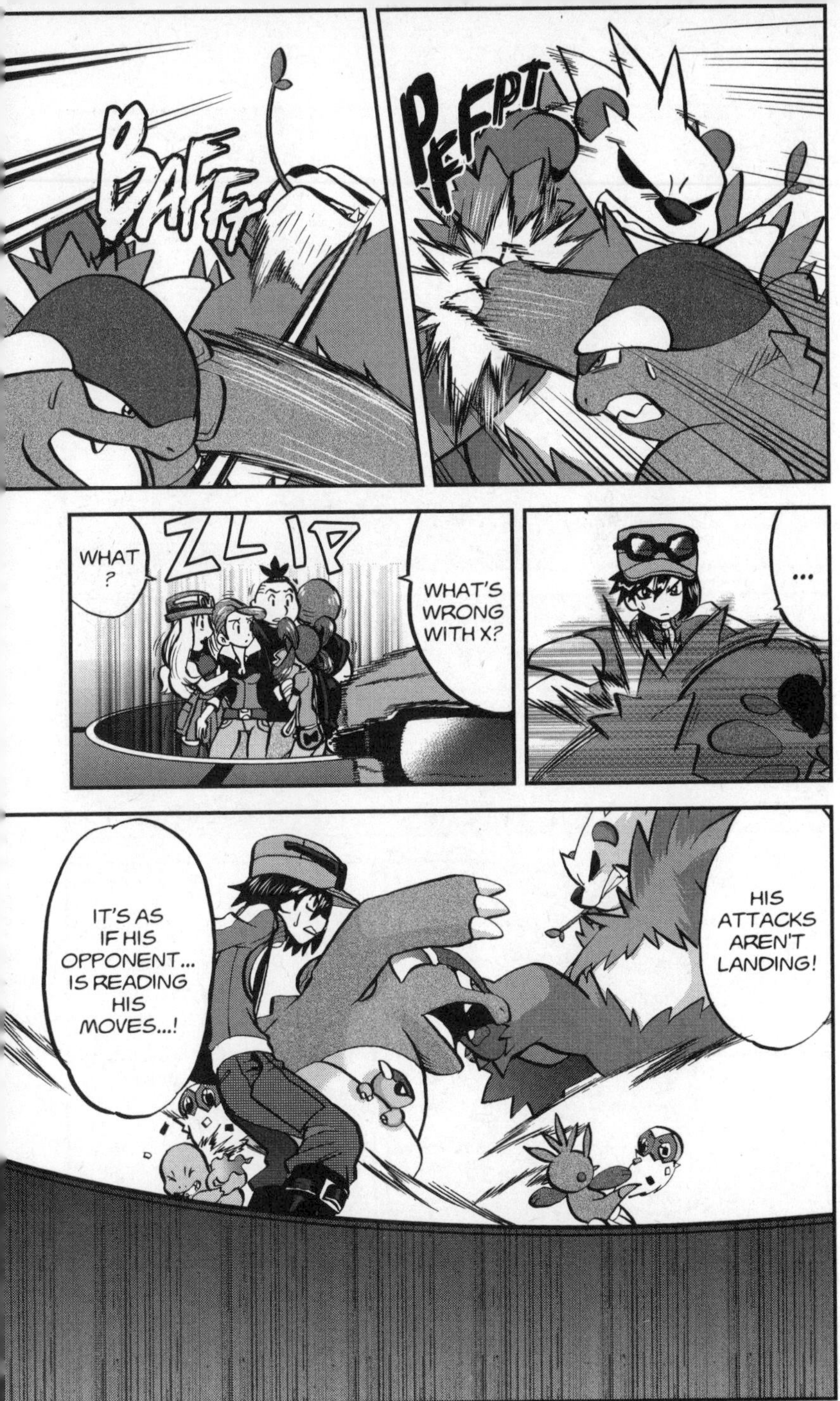
PFFPT
BAFFT
...
WHAT'S WRONG WITH X?
ZLIP
WHAT?
HIS ATTACKS AREN'T LANDING!
IT'S AS IF HIS OPPONENT... IS READING HIS MOVES...!

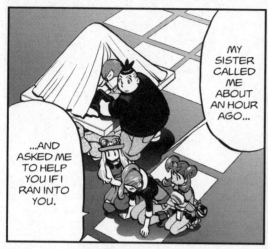

FSSST
MY SISTER CALLED ME ABOUT AN HOUR AGO...
...AND ASKED ME TO HELP YOU IF I RAN INTO YOU.
I NEVER DREAMED ...
...I'D BE THE ONE WHO NEEDED HELP!
I HAD NO IDEA THE EDITOR-IN-CHIEF WAS MY NEMESIS ...
SIGH ...
BUT THIS MAKES EVERYTHING CLEAR. THOSE TWO LEGENDARY POKÉMON...
IT'S NOT THAT THE TV STATION DIDN'T KNOW ANYTHING ABOUT THE INCIDENT... THEY DIDN'T REPORT IT ON PURPOSE!

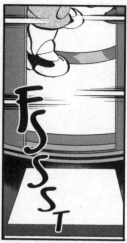

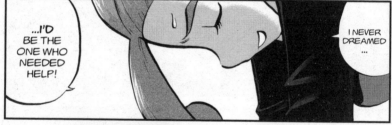

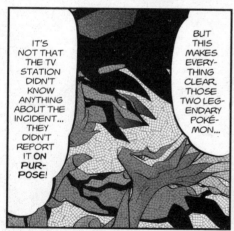

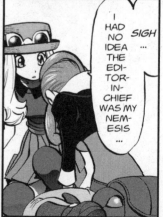

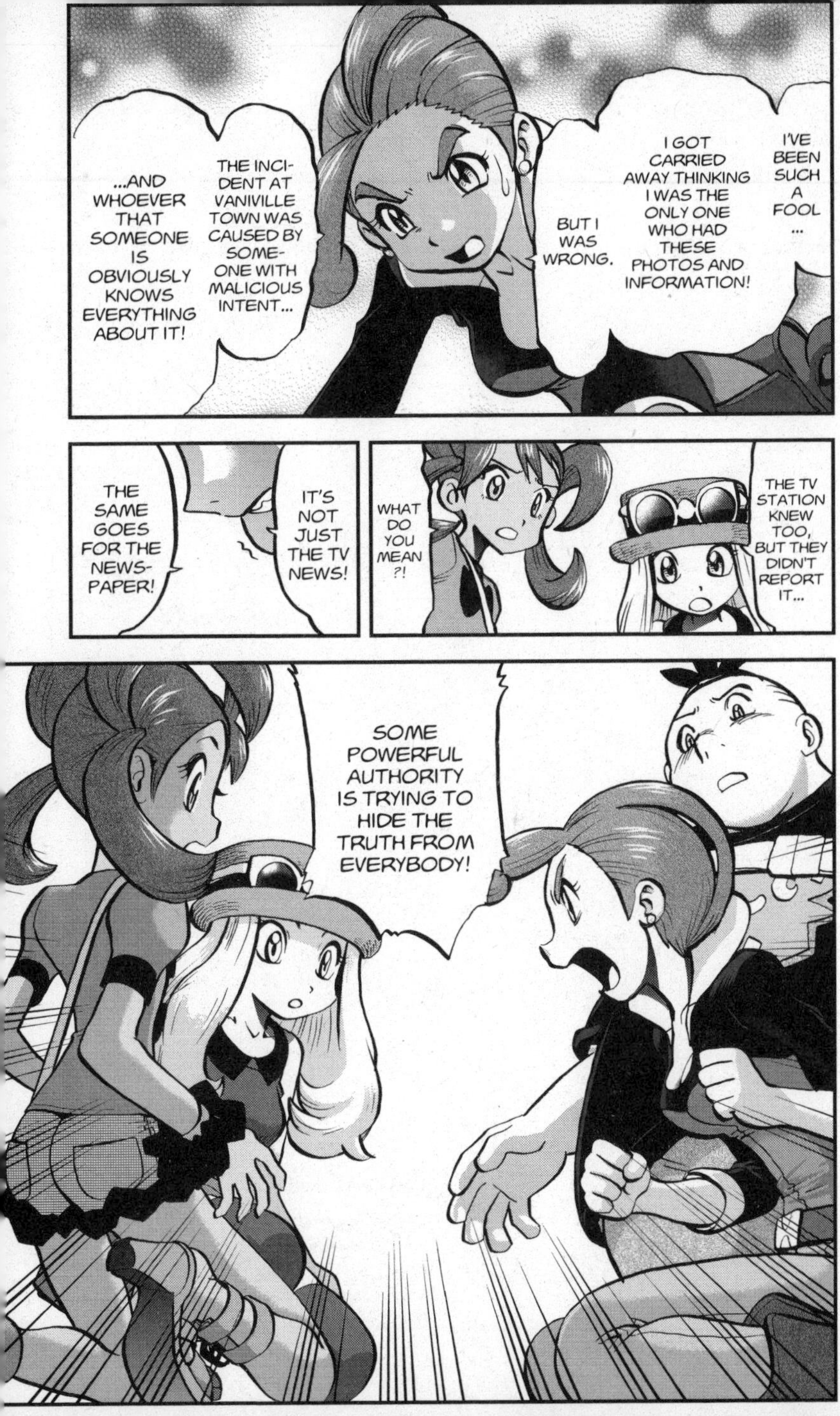
I'VE BEEN SUCH A FOOL...
I GOT CARRIED AWAY THINKING I WAS THE ONLY ONE WHO HAD THESE PHOTOS AND INFORMATION!
BUT I WAS WRONG.
THE INCIDENT AT VANIVILLE TOWN WAS CAUSED BY SOMEONE WITH MALICIOUS INTENT...
...AND WHOEVER THAT SOMEONE IS OBVIOUSLY KNOWS EVERYTHING ABOUT IT!
THE TV STATION KNEW TOO, BUT THEY DIDN'T REPORT IT...
WHAT DO YOU MEAN?!
IT'S NOT JUST THE TV NEWS!
THE SAME GOES FOR THE NEWSPAPER!
SOME POWERFUL AUTHORITY IS TRYING TO HIDE THE TRUTH FROM EVERYBODY!

## Current Location

**Lumiose City**

A dazzling metropolis of art and artifice, located in the very heart of the Kalos region.

Adventure #15
# Charging After Electrike

WZZZZZZ
MEGA!

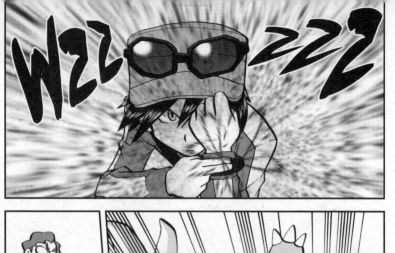

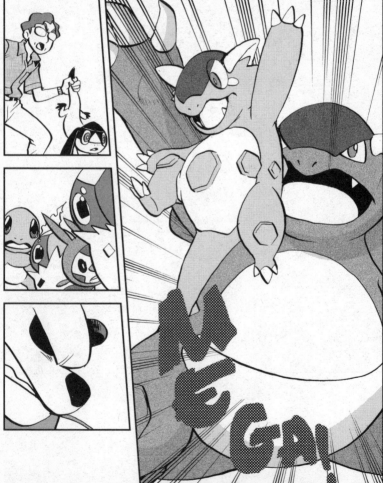

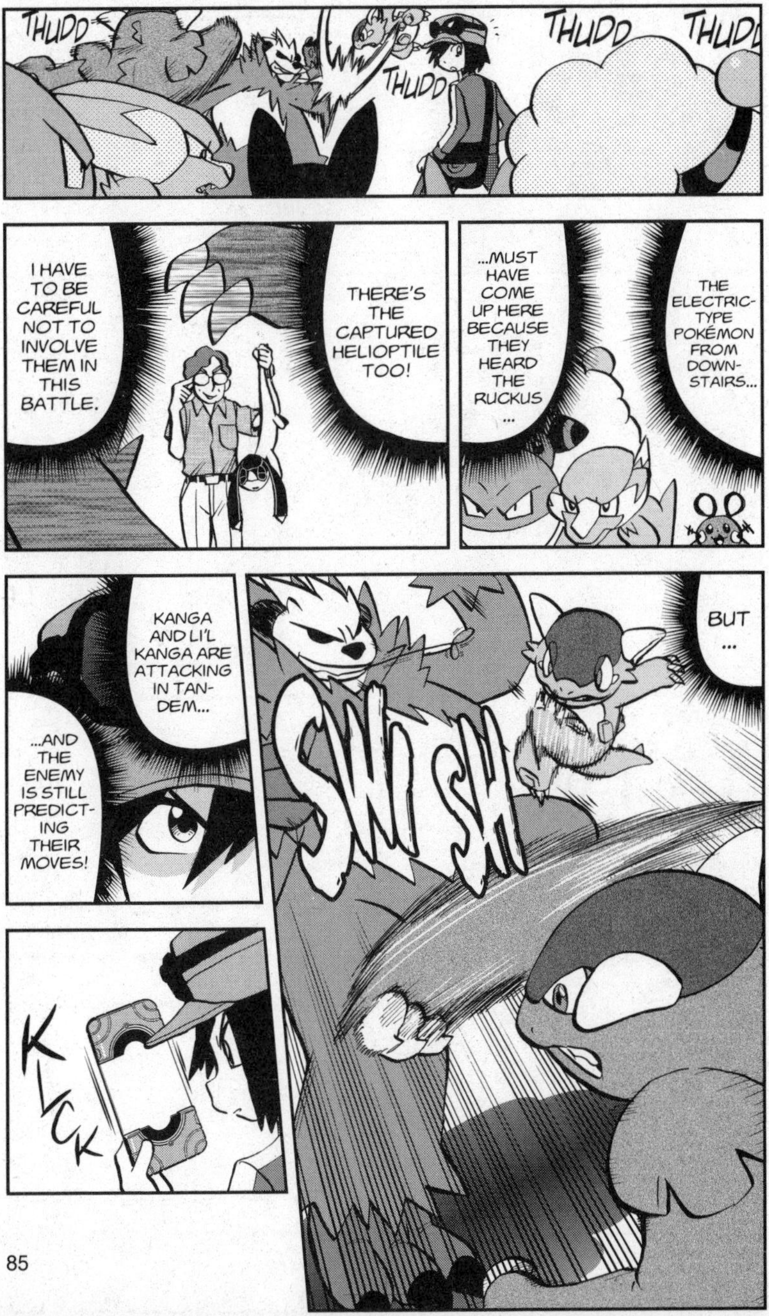
THUDD
THUDD
THUDD
THUDD
THE ELECTRIC-TYPE POKÉMON FROM DOWNSTAIRS...
...MUST HAVE COME UP HERE BECAUSE THEY HEARD THE RUCKUS...
THERE'S THE CAPTURED HELIOPTILE TOO!
I HAVE TO BE CAREFUL NOT TO INVOLVE THEM IN THIS BATTLE.
BUT ...
SWISH
KANGA AND LI'L KANGA ARE ATTACKING IN TANDEM...
...AND THE ENEMY IS STILL PREDICTING THEIR MOVES!
KLICK

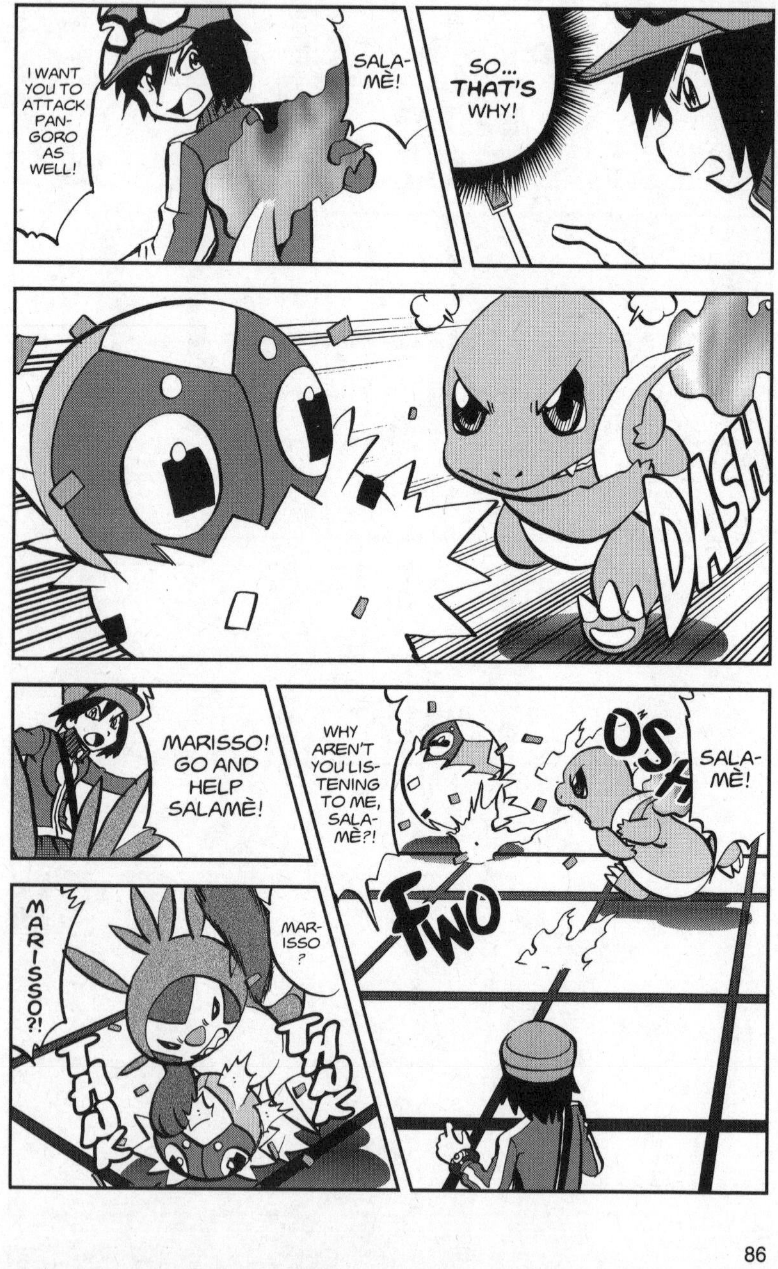
SO... THAT'S WHY!
SALA-MÈ!
I WANT YOU TO ATTACK PAN-GORO AS WELL!
DASH
SALA-MÈ!
OSH
WHY AREN'T YOU LIS-TENING TO ME, SALA-MÈ?!
MARISSO! GO AND HELP SALAMÈ!
FWO
MAR-ISSO?
MARISSO?!
THUK
THUK

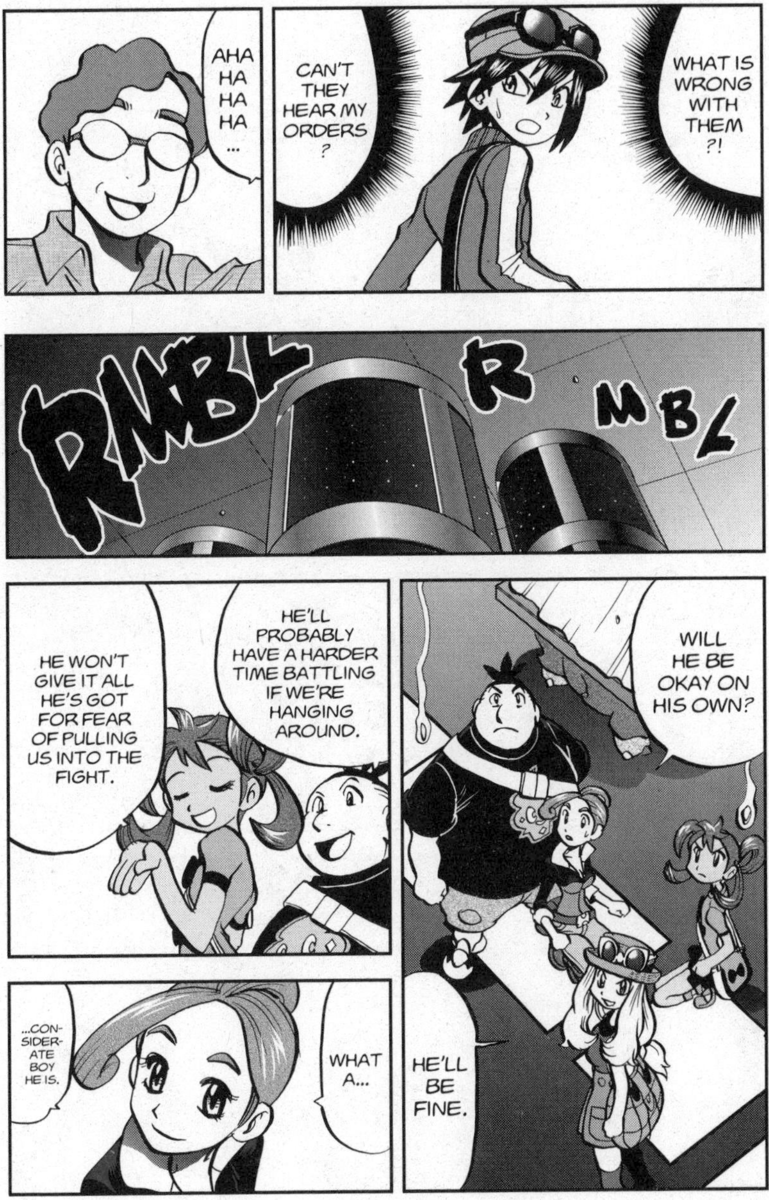
WHAT IS WRONG WITH THEM?!
CAN'T THEY HEAR MY ORDERS?
AHA HA HA HA...
RMBL
RMBL
WILL HE BE OKAY ON HIS OWN?
HE'LL BE FINE.
HE'LL PROBABLY HAVE A HARDER TIME BATTLING IF WE'RE HANGING AROUND.
HE WON'T GIVE IT ALL HE'S GOT FOR FEAR OF PULLING US INTO THE FIGHT.
WHAT A...
...CONSIDERATE BOY HE IS.

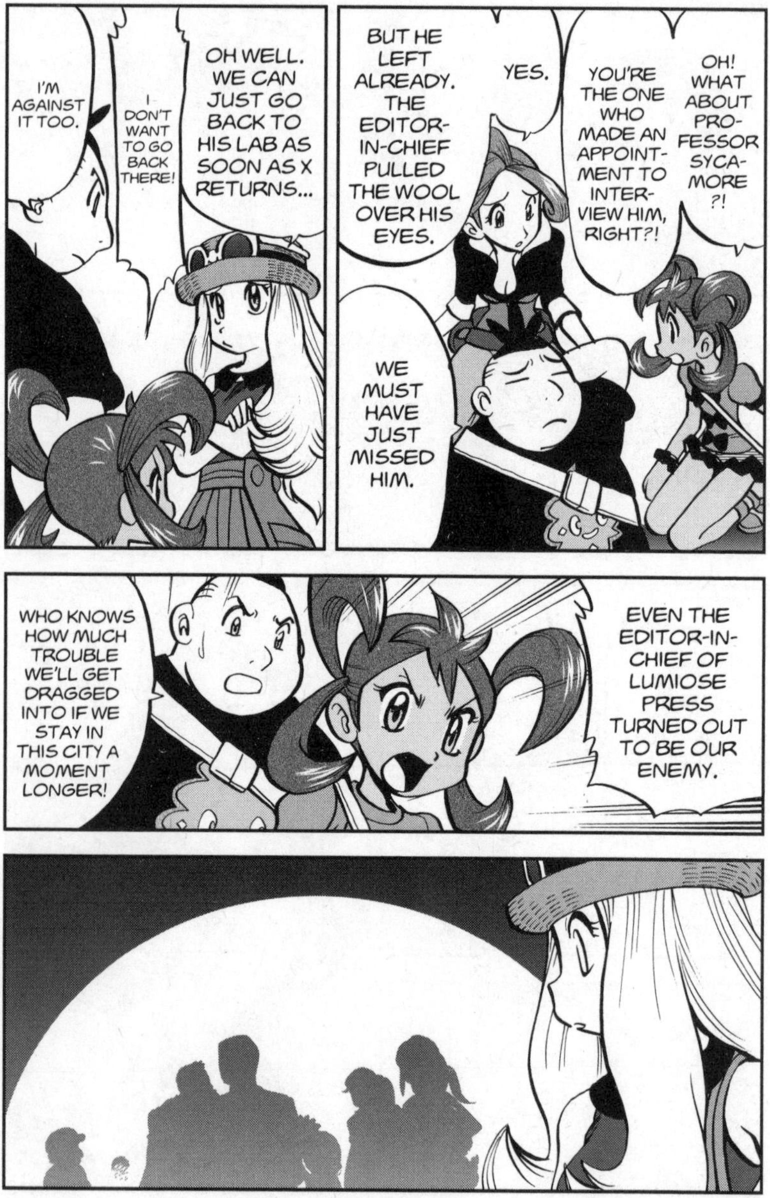
OH! WHAT ABOUT PROFESSOR SYCAMORE?!
YOU'RE THE ONE WHO MADE AN APPOINTMENT TO INTERVIEW HIM, RIGHT?!
YES.
BUT HE LEFT ALREADY. THE EDITOR-IN-CHIEF PULLED THE WOOL OVER HIS EYES.
WE MUST HAVE JUST MISSED HIM.
OH WELL. WE CAN JUST GO BACK TO HIS LAB AS SOON AS X RETURNS...
I- DON'T WANT TO GO BACK THERE!
I'M AGAINST IT TOO.
EVEN THE EDITOR-IN-CHIEF OF LUMIOSE PRESS TURNED OUT TO BE OUR ENEMY.
WHO KNOWS HOW MUCH TROUBLE WE'LL GET DRAGGED INTO IF WE STAY IN THIS CITY A MOMENT LONGER!

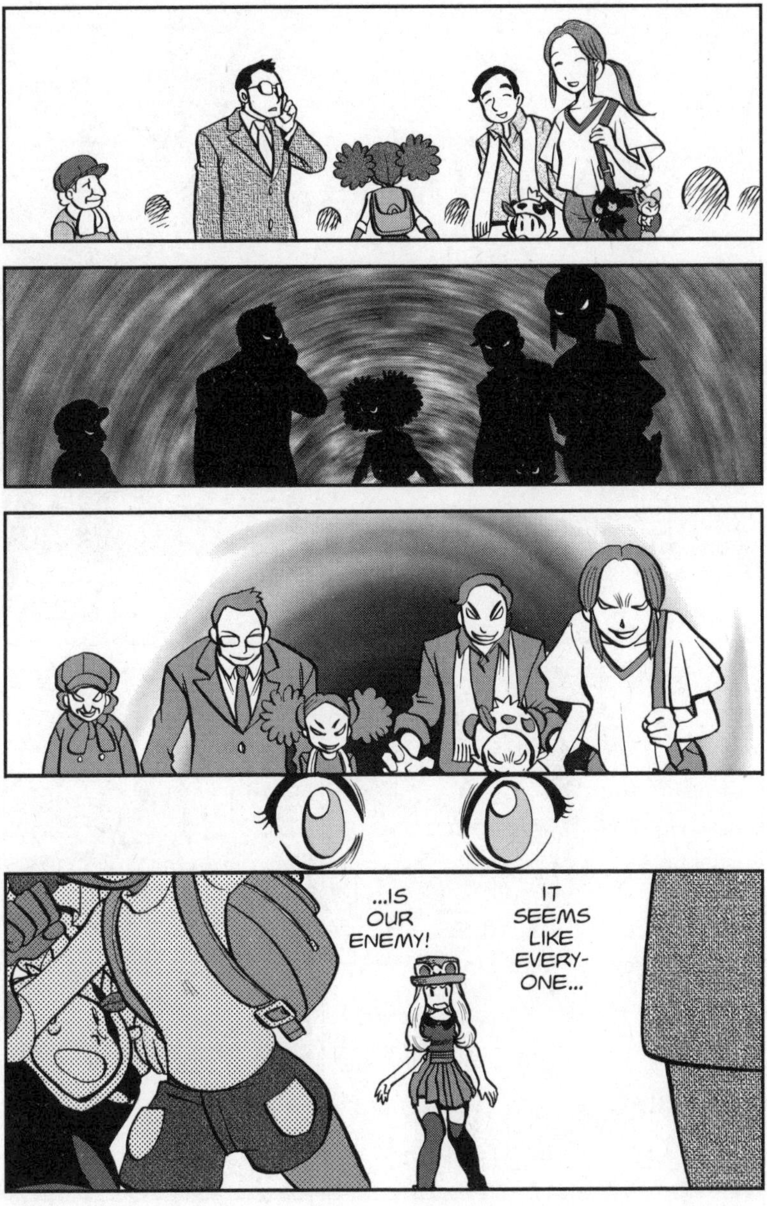
IT SEEMS LIKE EVERY-ONE...
...IS OUR ENEMY!

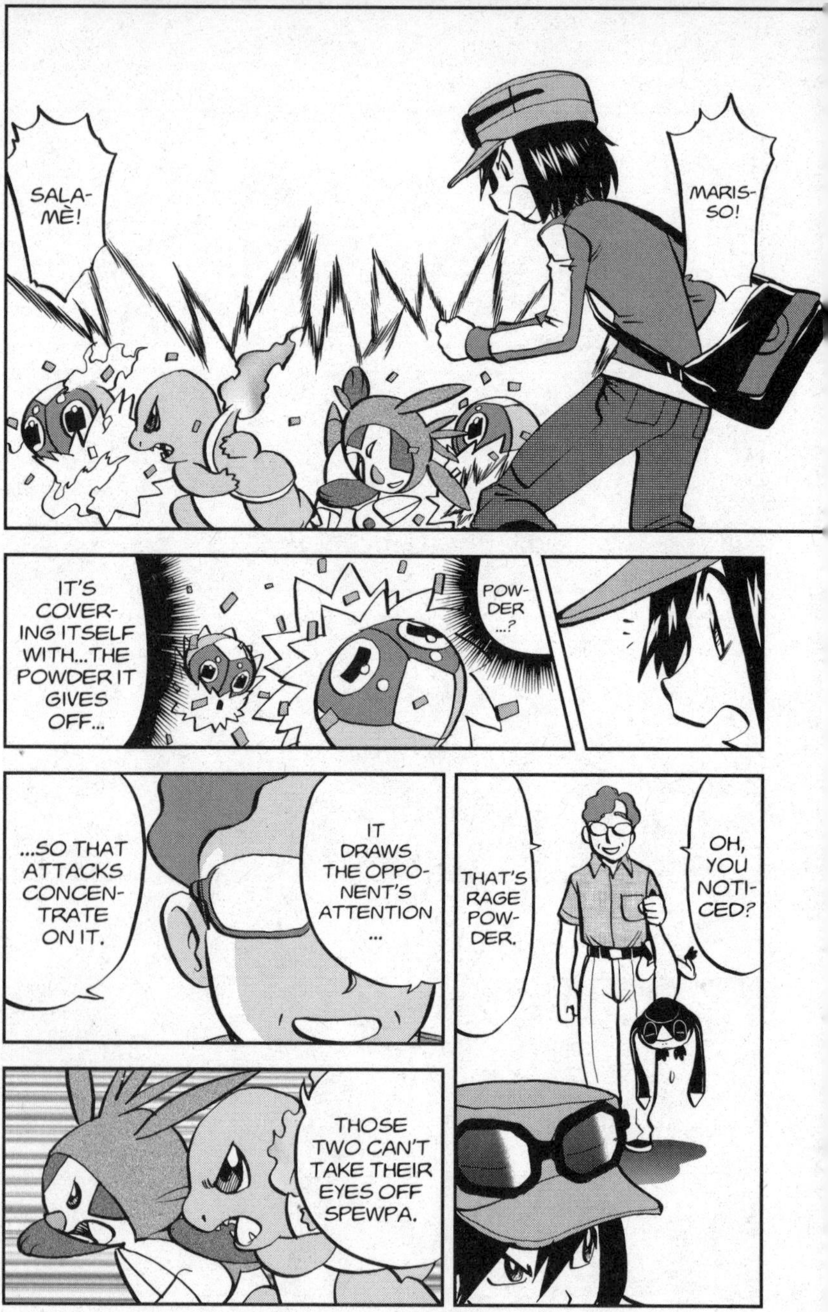
MARIS-SO!
SALA-MÈ!
POW-DER ...?
IT'S COVER-ING ITSELF WITH...THE POWDER IT GIVES OFF...
OH, YOU NOTI-CED?
THAT'S RAGE POW-DER.
IT DRAWS THE OPPO-NENT'S ATTENTION ...
...SO THAT ATTACKS CONCEN-TRATE ON IT.
THOSE TWO CAN'T TAKE THEIR EYES OFF SPEWPA.

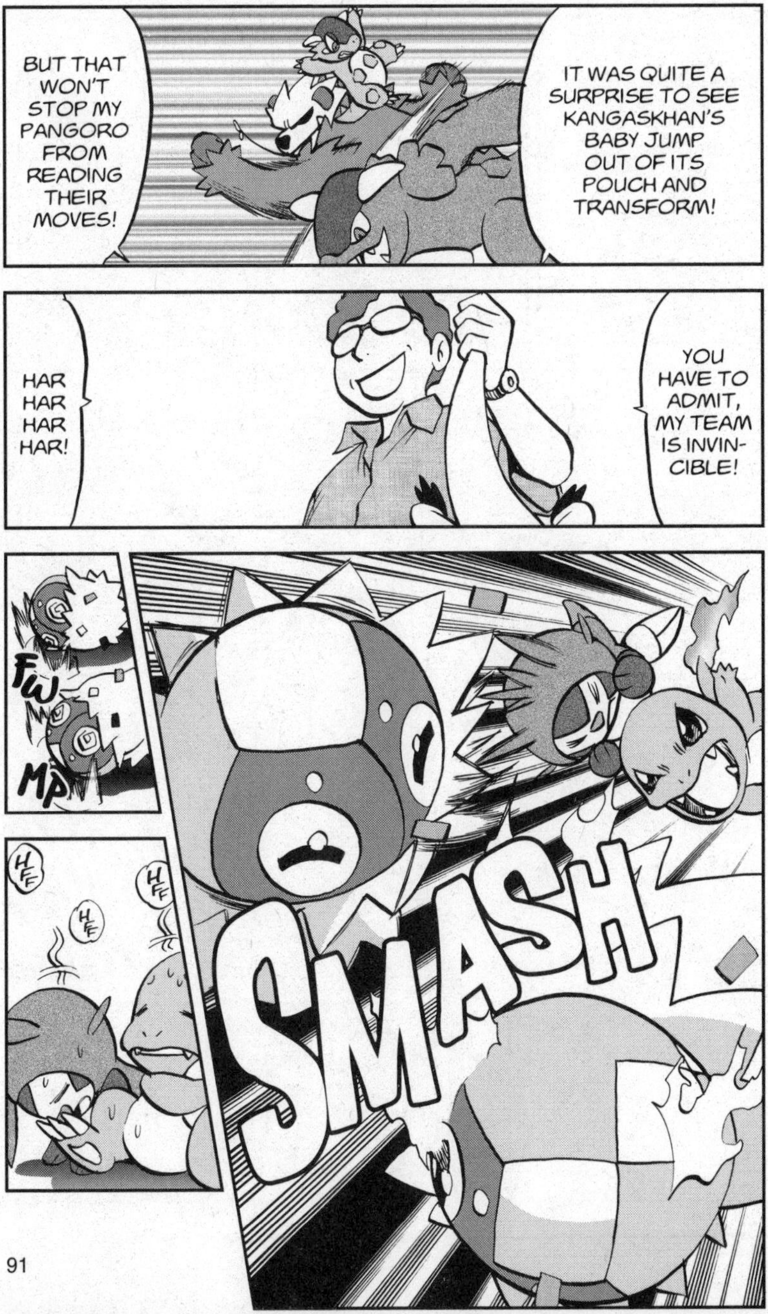
IT WAS QUITE A SURPRISE TO SEE KANGASKHAN'S BABY JUMP OUT OF ITS POUCH AND TRANSFORM!
BUT THAT WON'T STOP MY PANGORO FROM READING THEIR MOVES!
YOU HAVE TO ADMIT, MY TEAM IS INVIN-CIBLE!
HAR HAR HAR HAR!
SMASH
FWMP
HFF
HFF
HFF

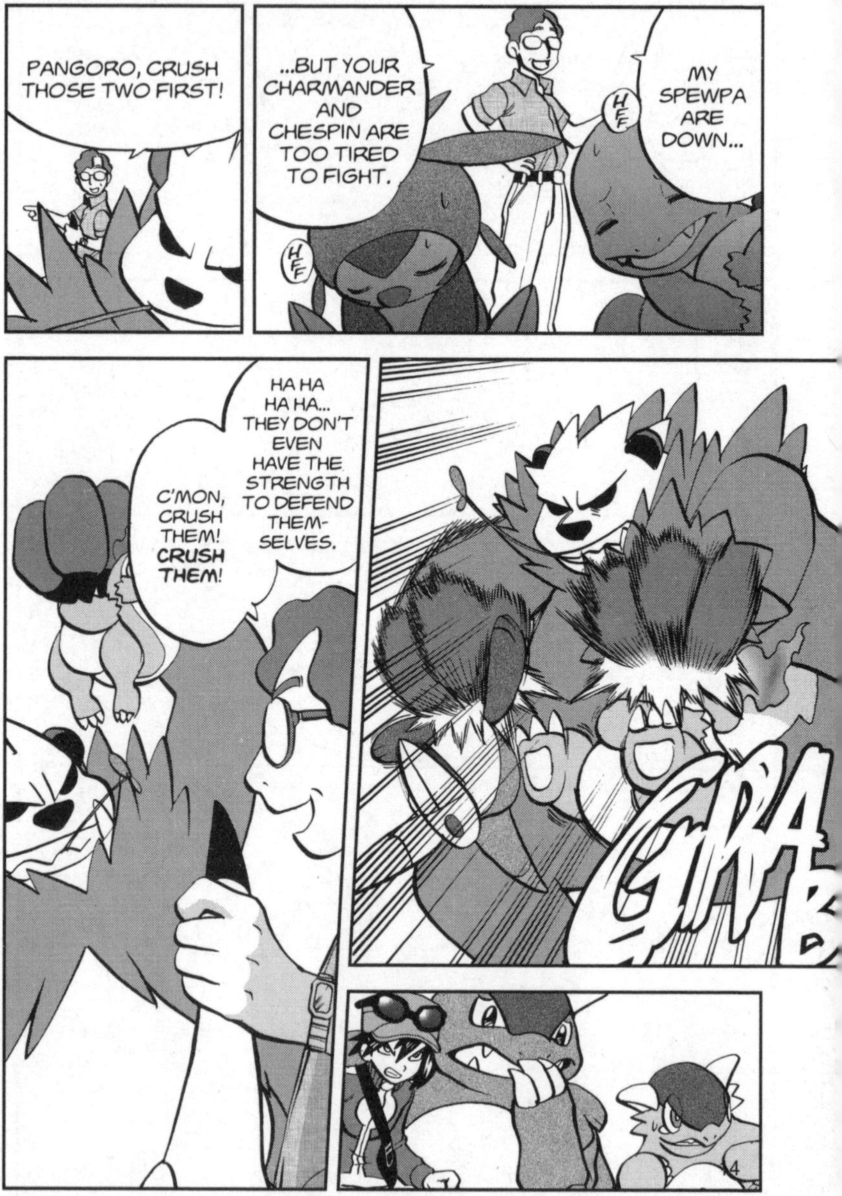
MY SPEWPA ARE DOWN...
HFF
...BUT YOUR CHARMANDER AND CHESPIN ARE TOO TIRED TO FIGHT.
HFF
PANGORO, CRUSH THOSE TWO FIRST!
GRAB
HA HA HA HA... THEY DON'T EVEN HAVE THE STRENGTH TO DEFEND THEM-SELVES.
C'MON, CRUSH THEM! **CRUSH THEM!**

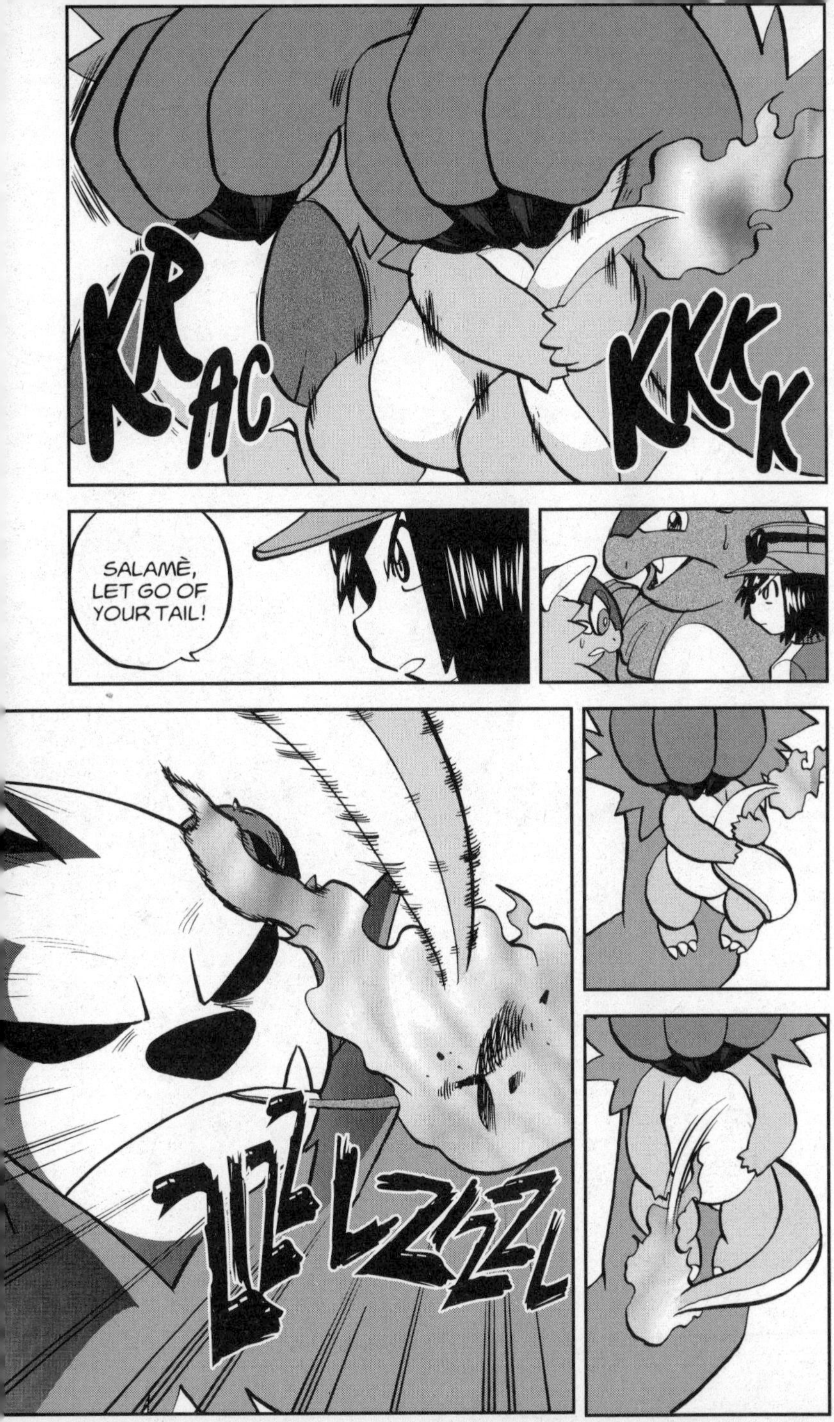
KRAC
KKKK
SALAMÈ, LET GO OF YOUR TAIL!
ZZZZLZZZZL

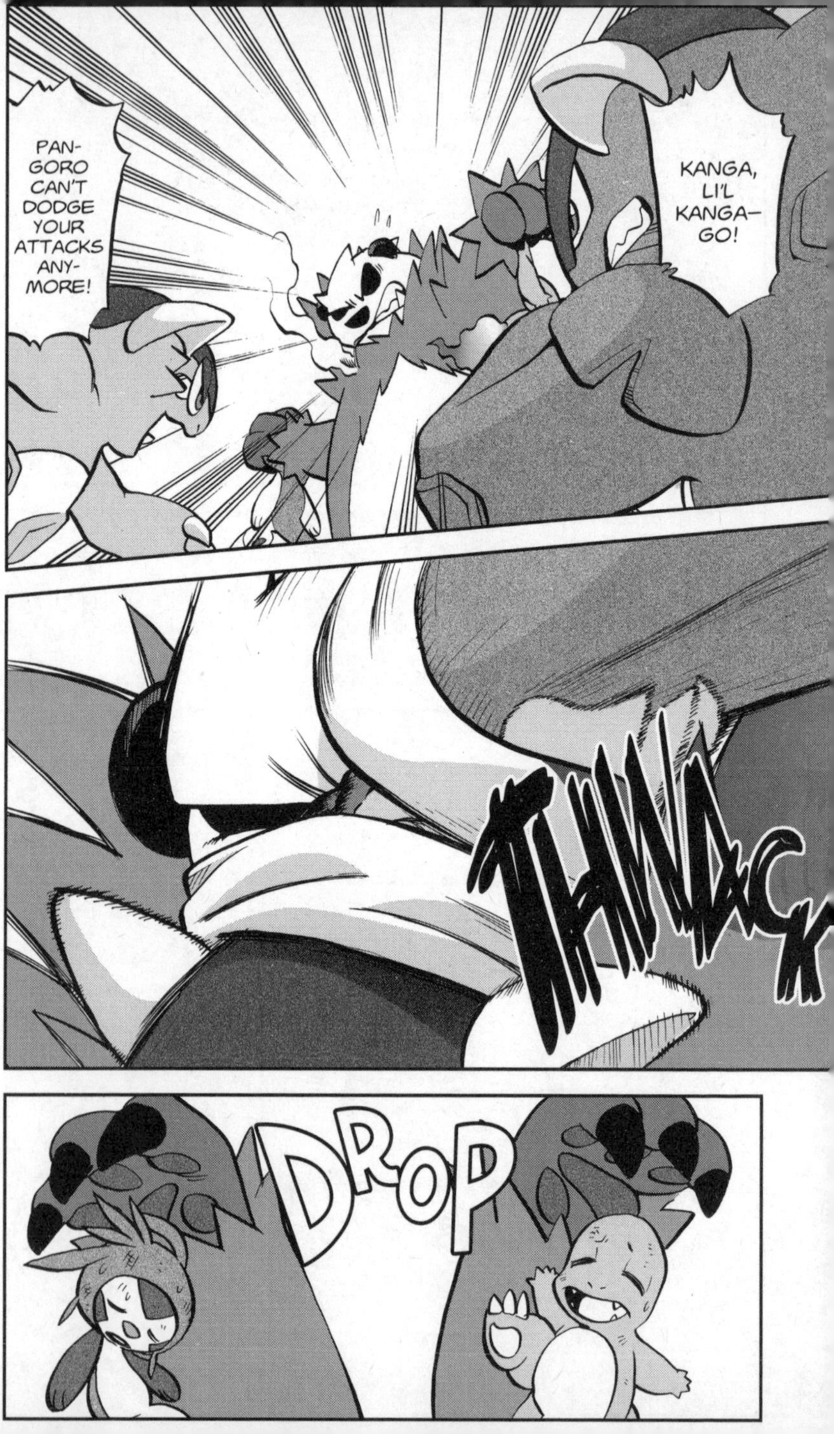
KANGA, LI'L KANGA-GO!
PAN-GORO CAN'T DODGE YOUR ATTACKS ANY-MORE!
THWACK
DROP

DOINK
YOU KNEW THE SECRET OF HOW PANGORO COULD READ THEIR MOVES?!
National Pokédex
Seen
Obtained
No.675
Pangoro
Daunting Pokémon
Type:
Fighting
Dark
Height: 6'11"
Weight: 299.8 lbs
Although it possesses a violent temperament, it won't put up with bullying. It uses the leaf in its mouth to sense the movements of its enemies.
YES. BY ANALYZING THE SUBTLE CHANGES IN THE FLOW OF AIR WHEN MY POKÉMON ATTACKED PANGORO.
THE LEAF IN PANGORO'S MOUTH CAN DETECT THOSE CHANGES.
THAT'S HOW IT DODGED ALL OF MY ATTACKS.
SO YOU MADE IT CAPTURE YOUR POKÉMON ON PURPOSE?! SO YOU COULD BURN ITS LEAF?!

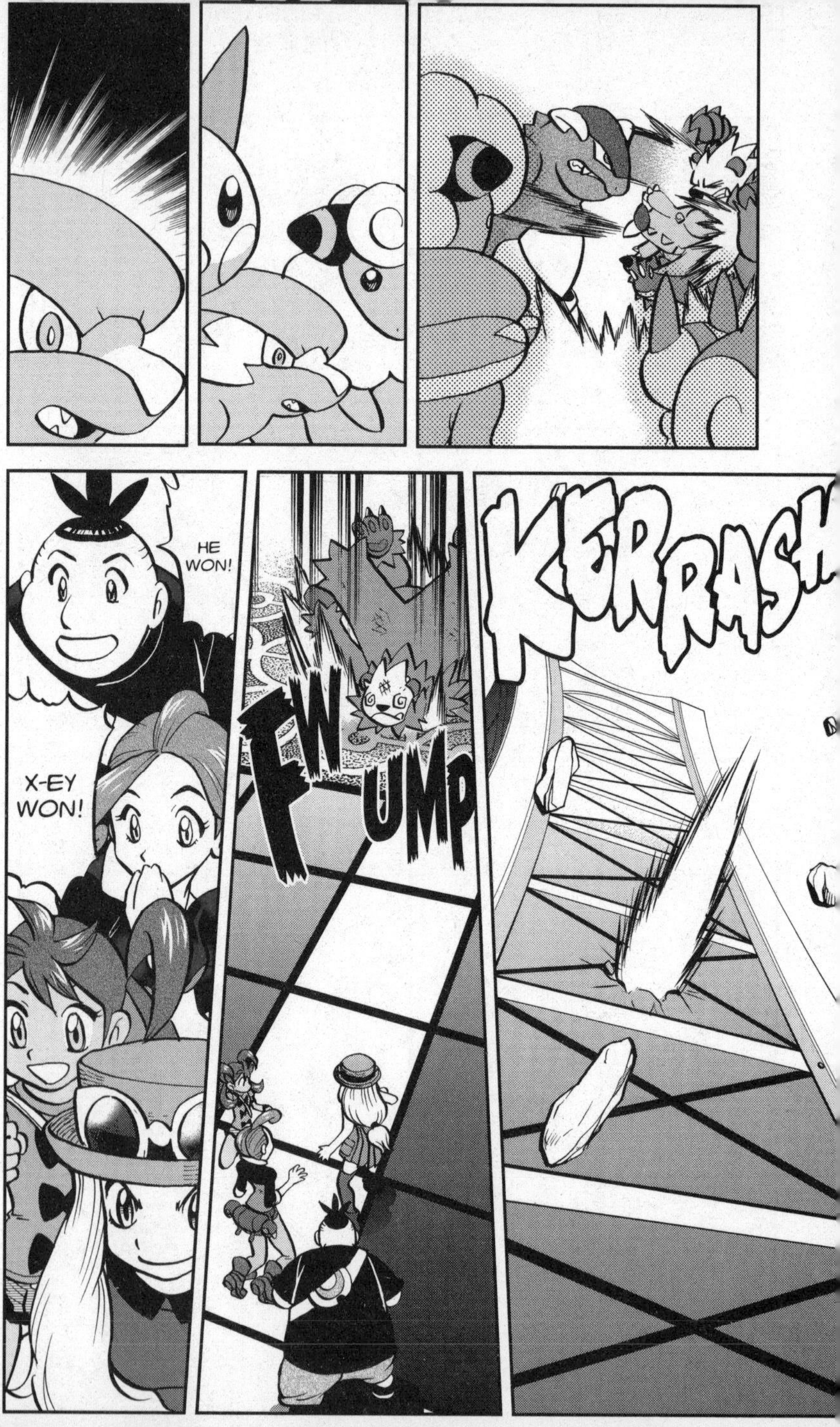
KERRASH
FWUMP
HE WON!
X-EY WON!

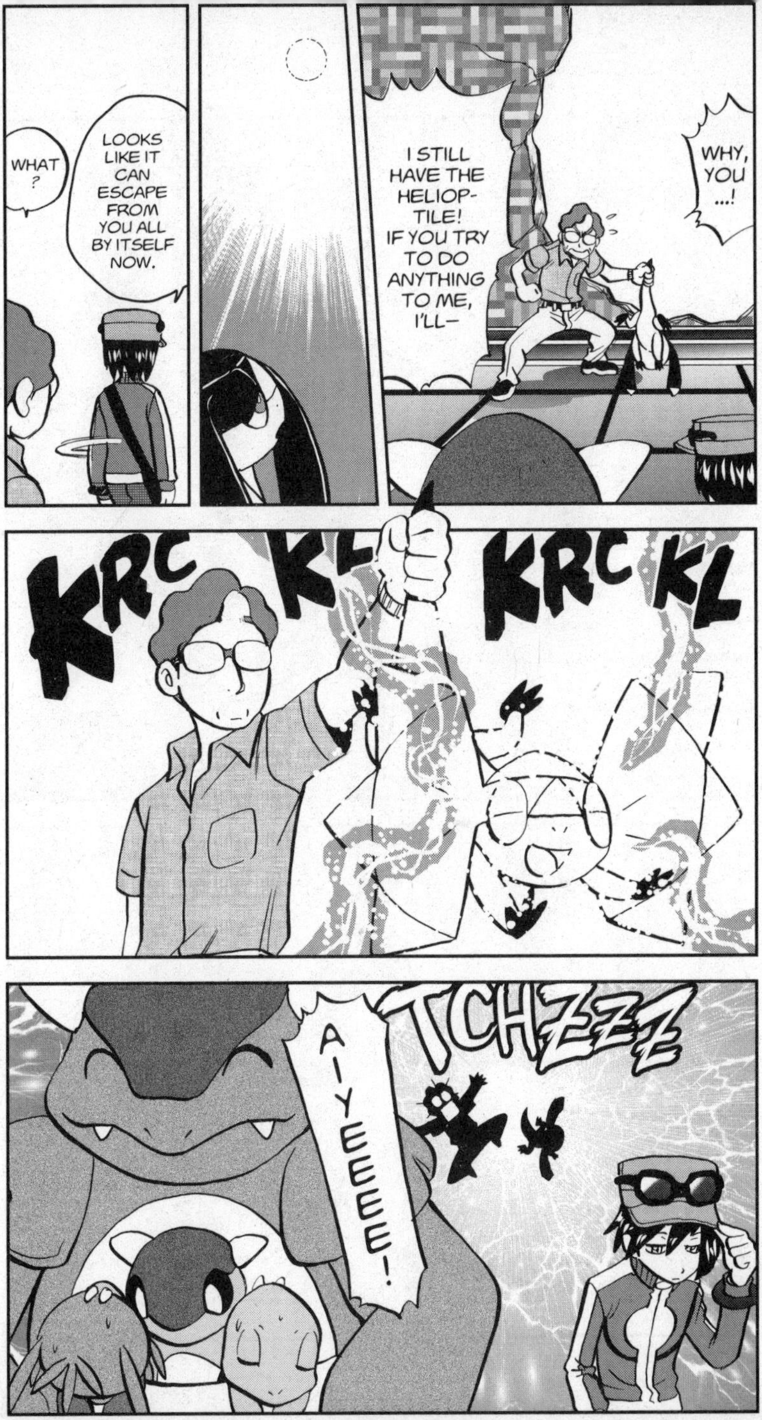
WHY, YOU ...!
I STILL HAVE THE HELIOPTILE! IF YOU TRY TO DO ANYTHING TO ME, I'LL—
LOOKS LIKE IT CAN ESCAPE FROM YOU ALL BY ITSELF NOW.
WHAT?
KRCKL KRCKL
TCHZZZ
AIYEEEE!

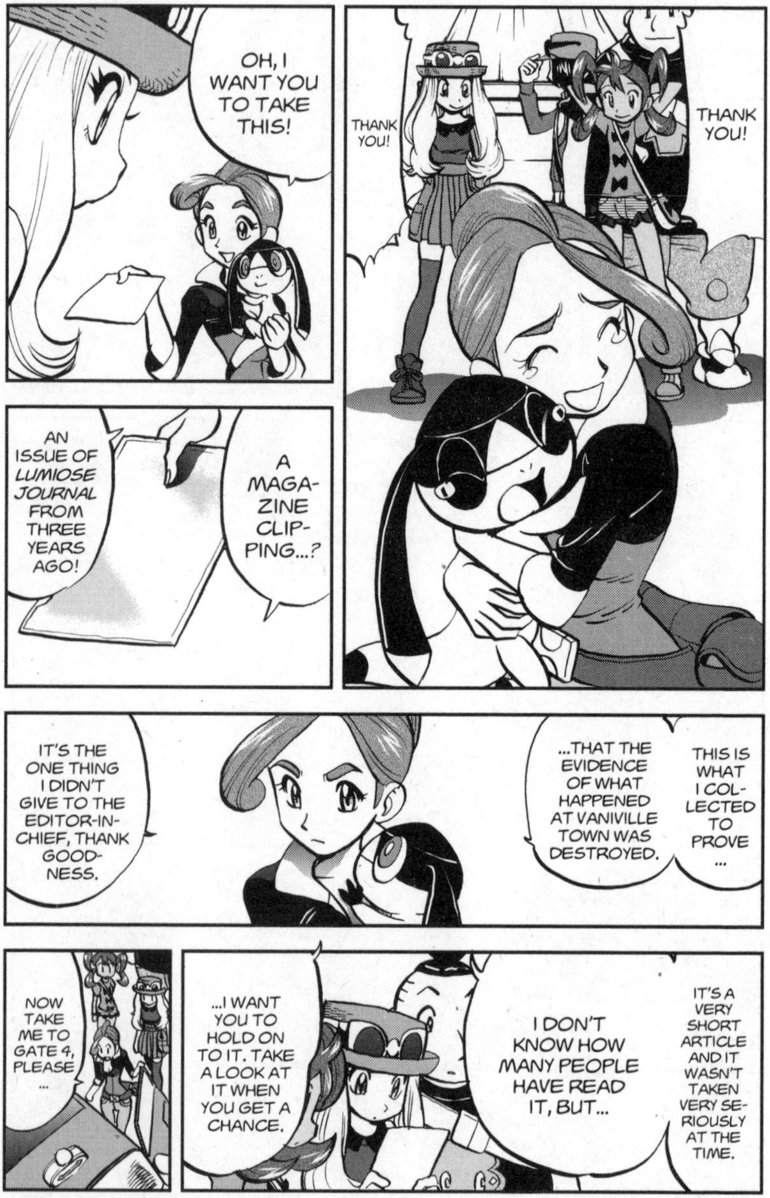
THANK YOU!
THANK YOU!
OH, I WANT YOU TO TAKE THIS!
A MAGAZINE CLIPPING...?
AN ISSUE OF *LUMIOSE JOURNAL* FROM THREE YEARS AGO!
THIS IS WHAT I COLLECTED TO PROVE ...
...THAT THE EVIDENCE OF WHAT HAPPENED AT VANIVILLE TOWN WAS DESTROYED.
IT'S THE ONE THING I DIDN'T GIVE TO THE EDITOR-IN-CHIEF, THANK GOODNESS.
IT'S A VERY SHORT ARTICLE AND IT WASN'T TAKEN VERY SERIOUSLY AT THE TIME.
I DON'T KNOW HOW MANY PEOPLE HAVE READ IT, BUT...
...I WANT YOU TO HOLD ON TO IT. TAKE A LOOK AT IT WHEN YOU GET A CHANCE.
NOW TAKE ME TO GATE 4, PLEASE ...

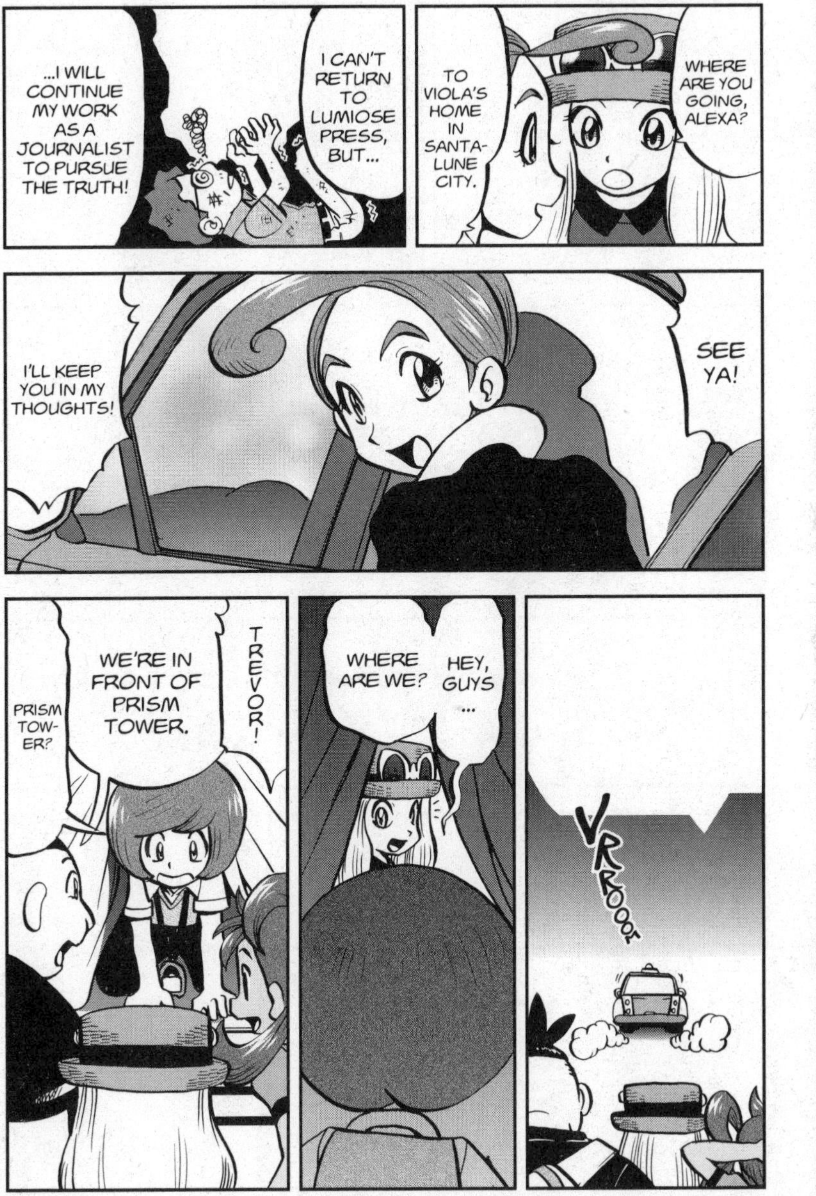
WHERE ARE YOU GOING, ALEXA?
TO VIOLA'S HOME IN SANTA-LUNE CITY.
I CAN'T RETURN TO LUMIOSE PRESS, BUT...
...I WILL CONTINUE MY WORK AS A JOURNALIST TO PURSUE THE TRUTH!
SEE YA!
I'LL KEEP YOU IN MY THOUGHTS!
VRROOOO
HEY, GUYS...
WHERE ARE WE?
TREVOR!
WE'RE IN FRONT OF PRISM TOWER.
PRISM TOW-ER?

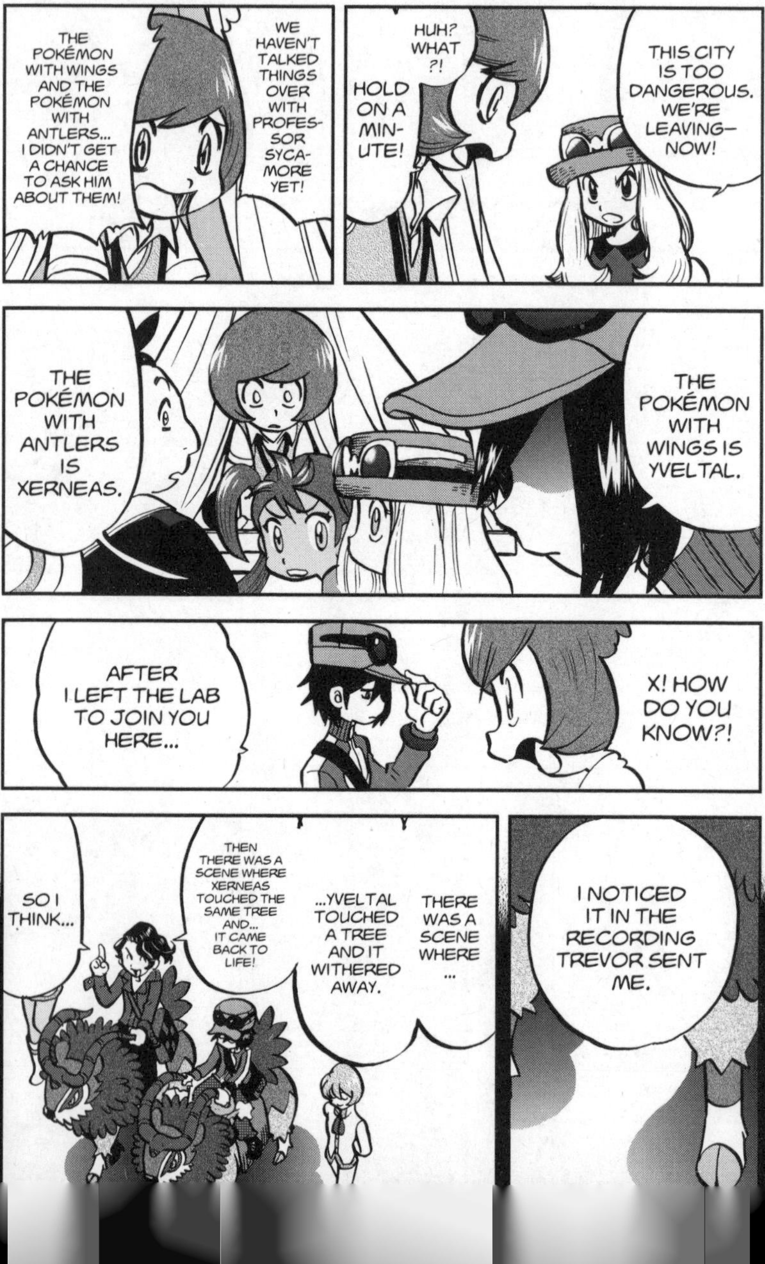
THIS CITY IS TOO DANGEROUS. WE'RE LEAVING—NOW!
HUH? WHAT?!
HOLD ON A MIN-UTE!
WE HAVEN'T TALKED THINGS OVER WITH PROFES-SOR SYCA-MORE YET!
THE POKÉMON WITH WINGS AND THE POKÉMON WITH ANTLERS... I DIDN'T GET A CHANCE TO ASK HIM ABOUT THEM!
THE POKÉMON WITH WINGS IS YVELTAL.
THE POKÉMON WITH ANTLERS IS XERNEAS.
X! HOW DO YOU KNOW?!
AFTER I LEFT THE LAB TO JOIN YOU HERE...
I NOTICED IT IN THE RECORDING TREVOR SENT ME.
THERE WAS A SCENE WHERE ...
...YVELTAL TOUCHED A TREE AND IT WITHERED AWAY.
THEN THERE WAS A SCENE WHERE XERNEAS TOUCHED THE SAME TREE AND... IT CAME BACK TO LIFE!
SO I THINK...

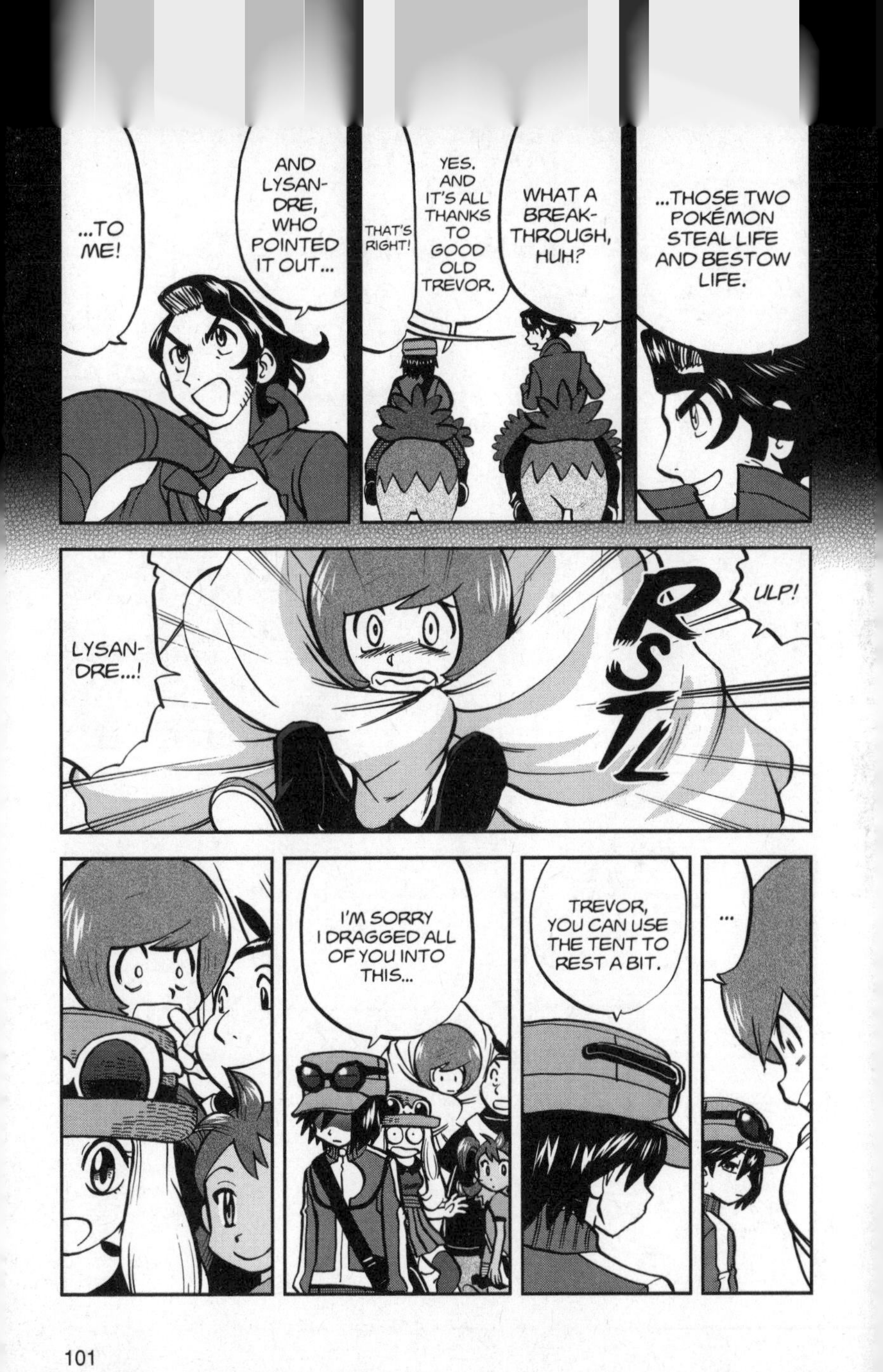
...THOSE TWO POKÉMON STEAL LIFE AND BESTOW LIFE.
WHAT A BREAK-THROUGH, HUH?
YES. AND IT'S ALL THANKS TO GOOD OLD TREVOR.
THAT'S RIGHT!
AND LYSAN-DRE, WHO POINTED IT OUT...
...TO ME!
ULP!
RSTL
LYSAN-DRE...!
...
TREVOR, YOU CAN USE THE TENT TO REST A BIT.
I'M SORRY I DRAGGED ALL OF YOU INTO THIS...

OW...
WHAT'S THIS?!
ALL THE POKÉMON WHO WERE CREATING ELECTRICITY ON THE FIRST FLOOR ARE HERE NOW. AND THERE'S A STRANGE GUY OVER THERE ...
I WAS GUARDING THE TOWER ON THE UPPER FLOOR LIKE CLEMONT TOLD ME TO...
HE SAID TO STAY THERE AND I KEPT THAT PROMISE...
THIS ISN'T MY FAULT!
I'M SURE IT'S HERE... SOME-PLACE...
UMM ...
ONE... TWO... THREE... FOUR...
TWENTY-THREE... TWENTY-FOUR...

THERE'S ONE MISSING! DID IT RUN AWAY?!

AHHH!!

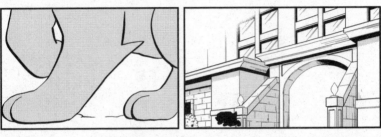

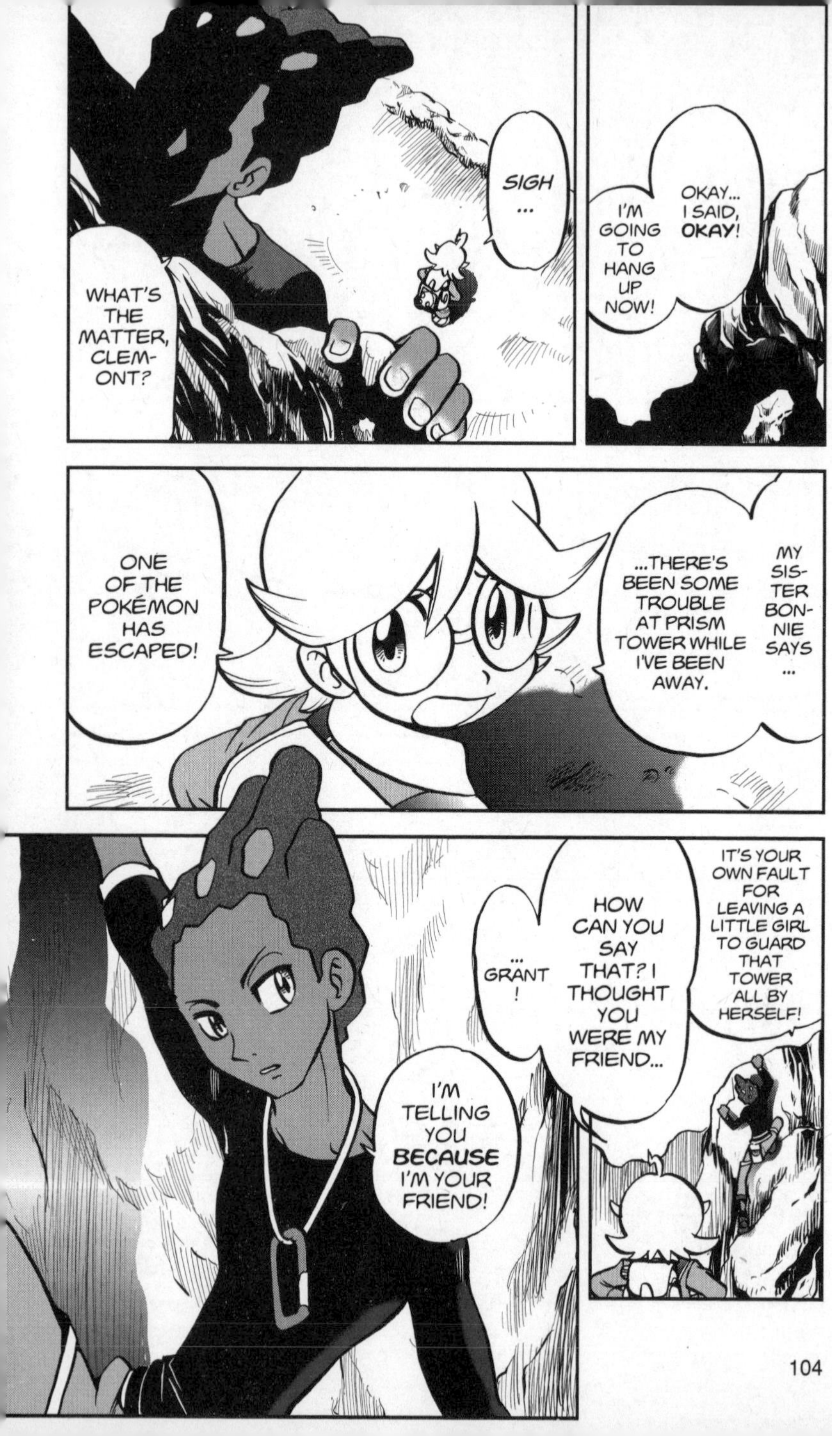

OKAY... I SAID, **OKAY**!
I'M GOING TO HANG UP NOW!
SIGH...
WHAT'S THE MATTER, CLEMONT?
MY SISTER BONNIE SAYS...
...THERE'S BEEN SOME TROUBLE AT PRISM TOWER WHILE I'VE BEEN AWAY.
ONE OF THE POKÉMON HAS ESCAPED!
IT'S YOUR OWN FAULT FOR LEAVING A LITTLE GIRL TO GUARD THAT TOWER ALL BY HERSELF!
HOW CAN YOU SAY THAT? I THOUGHT YOU WERE MY FRIEND...
...GRANT!
I'M TELLING YOU **BECAUSE** I'M YOUR FRIEND!

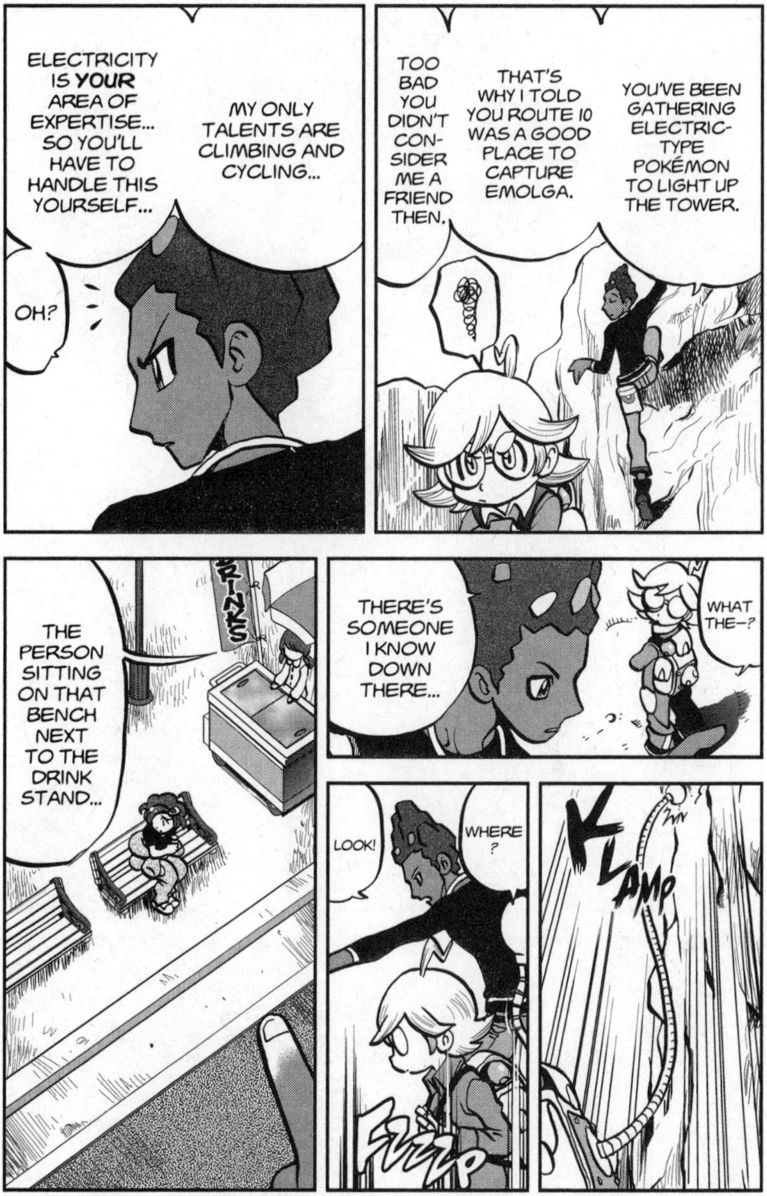

YOU'VE BEEN GATHERING ELECTRIC-TYPE POKÉMON TO LIGHT UP THE TOWER.
THAT'S WHY I TOLD YOU ROUTE 10 WAS A GOOD PLACE TO CAPTURE EMOLGA.
TOO BAD YOU DIDN'T CONSIDER ME A FRIEND THEN.
MY ONLY TALENTS ARE CLIMBING AND CYCLING...
ELECTRICITY IS **YOUR** AREA OF EXPERTISE... SO YOU'LL HAVE TO HANDLE THIS YOURSELF...
OH?
WHAT THE–?
THERE'S SOMEONE I KNOW DOWN THERE...
KLAMP
WHERE?
LOOK!
FZZZP
DRINKS
THE PERSON SITTING ON THAT BENCH NEXT TO THE DRINK STAND...

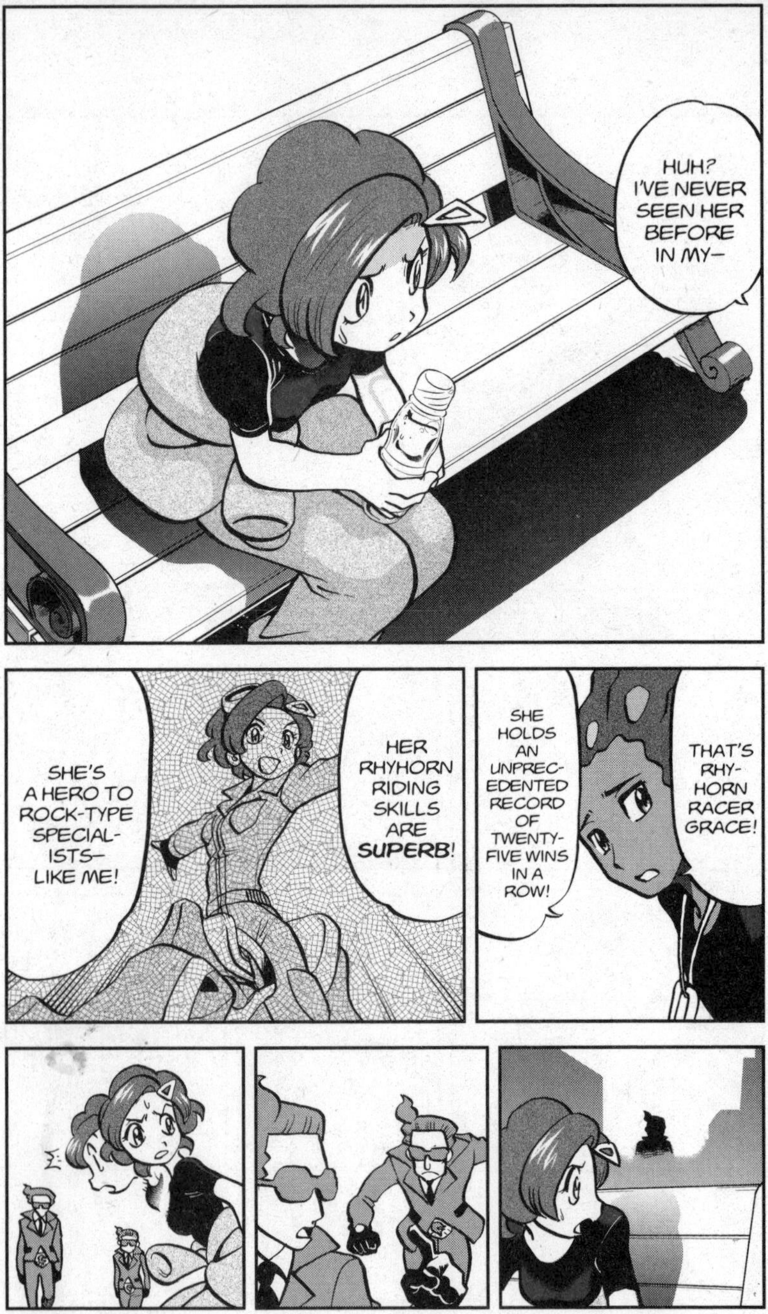
HUH? I'VE NEVER SEEN HER BEFORE IN MY—
THAT'S RHYHORN RACER GRACE!
SHE HOLDS AN UNPRECEDENTED RECORD OF TWENTY-FIVE WINS IN A ROW!
HER RHYHORN RIDING SKILLS ARE **SUPERB**!
SHE'S A HERO TO ROCK-TYPE SPECIALISTS— LIKE ME!

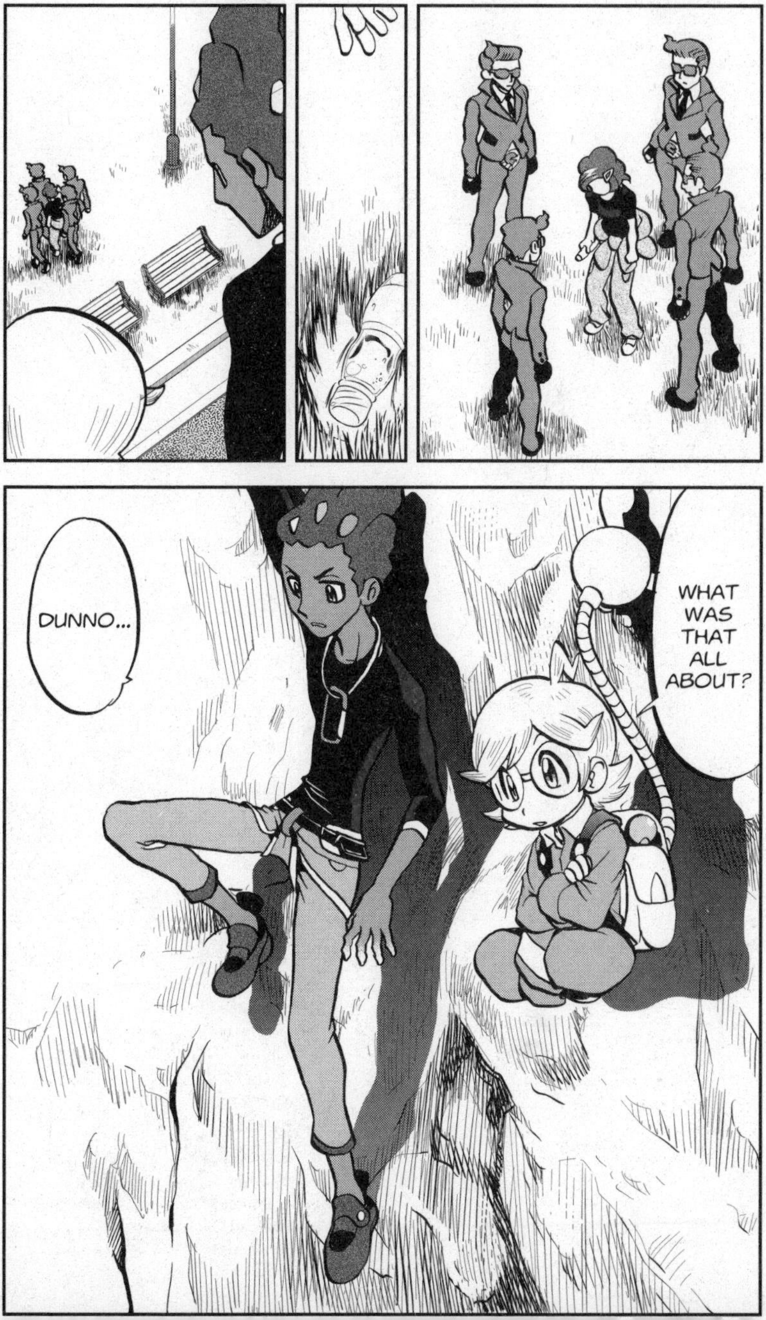
WHAT WAS THAT ALL ABOUT?
DUNNO...

## Current Location

**Lumiose City**

A dazzling metropolis of art and artifice, located in the very heart of the Kalos region.

**Route 5
Versant Road**

Roller Skaters from across the Kalos region gather on this hilly path to demonstrate their best skills.

# Adventure #16
## Corphish Pinches

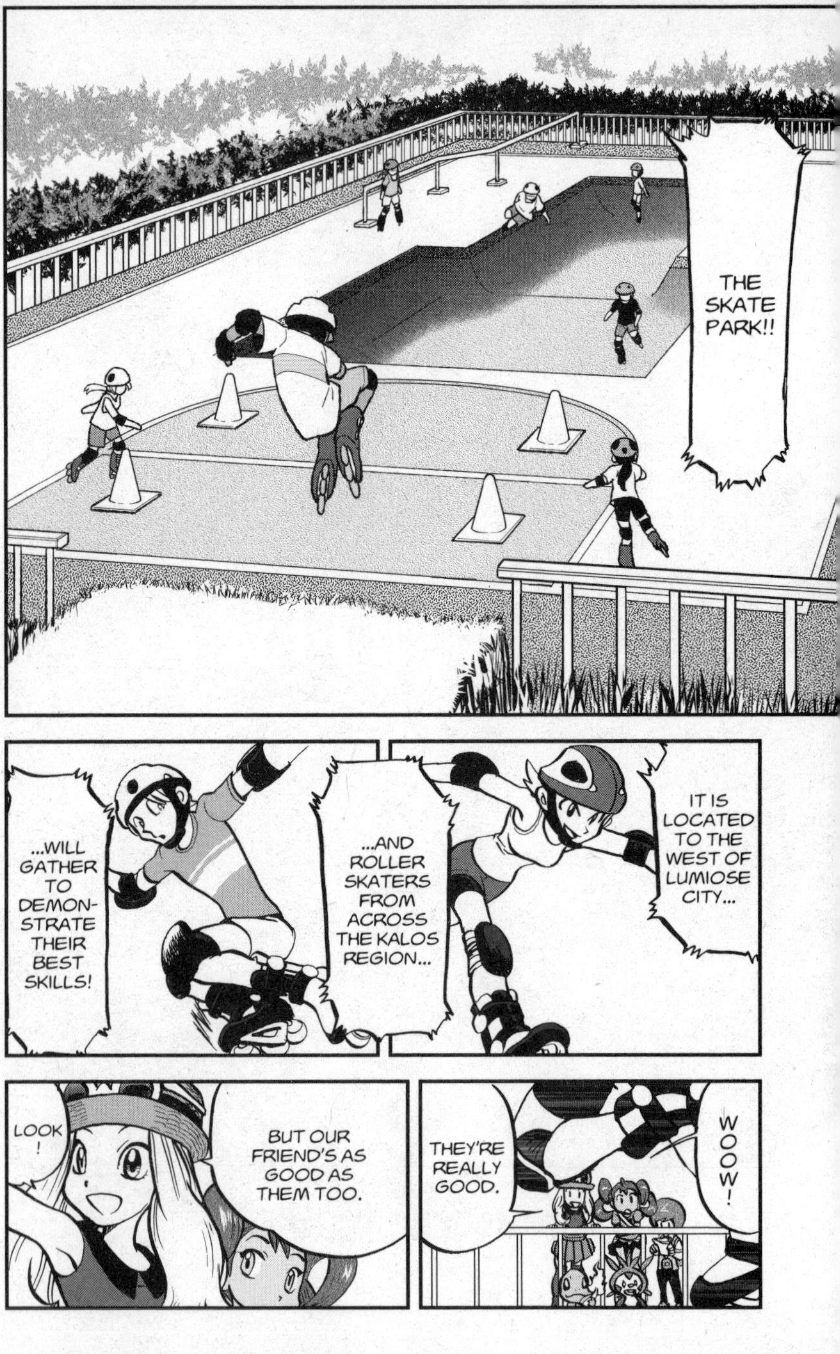
THE SKATE PARK!!
IT IS LOCATED TO THE WEST OF LUMIOSE CITY...
...AND ROLLER SKATERS FROM ACROSS THE KALOS REGION...
...WILL GATHER TO DEMON-STRATE THEIR BEST SKILLS!
WOOOW!
THEY'RE REALLY GOOD.
BUT OUR FRIEND'S AS GOOD AS THEM TOO.
LOOK!

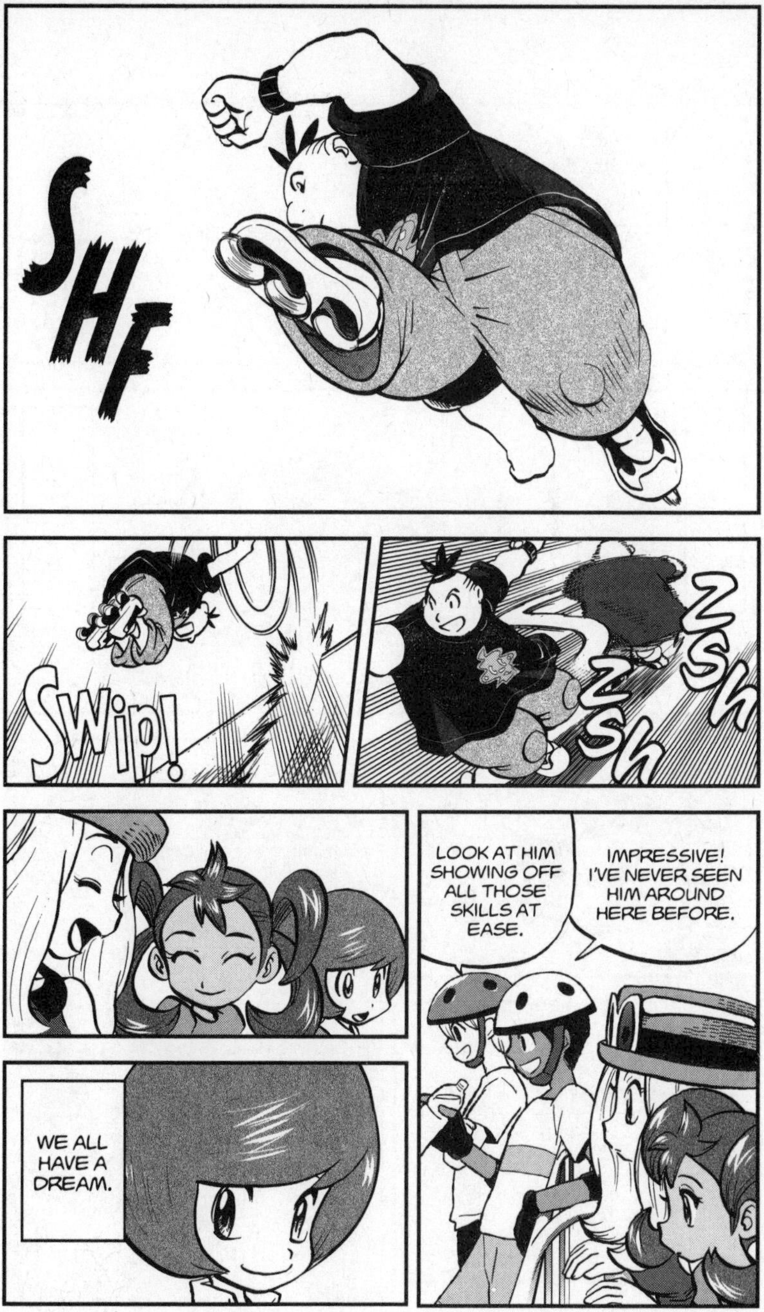

SHF
ZSH
ZSH
SWIP!
IMPRESSIVE! I'VE NEVER SEEN HIM AROUND HERE BEFORE.
LOOK AT HIM SHOWING OFF ALL THOSE SKILLS AT EASE.
WE ALL HAVE A DREAM.

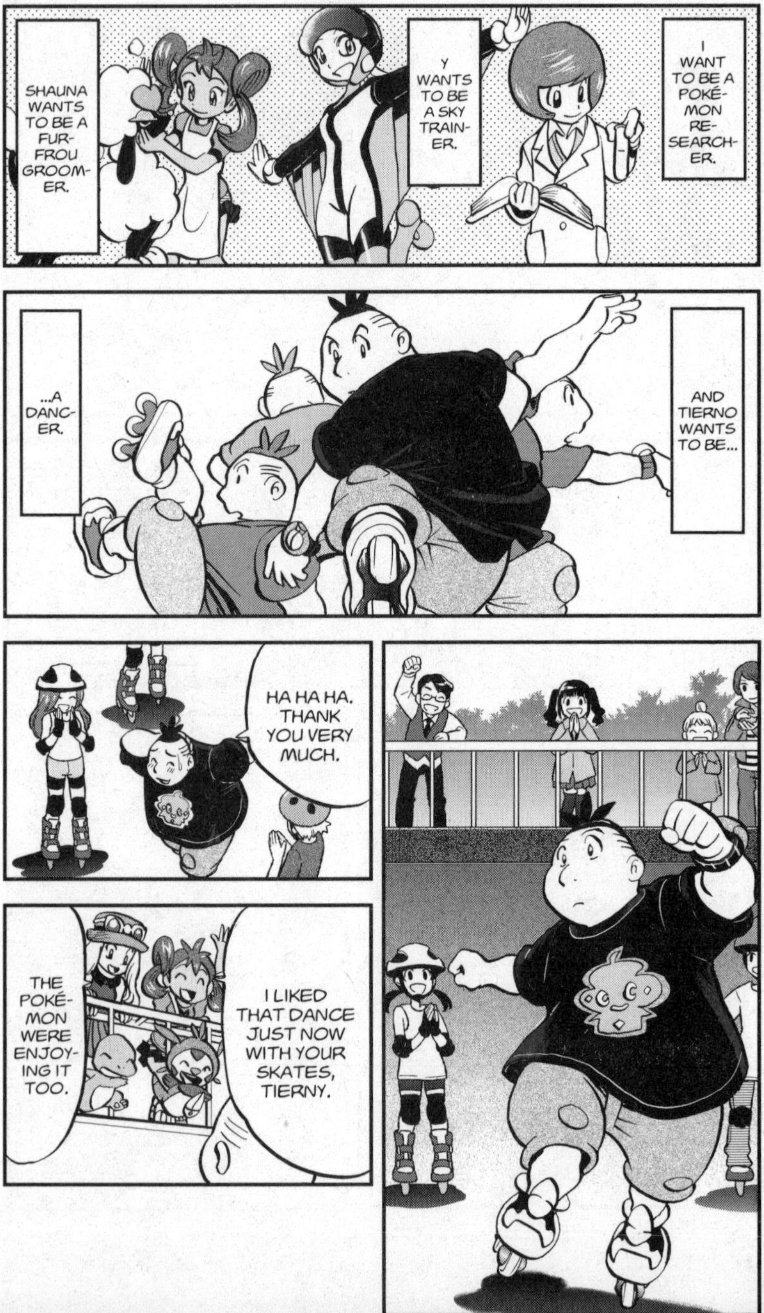
I WANT TO BE A POKÉMON RESEARCHER.
Y WANTS TO BE A SKY TRAINER.
SHAUNA WANTS TO BE A FURFROU GROOMER.
AND TIERNO WANTS TO BE...
...A DANCER.
HA HA HA. THANK YOU VERY MUCH.
I LIKED THAT DANCE JUST NOW WITH YOUR SKATES, TIERNY.
THE POKÉMON WERE ENJOYING IT TOO.

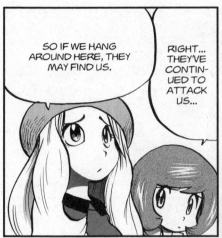

YEAH, THANKS.
BUT MAYBE I SHOULDN'T HAVE DONE IT.
YOU MEAN THE RED SUITS... TEAM FLARE?
UH-HUH.
RIGHT... THEY'VE CONTINUED TO ATTACK US...
SO IF WE HANG AROUND HERE, THEY MAY FIND US.
BUT X-EY'S THE ONE WHO SAID "LET'S VISIT IT."
TEAM FLARE'S PRIME TARGET IS SAYING "OKAY," SO WHAT IS THERE TO WORRY ABOUT?
HUMPH, WHAT IS HE THINKING OF...?
WHAT'S X DOING?
HE'S BEEN STARING AT THE POKÉDEX.
IT LOOKS LIKE HE'S FINALLY INTERESTED IN IT.
HE'S BEEN AT IT FOR AGES NOW.
HE ALWAYS LIKED READING DATA AND WHAT-NOT.

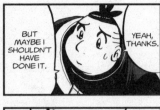

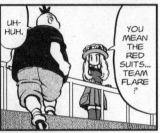

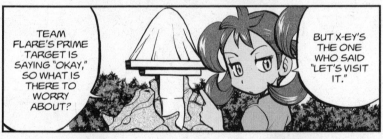

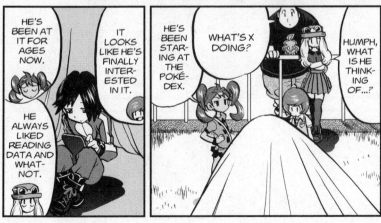

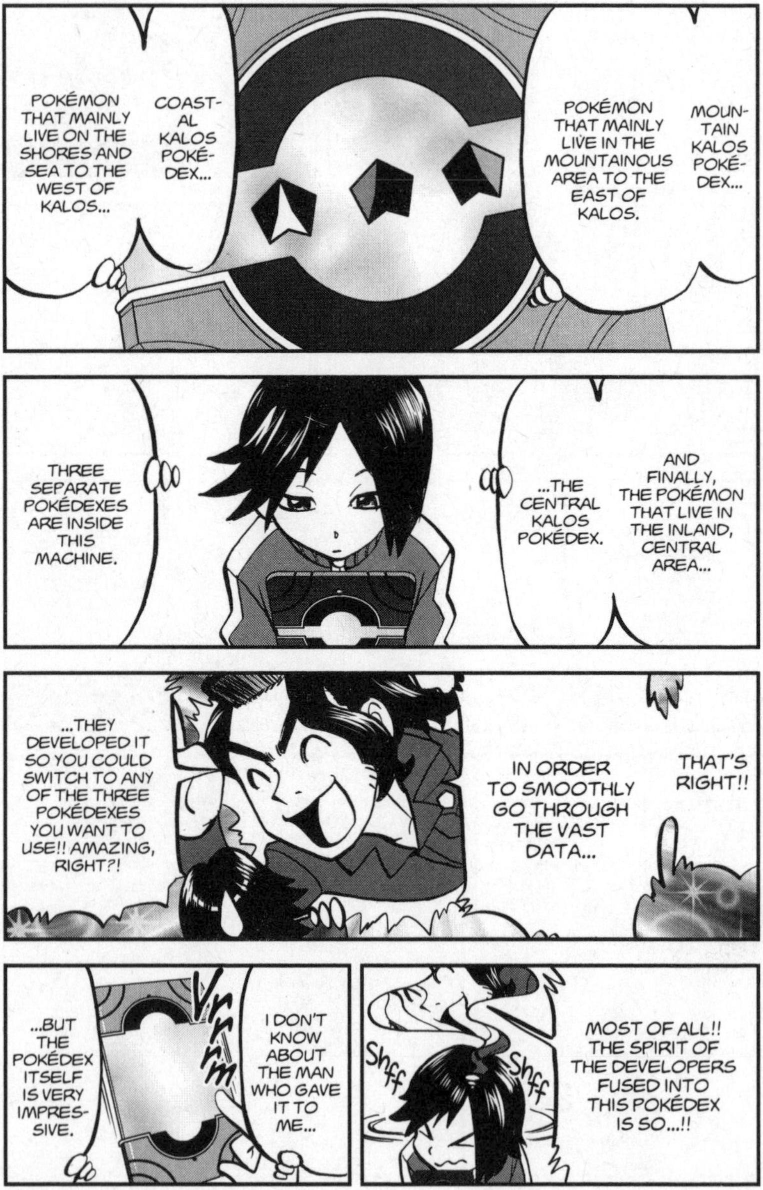

MOUNTAIN KALOS POKÉDEX...
POKÉMON THAT MAINLY LIVE IN THE MOUNTAINOUS AREA TO THE EAST OF KALOS.
COASTAL KALOS POKÉDEX...
POKÉMON THAT MAINLY LIVE ON THE SHORES AND SEA TO THE WEST OF KALOS...
AND FINALLY, THE POKÉMON THAT LIVE IN THE INLAND, CENTRAL AREA...
...THE CENTRAL KALOS POKÉDEX.
THREE SEPARATE POKÉDEXES ARE INSIDE THIS MACHINE.
THAT'S RIGHT!!
IN ORDER TO SMOOTHLY GO THROUGH THE VAST DATA...
...THEY DEVELOPED IT SO YOU COULD SWITCH TO ANY OF THE THREE POKÉDEXES YOU WANT TO USE!! AMAZING, RIGHT?!
MOST OF ALL!! THE SPIRIT OF THE DEVELOPERS FUSED INTO THIS POKÉDEX IS SO...!!
Shff
Shff
I DON'T KNOW ABOUT THE MAN WHO GAVE IT TO ME...
Vrrrm
...BUT THE POKÉDEX ITSELF IS VERY IMPRESSIVE.

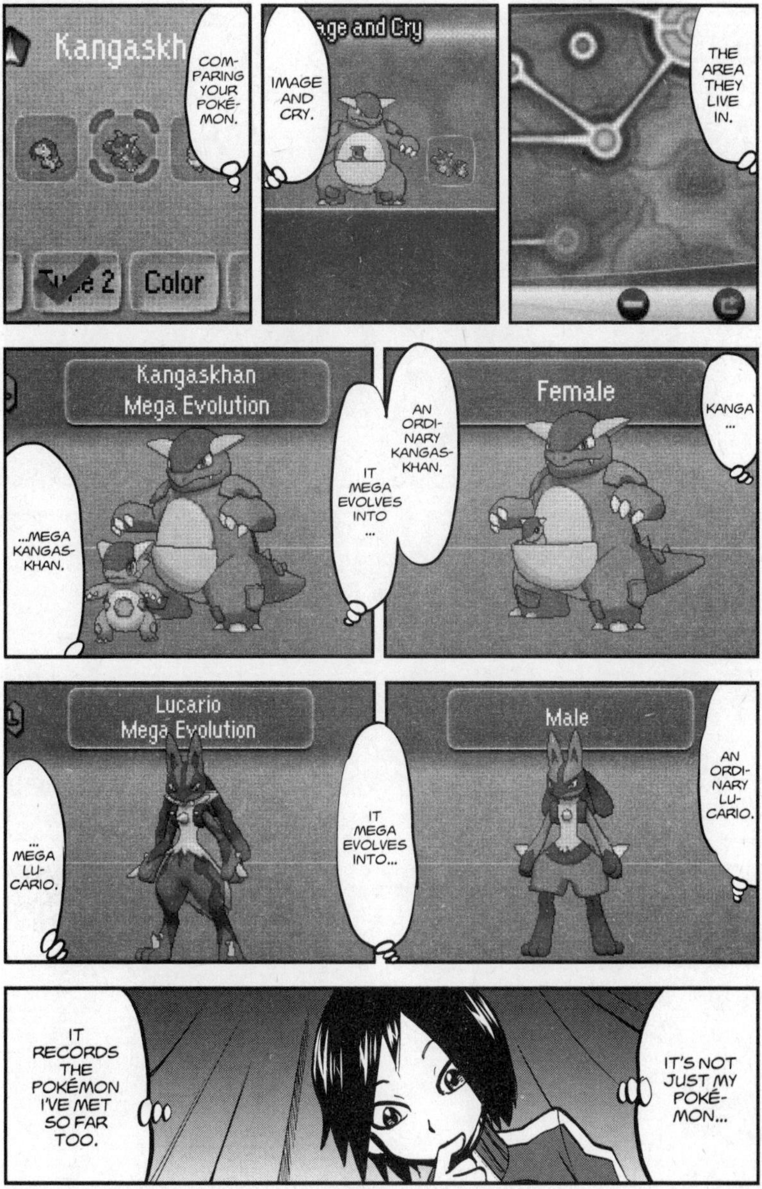
THE AREA THEY LIVE IN.
age and Cry
IMAGE AND CRY.
Kangaskh
COMPARING YOUR POKÉMON.
Type 2
Color
Female
KANGA...
AN ORDINARY KANGASKHAN.
Kangaskhan Mega Evolution
IT MEGA EVOLVES INTO...
...MEGA KANGASKHAN.
Male
AN ORDINARY LUCARIO.
Lucario Mega Evolution
IT MEGA EVOLVES INTO...
...MEGA LUCARIO.
IT'S NOT JUST MY POKÉMON...
IT RECORDS THE POKÉMON I'VE MET SO FAR TOO.

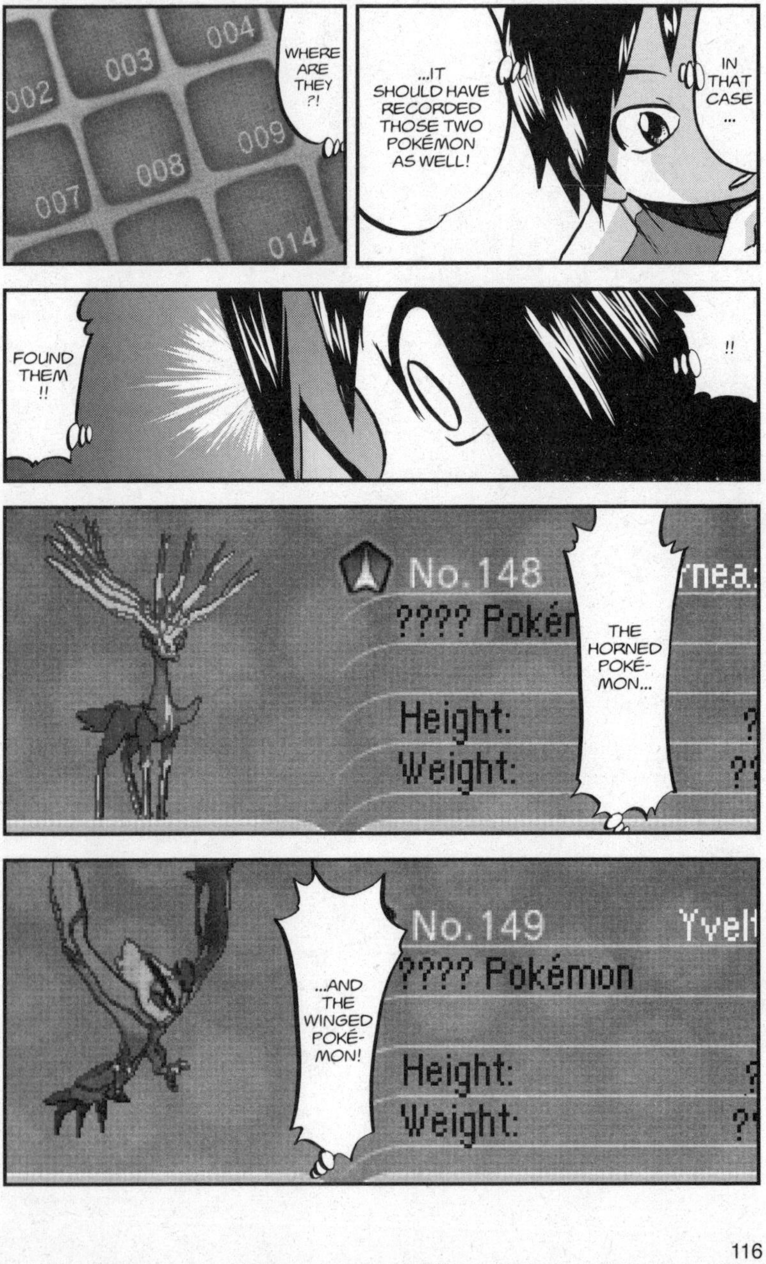
IN THAT CASE ...
...IT SHOULD HAVE RECORDED THOSE TWO POKéMON AS WELL!
WHERE ARE THEY ?!
!!
FOUND THEM !!
No.148
???? Pokém
THE HORNED POKÉ-MON...
Height:
Weight:
No.149
???? Pokémon
...AND THE WINGED POKÉ-MON!
Height:
Weight:

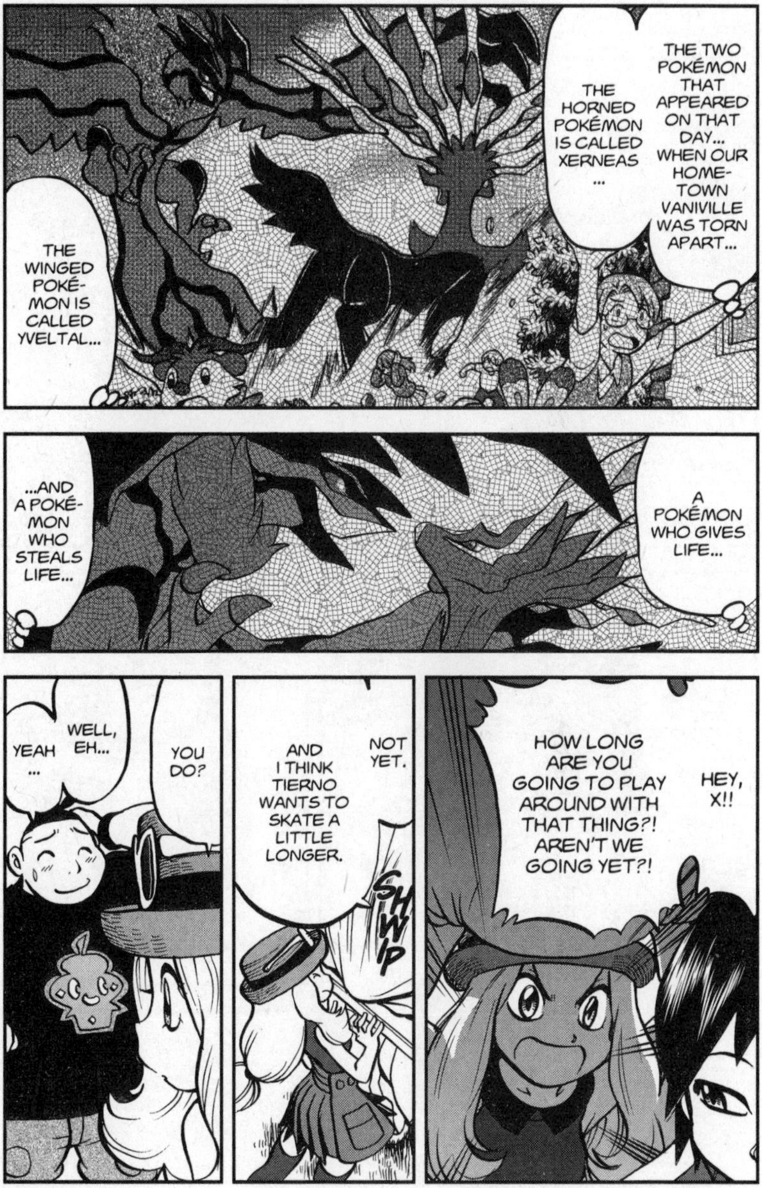
THE TWO POKÉMON THAT APPEARED ON THAT DAY... WHEN OUR HOME-TOWN VANIVILLE WAS TORN APART...
THE HORNED POKÉMON IS CALLED XERNEAS ...
THE WINGED POKÉ-MON IS CALLED YVELTAL...
A POKÉMON WHO GIVES LIFE...
...AND A POKÉ-MON WHO STEALS LIFE...
HEY, X!!
HOW LONG ARE YOU GOING TO PLAY AROUND WITH THAT THING?! AREN'T WE GOING YET?!
NOT YET.
AND I THINK TIERNO WANTS TO SKATE A LITTLE LONGER.
SHWIP
YOU DO?
WELL, EH...
YEAH ...

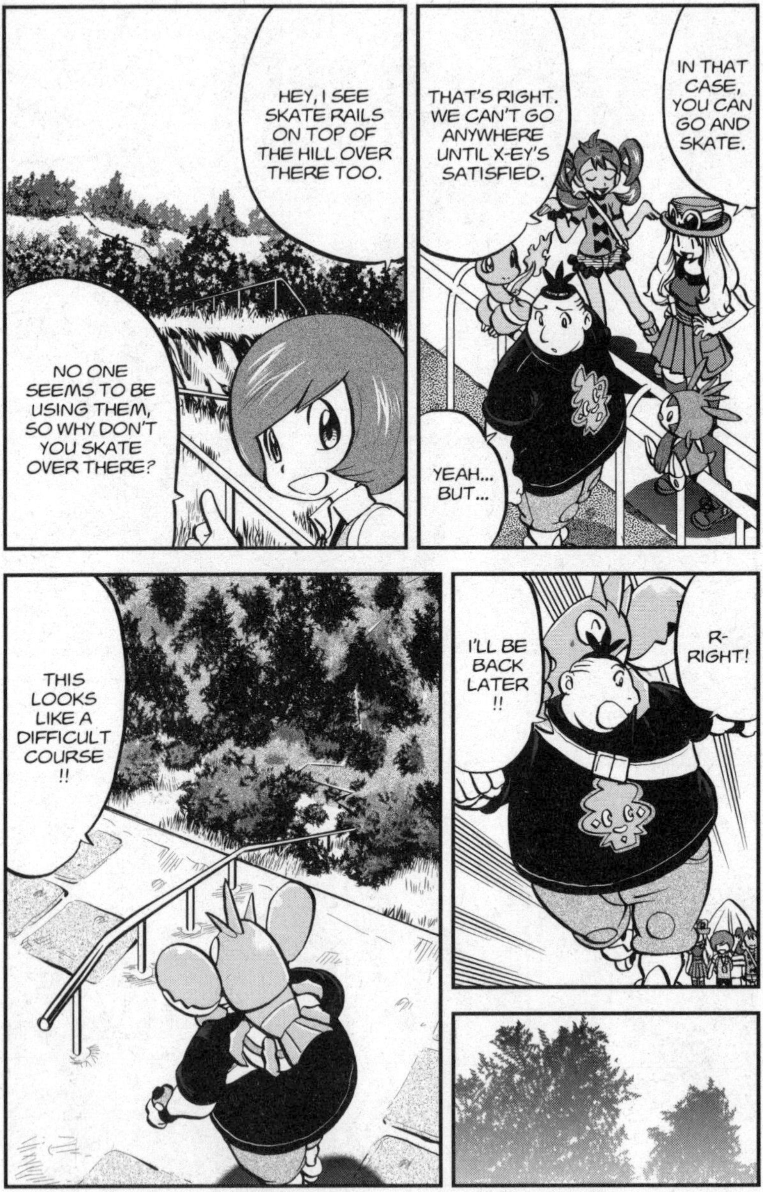
IN THAT CASE, YOU CAN GO AND SKATE.
THAT'S RIGHT. WE CAN'T GO ANYWHERE UNTIL X-EY'S SATISFIED.
YEAH... BUT...
HEY, I SEE SKATE RAILS ON TOP OF THE HILL OVER THERE TOO.
NO ONE SEEMS TO BE USING THEM, SO WHY DON'T YOU SKATE OVER THERE?
R-RIGHT!
I'LL BE BACK LATER !!
THIS LOOKS LIKE A DIFFICULT COURSE !!

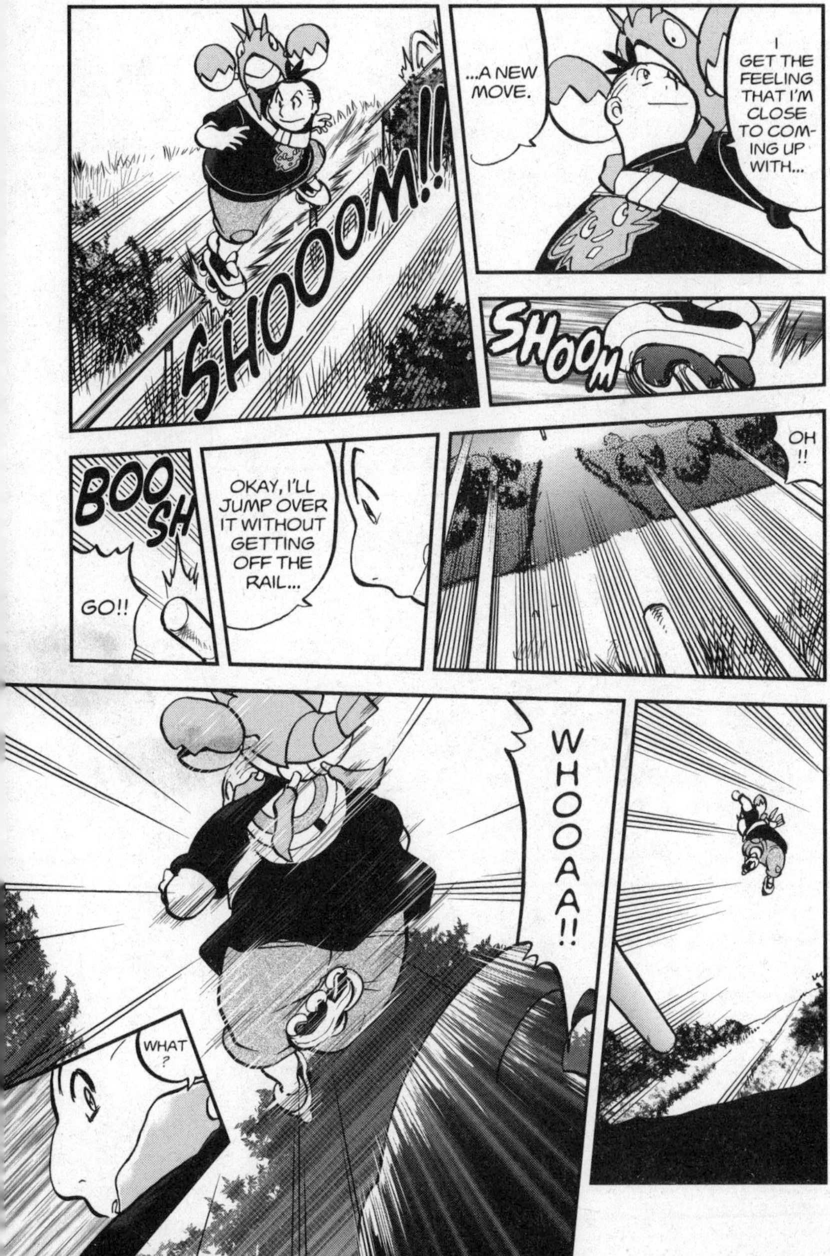
I GET THE FEELING THAT I'M CLOSE TO COMING UP WITH...
...A NEW MOVE.
SHOOM
SHOOOM!!!
OH!!
OKAY, I'LL JUMP OVER IT WITHOUT GETTING OFF THE RAIL...
BOOSH
GO!!
WHOOAA!!
WHAT?

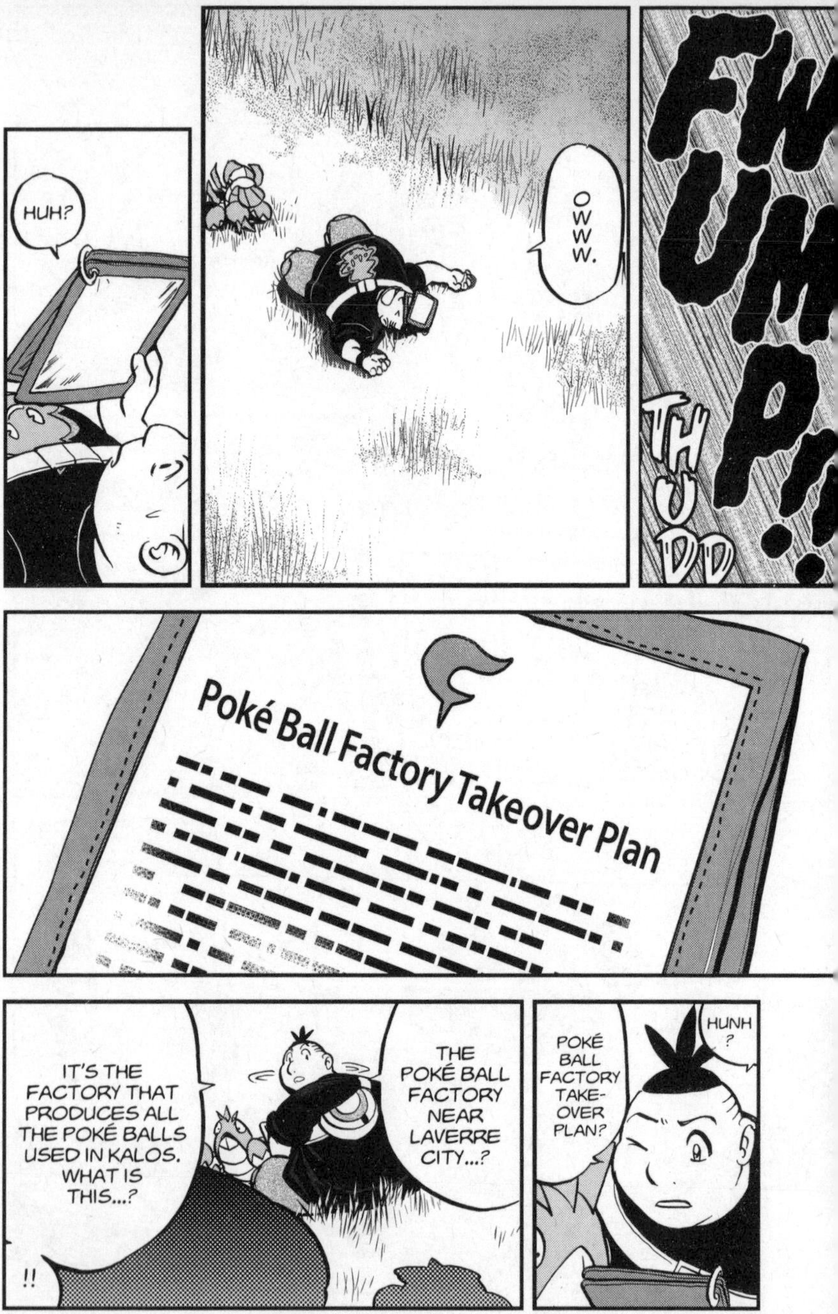
FWUMP!!
THUDD
OWWW.
HUH?
Poké Ball Factory Takeover Plan
HUNH?
POKÉ BALL FACTORY TAKE-OVER PLAN?
THE POKÉ BALL FACTORY NEAR LAVERRE CITY...?
IT'S THE FACTORY THAT PRODUCES ALL THE POKÉ BALLS USED IN KALOS. WHAT IS THIS...?
!!

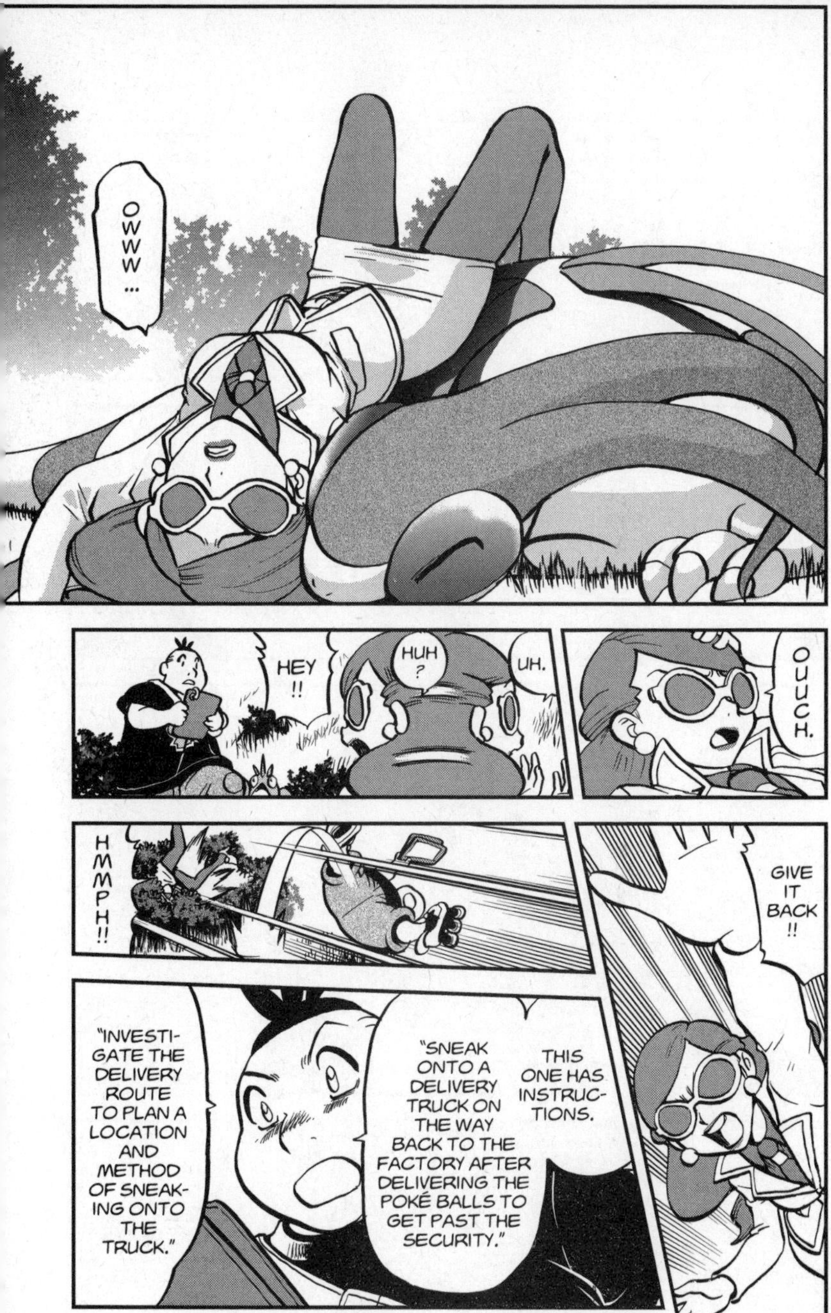
OWWW...
OUUCH.
UH.
HUH ?
HEY !!
GIVE IT BACK !!
HMMPH!!
THIS ONE HAS INSTRUC-TIONS.
"SNEAK ONTO A DELIVERY TRUCK ON THE WAY BACK TO THE FACTORY AFTER DELIVERING THE POKÉ BALLS TO GET PAST THE SECURITY."
"INVESTI-GATE THE DELIVERY ROUTE TO PLAN A LOCATION AND METHOD OF SNEAK-ING ONTO THE TRUCK."

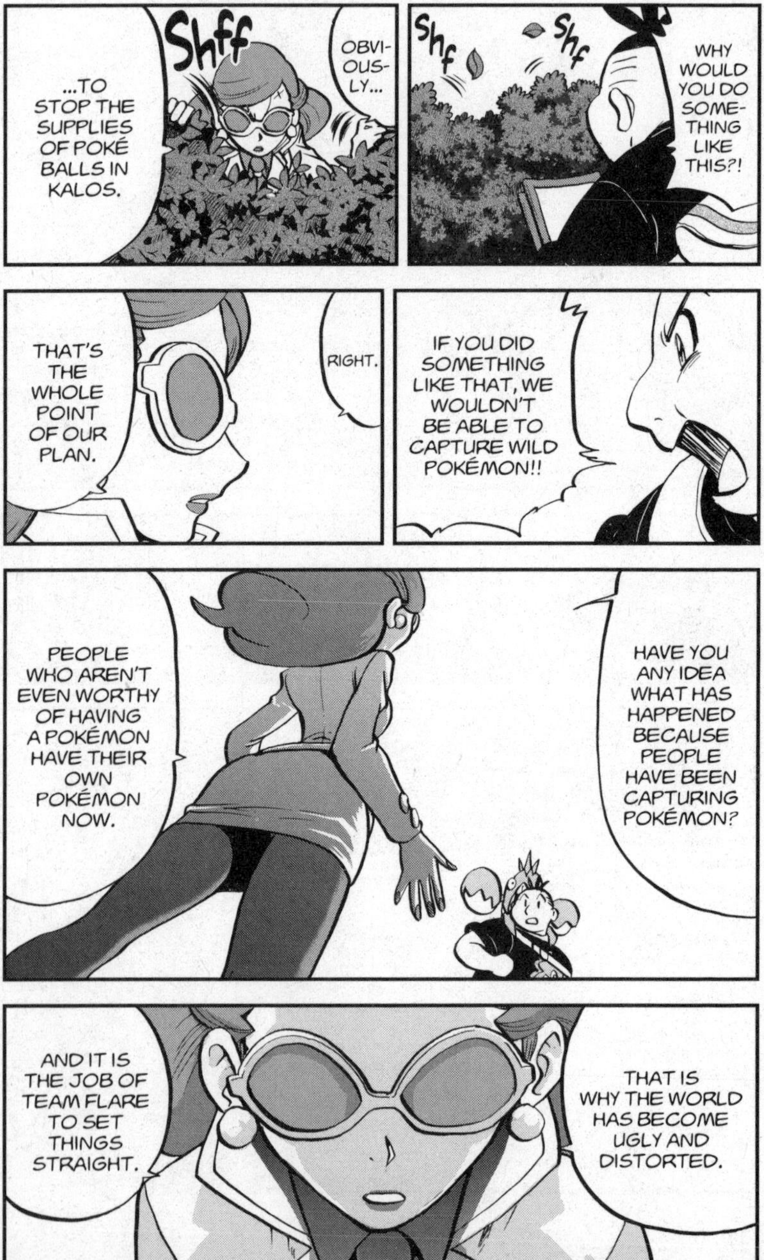
Shf
Shf
WHY WOULD YOU DO SOMETHING LIKE THIS?!
OBVIOUSLY...
Shff
...TO STOP THE SUPPLIES OF POKÉ BALLS IN KALOS.
IF YOU DID SOMETHING LIKE THAT, WE WOULDN'T BE ABLE TO CAPTURE WILD POKÉMON!!
RIGHT.
THAT'S THE WHOLE POINT OF OUR PLAN.
HAVE YOU ANY IDEA WHAT HAS HAPPENED BECAUSE PEOPLE HAVE BEEN CAPTURING POKÉMON?
PEOPLE WHO AREN'T EVEN WORTHY OF HAVING A POKÉMON HAVE THEIR OWN POKÉMON NOW.
THAT IS WHY THE WORLD HAS BECOME UGLY AND DISTORTED.
AND IT IS THE JOB OF TEAM FLARE TO SET THINGS STRAIGHT.

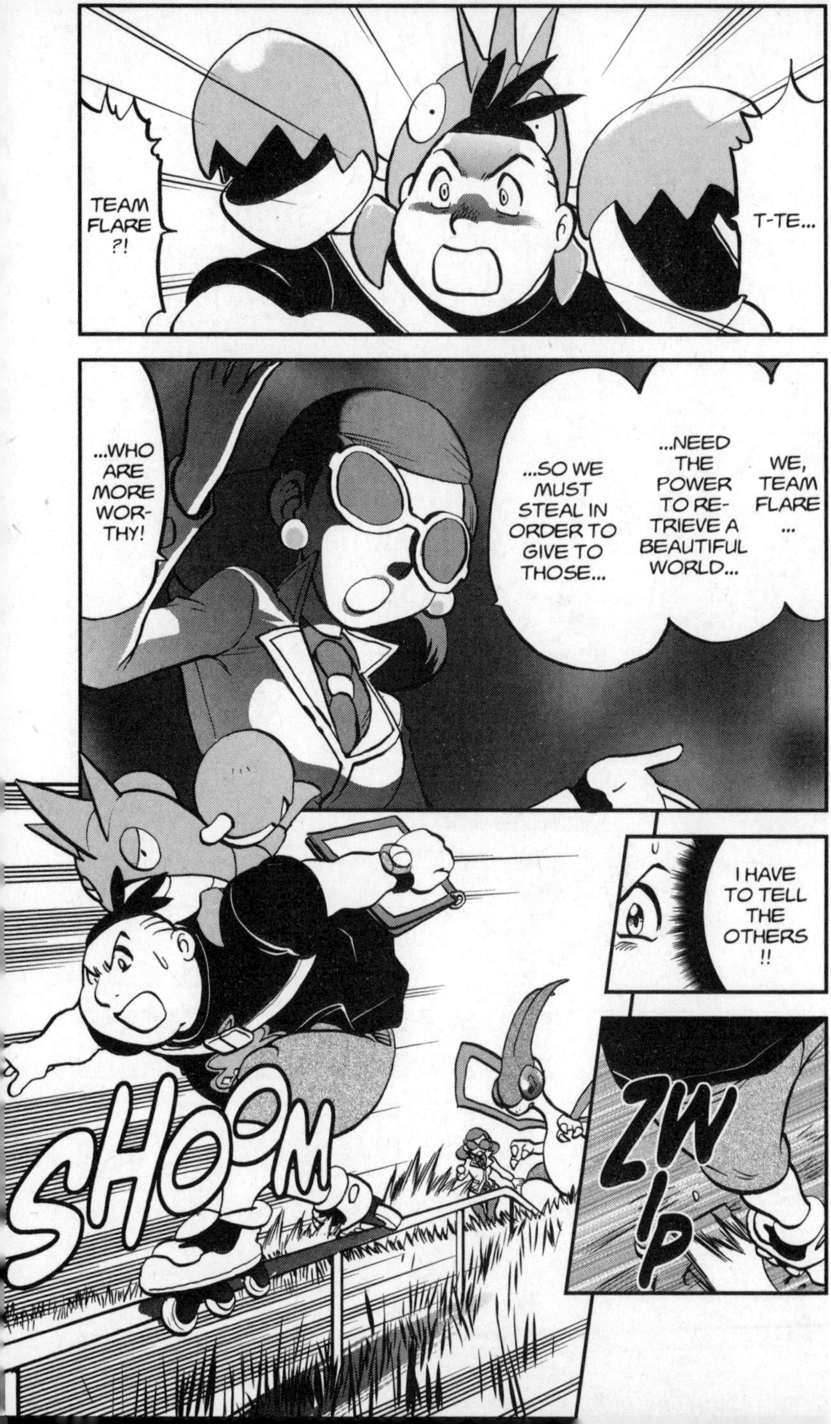

T-TE...
TEAM FLARE ?!
WE, TEAM FLARE ...
...NEED THE POWER TO RE-TRIEVE A BEAUTIFUL WORLD...
...SO WE MUST STEAL IN ORDER TO GIVE TO THOSE...
...WHO ARE MORE WOR-THY!
I HAVE TO TELL THE OTHERS !!
ZWIP
SHOOM

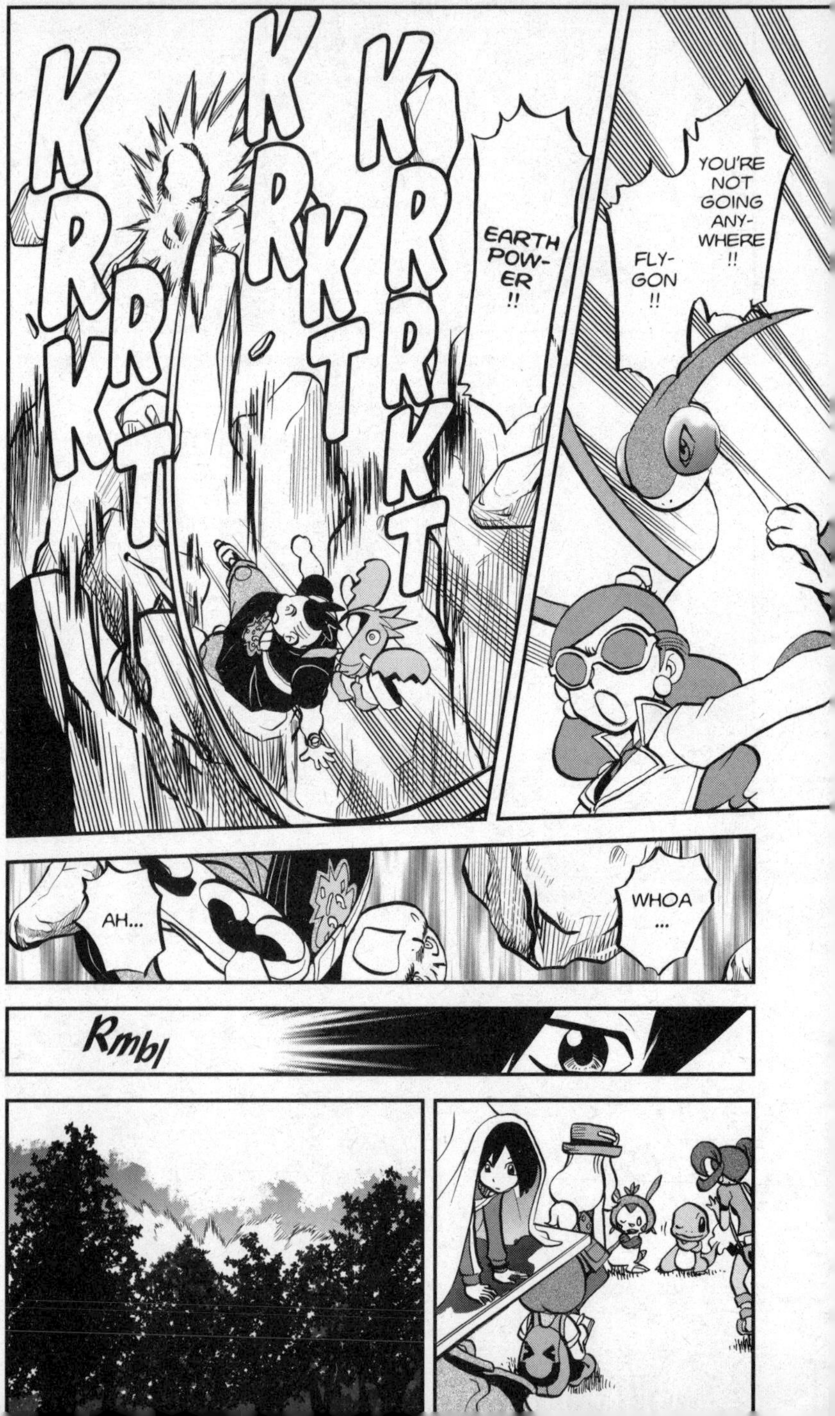
YOU'RE NOT GOING ANY-WHERE!!
FLY-GON!!
EARTH POW-ER!!
KRRKT
KRKT
KRRKT
WHOA...
AH...
Rmbl

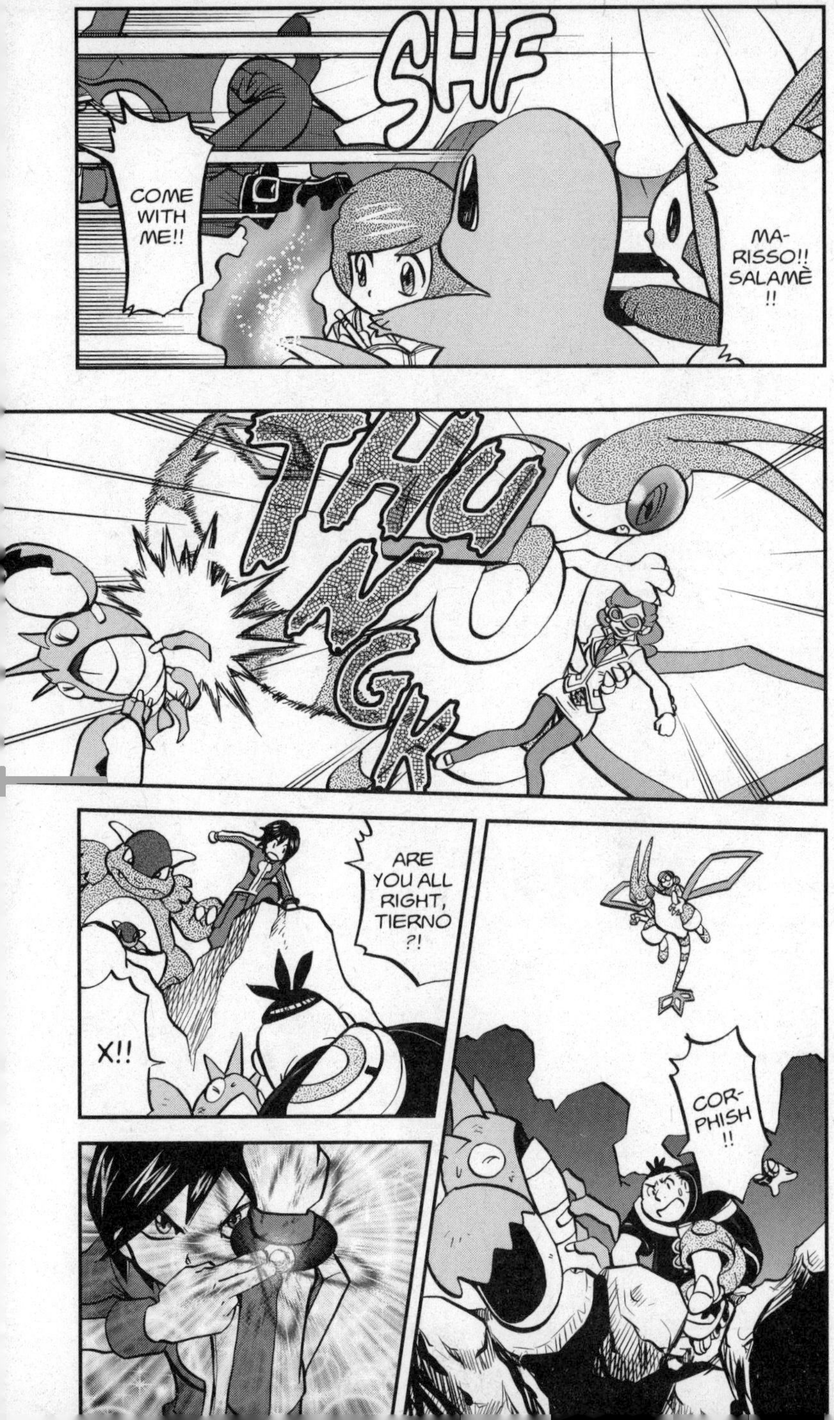
SHF
MA-RISSO!! SALAMÈ!!
COME WITH ME!!
THWGK
CORPHISH!!
ARE YOU ALL RIGHT, TIERNO?!
X!!

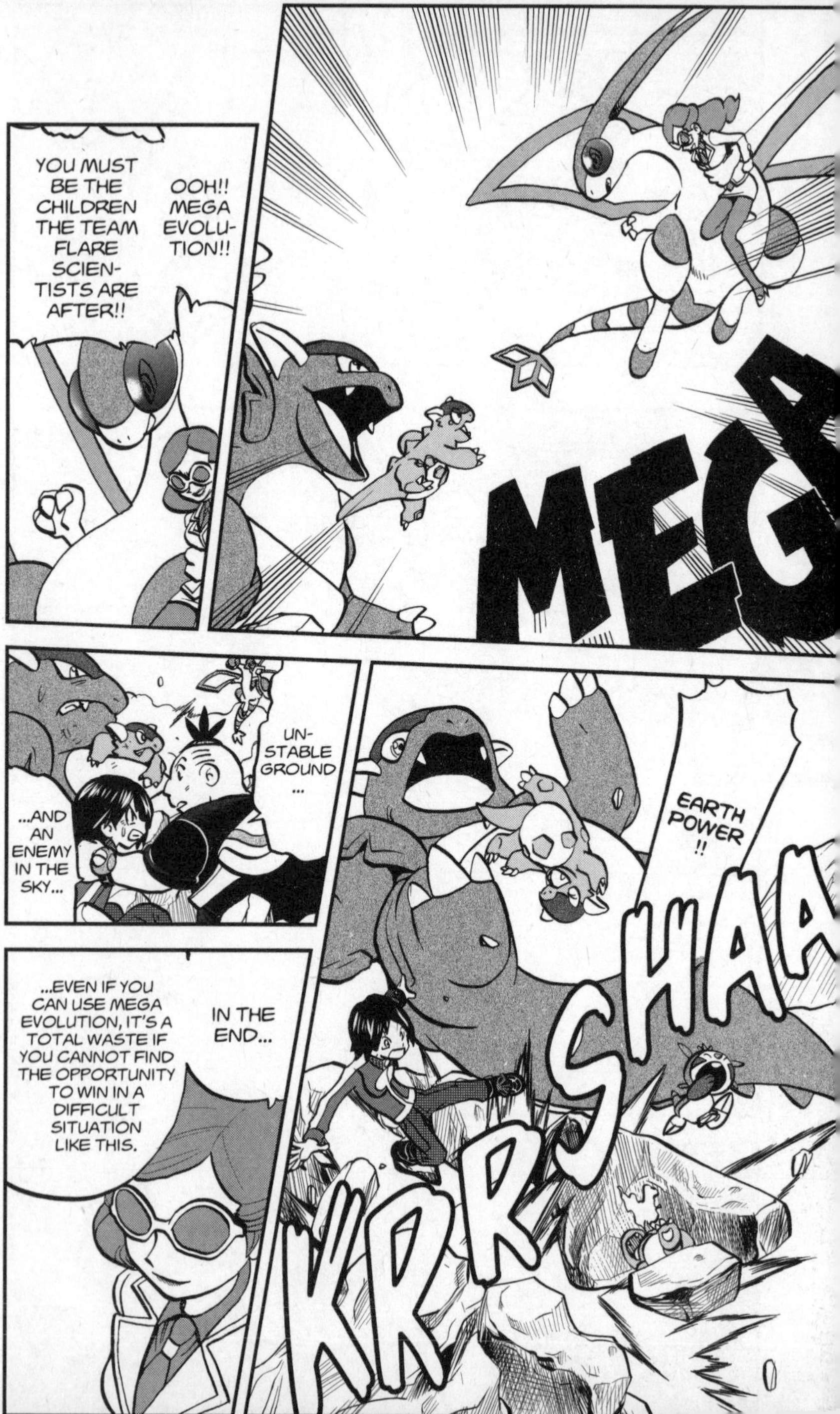
MEGA
OOH!! MEGA EVOLU-TION!!
YOU MUST BE THE CHILDREN THE TEAM FLARE SCIEN-TISTS ARE AFTER!!
EARTH POWER!!
SHAA
KRR
UN-STABLE GROUND...
...AND AN ENEMY IN THE SKY...
IN THE END...
...EVEN IF YOU CAN USE MEGA EVOLUTION, IT'S A TOTAL WASTE IF YOU CANNOT FIND THE OPPORTUNITY TO WIN IN A DIFFICULT SITUATION LIKE THIS.

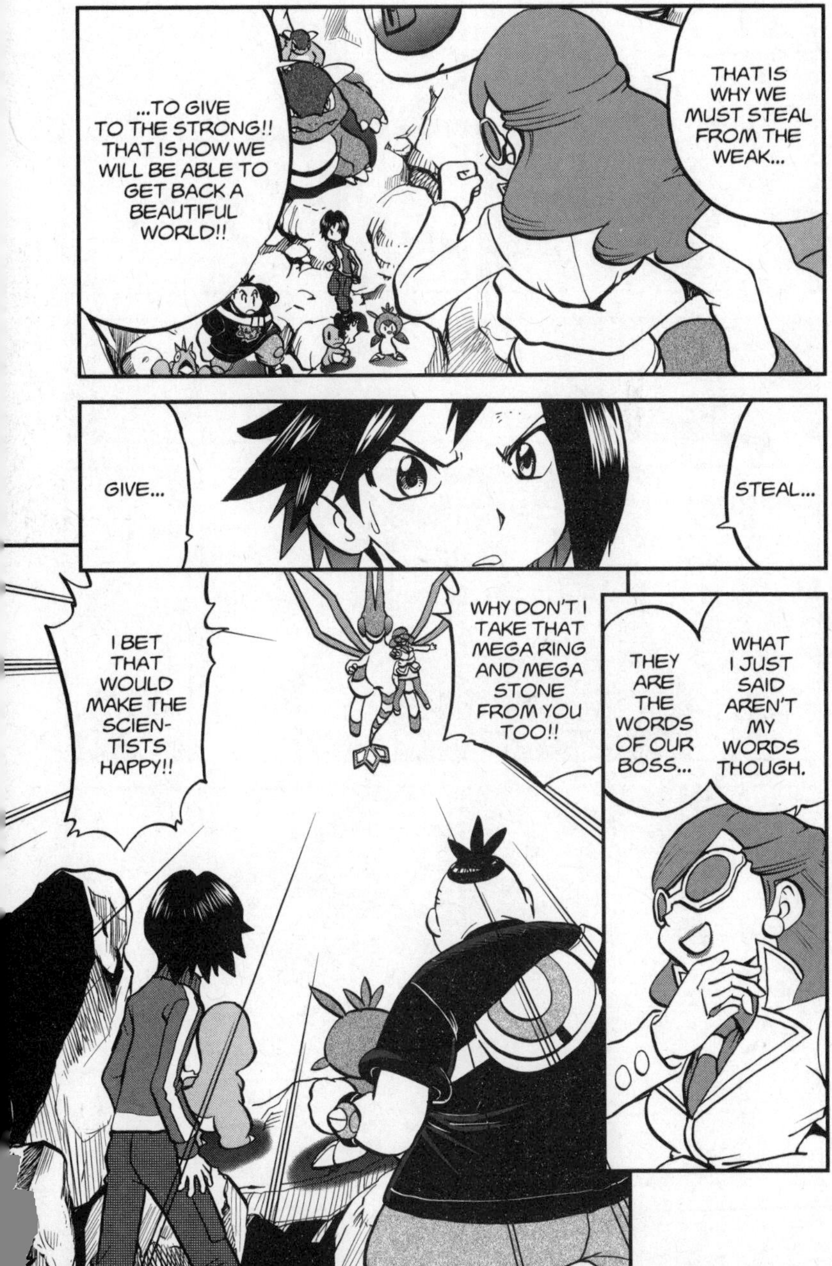
THAT IS WHY WE MUST STEAL FROM THE WEAK...
...TO GIVE TO THE STRONG!! THAT IS HOW WE WILL BE ABLE TO GET BACK A BEAUTIFUL WORLD!!
STEAL...
GIVE...
WHAT I JUST SAID AREN'T MY WORDS THOUGH.
THEY ARE THE WORDS OF OUR BOSS...
WHY DON'T I TAKE THAT MEGA RING AND MEGA STONE FROM YOU TOO!!
I BET THAT WOULD MAKE THE SCIEN-TISTS HAPPY!!

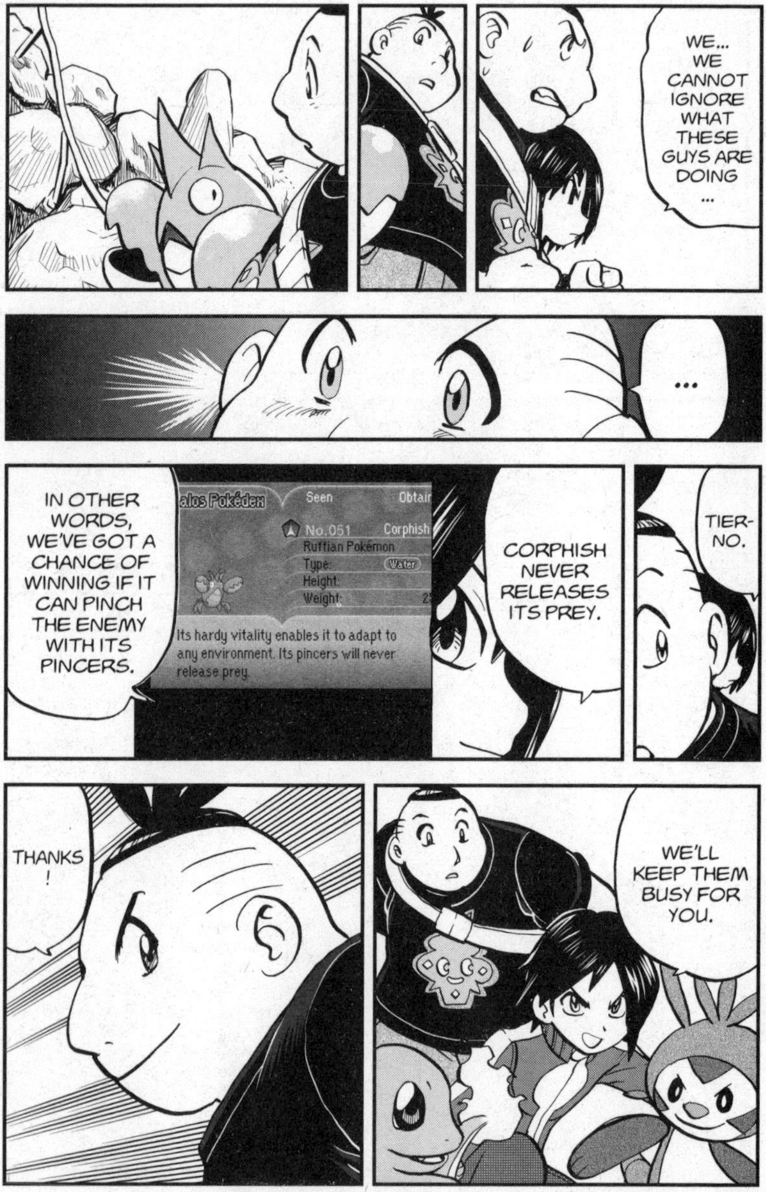
WE... WE CANNOT IGNORE WHAT THESE GUYS ARE DOING ...
...
TIER-NO.
CORPHISH NEVER RELEASES ITS PREY.
alos Pokédex
Seen
Obtain
No.051
Corphish
Ruffian Pokémon
Type:
Water
Height:
Weight:
Its hardy vitality enables it to adapt to any environment. Its pincers will never release prey.
IN OTHER WORDS, WE'VE GOT A CHANCE OF WINNING IF IT CAN PINCH THE ENEMY WITH ITS PINCERS.
WE'LL KEEP THEM BUSY FOR YOU.
THANKS!

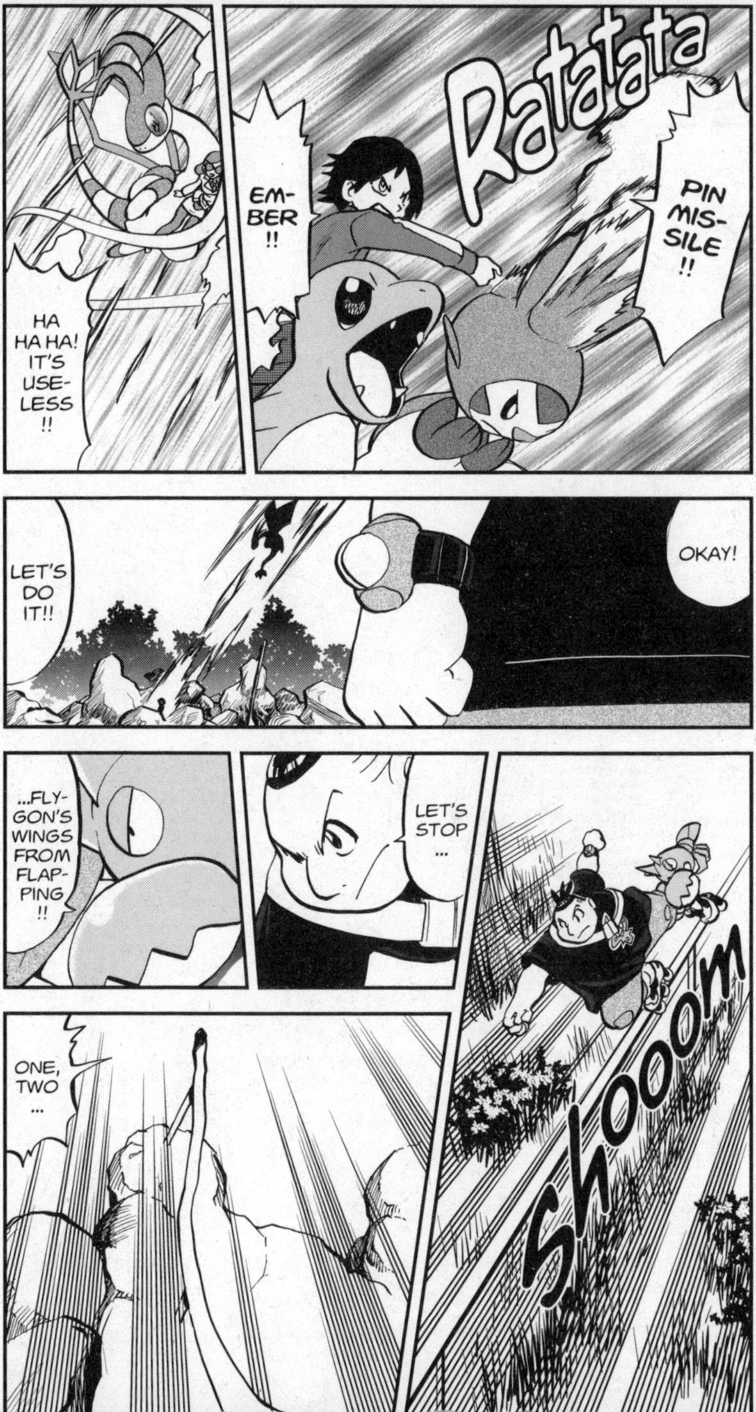
Ratatata
PIN MIS-SILE!!
EM-BER!!
HA HA HA! IT'S USE-LESS!!
OKAY!
LET'S DO IT!!
Shooom
LET'S STOP...
...FLY-GON'S WINGS FROM FLAP-PING!!
ONE, TWO...

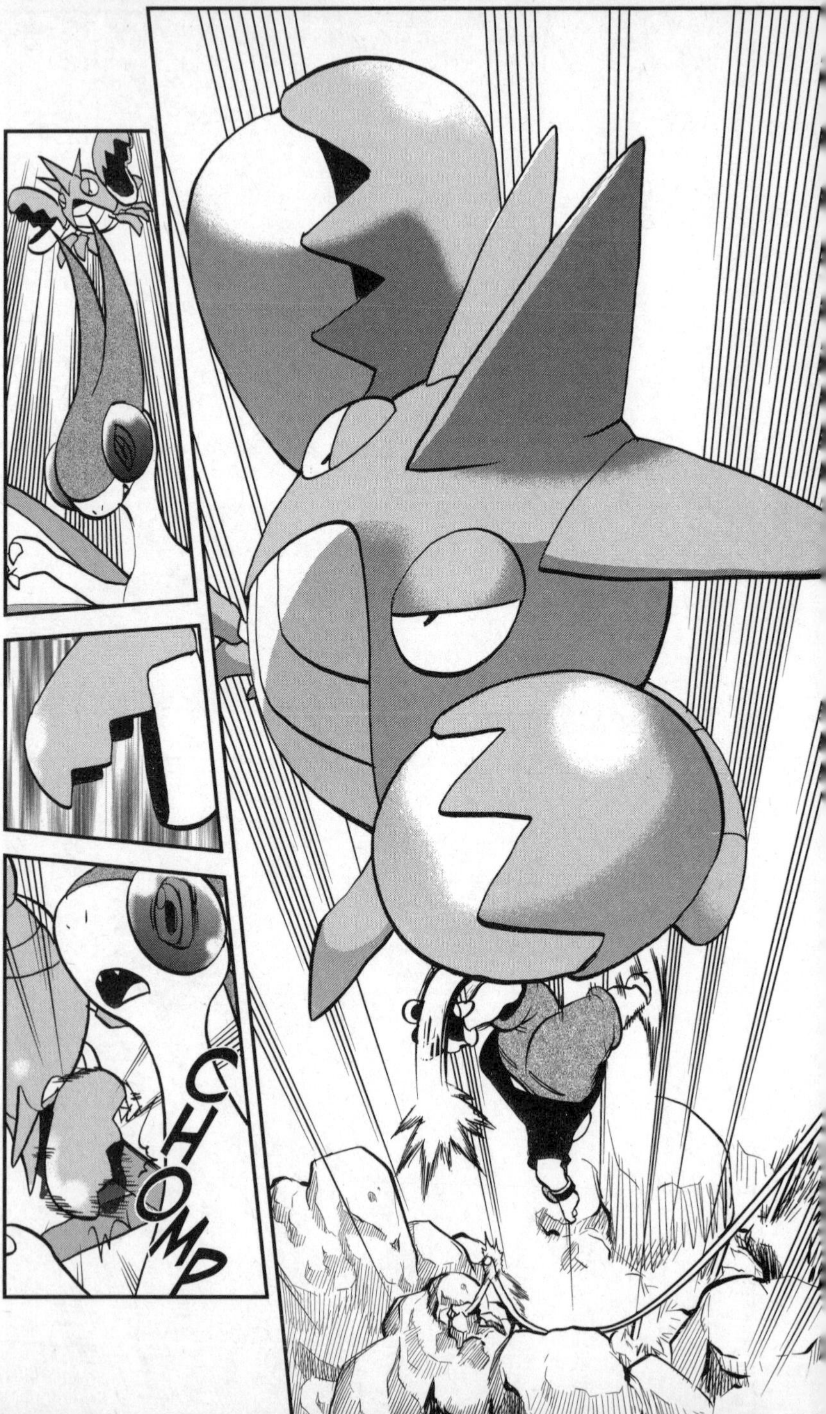
CHOMP

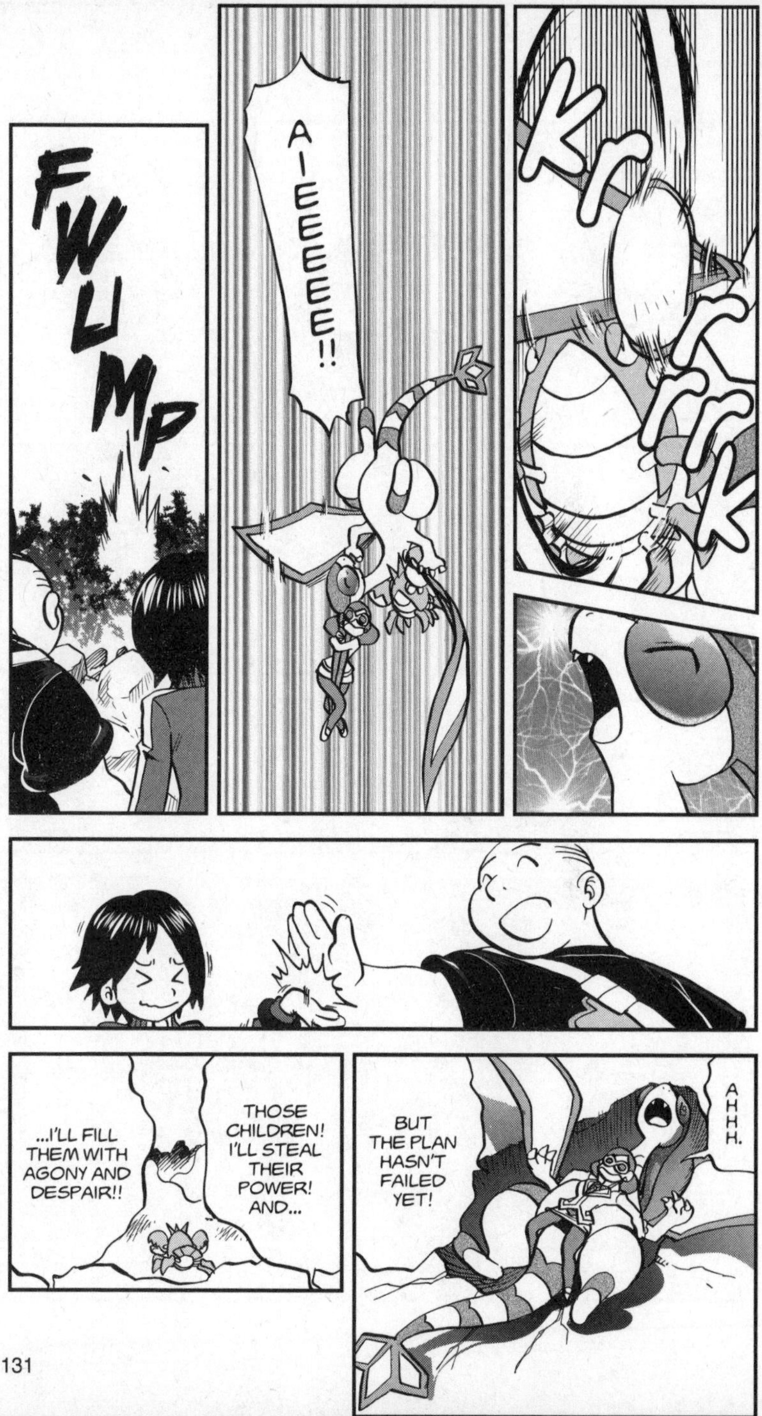
Krrrrk
AIEEEEEE!!
FWUMP
AHHH.
BUT THE PLAN HASN'T FAILED YET!
THOSE CHILDREN! I'LL STEAL THEIR POWER! AND...
...I'LL FILL THEM WITH AGONY AND DESPAIR!!

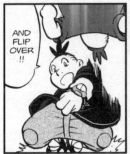

PINCH.
TWIST.
AND FLIP OVER!!
HMM!!
NICE! NICE!
YOU GOT THAT MOVE FROM CORPHISH, RIGHT?
UH-HUH.
IT'S A NEW MOVE I CAME UP WITH DURING THE BATTLE TODAY.
WE...
...ALL HAVE A DREAM.
I HOPE THIS JOURNEY IS NOT JUST A JOURNEY OF BATTLES AND ESCAPE...
...BUT A JOURNEY FOR US TO MOVE A STEP CLOSER TO OUR DREAMS AS WELL.

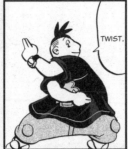

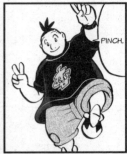

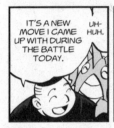

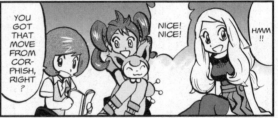

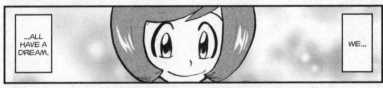

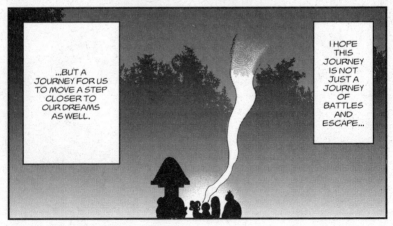

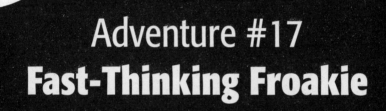

Adventure #17
**Fast-Thinking Froakie**

X●Y

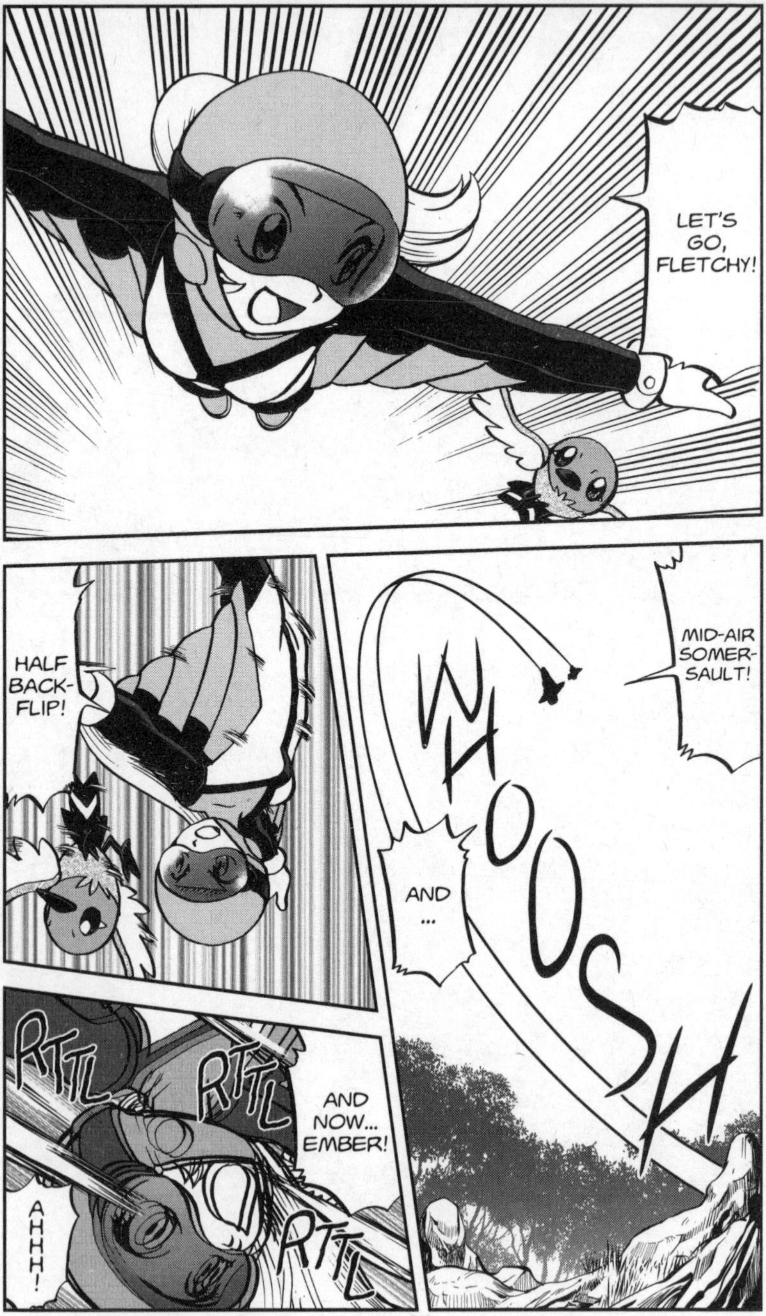
LET'S GO, FLETCHY!
MID-AIR SOMER-SAULT!
WHOOOSH
AND ...
HALF BACK-FLIP!
RTTL
RTTL
AND NOW... EMBER!
RTTL
AHHH!

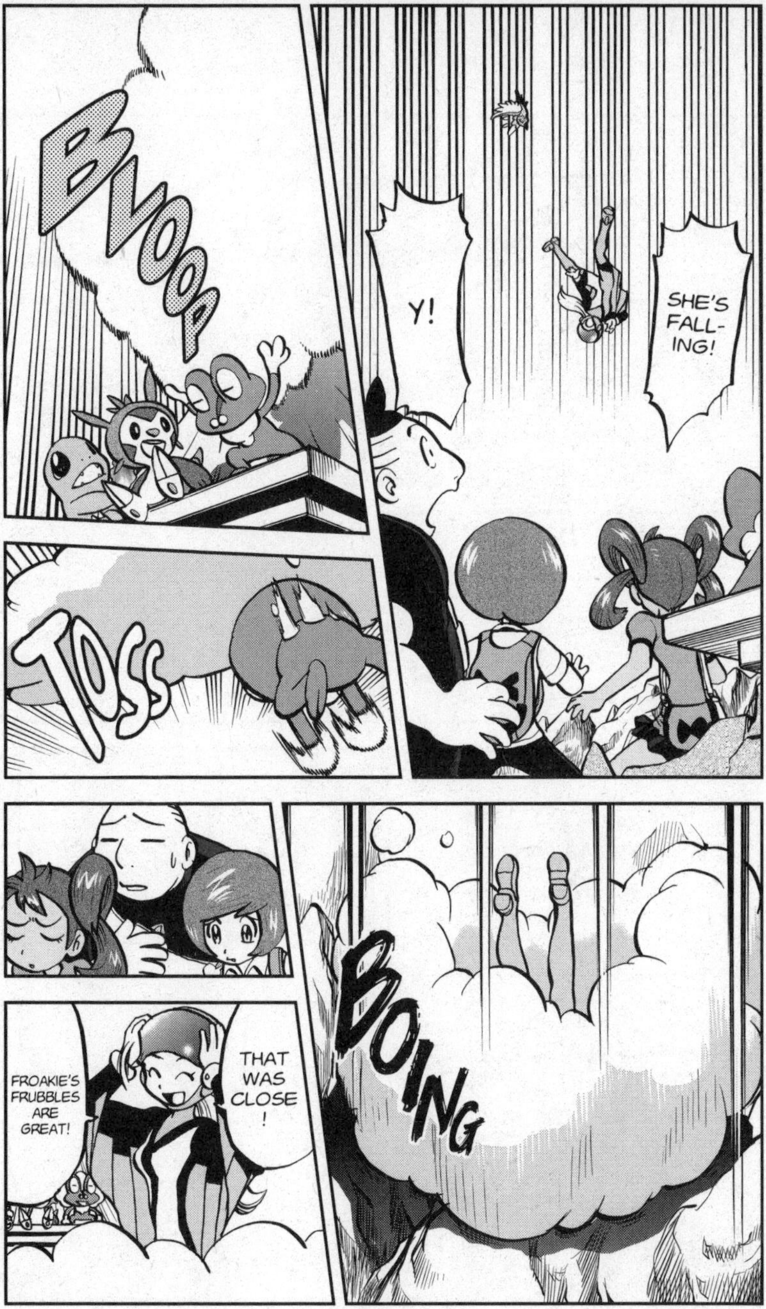
SHE'S FALL-ING!
Y!
BVOOP
TOSS
BOING
THAT WAS CLOSE!
FROAKIE'S FRUBBLES ARE GREAT!

I CAN TRAIN IN THE SKY WITHOUT A CARE IN THE WORLD NOW THAT **YOU'VE** JOINED OUR GROUP!
SMOOCH♡
THANKS ... ...CROAKY!
Dramatic much?
PROFESSOR SYCAMORE...
KLICK
THE FROAKIE YOU GAVE ME TO WATCH OVER HAS BECOME Y'S POKÉMON.
SHE SAYS SHE'S BEEN INSPIRED BY X.
BUT IT'S STRANGE... IT'S LIKE THEY WERE **MEANT** TO BE TOGETHER FROM THE START.
DID YOU FILM IT, TREVOR?
UH-HUH. I'LL SEND IT TO PROFESSOR SYCAMORE.
OKAY! TELL HIM I SAID "HI"!
WELL, THAT'S IT FOR TRAINING TODAY!
Time to get changed!
RSTL
HEY! DON'T CHANGE IN THE MIDDLE OF THE ROAD!

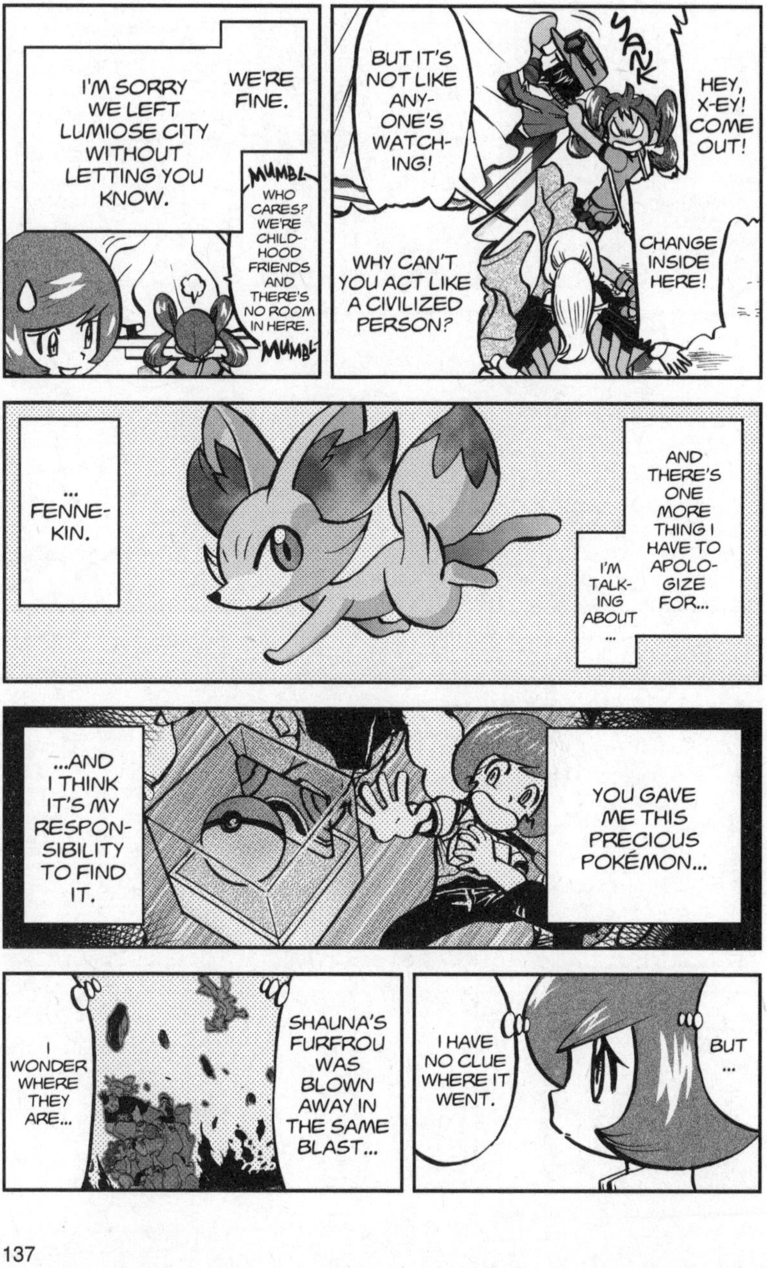
YANK
HEY, X-EY! COME OUT!
CHANGE INSIDE HERE!
BUT IT'S NOT LIKE ANY-ONE'S WATCH-ING!
WHY CAN'T YOU ACT LIKE A CIVILIZED PERSON?
WE'RE FINE.
I'M SORRY WE LEFT LUMIOSE CITY WITHOUT LETTING YOU KNOW.
MUMBL
WHO CARES? WE'RE CHILD-HOOD FRIENDS AND THERE'S NO ROOM IN HERE.
MUMBL
AND THERE'S ONE MORE THING I HAVE TO APOLO-GIZE FOR...
I'M TALK-ING ABOUT ...
... FENNE-KIN.
YOU GAVE ME THIS PRECIOUS POKÉMON...
...AND I THINK IT'S MY RESPON-SIBILITY TO FIND IT.
BUT ...
I HAVE NO CLUE WHERE IT WENT.
SHAUNA'S FURFROU WAS BLOWN AWAY IN THE SAME BLAST...
I WONDER WHERE THEY ARE...

AT ANY RATE... I'LL KEEP YOU UPDATED ON OUR SITUATION.
THE HOLO CASTER HAS BEEN FIXED. IT'S WORKING FINE NOW.
SHVR
SEE YOU LATER.
AHHH!
SOME-THING JUMPED INTO THE TENT!
WHOA!
WHOA!
WHAT JUMPED INTO THE TENT?!
I DON'T KNOW! BUT IT... TINGLES!
SNAG

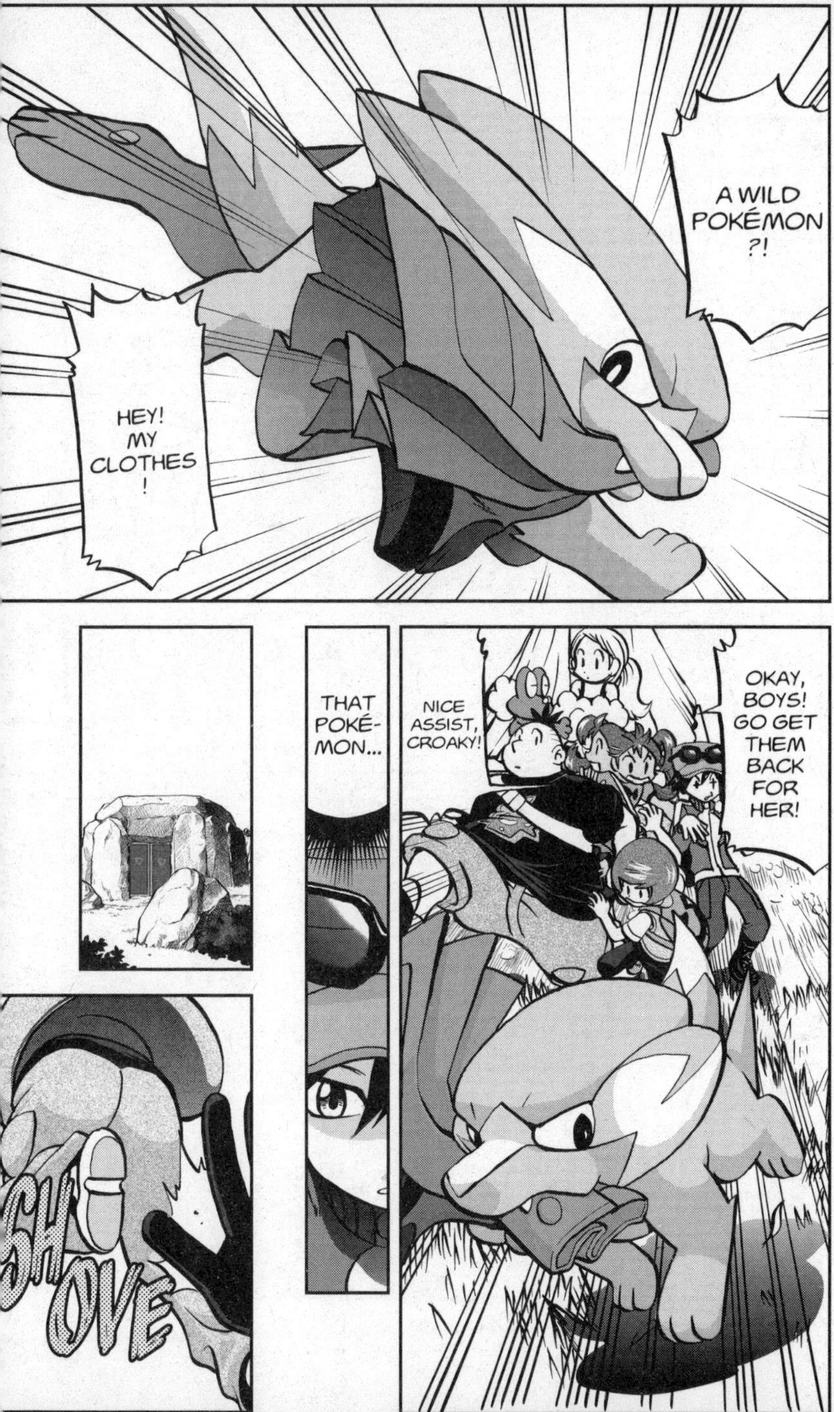
A WILD POKÉMON ?!
HEY! MY CLOTHES !
OKAY, BOYS! GO GET THEM BACK FOR HER!
NICE ASSIST, CROAKY!
THAT POKÉ-MON...
SHOVE

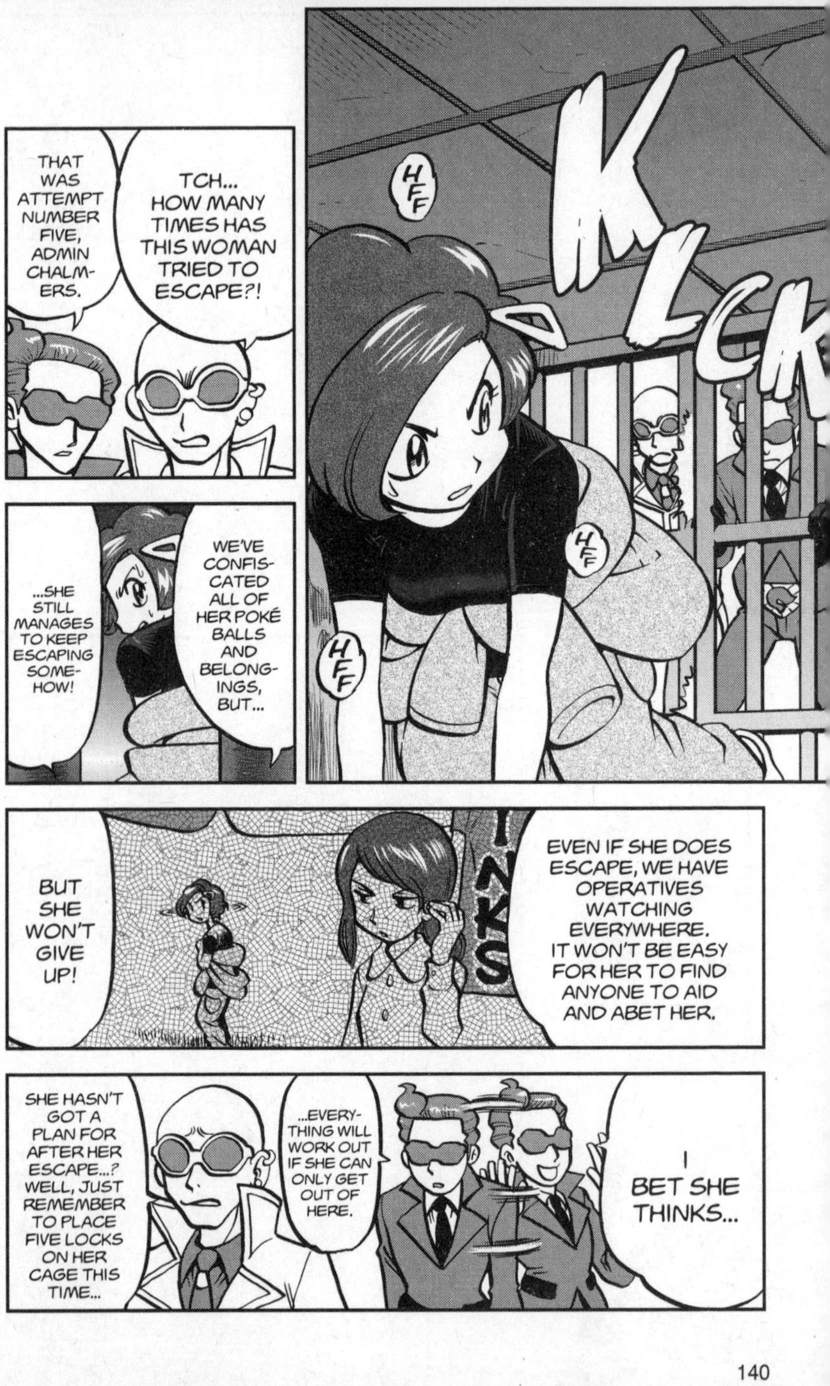
KLCK
HFF
HFF
HFF
TCH... HOW MANY TIMES HAS THIS WOMAN TRIED TO ESCAPE?!
THAT WAS ATTEMPT NUMBER FIVE, ADMIN CHALMERS.
WE'VE CONFISCATED ALL OF HER POKÉ BALLS AND BELONGINGS, BUT...
...SHE STILL MANAGES TO KEEP ESCAPING SOMEHOW!
EVEN IF SHE DOES ESCAPE, WE HAVE OPERATIVES WATCHING EVERYWHERE. IT WON'T BE EASY FOR HER TO FIND ANYONE TO AID AND ABET HER.
BUT SHE WON'T GIVE UP!
I BET SHE THINKS...
...EVERYTHING WILL WORK OUT IF SHE CAN ONLY GET OUT OF HERE.
SHE HASN'T GOT A PLAN FOR AFTER HER ESCAPE...? WELL, JUST REMEMBER TO PLACE FIVE LOCKS ON HER CAGE THIS TIME...

HANG IN THERE, GRACE!

ARE YOU ALL RIGHT, GRACE?

JINGL JINGL

I THOUGHT I'D MAKE IT THIS TIME...

I'M FINE... THANKS.

THAT FATEFUL DAY...

SORRY... I DIDN'T FIND OUT ANYTHING. I WAS CAPTURED RIGHT AWAY AGAIN.

IS THERE ANYONE OUT THERE LOOKING FOR US?

WERE YOU ABLE TO CONTACT YOUR DAUGHTER?

DID YOU FIND OUT ANYTHING? LIKE HOW MANY DAYS IT'S BEEN SINCE...THE INCIDENT.

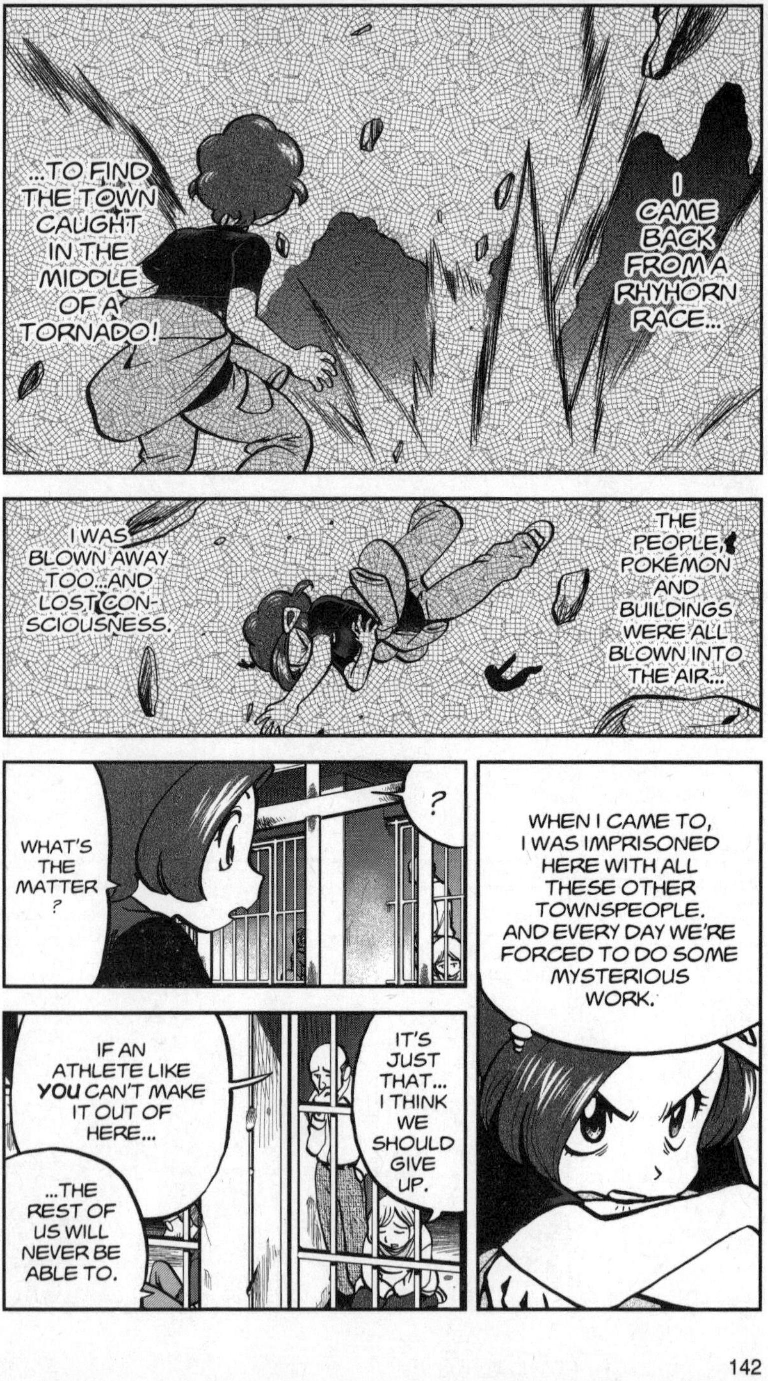
I CAME BACK FROM A RHYHORN RACE...
...TO FIND THE TOWN CAUGHT IN THE MIDDLE OF A TORNADO!
THE PEOPLE, POKÉMON AND BUILDINGS WERE ALL BLOWN INTO THE AIR...
I WAS BLOWN AWAY TOO...AND LOST CON-SCIOUSNESS.
WHEN I CAME TO, I WAS IMPRISONED HERE WITH ALL THESE OTHER TOWNSPEOPLE. AND EVERY DAY WE'RE FORCED TO DO SOME MYSTERIOUS WORK.
?
WHAT'S THE MATTER?
IT'S JUST THAT... I THINK WE SHOULD GIVE UP.
IF AN ATHLETE LIKE **YOU** CAN'T MAKE IT OUT OF HERE...
...THE REST OF US WILL NEVER BE ABLE TO.

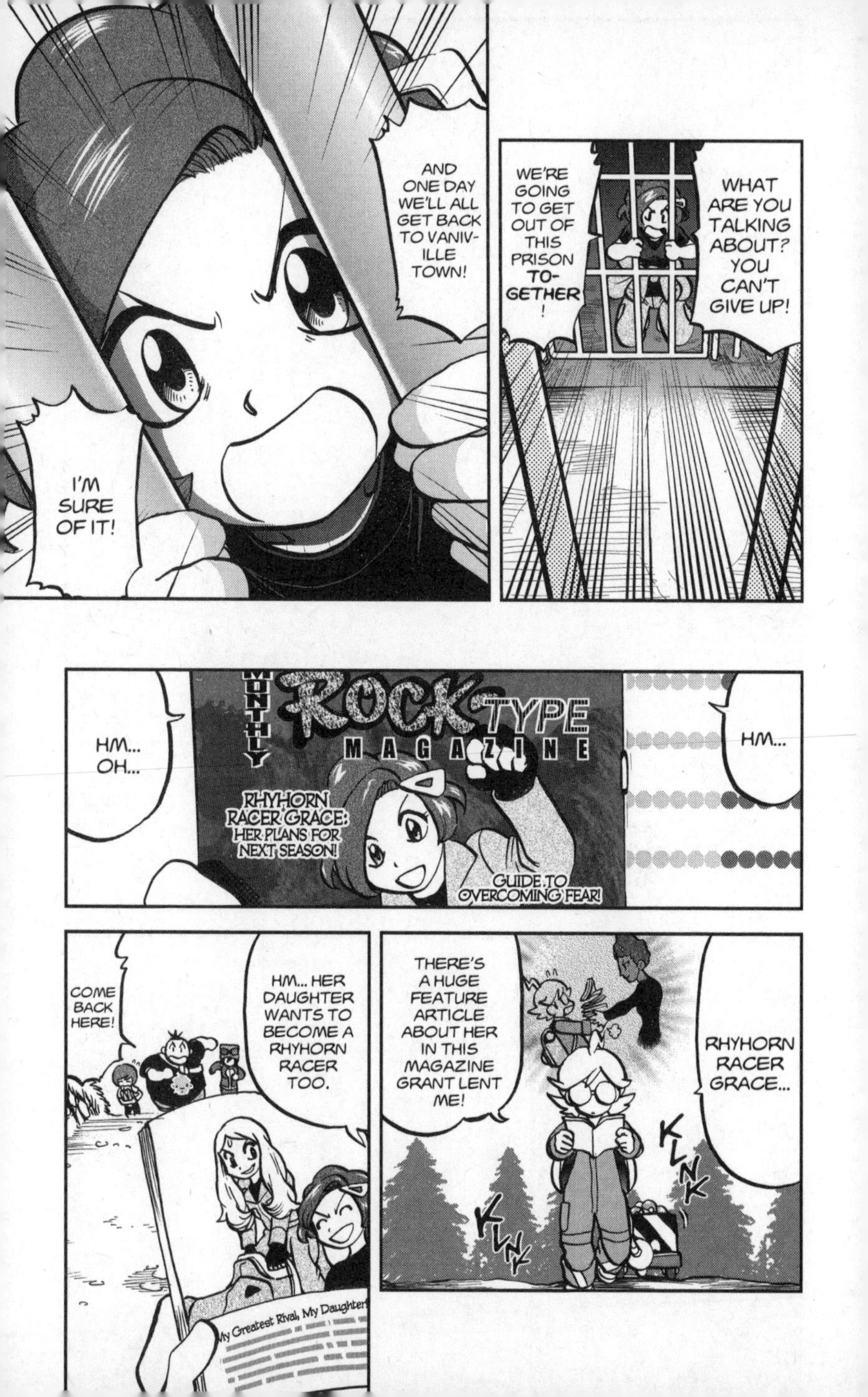
WHAT ARE YOU TALKING ABOUT? YOU CAN'T GIVE UP!
WE'RE GOING TO GET OUT OF THIS PRISON TO-GETHER!
AND ONE DAY WE'LL ALL GET BACK TO VANIV-ILLE TOWN!
I'M SURE OF IT!
HM...
MONTHLY ROCK TYPE MAGAZINE
RHYHORN RACER GRACE: HER PLANS FOR NEXT SEASON!
GUIDE TO OVERCOMING FEAR!
HM... OH...
RHYHORN RACER GRACE...
THERE'S A HUGE FEATURE ARTICLE ABOUT HER IN THIS MAGAZINE GRANT LENT ME!
KLNK
KLNK
HM... HER DAUGHTER WANTS TO BECOME A RHYHORN RACER TOO.
COME BACK HERE!
My Greatest Rival, My Daughter!

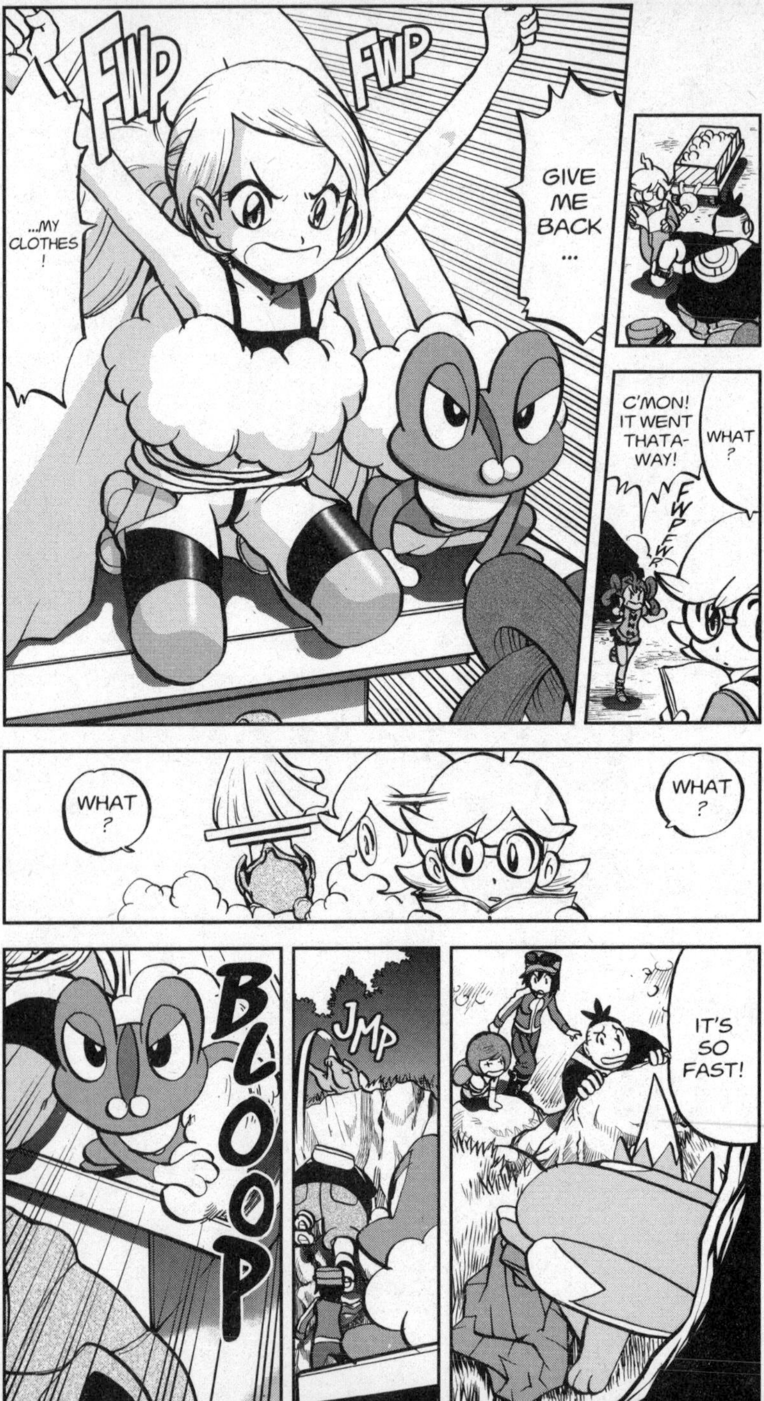
WHAT?
C'MON! IT WENT THATA-WAY!
FWPFWR
FWP
GIVE ME BACK...
FWP
...MY CLOTHES!
WHAT?
WHAT?
IT'S SO FAST!
JMP
BLOOP

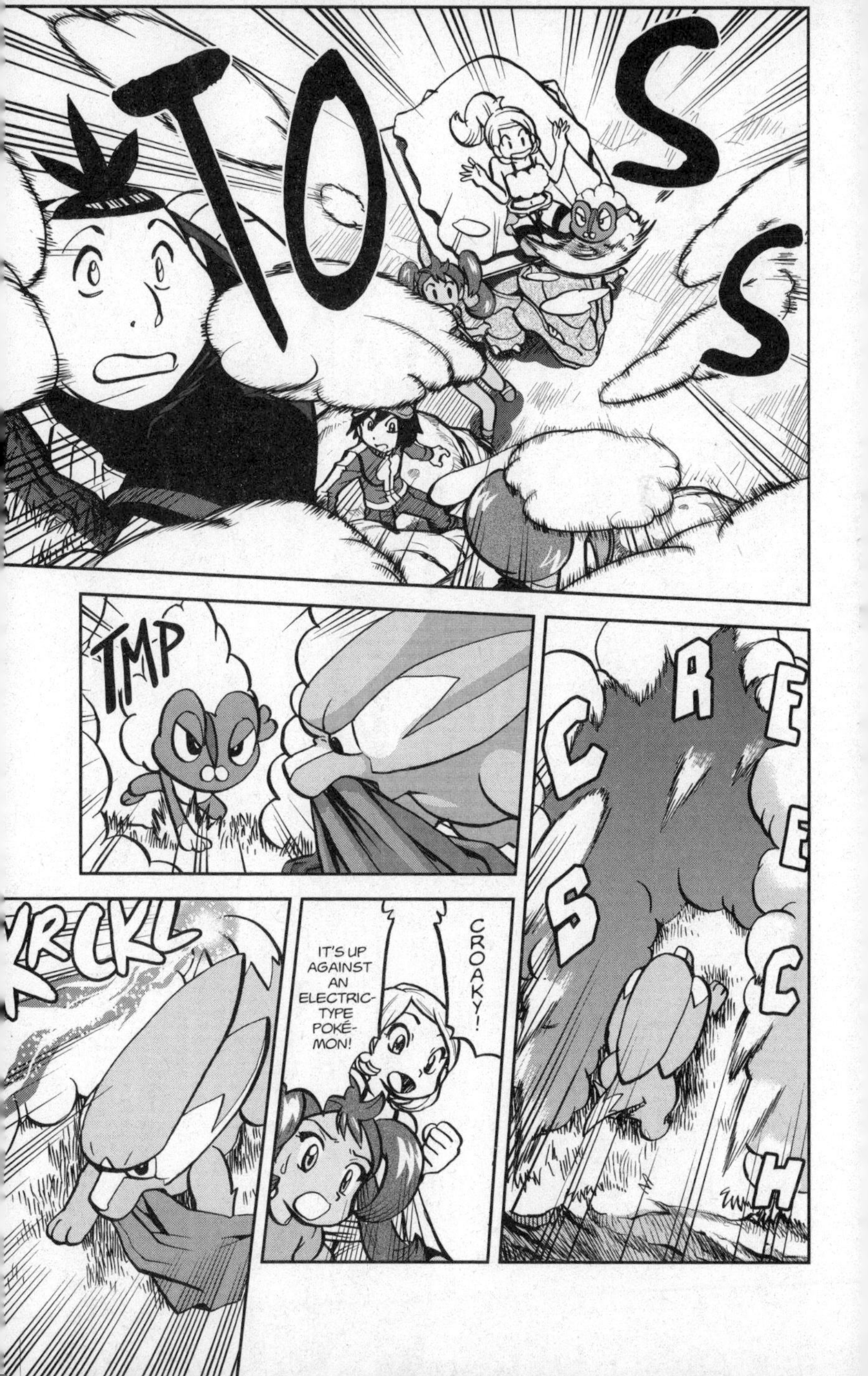
TOSS
SCREECH
TMP
CROAKY!
IT'S UP AGAINST AN ELECTRIC-TYPE POKÉMON!
KRCKL

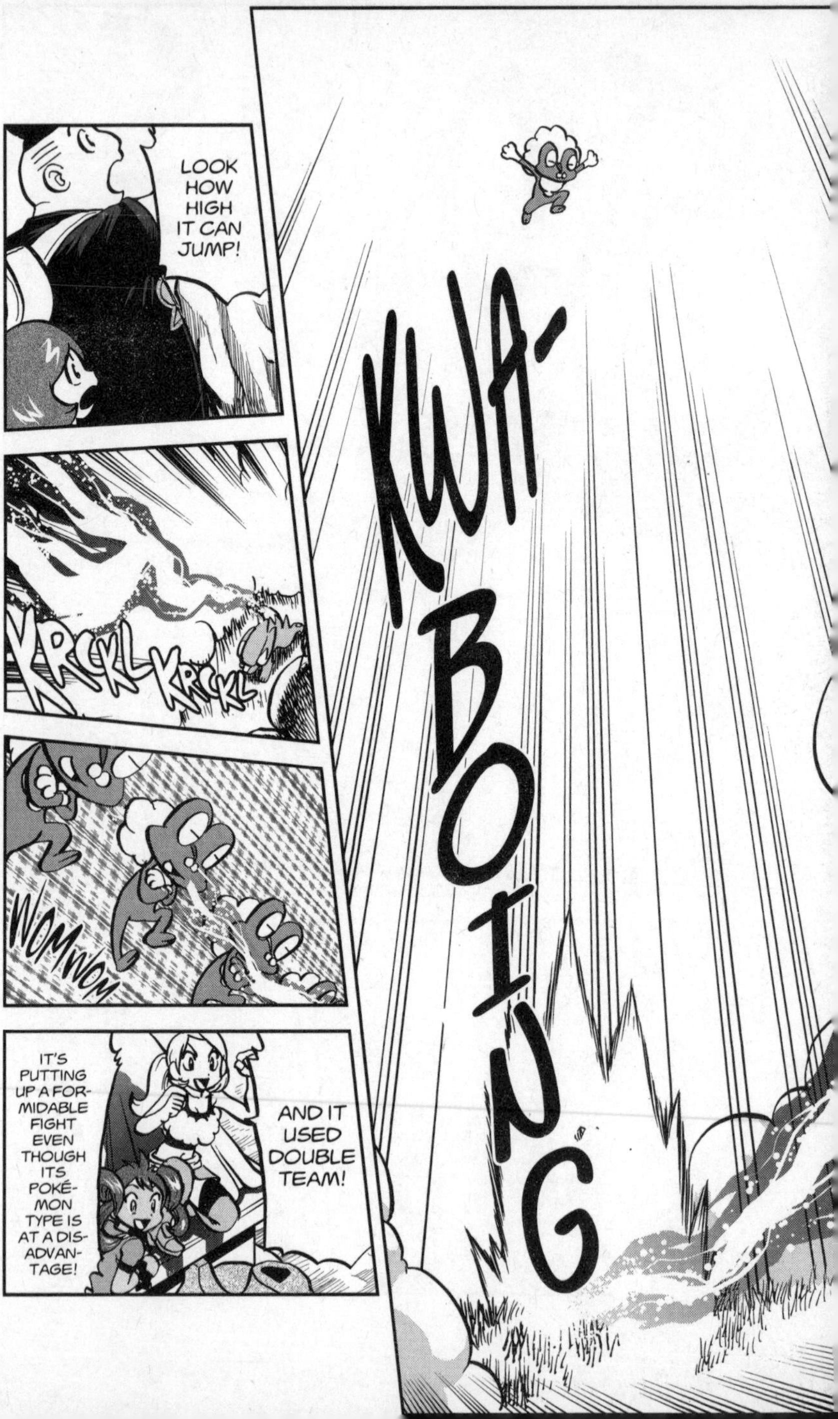
KWA-BOING
LOOK HOW HIGH IT CAN JUMP!
KRCKL KRCKL
WOM WOM
AND IT USED DOUBLE TEAM!
IT'S PUTTING UP A FORMIDABLE FIGHT EVEN THOUGH ITS POKÉMON TYPE IS AT A DISADVANTAGE!

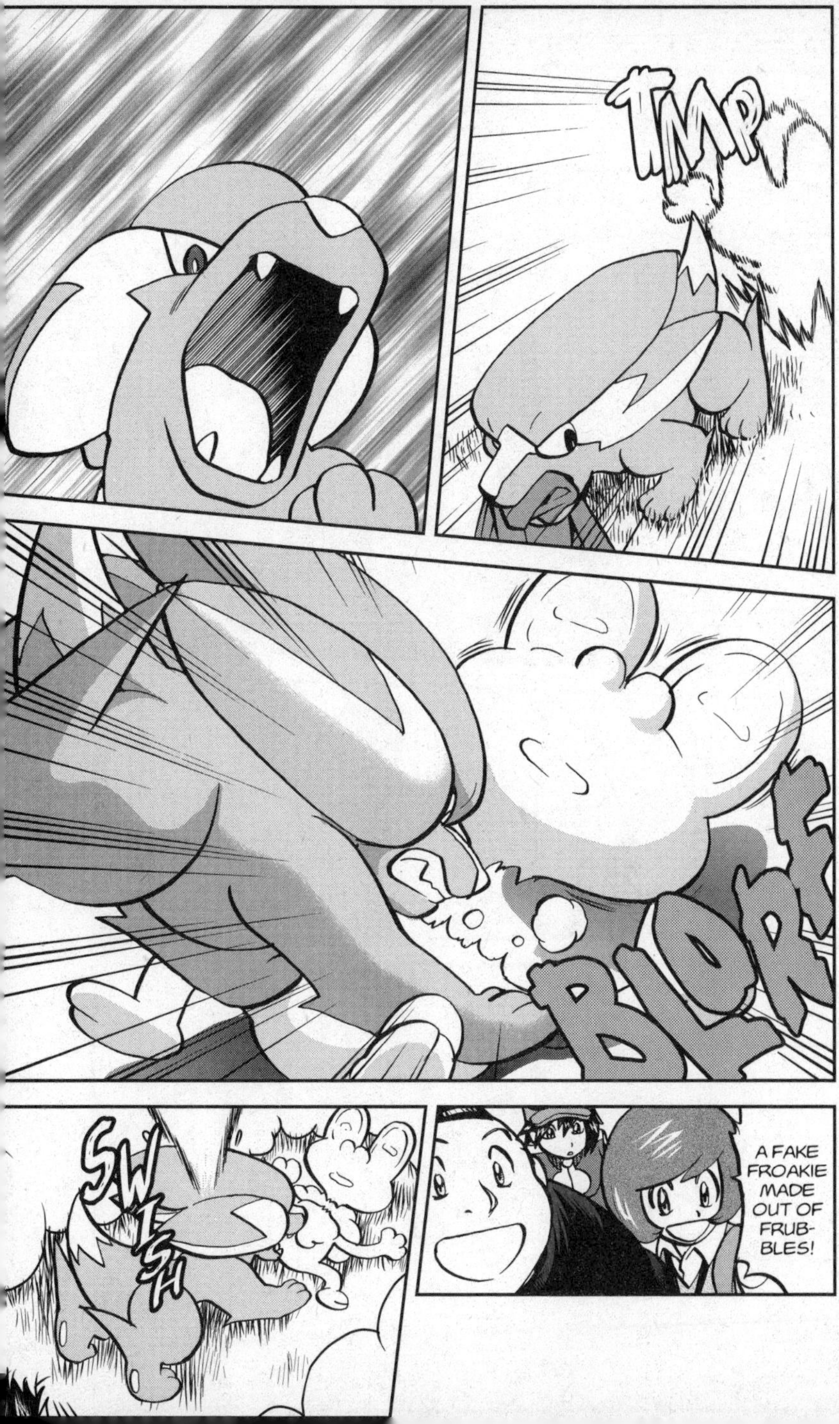
TMP
BLORF
A FAKE FROAKIE MADE OUT OF FRUB-BLES!
SWISH

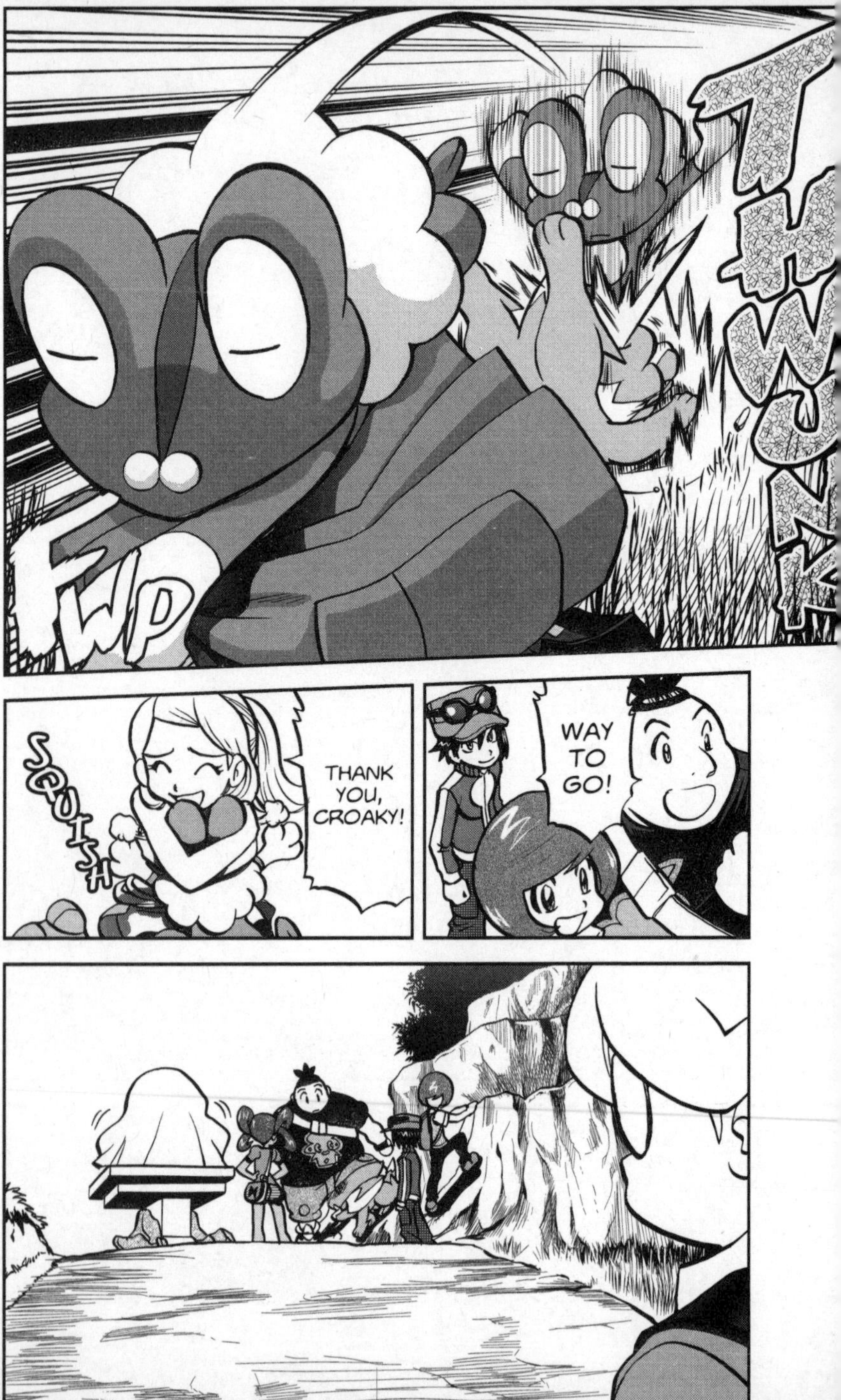
THWUNK
FWP
WAY TO GO!
THANK YOU, CROAKY!
SQUISH

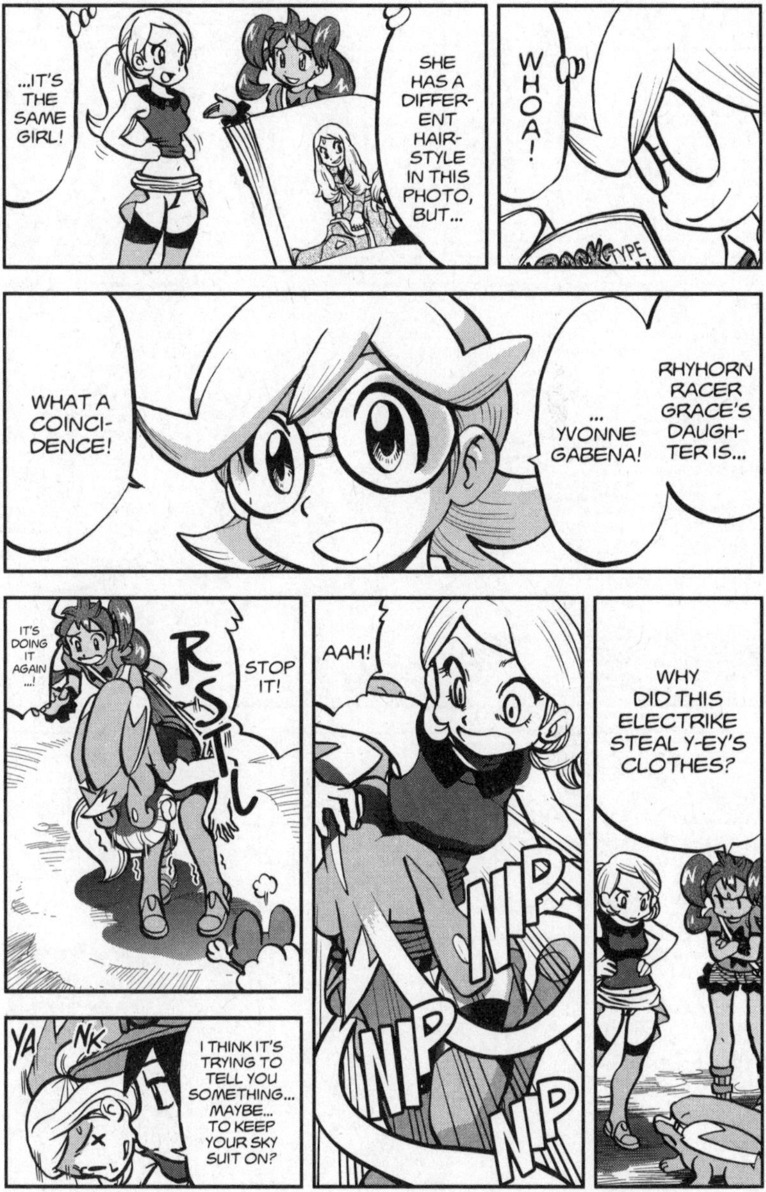
WHOA!
SHE HAS A DIFFERENT HAIRSTYLE IN THIS PHOTO, BUT...
...IT'S THE SAME GIRL!
RHYHORN RACER GRACE'S DAUGHTER IS...
... YVONNE GABENA!
WHAT A COINCIDENCE!
WHY DID THIS ELECTRIKE STEAL Y-EY'S CLOTHES?
AAH!
NIP
NIP
NIP
NIP
STOP IT!
RSTL
IT'S DOING IT AGAIN ...!
YANK
I THINK IT'S TRYING TO TELL YOU SOMETHING... MAYBE... TO KEEP YOUR SKY SUIT ON?

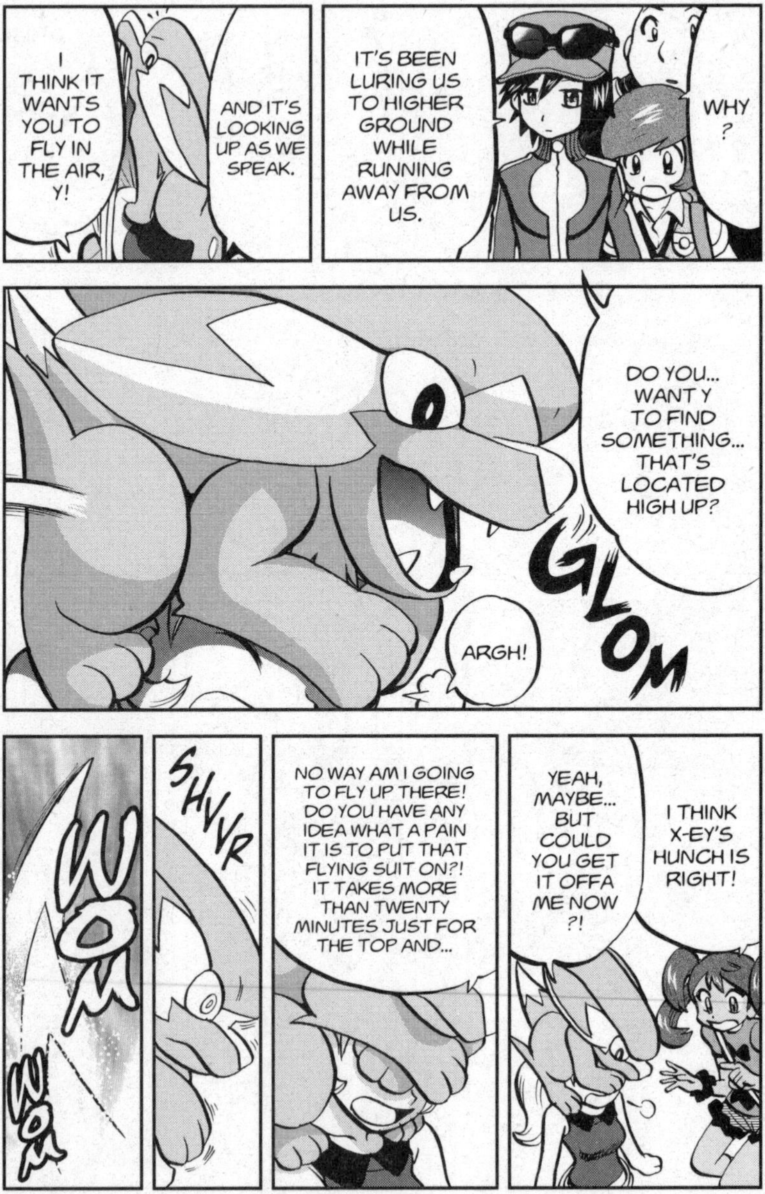
WHY?
IT'S BEEN LURING US TO HIGHER GROUND WHILE RUNNING AWAY FROM US.
AND IT'S LOOKING UP AS WE SPEAK.
I THINK IT WANTS YOU TO FLY IN THE AIR, Y!
DO YOU... WANT Y TO FIND SOMETHING... THAT'S LOCATED HIGH UP?
GLOM
ARGH!
I THINK X-EY'S HUNCH IS RIGHT!
YEAH, MAYBE... BUT COULD YOU GET IT OFFA ME NOW?!
NO WAY AM I GOING TO FLY UP THERE! DO YOU HAVE ANY IDEA WHAT A PAIN IT IS TO PUT THAT FLYING SUIT ON?! IT TAKES MORE THAN TWENTY MINUTES JUST FOR THE TOP AND...
SHVVR
WOM
WOM

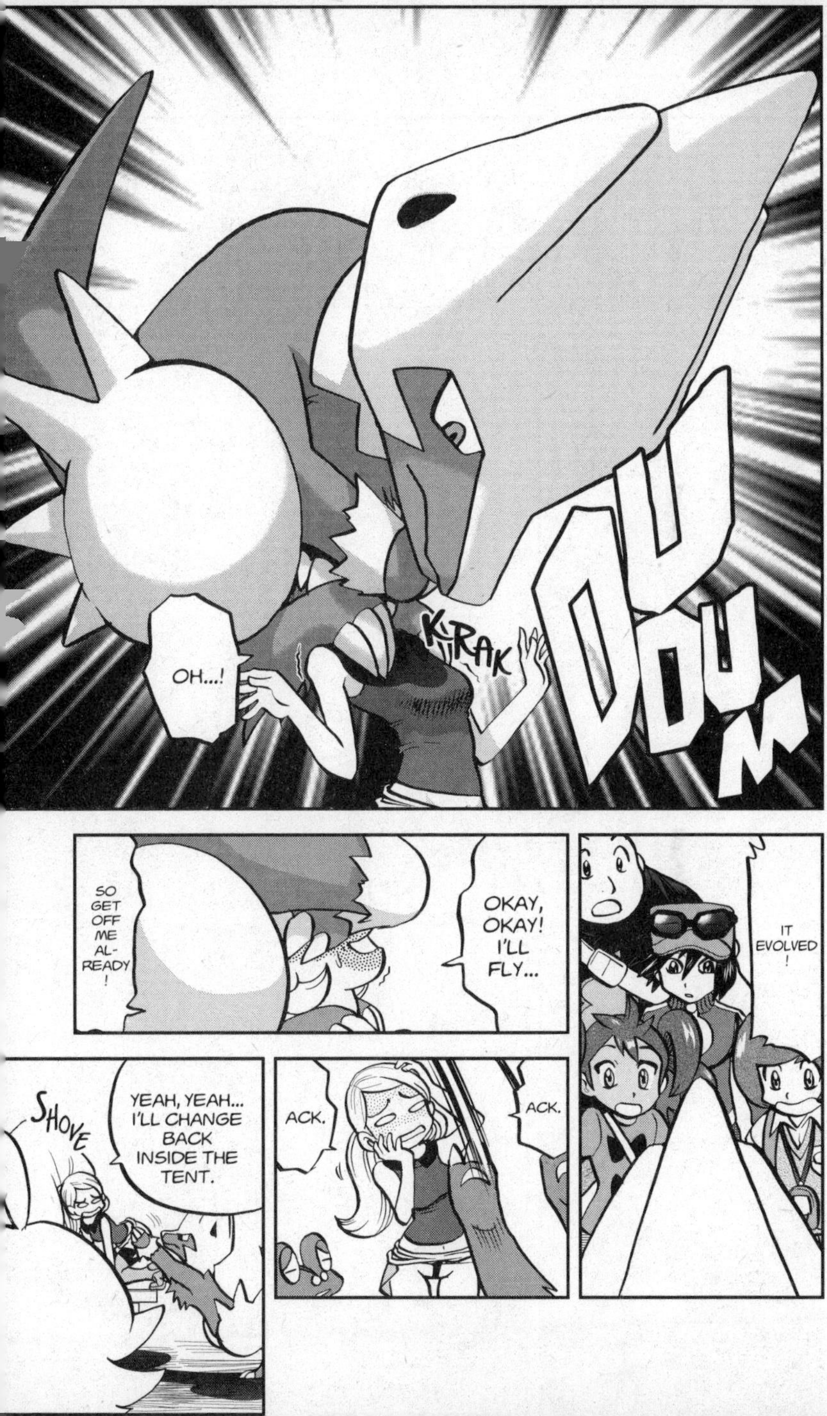
DOUDOUM
KRAK
OH...!
IT EVOLVED!
OKAY, OKAY! I'LL FLY...
SO GET OFF ME AL-READY!
ACK.
ACK.
YEAH, YEAH... I'LL CHANGE BACK INSIDE THE TENT.
SHOVE

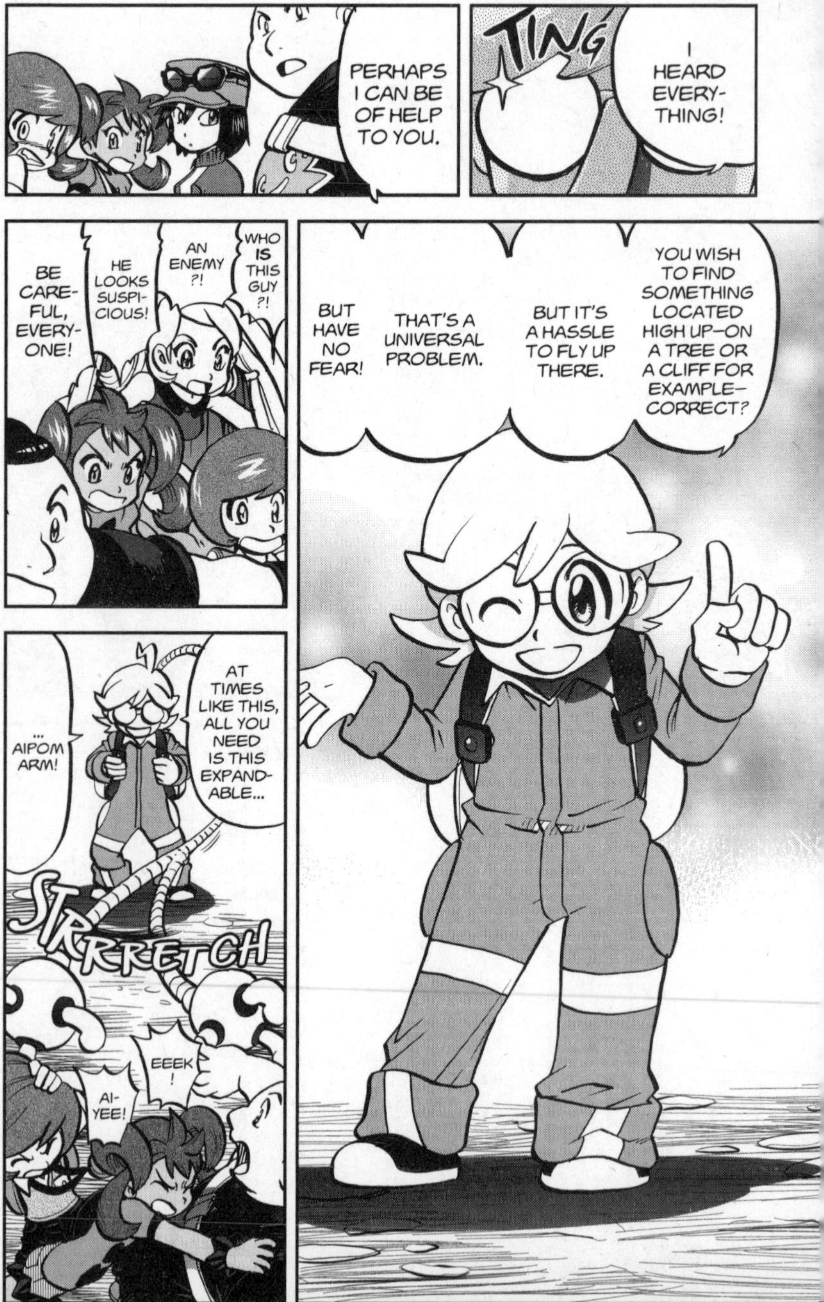
TING
I HEARD EVERYTHING!
PERHAPS I CAN BE OF HELP TO YOU.
YOU WISH TO FIND SOMETHING LOCATED HIGH UP—ON A TREE OR A CLIFF FOR EXAMPLE—CORRECT?
BUT IT'S A HASSLE TO FLY UP THERE.
THAT'S A UNIVERSAL PROBLEM.
BUT HAVE NO FEAR!
WHO IS THIS GUY?!
AN ENEMY?!
HE LOOKS SUSPICIOUS!
BE CAREFUL, EVERYONE!
AT TIMES LIKE THIS, ALL YOU NEED IS THIS EXPANDABLE...
...AIPOM ARM!
STRRRETCH
EEEK!
AI-YEE!

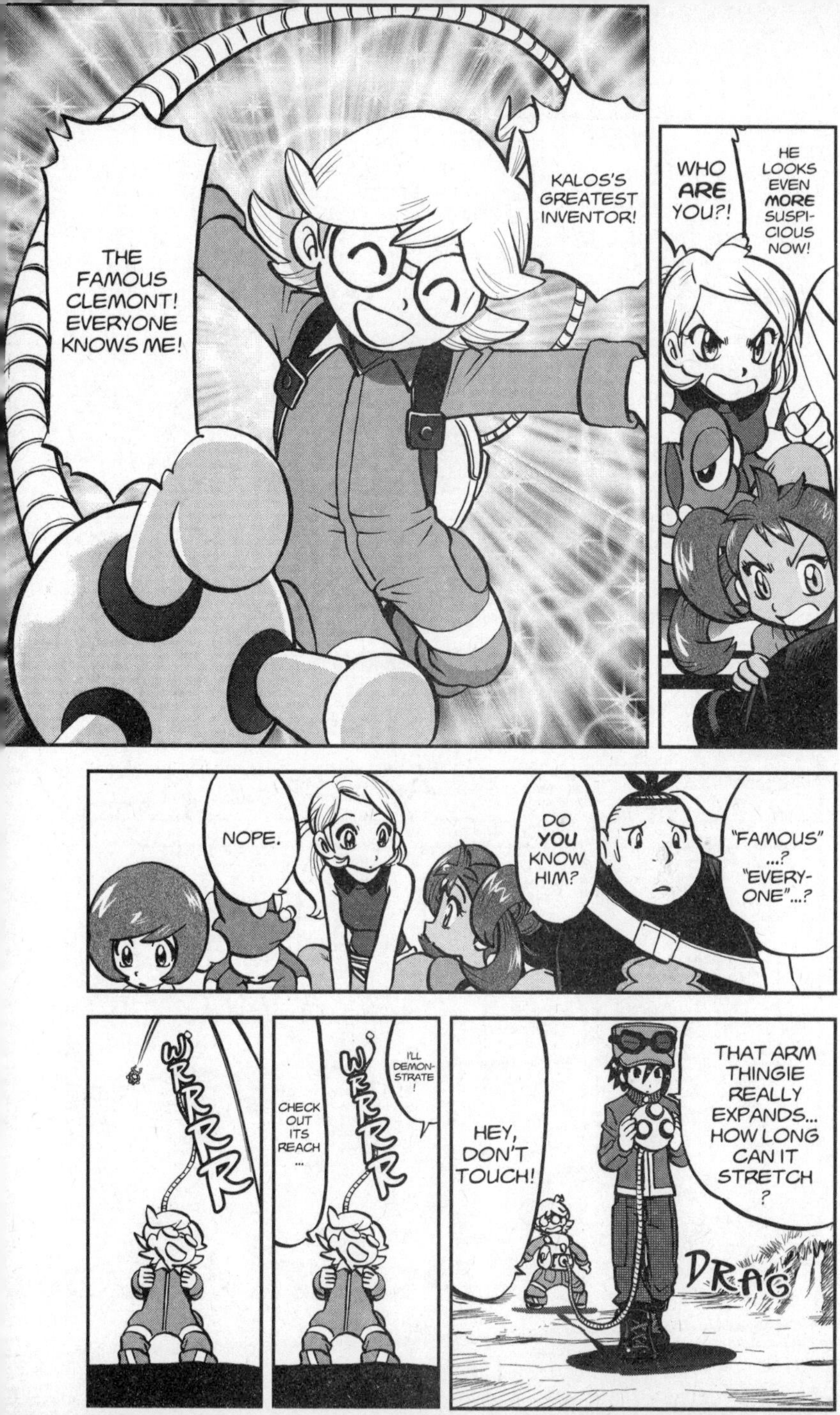
HE LOOKS EVEN MORE SUSPICIOUS NOW!
WHO ARE YOU?!
KALOS'S GREATEST INVENTOR!
THE FAMOUS CLEMONT! EVERYONE KNOWS ME!
"FAMOUS"...? "EVERYONE"...?
DO YOU KNOW HIM?
NOPE.
THAT ARM THINGIE REALLY EXPANDS... HOW LONG CAN IT STRETCH?
DRAG
HEY, DON'T TOUCH!
I'LL DEMONSTRATE!
WRRRR
CHECK OUT ITS REACH...
WRRRR

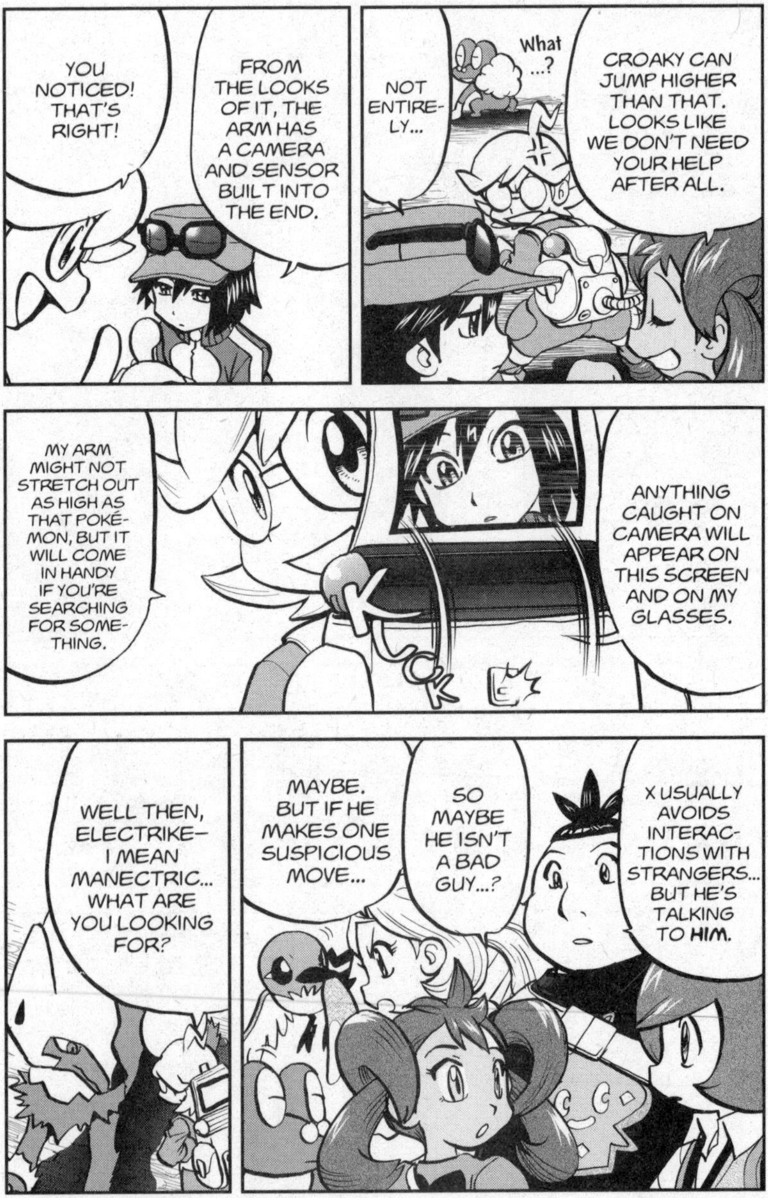
CROAKY CAN JUMP HIGHER THAN THAT. LOOKS LIKE WE DON'T NEED YOUR HELP AFTER ALL.
What ...?
NOT ENTIRELY...
FROM THE LOOKS OF IT, THE ARM HAS A CAMERA AND SENSOR BUILT INTO THE END.
YOU NOTICED! THAT'S RIGHT!
ANYTHING CAUGHT ON CAMERA WILL APPEAR ON THIS SCREEN AND ON MY GLASSES.
MY ARM MIGHT NOT STRETCH OUT AS HIGH AS THAT POKÉMON, BUT IT WILL COME IN HANDY IF YOU'RE SEARCHING FOR SOMETHING.
X USUALLY AVOIDS INTERACTIONS WITH STRANGERS... BUT HE'S TALKING TO **HIM**.
SO MAYBE HE ISN'T A BAD GUY...?
MAYBE. BUT IF HE MAKES ONE SUSPICIOUS MOVE...
WELL THEN, ELECTRIKE— I MEAN MANECTRIC... WHAT ARE YOU LOOKING FOR?

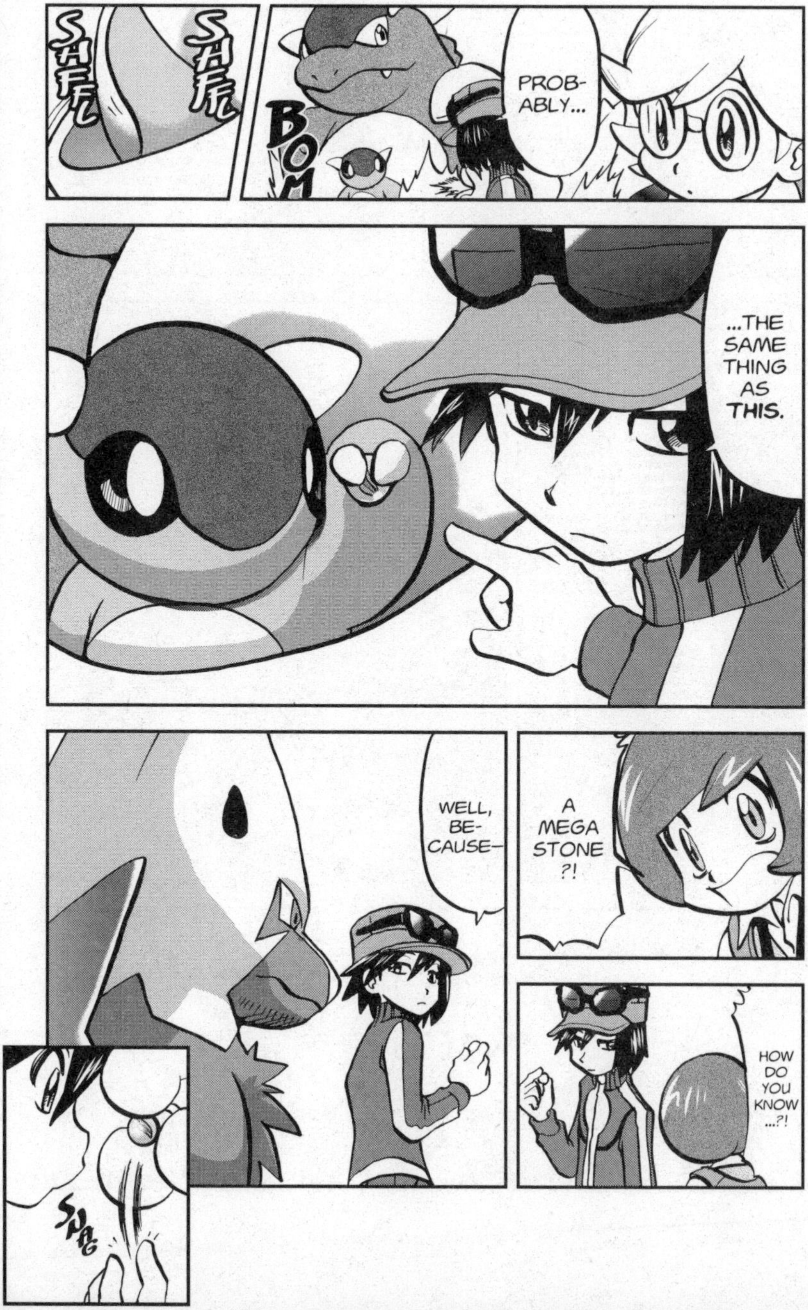
PROBABLY...
BOM
SHFFL
SHFFL
...THE SAME THING AS THIS.
A MEGA STONE?!
HOW DO YOU KNOW...?!
WELL, BECAUSE—
SNAG

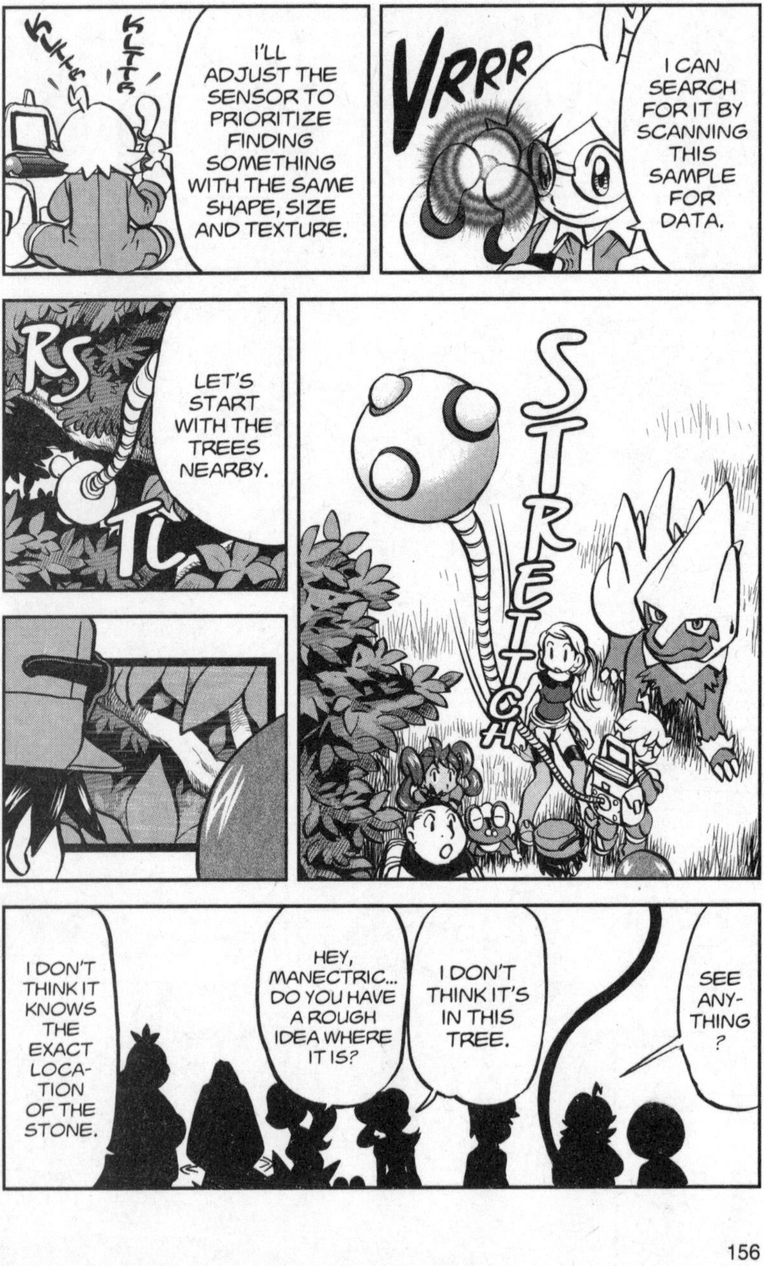
VRRR
I CAN SEARCH FOR IT BY SCANNING THIS SAMPLE FOR DATA.
KLTTR
I'LL ADJUST THE SENSOR TO PRIORITIZE FINDING SOMETHING WITH THE SAME SHAPE, SIZE AND TEXTURE.
STRETCH
RS
TL
LET'S START WITH THE TREES NEARBY.
SEE ANYTHING?
I DON'T THINK IT'S IN THIS TREE.
HEY, MANECTRIC... DO YOU HAVE A ROUGH IDEA WHERE IT IS?
I DON'T THINK IT KNOWS THE EXACT LOCATION OF THE STONE.

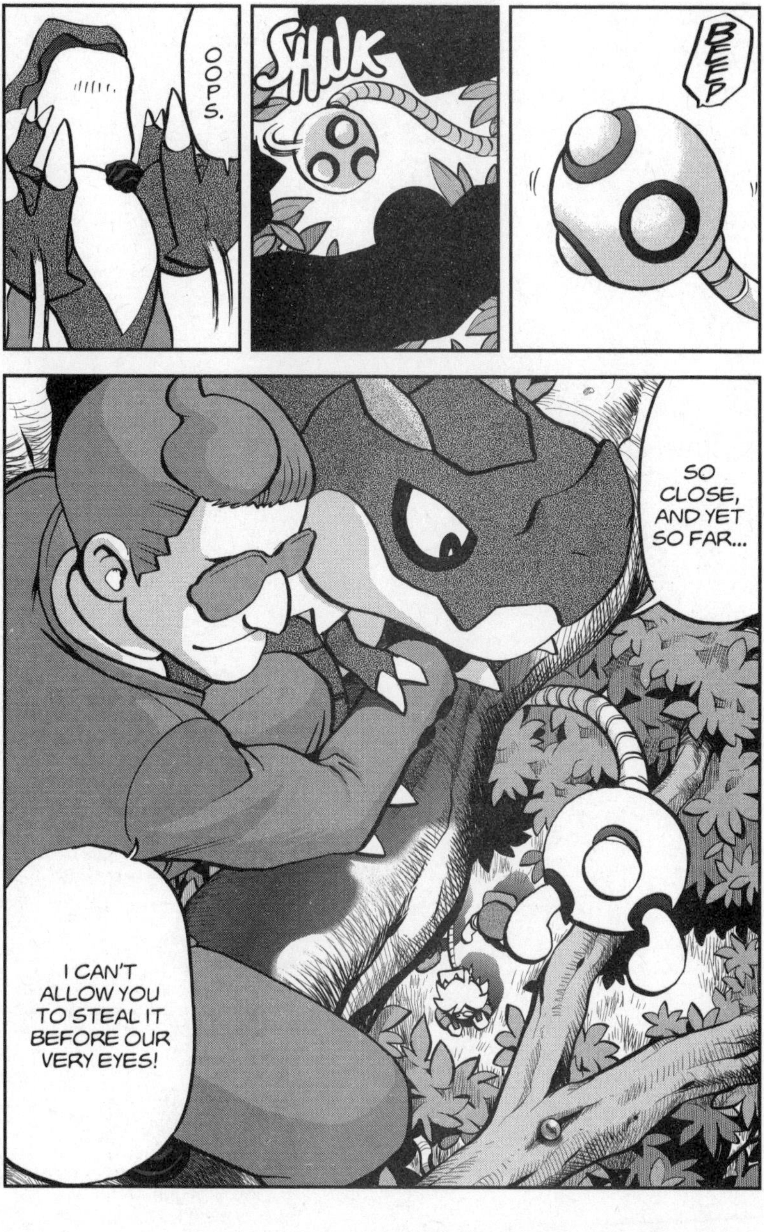
BEEP
SHNK
OOPS.
SO CLOSE, AND YET SO FAR...
I CAN'T ALLOW YOU TO STEAL IT BEFORE OUR VERY EYES!

## Current Location

### Route 5
### Versant Road

Roller Skaters from across the Kalos region gather on this hilly path to demonstrate their best skills.

▼

### Camphrier Town

This ancient town was once famous for the long-neglected manor home of a noble family.

▼

### Route 6
### Palais Lane

This tree-lined path was once covered with grass as tall as a person, but it was cleared by the palace.

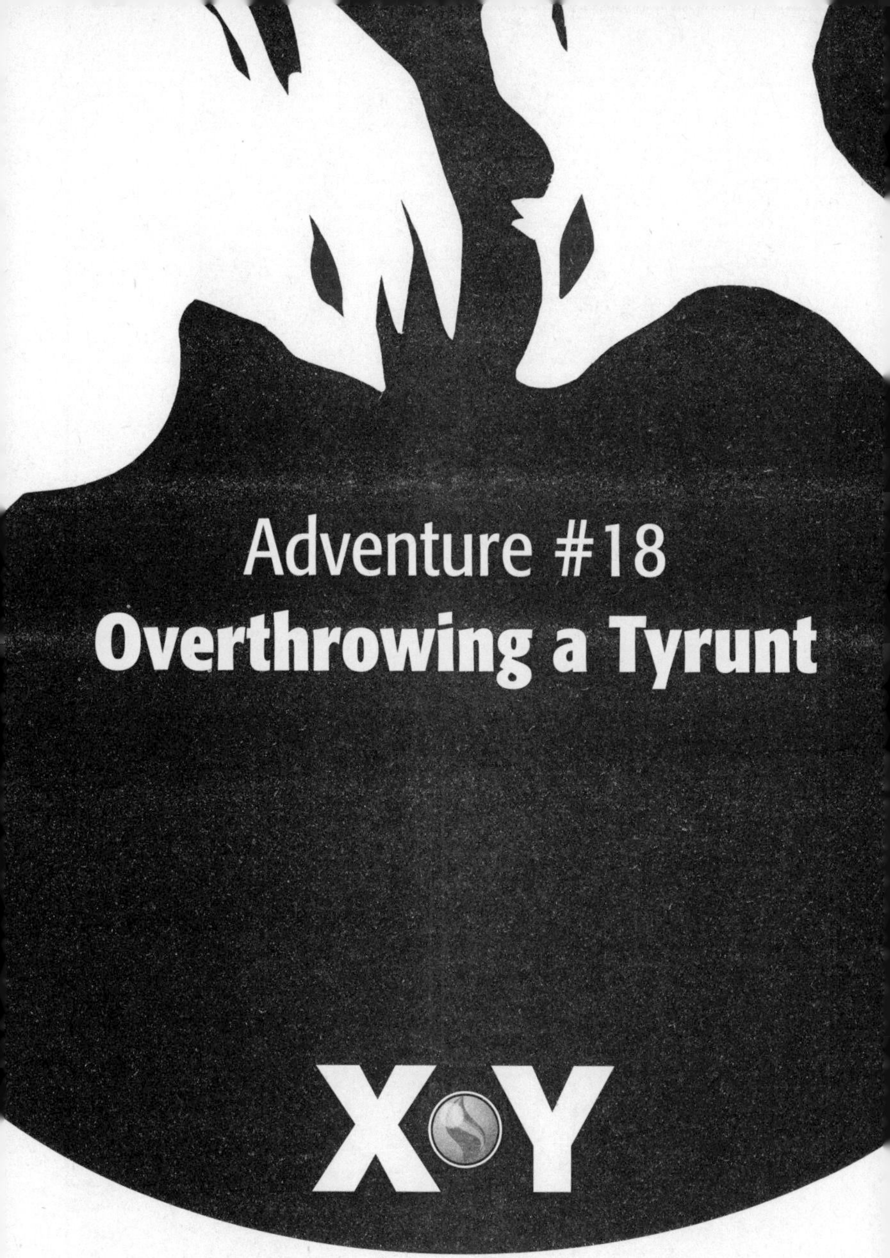

# Adventure #18
# Overthrowing a Tyrunt

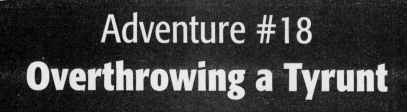

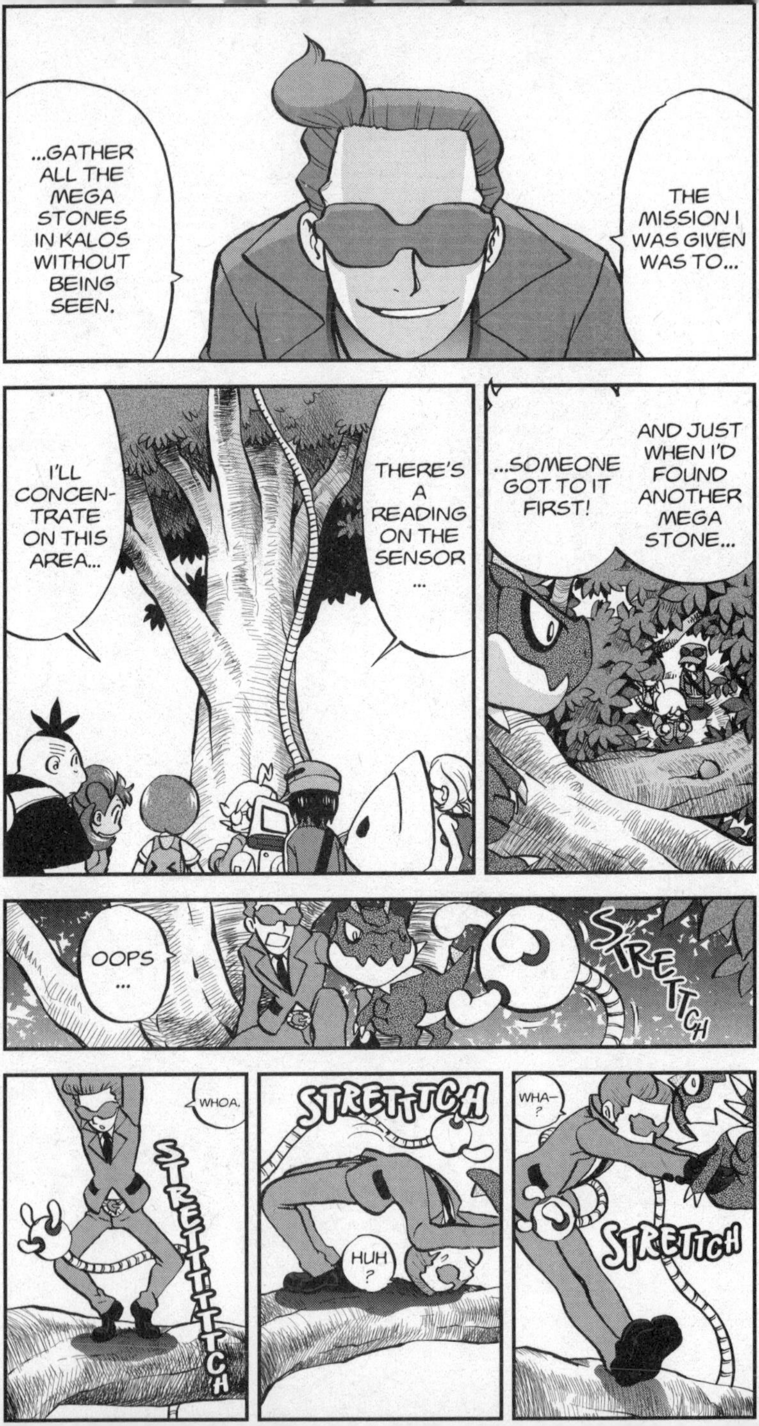
THE MISSION I WAS GIVEN WAS TO...
...GATHER ALL THE MEGA STONES IN KALOS WITHOUT BEING SEEN.
AND JUST WHEN I'D FOUND ANOTHER MEGA STONE...
...SOMEONE GOT TO IT FIRST!
THERE'S A READING ON THE SENSOR ...
I'LL CONCENTRATE ON THIS AREA...
STRETTCH
OOPS ...
WHA-?
STRETTCH
STRETTTCH
HUH ?
WHOA.
STRETTTTTTTCH

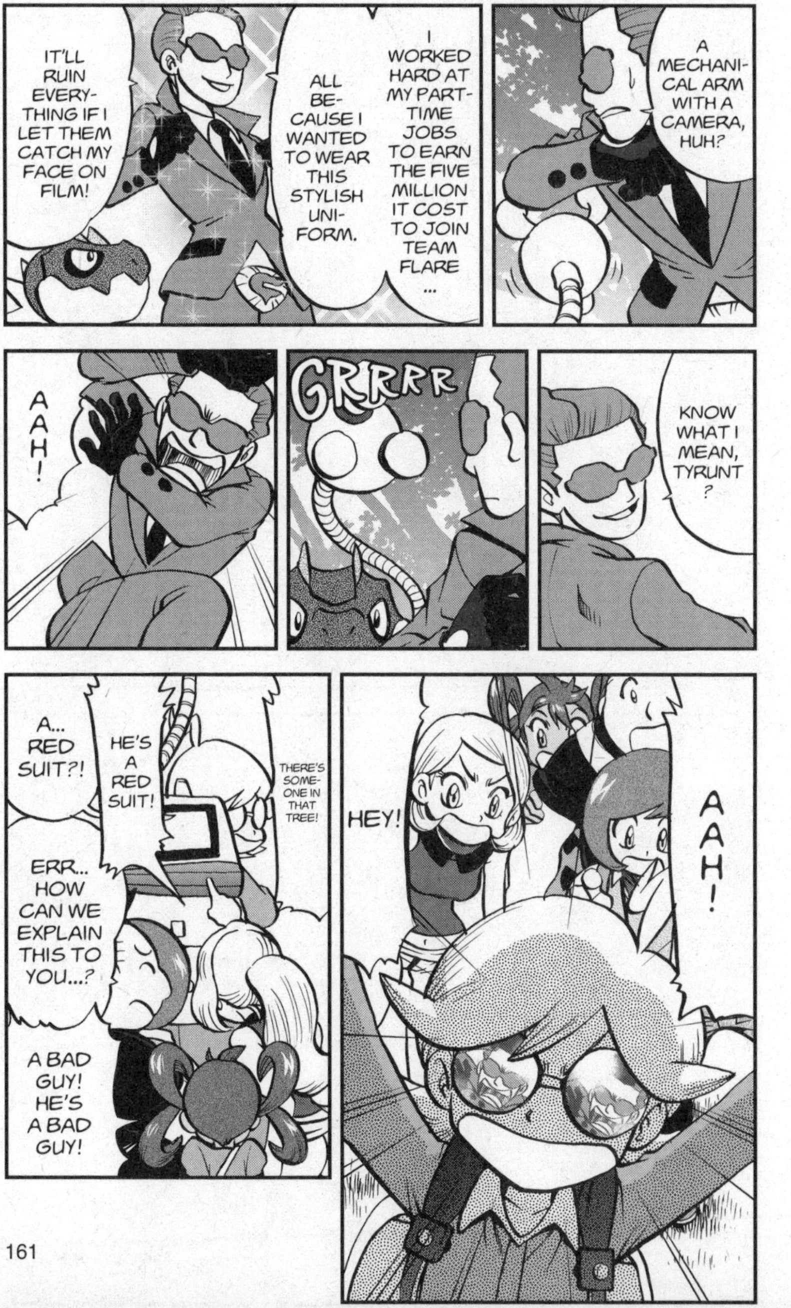
A MECHANICAL ARM WITH A CAMERA, HUH?
I WORKED HARD AT MY PART-TIME JOBS TO EARN THE FIVE MILLION IT COST TO JOIN TEAM FLARE...
ALL BECAUSE I WANTED TO WEAR THIS STYLISH UNIFORM.
IT'LL RUIN EVERYTHING IF I LET THEM CATCH MY FACE ON FILM!
KNOW WHAT I MEAN, TYRUNT?
GRRRR
AAH!
AAH!
HEY!
THERE'S SOMEONE IN THAT TREE!
HE'S A RED SUIT!
A... RED SUIT?!
ERR... HOW CAN WE EXPLAIN THIS TO YOU...?
A BAD GUY! HE'S A BAD GUY!

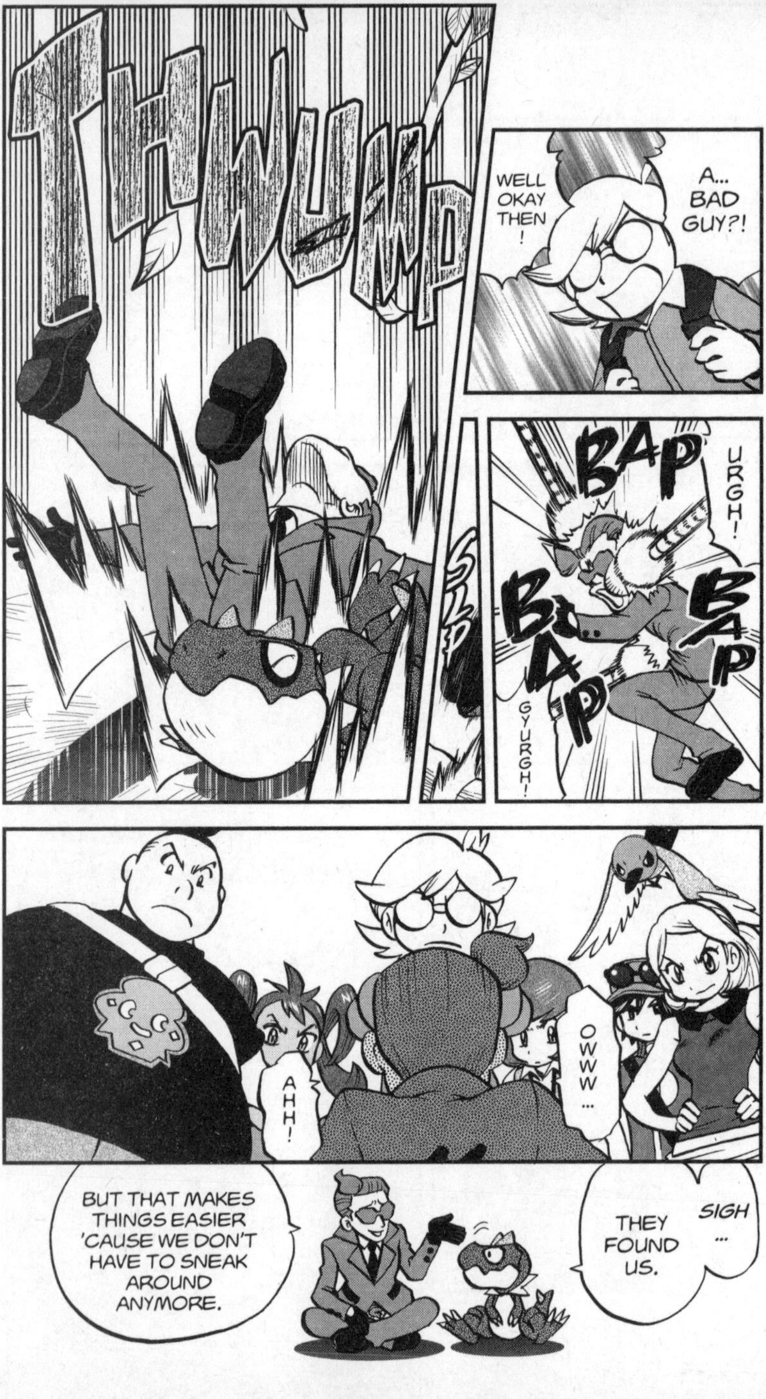
A... BAD GUY?!
WELL OKAY THEN!
URGH!
BAP
BAP
BAP
BAP
GYURGH!
SLIP
THWUMP
OWWW...
AHH!
SIGH...
THEY FOUND US.
BUT THAT MAKES THINGS EASIER 'CAUSE WE DON'T HAVE TO SNEAK AROUND ANYMORE.

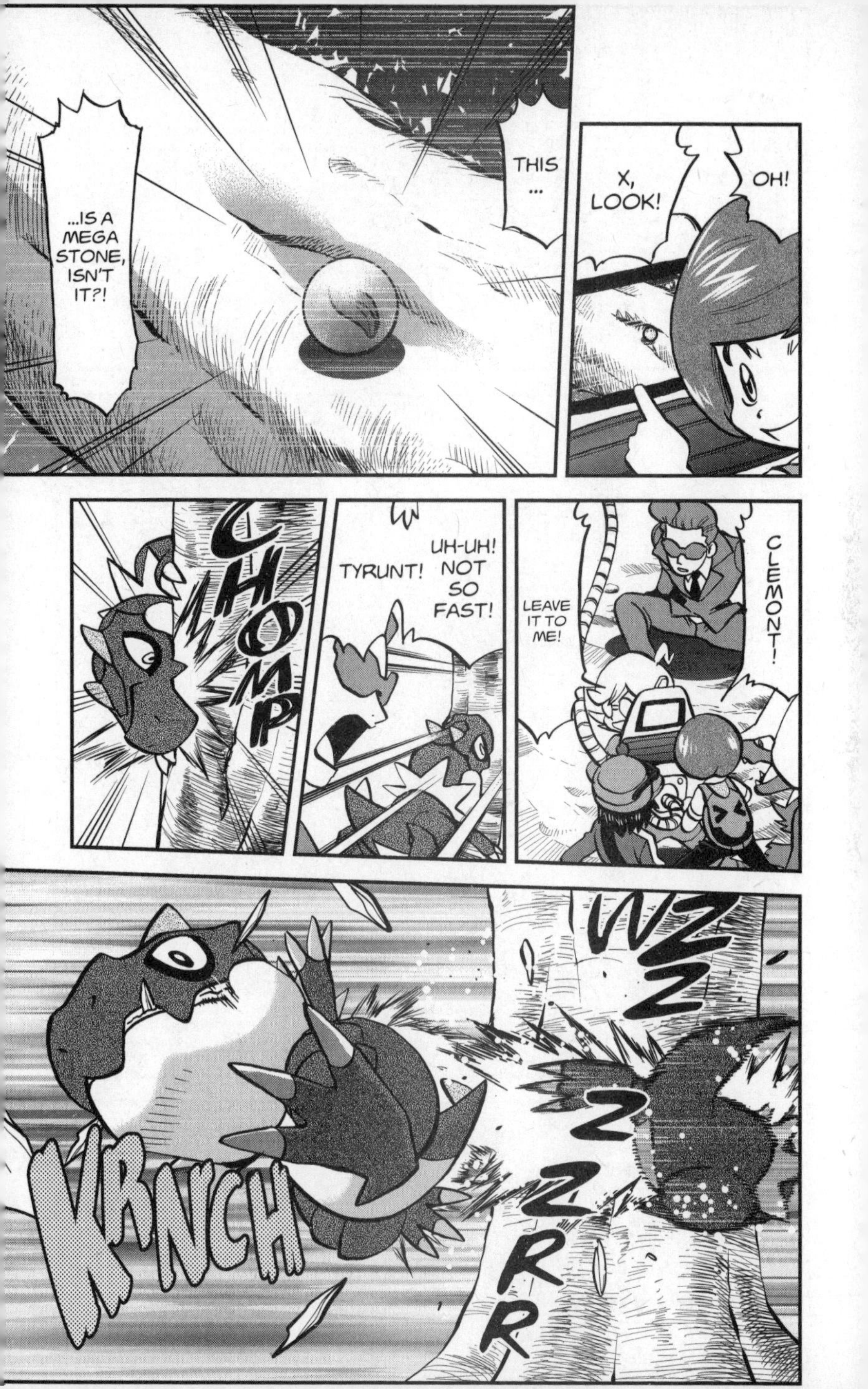
OH!
X, LOOK!
THIS...
...IS A MEGA STONE, ISN'T IT?!
CLEMONT!
LEAVE IT TO ME!
UH-UH! NOT SO FAST!
TYRUNT!
CHOMP
WZZZZRRR
KRNCH

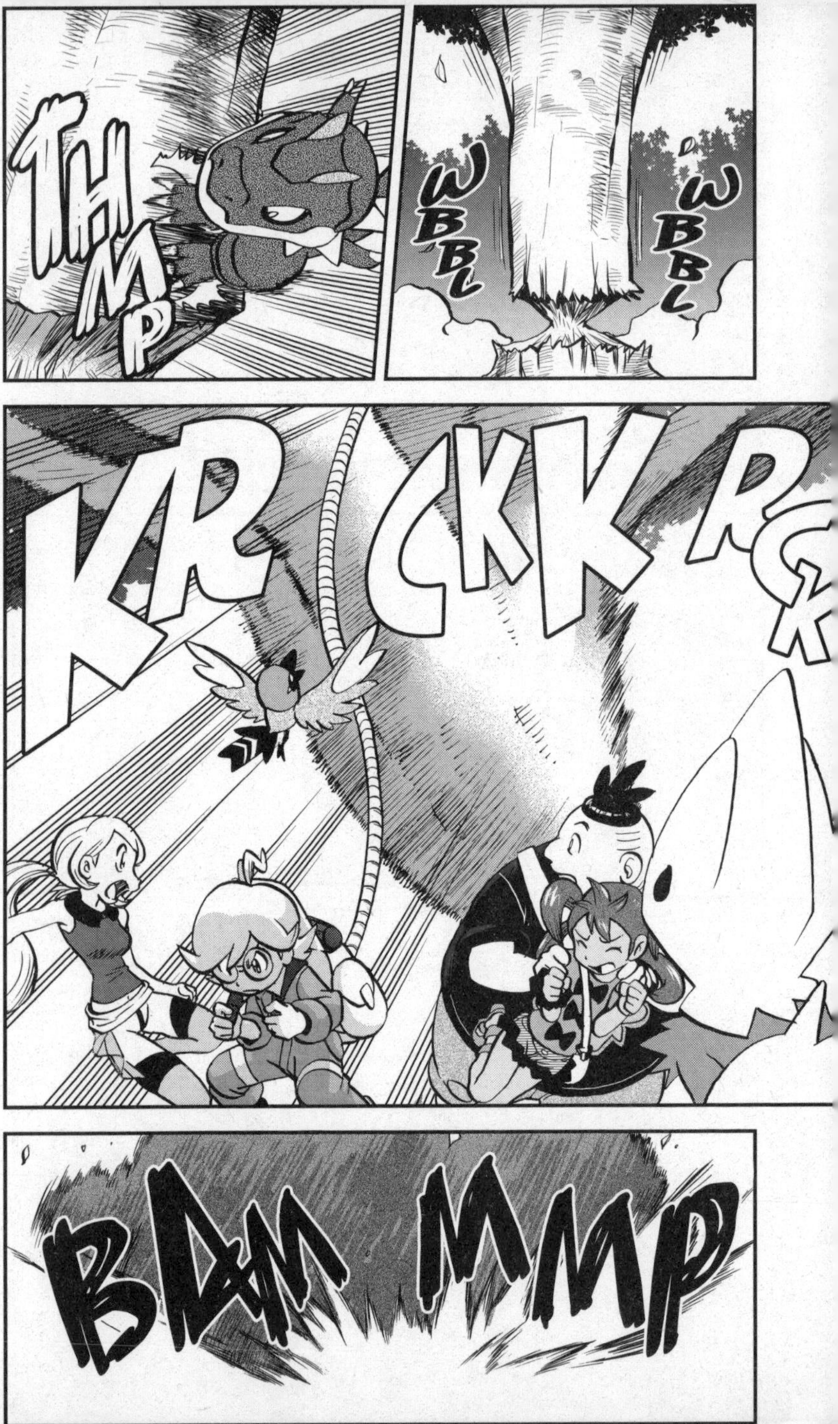
WBBL
WBBL
THMP
KRCKK
RCK
BAMMMP

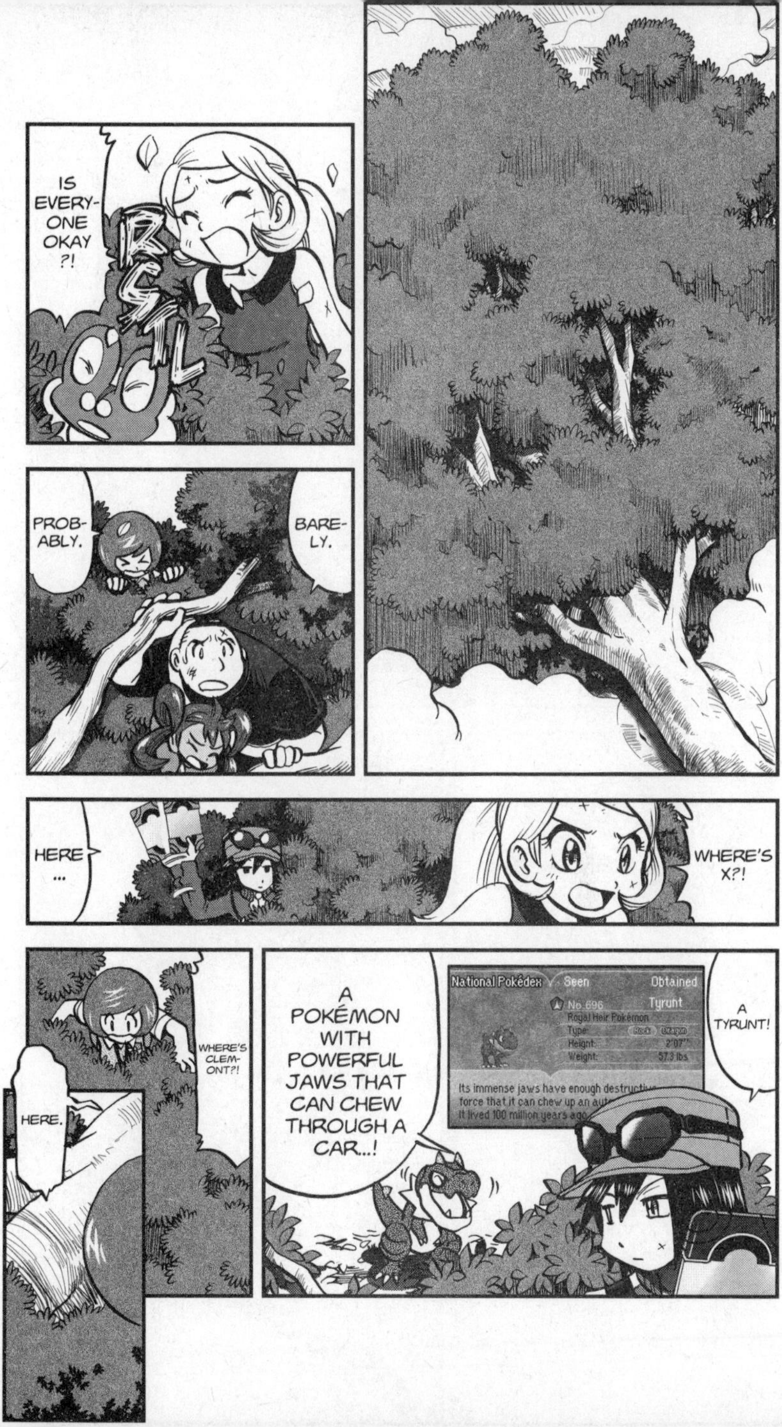
IS EVERYONE OKAY?!
BARELY.
PROBABLY.
WHERE'S X?!
HERE...
A TYRUNT!
National Pokédex
Seen
Obtained
No. 696
Tyrunt
Royal Heir Pokémon
Type:
Rock
Dragon
Height:
2'07''
Weight:
57.3 lbs
Its immense jaws have enough destructiv
force that it can chew up an aut
It lived 100 million years ago
A POKÉMON WITH POWERFUL JAWS THAT CAN CHEW THROUGH A CAR...!
WHERE'S CLEMONT?!
HERE.

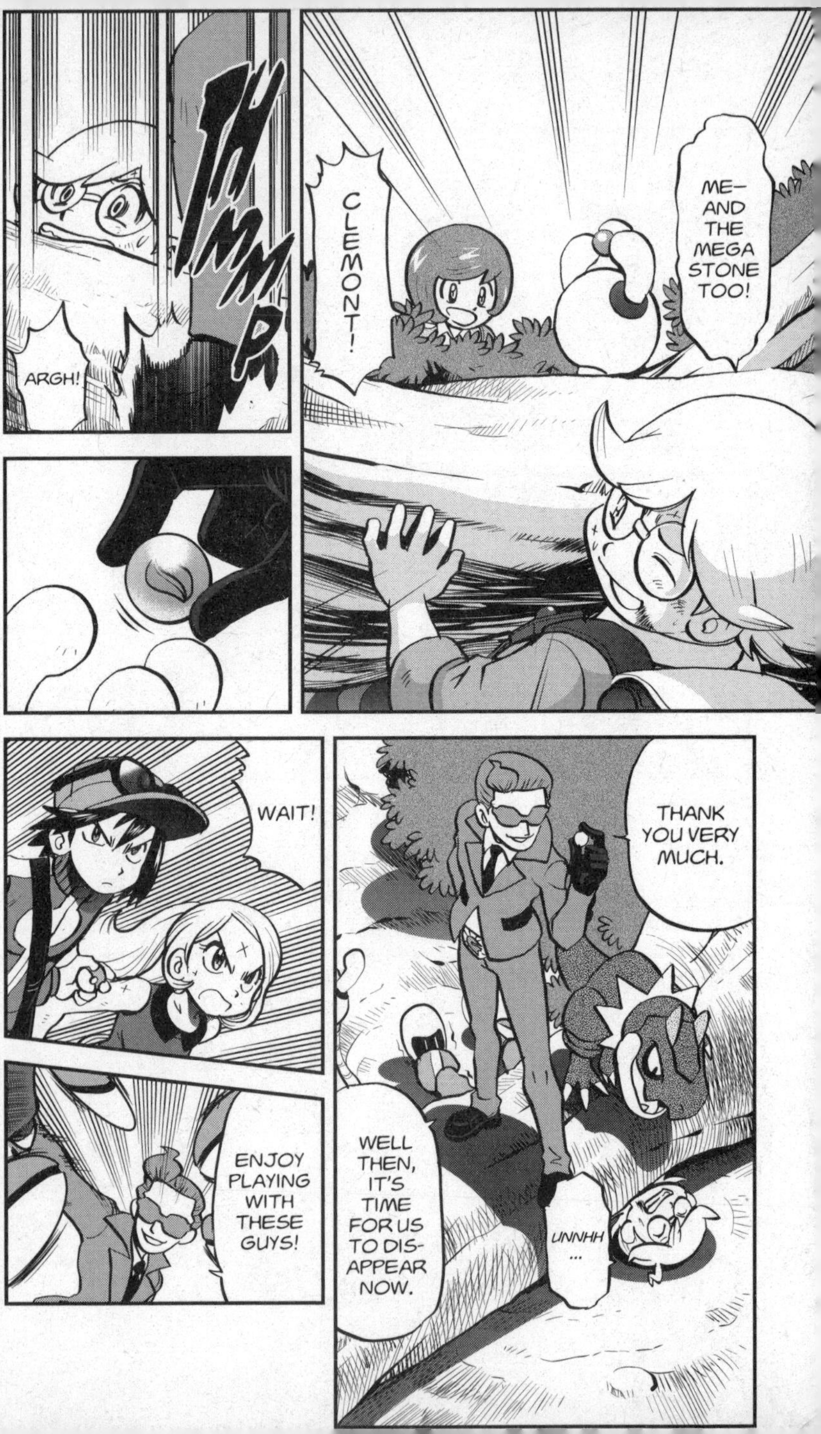
ME— AND THE MEGA STONE TOO!
CLEMONT!
THMMP!
ARGH!
THANK YOU VERY MUCH.
WELL THEN, IT'S TIME FOR US TO DIS-APPEAR NOW.
UNNHH ...
WAIT!
ENJOY PLAYING WITH THESE GUYS!

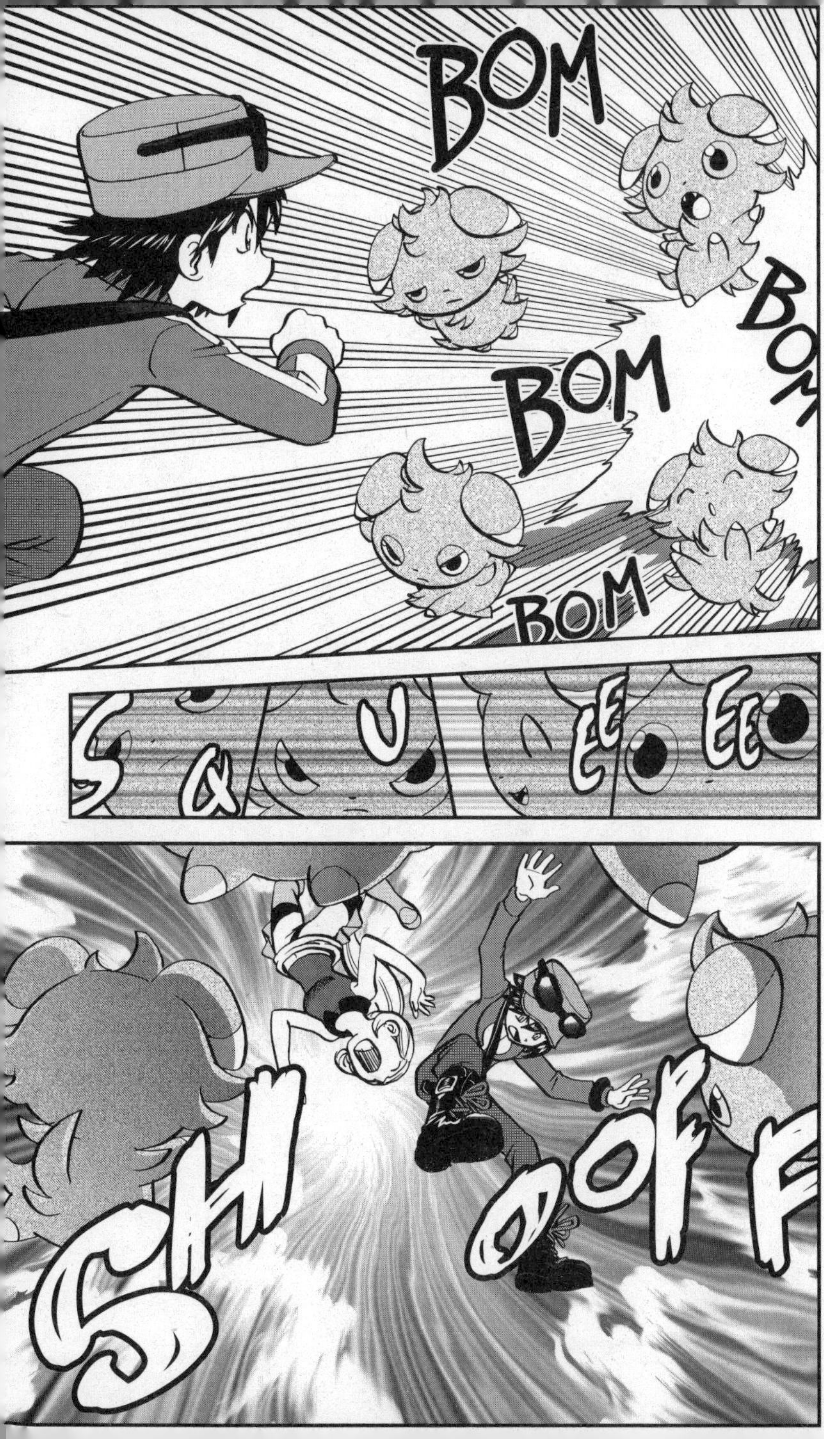
BOM
BOM
BOM
BOM
SQUEEEE
SHOOFF

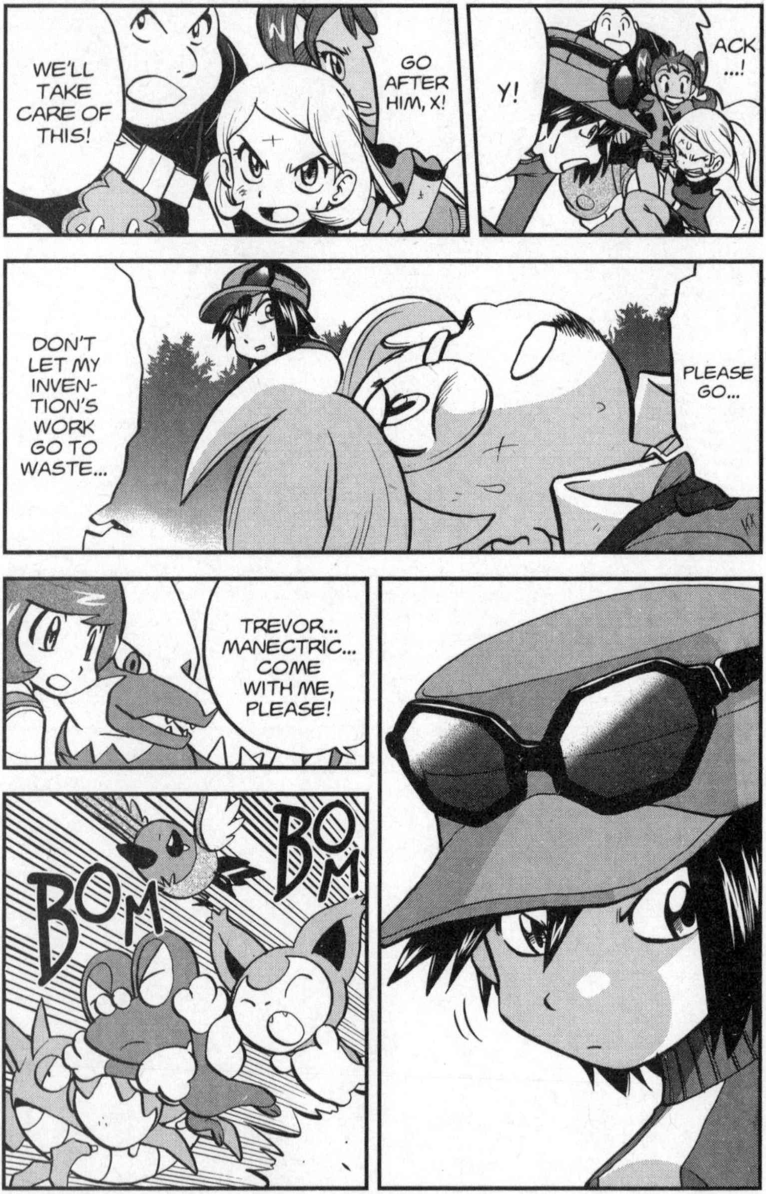
ACK ...!
Y!
GO AFTER HIM, X!
WE'LL TAKE CARE OF THIS!
PLEASE GO...
DON'T LET MY INVEN-TION'S WORK GO TO WASTE...
TREVOR... MANECTRIC... COME WITH ME, PLEASE!
BOM
BOM

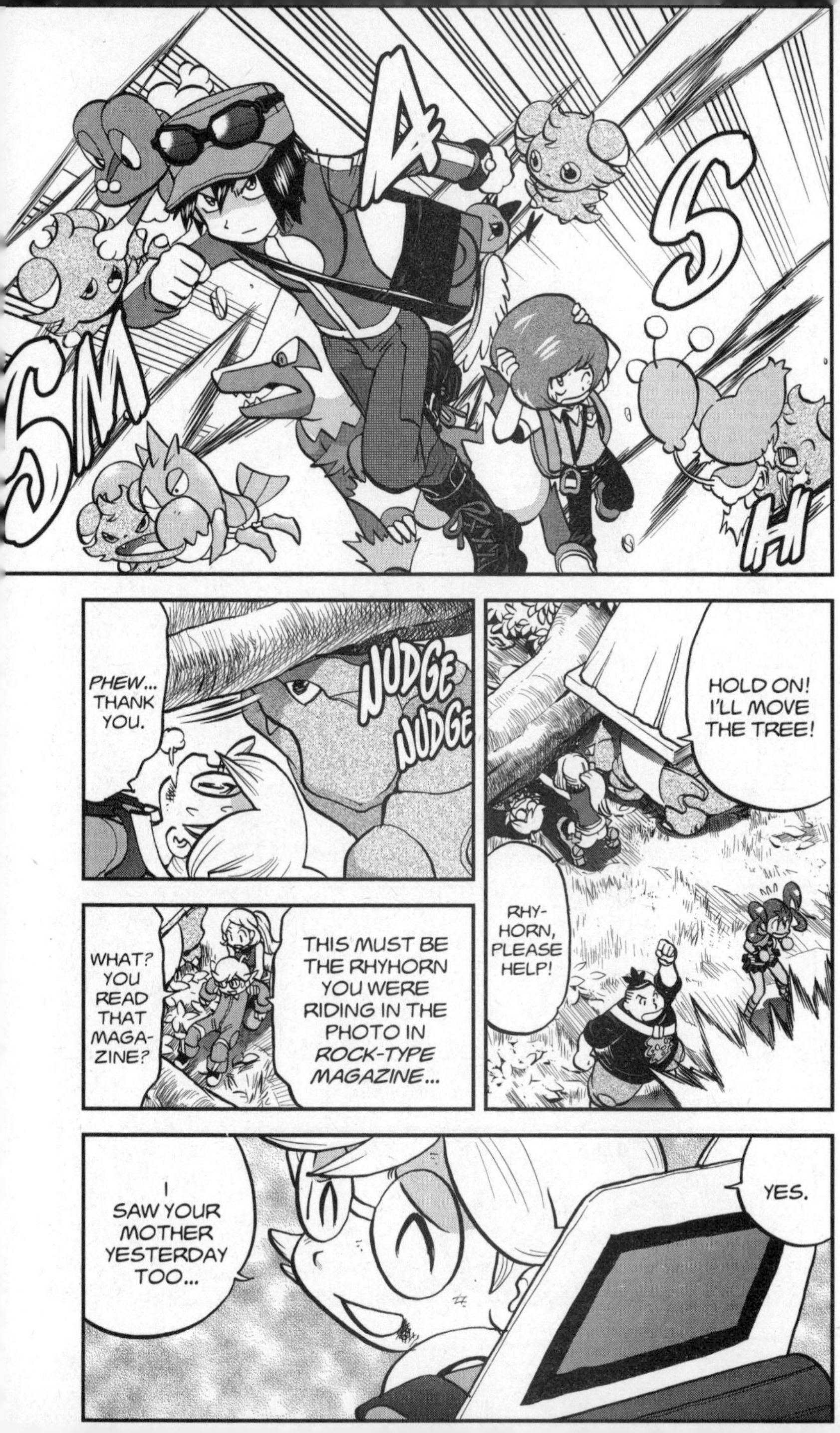
SMASH
HOLD ON! I'LL MOVE THE TREE!
RHY-HORN, PLEASE HELP!
NUDGE NUDGE
PHEW... THANK YOU.
THIS MUST BE THE RHYHORN YOU WERE RIDING IN THE PHOTO IN *ROCK-TYPE MAGAZINE*...
WHAT? YOU READ THAT MAGA-ZINE?
YES.
I SAW YOUR MOTHER YESTERDAY TOO...

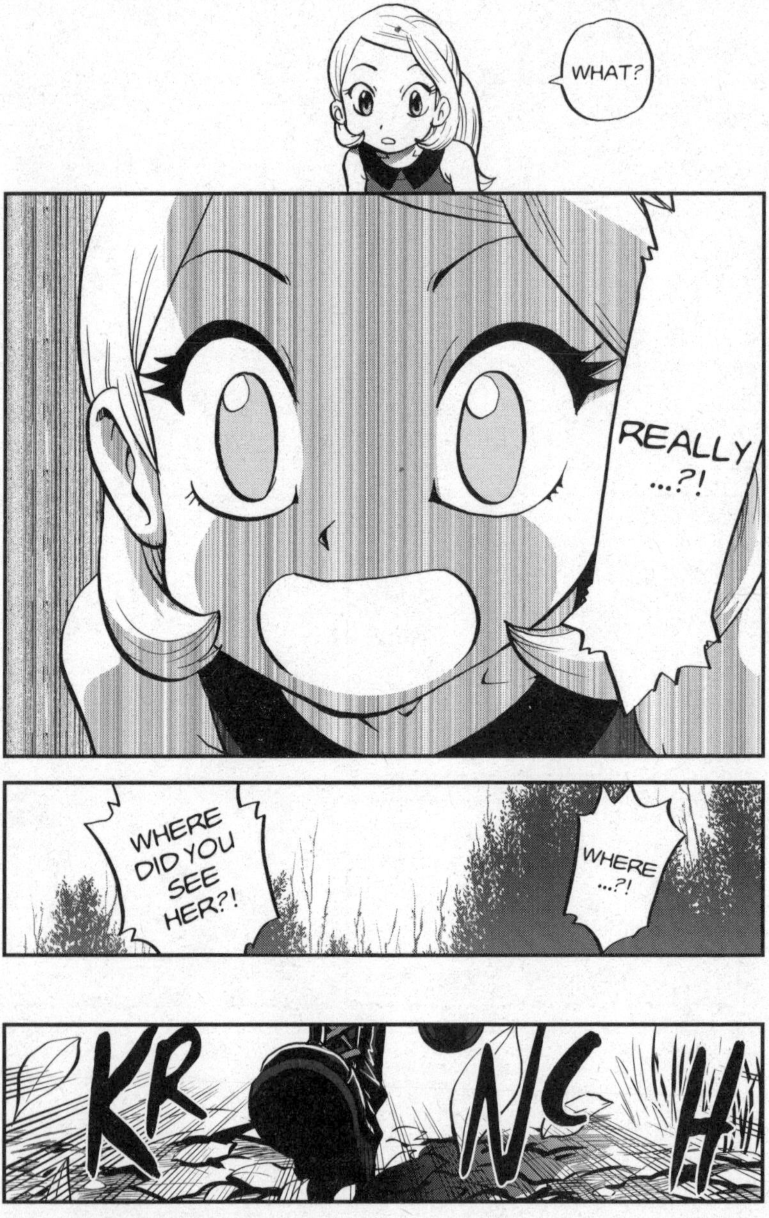
WHAT?
REALLY ...?!
WHERE ...?!
WHERE DID YOU SEE HER?!
KRNCH

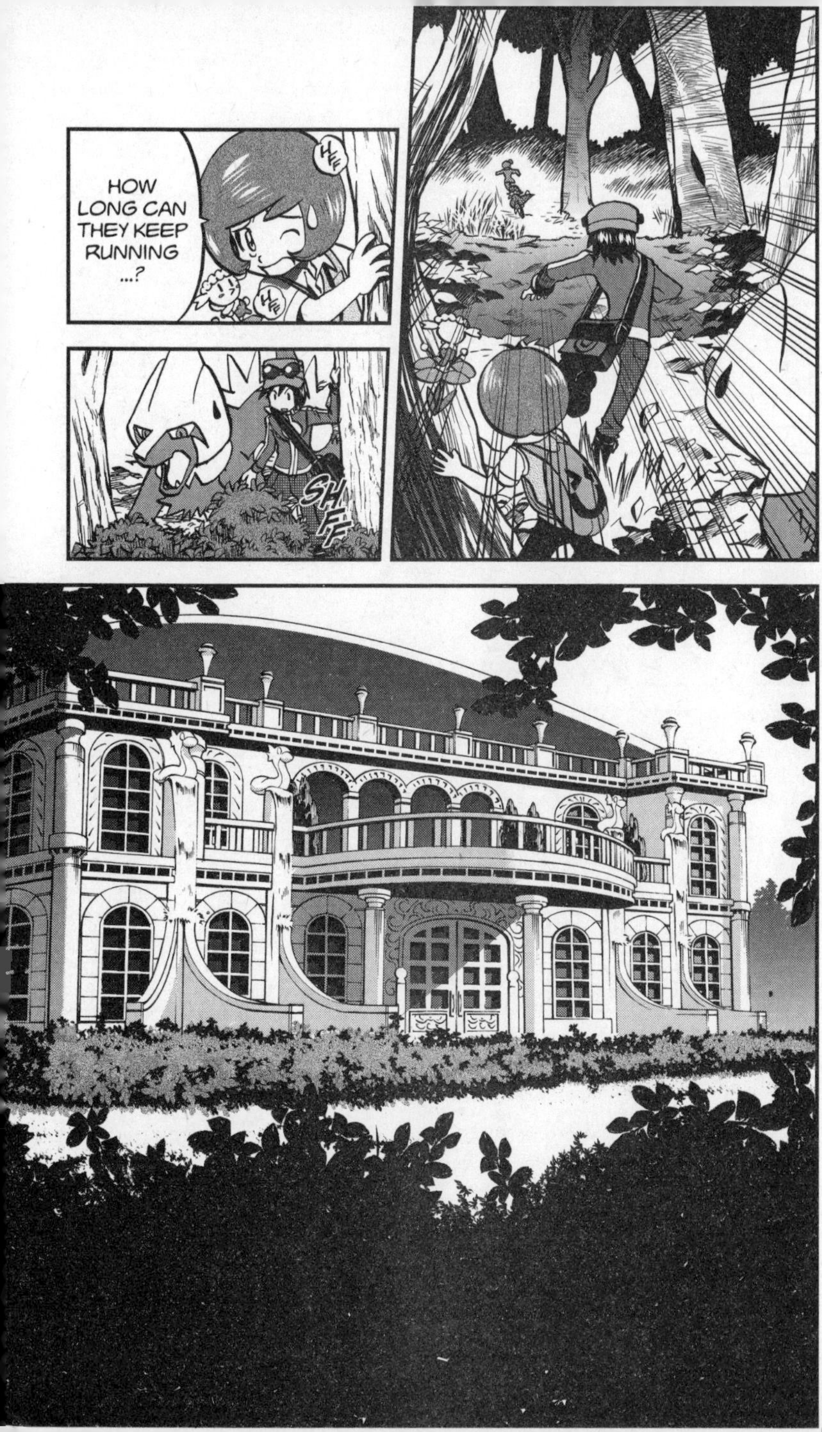
HEFF
HOW LONG CAN THEY KEEP RUNNING ...?
HEFF
SHFF

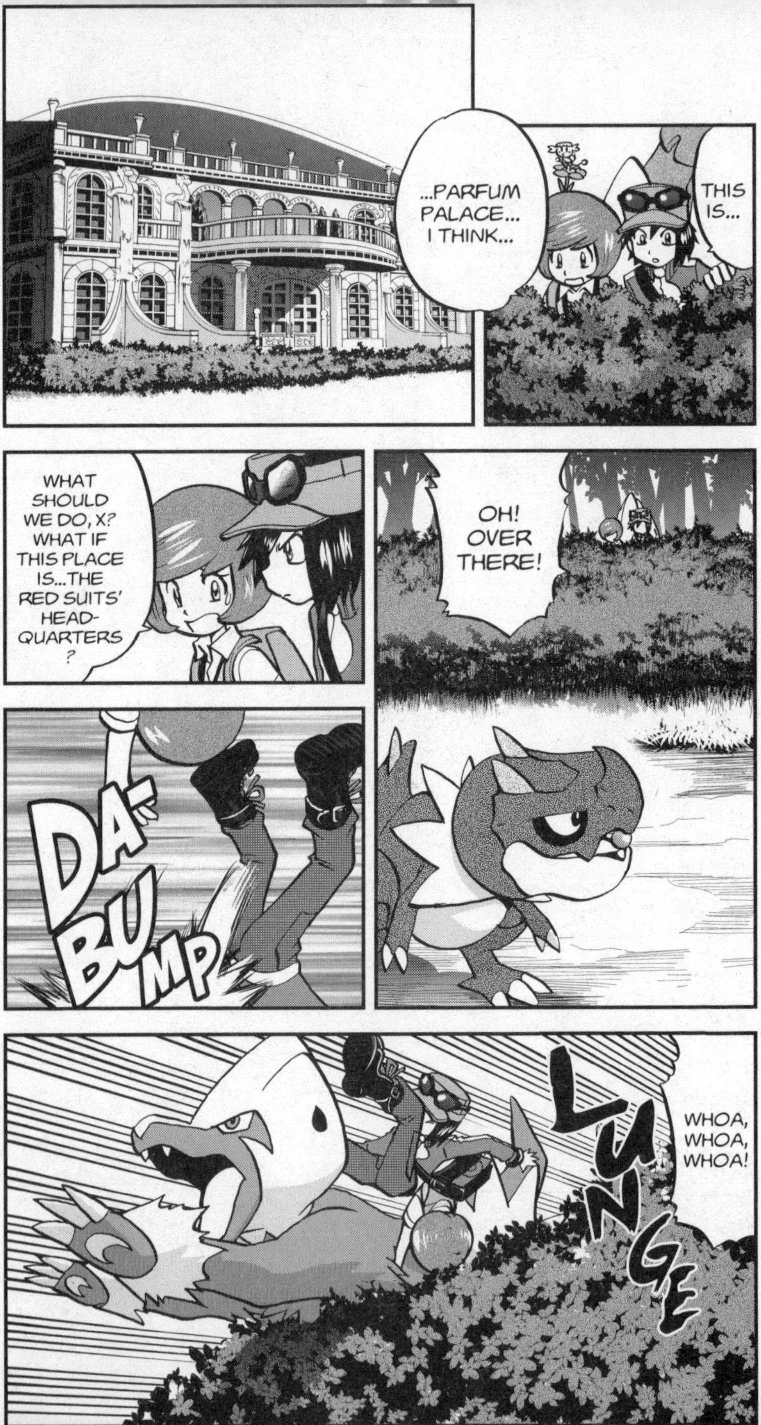
THIS IS...
...PARFUM PALACE... I THINK...
OH! OVER THERE!
WHAT SHOULD WE DO, X? WHAT IF THIS PLACE IS...THE RED SUITS' HEAD-QUARTERS?
DA-BUMP
WHOA, WHOA, WHOA!
LUNGE

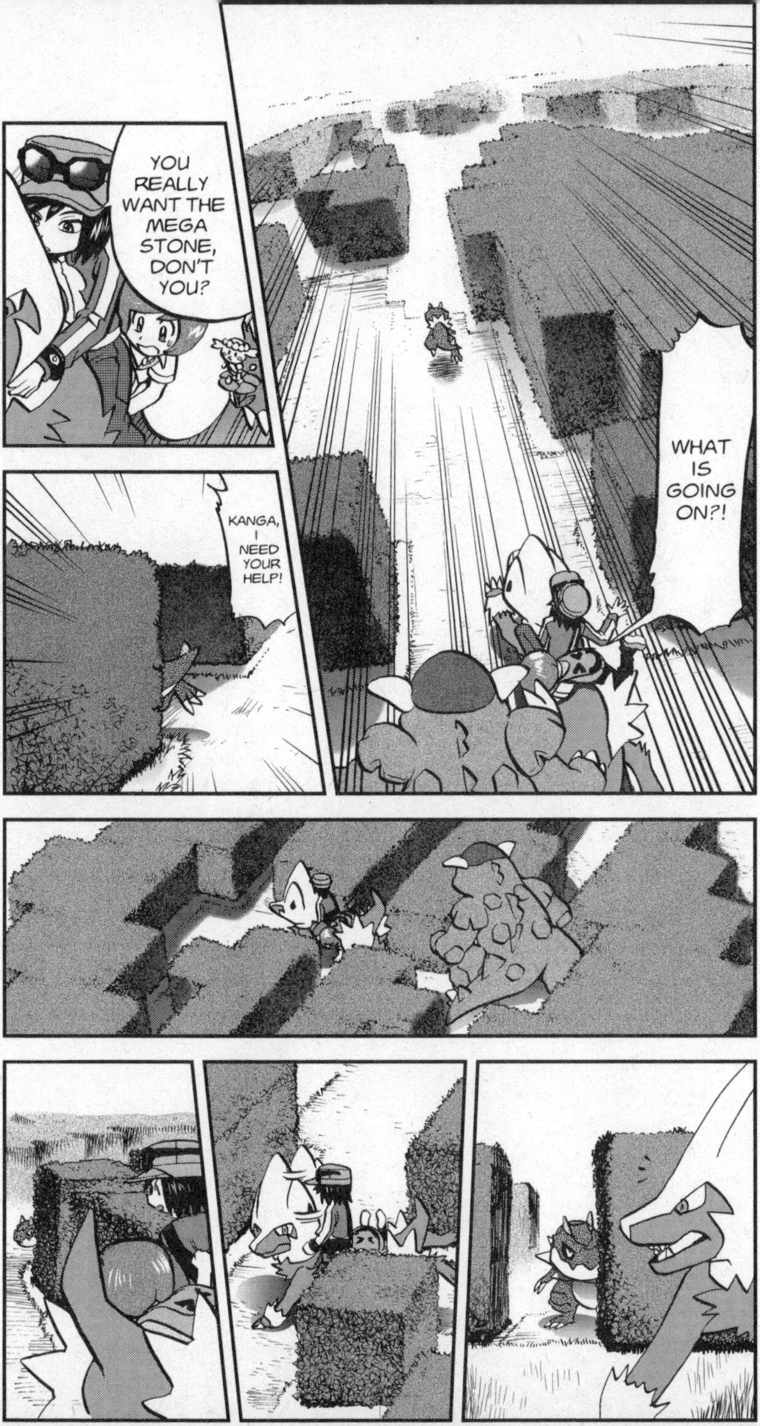
WHAT IS GOING ON?!
YOU REALLY WANT THE MEGA STONE, DON'T YOU?
KANGA, I NEED YOUR HELP!

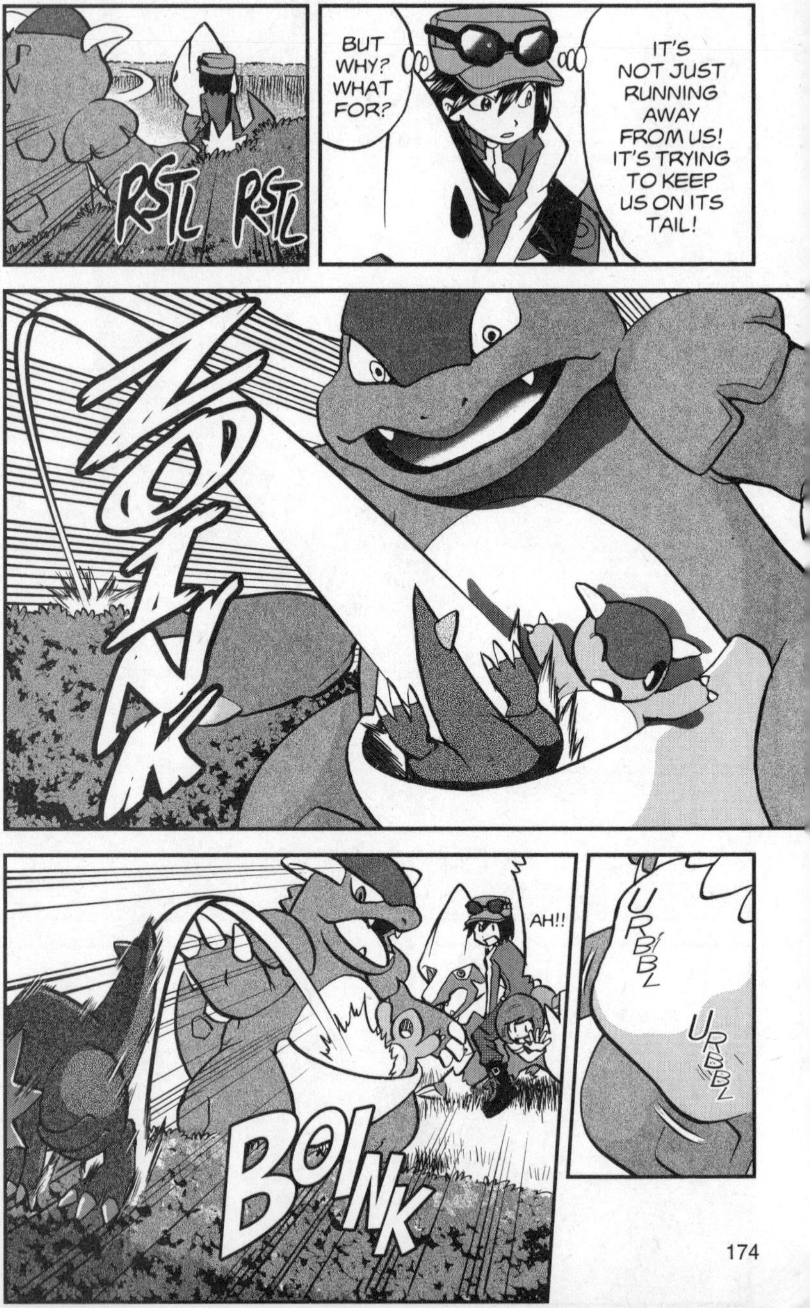
IT'S NOT JUST RUNNING AWAY FROM US! IT'S TRYING TO KEEP US ON ITS TAIL!
BUT WHY? WHAT FOR?
RSTL RSTL
ZOINK
URBBL
URBBL
AH!!
BOINK

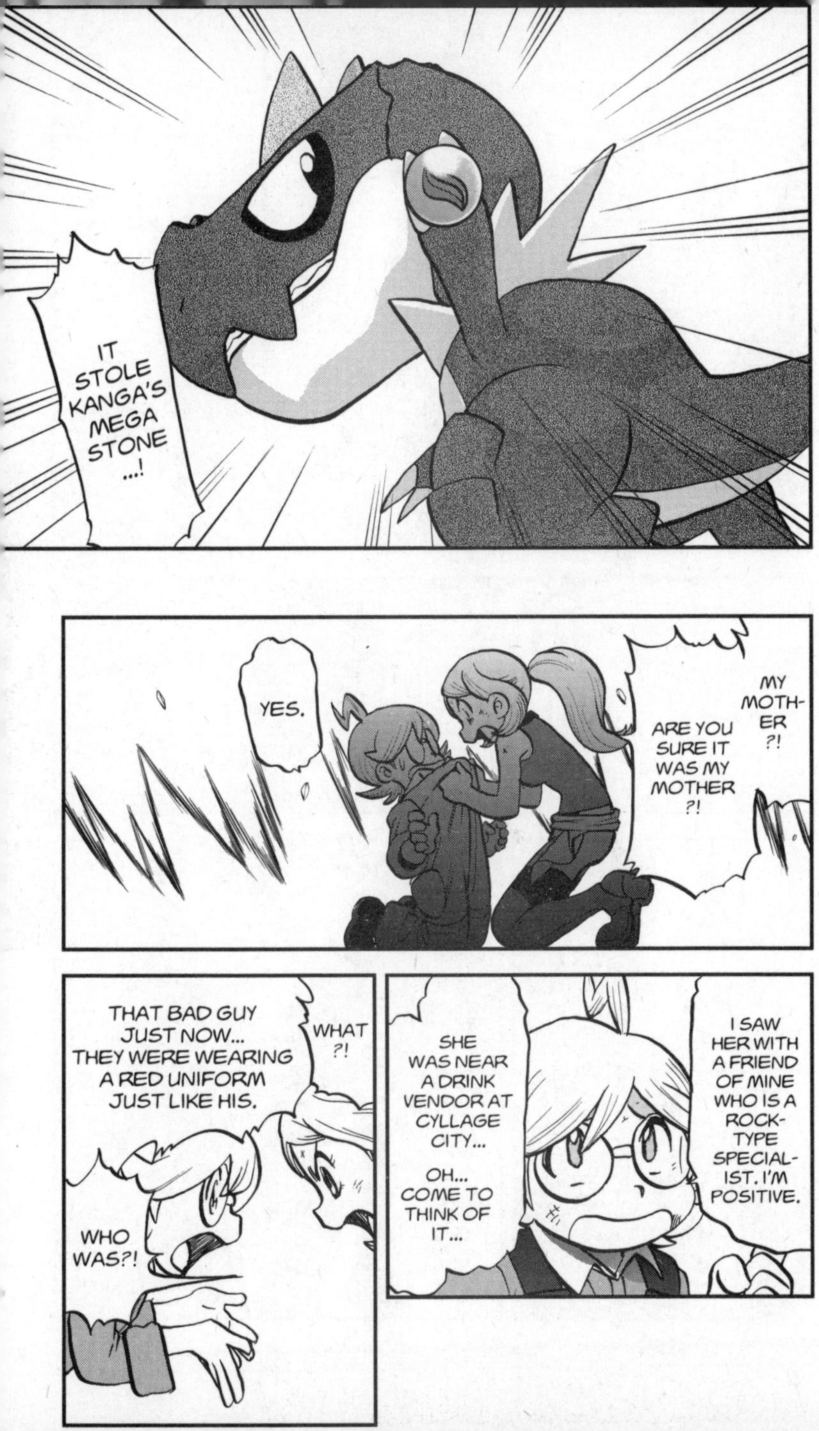
IT STOLE KANGA'S MEGA STONE ...!
MY MOTHER?!
ARE YOU SURE IT WAS MY MOTHER?!
YES.
I SAW HER WITH A FRIEND OF MINE WHO IS A ROCK-TYPE SPECIALIST. I'M POSITIVE.
SHE WAS NEAR A DRINK VENDOR AT CYLLAGE CITY...
OH... COME TO THINK OF IT...
WHAT?!
THAT BAD GUY JUST NOW... THEY WERE WEARING A RED UNIFORM JUST LIKE HIS.
WHO WAS?!

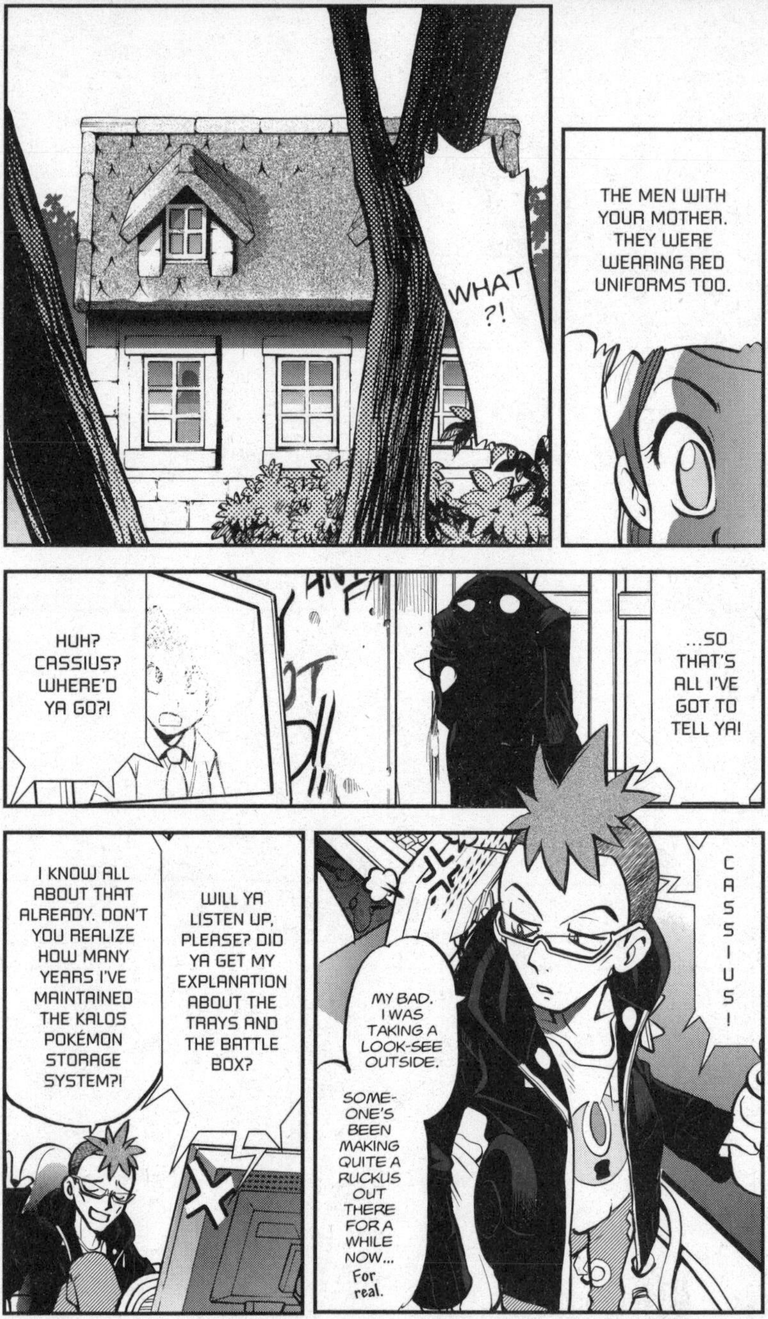
THE MEN WITH YOUR MOTHER. THEY WERE WEARING RED UNIFORMS TOO.
WHAT ?!
...SO THAT'S ALL I'VE GOT TO TELL YA!
HUH? CASSIUS? WHERE'D YA GO?!
CASSIUS!
MY BAD. I WAS TAKING A LOOK-SEE OUTSIDE.
SOME-ONE'S BEEN MAKING QUITE A RUCKUS OUT THERE FOR A WHILE NOW... For real.
WILL YA LISTEN UP, PLEASE? DID YA GET MY EXPLANATION ABOUT THE TRAYS AND THE BATTLE BOX?
I KNOW ALL ABOUT THAT ALREADY. DON'T YOU REALIZE HOW MANY YEARS I'VE MAINTAINED THE KALOS POKÉMON STORAGE SYSTEM?!

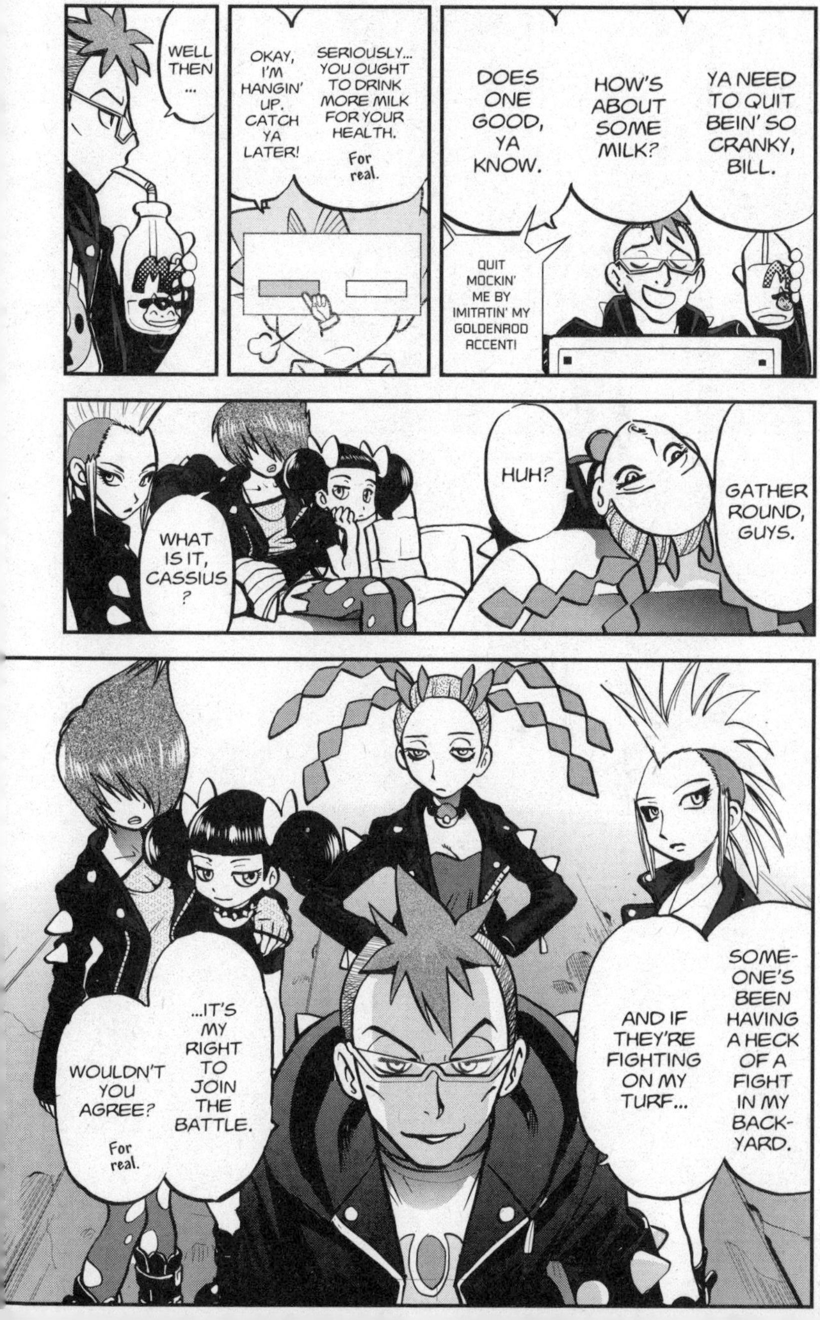
YA NEED TO QUIT BEIN' SO CRANKY, BILL.
HOW'S ABOUT SOME MILK?
DOES ONE GOOD, YA KNOW.
QUIT MOCKIN' ME BY IMITATIN' MY GOLDENROD ACCENT!
SERIOUSLY... YOU OUGHT TO DRINK MORE MILK FOR YOUR HEALTH.
For real.
OKAY, I'M HANGIN' UP. CATCH YA LATER!
WELL THEN ...
GATHER ROUND, GUYS.
HUH?
WHAT IS IT, CASSIUS?
SOMEONE'S BEEN HAVING A HECK OF A FIGHT IN MY BACKYARD.
AND IF THEY'RE FIGHTING ON MY TURF...
...IT'S MY RIGHT TO JOIN THE BATTLE.
WOULDN'T YOU AGREE?
For real.

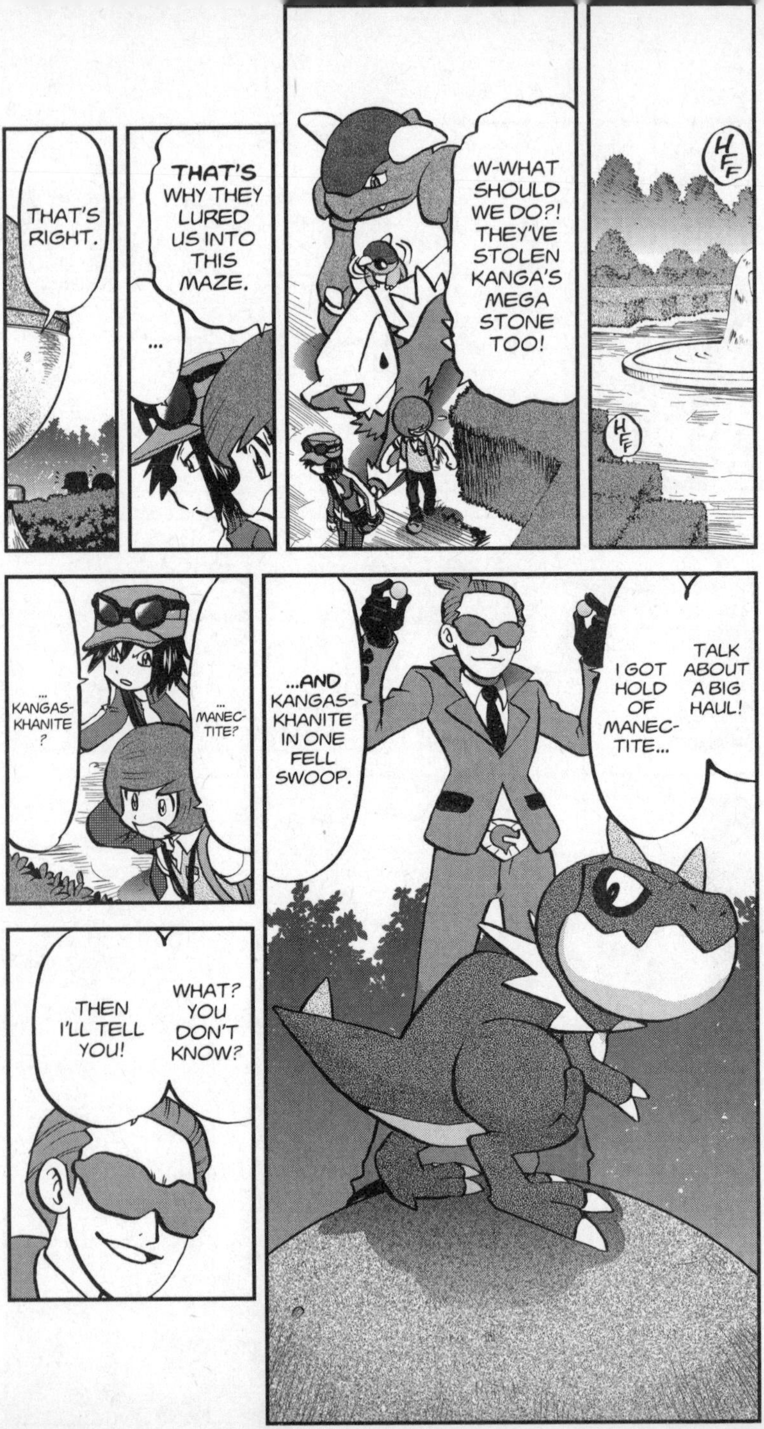
HFF
HFF
W-WHAT SHOULD WE DO?! THEY'VE STOLEN KANGA'S MEGA STONE TOO!
THAT'S WHY THEY LURED US INTO THIS MAZE.
...
THAT'S RIGHT.
TALK ABOUT A BIG HAUL!
I GOT HOLD OF MANEC-TITE...
...AND KANGAS-KHANITE IN ONE FELL SWOOP.
... MANEC-TITE?
... KANGAS-KHANITE?
WHAT? YOU DON'T KNOW?
THEN I'LL TELL YOU!

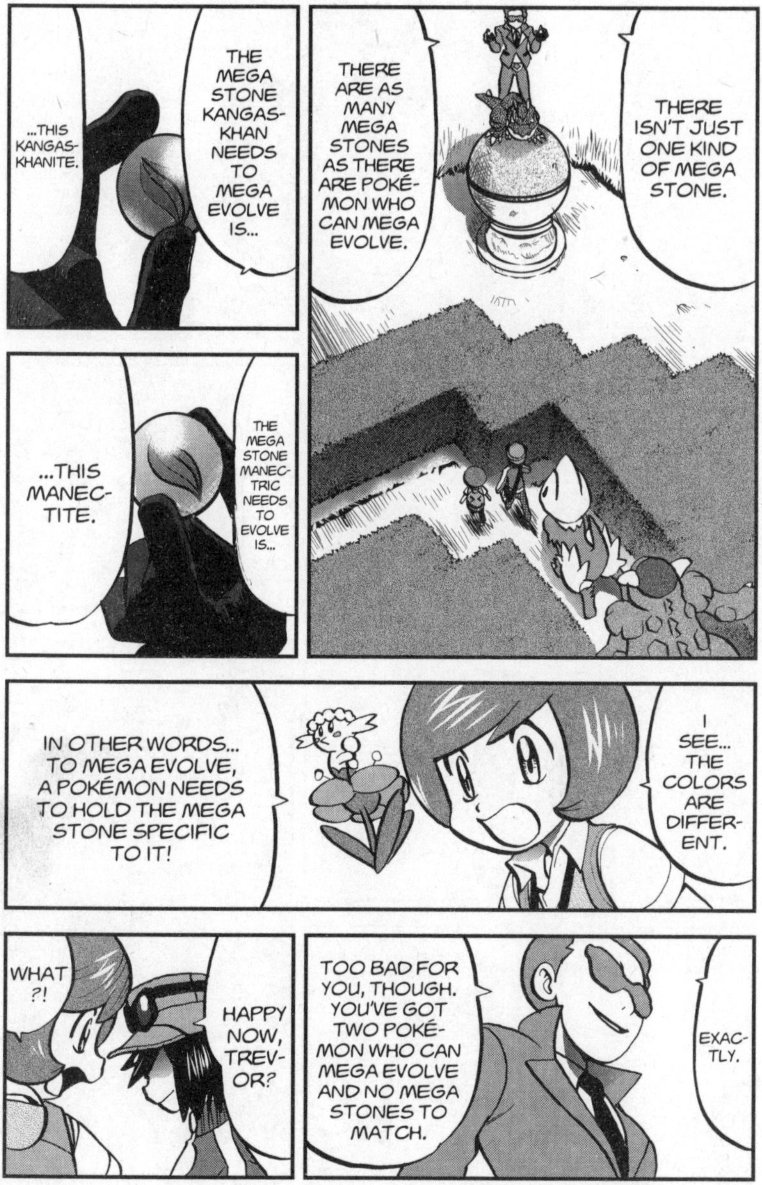
THERE ISN'T JUST ONE KIND OF MEGA STONE.
THERE ARE AS MANY MEGA STONES AS THERE ARE POKÉMON WHO CAN MEGA EVOLVE.
THE MEGA STONE KANGASKHAN NEEDS TO MEGA EVOLVE IS...
...THIS KANGASKHANITE.
THE MEGA STONE MANECTRIC NEEDS TO EVOLVE IS...
...THIS MANECTITE.
I SEE... THE COLORS ARE DIFFERENT.
IN OTHER WORDS... TO MEGA EVOLVE, A POKÉMON NEEDS TO HOLD THE MEGA STONE SPECIFIC TO IT!
EXACTLY.
TOO BAD FOR YOU, THOUGH. YOU'VE GOT TWO POKÉMON WHO CAN MEGA EVOLVE AND NO MEGA STONES TO MATCH.
HAPPY NOW, TREVOR?
WHAT?!

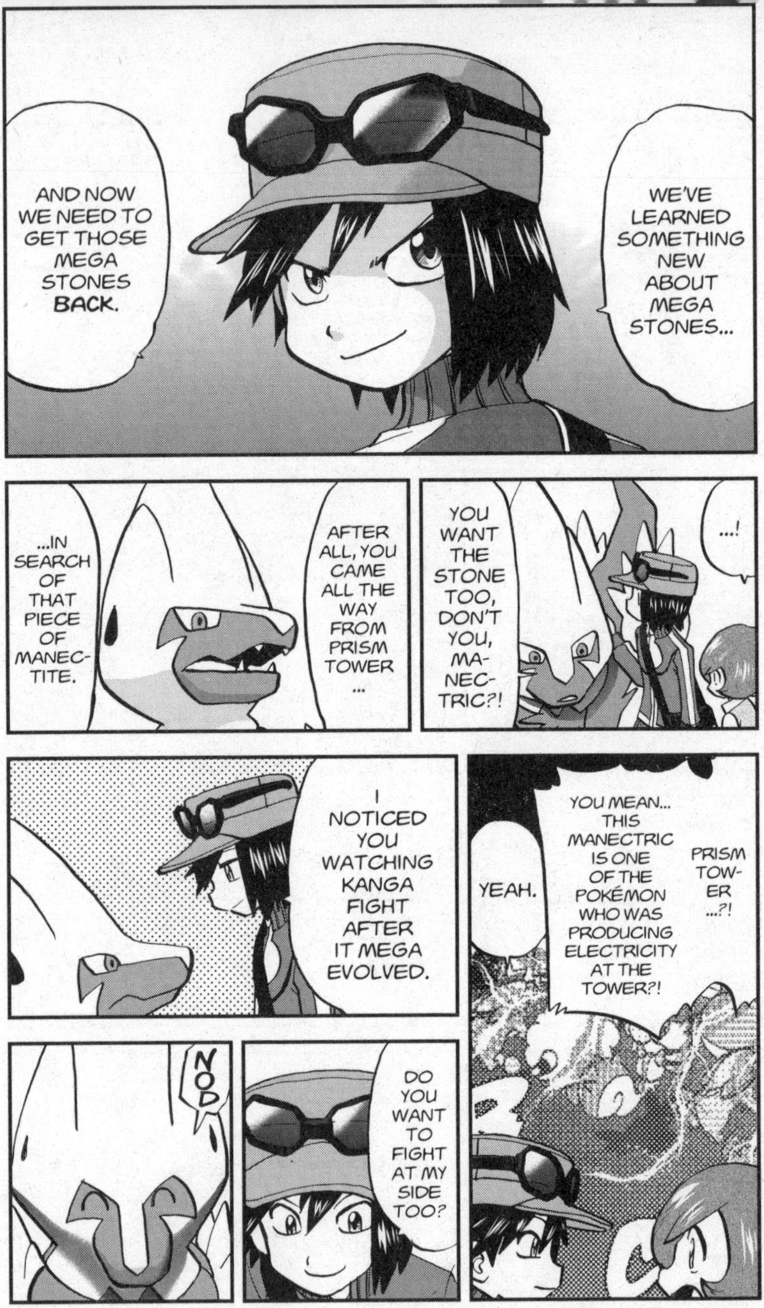
WE'VE LEARNED SOMETHING NEW ABOUT MEGA STONES...
AND NOW WE NEED TO GET THOSE MEGA STONES **BACK.**
...!
YOU WANT THE STONE TOO, DON'T YOU, MANECTRIC?!
AFTER ALL, YOU CAME ALL THE WAY FROM PRISM TOWER...
...IN SEARCH OF THAT PIECE OF MANECTITE.
PRISM TOWER...?!
YOU MEAN... THIS MANECTRIC IS ONE OF THE POKÉMON WHO WAS PRODUCING ELECTRICITY AT THE TOWER?!
YEAH.
I NOTICED YOU WATCHING KANGA FIGHT AFTER IT MEGA EVOLVED.
DO YOU WANT TO FIGHT AT MY SIDE TOO?
NOD

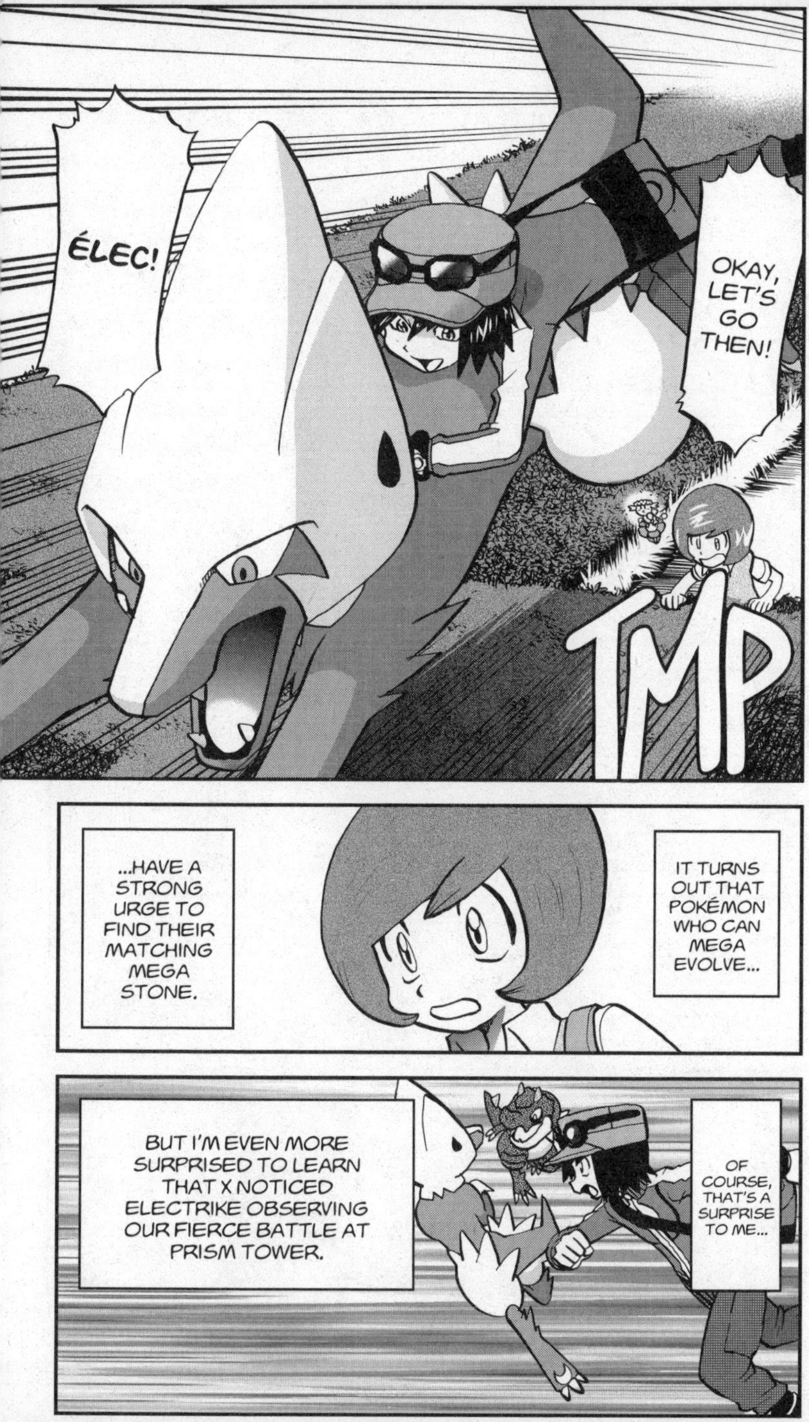
OKAY, LET'S GO THEN!
ÉLEC!
TMP
IT TURNS OUT THAT POKÉMON WHO CAN MEGA EVOLVE...
...HAVE A STRONG URGE TO FIND THEIR MATCHING MEGA STONE.
OF COURSE, THAT'S A SURPRISE TO ME...
BUT I'M EVEN MORE SURPRISED TO LEARN THAT X NOTICED ELECTRIKE OBSERVING OUR FIERCE BATTLE AT PRISM TOWER.

COME TO THINK OF IT, THERE HAVE BEEN A LOT OF MOMENTS DURING THIS JOURNEY WHEN X'S HUNCHES HAVE PROVED RIGHT!
AND I THINK I KNOW WHY!
X LOCKED HIMSELF IN HIS ROOM AND BROKE OFF CONTACT WITH THE OUTSIDE WORLD AND PEOPLE FOR A LONG TIME.
HIS LIFE WAS DEVOID OF STIMULATION...
...WHICH LED TO AN ALREADY SENSITIVE PERSON...
...BECOMING **EXTRA** SENSITIVE.
SIGHT, HEARING, SMELL, TASTE, TOUCH...
HIS FIVE SENSES MUST HAVE BEEN AMPLIFIED!
X HAS BEEN SKILLED AT POKÉMON BATTLES SINCE HE WAS A LITTLE KID.
HE'S ALWAYS HAD EXCELLENT OBSERVATION SKILLS, INSIGHT, JUDGMENT AND THE ABILITY TO THINK ON HIS FEET.

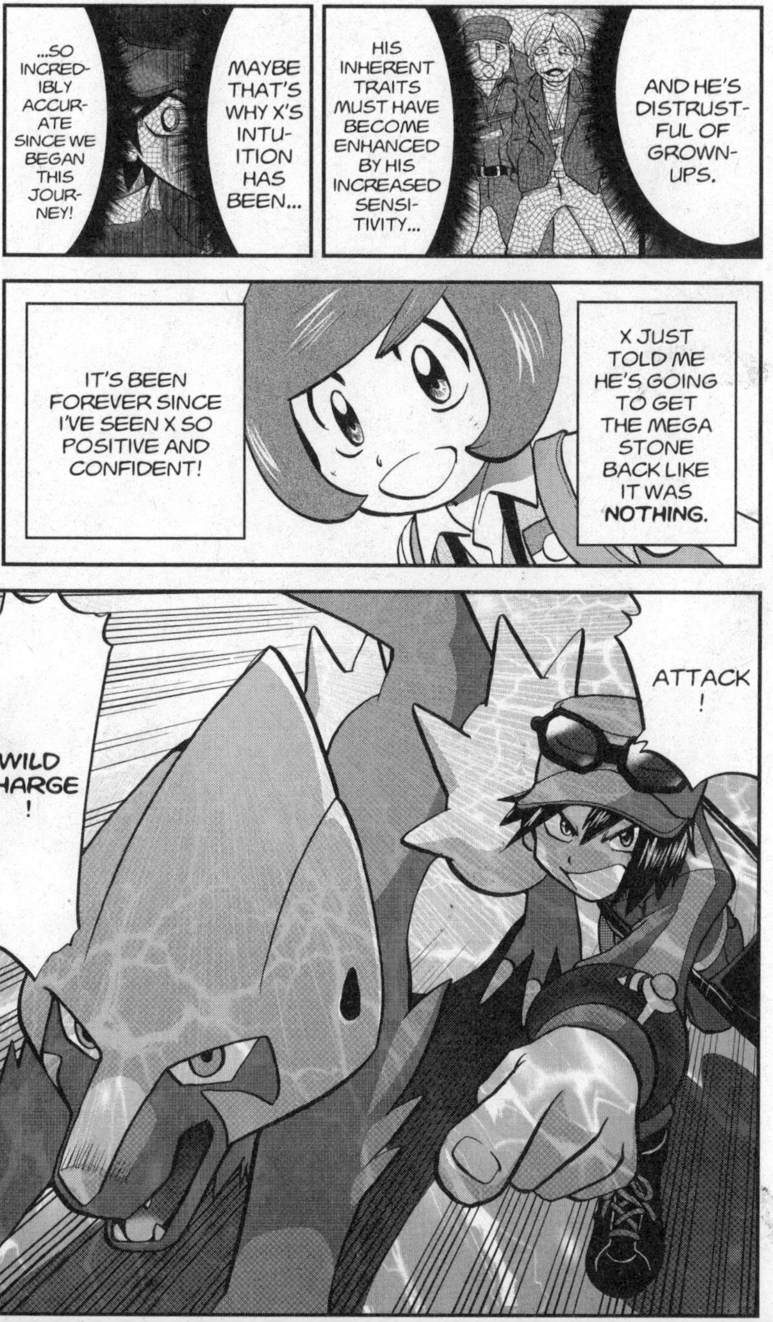
AND HE'S DISTRUSTFUL OF GROWN-UPS.
HIS INHERENT TRAITS MUST HAVE BECOME ENHANCED BY HIS INCREASED SENSITIVITY...
MAYBE THAT'S WHY X'S INTUITION HAS BEEN...
...SO INCREDIBLY ACCURATE SINCE WE BEGAN THIS JOURNEY!
X JUST TOLD ME HE'S GOING TO GET THE MEGA STONE BACK LIKE IT WAS **NOTHING.**
IT'S BEEN FOREVER SINCE I'VE SEEN X SO POSITIVE AND CONFIDENT!
ATTACK!
**WILD CHARGE!**

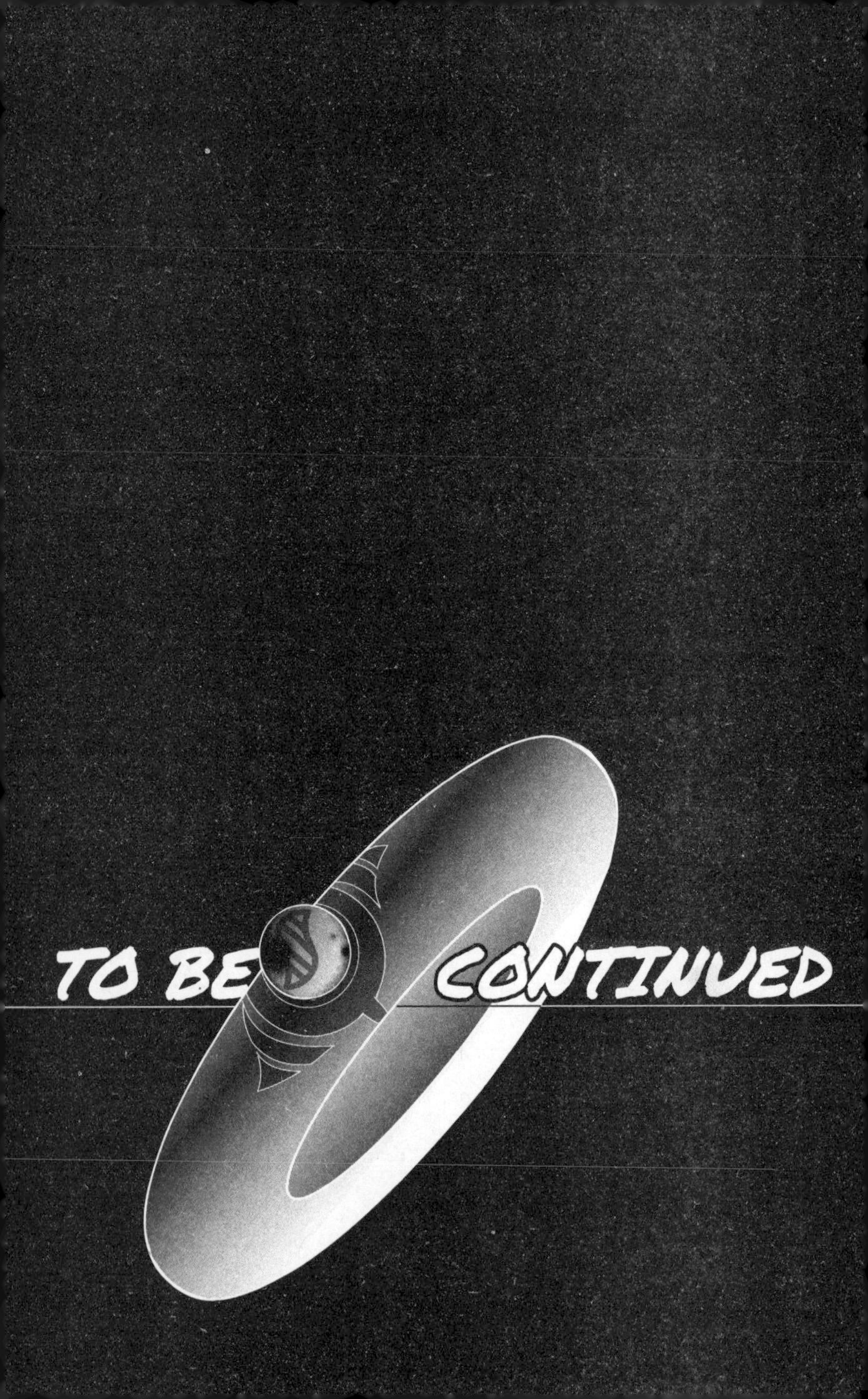
TO BE CONTINUED

#  ILLUSTRATION COLLECTION

Presenting title page illustrations
originally drawn for some of the
chapters of *Pokémon Adventures: X·Y*
when they were first published in
Japanese children's magazines *Pokémon
Fan Magazine* and *Coro Coro Ichiban!*

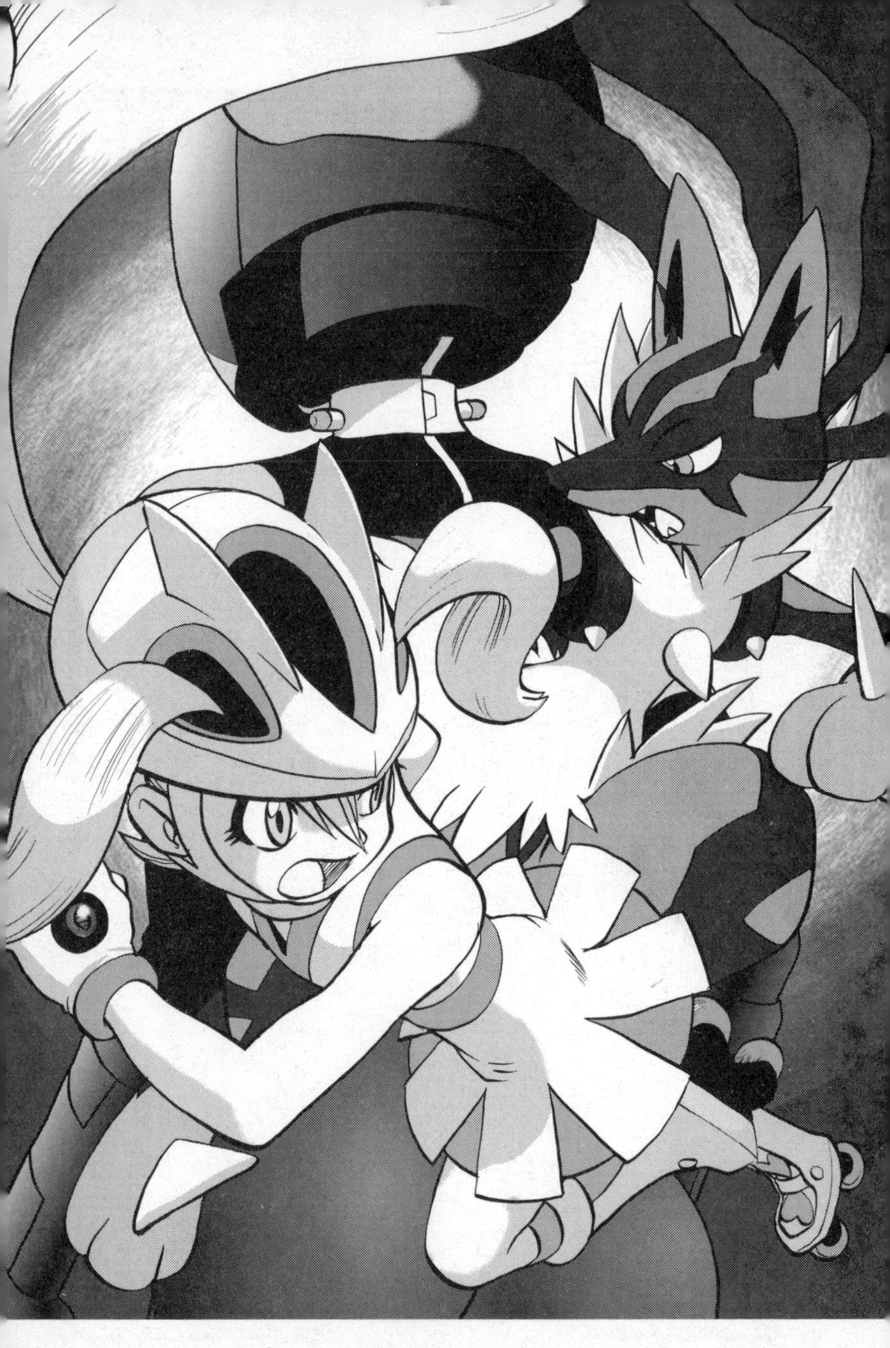

Adventure 12, *Pokémon Fan Magazine*, Issue 35

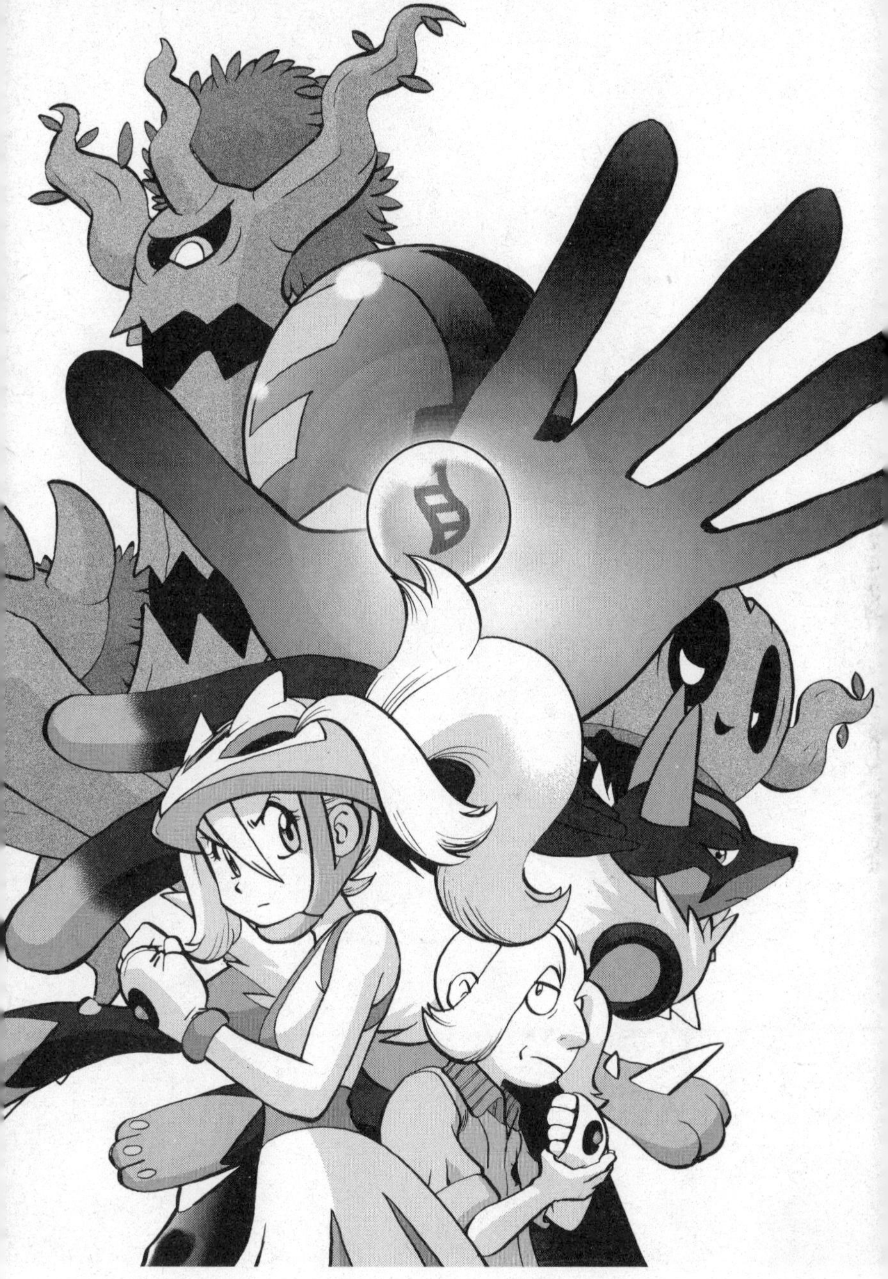

Adventure 13, *Pokémon Fan Magazine*, Issue 36

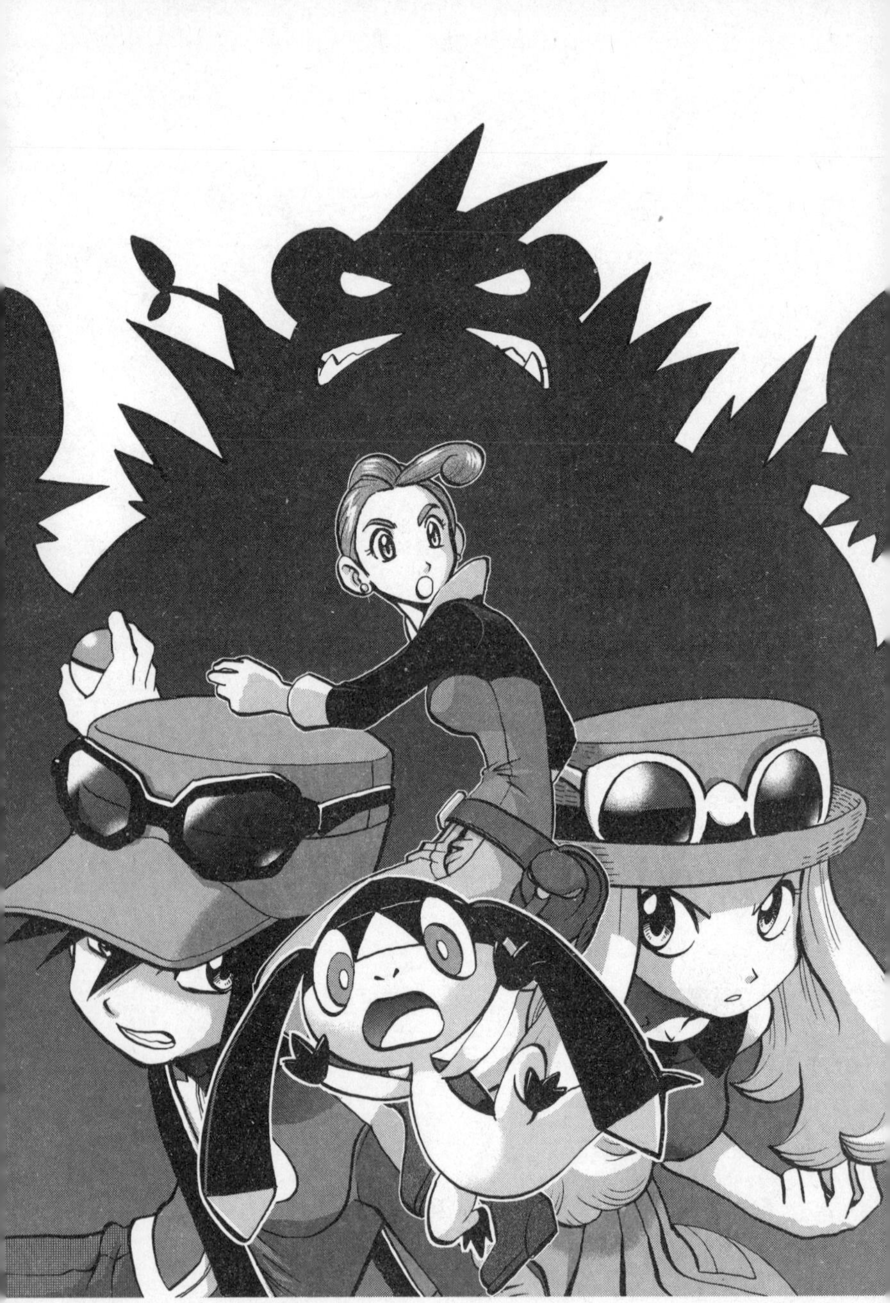

Adventure 14, *Coro Coro Ichiban!*, August 2014 Issue

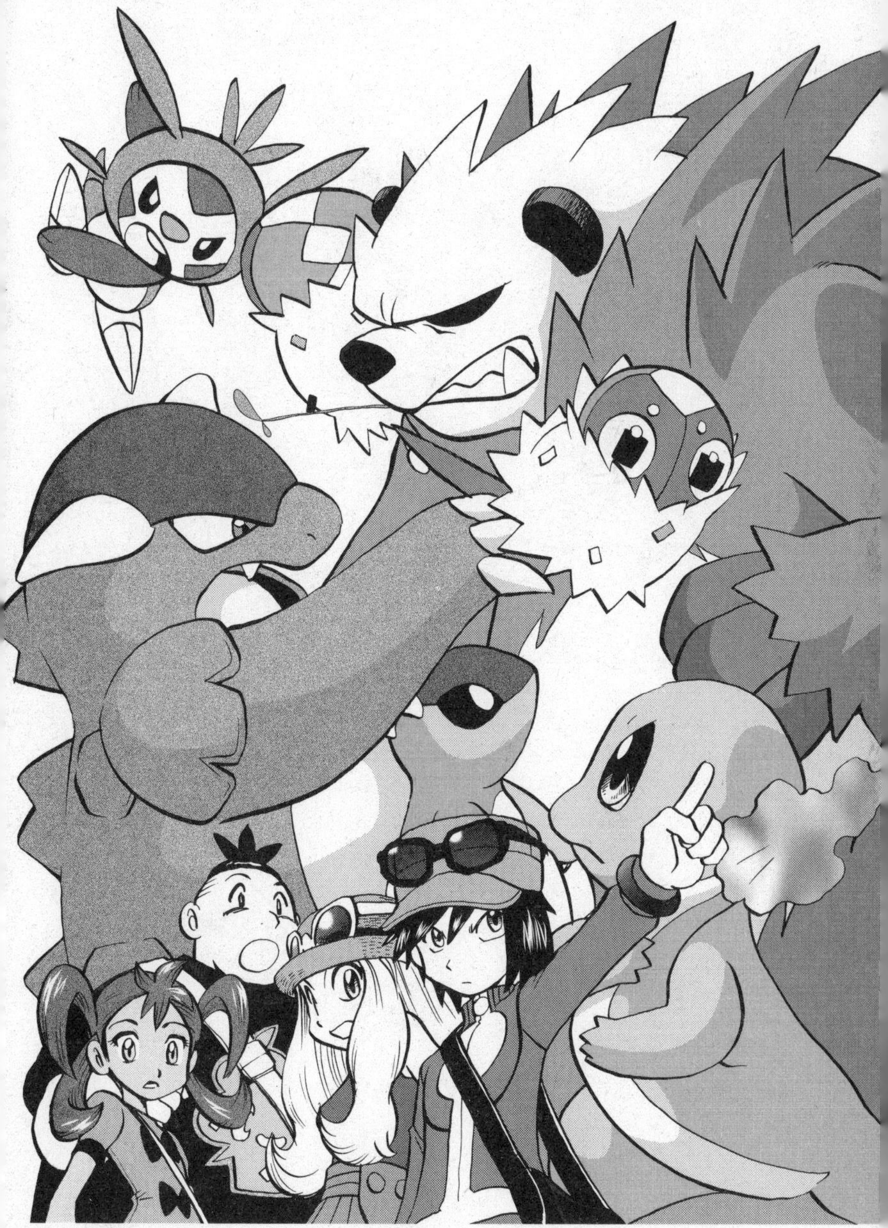

Adventure 15, *Coro Coro Ichiban!*, September 2014 Issue

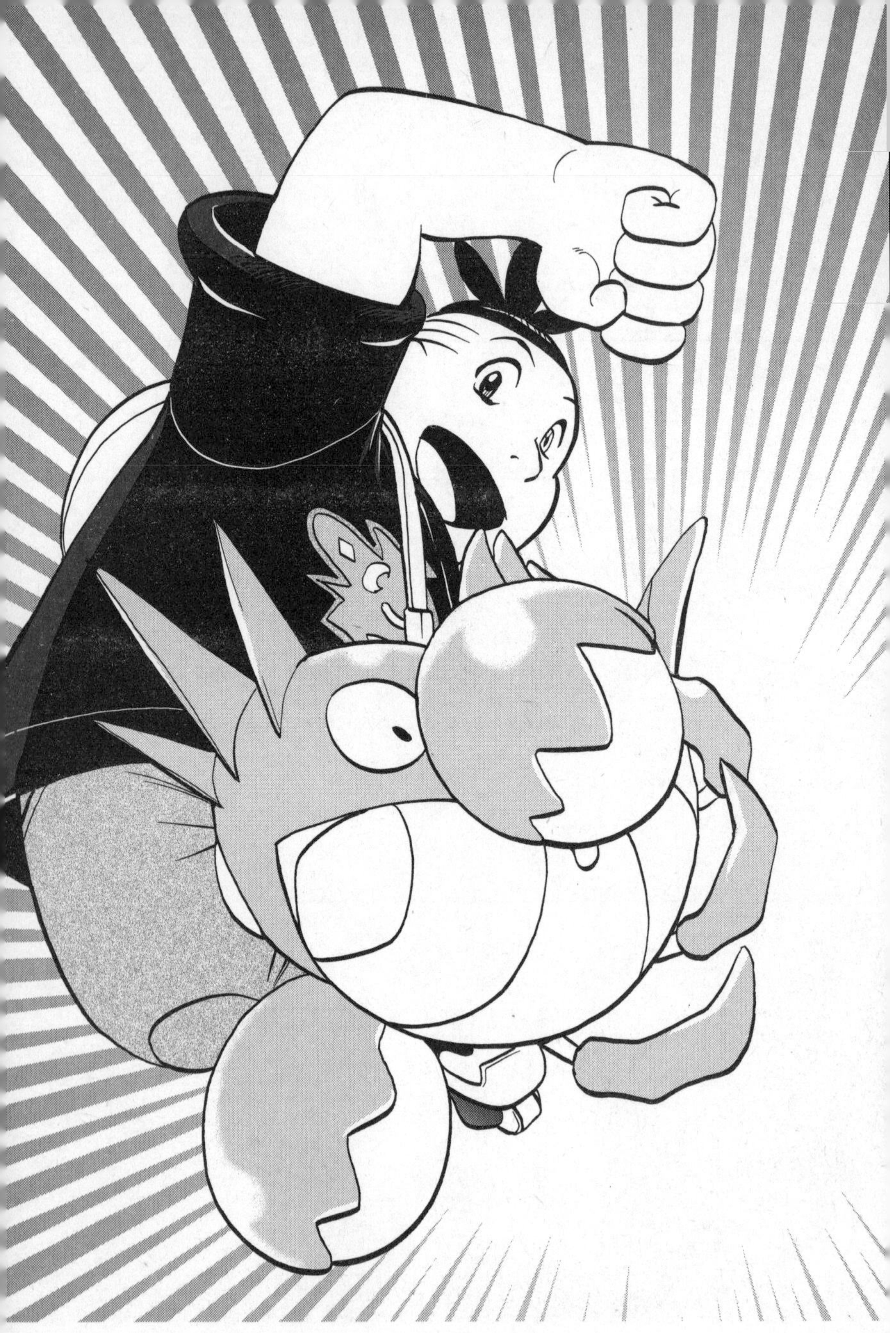

Adventure 16, *Pokémon Fan Magazine*, Issue 38

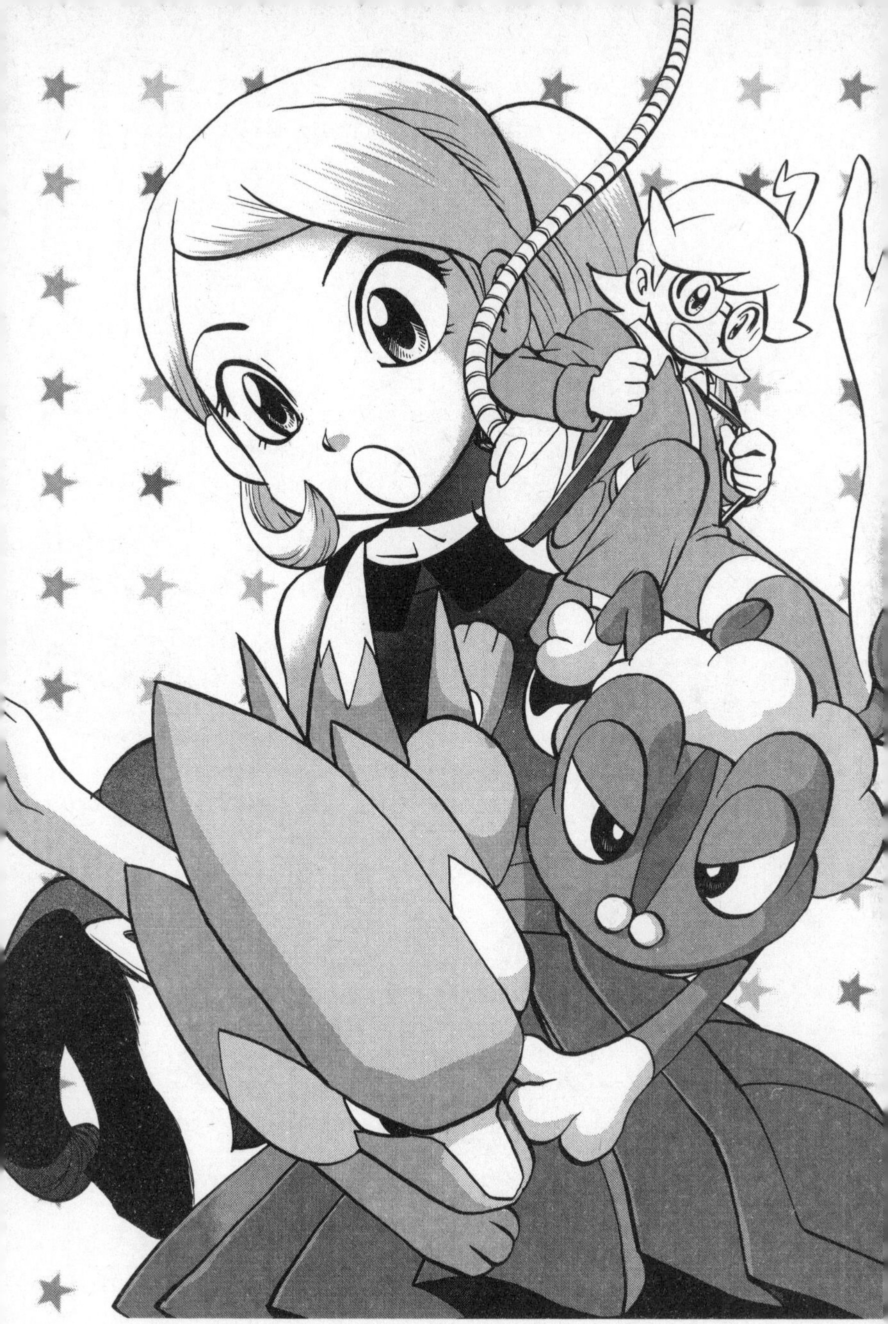

Adventure 17, *Coro Coro Ichiban!*, October 2014 Issue

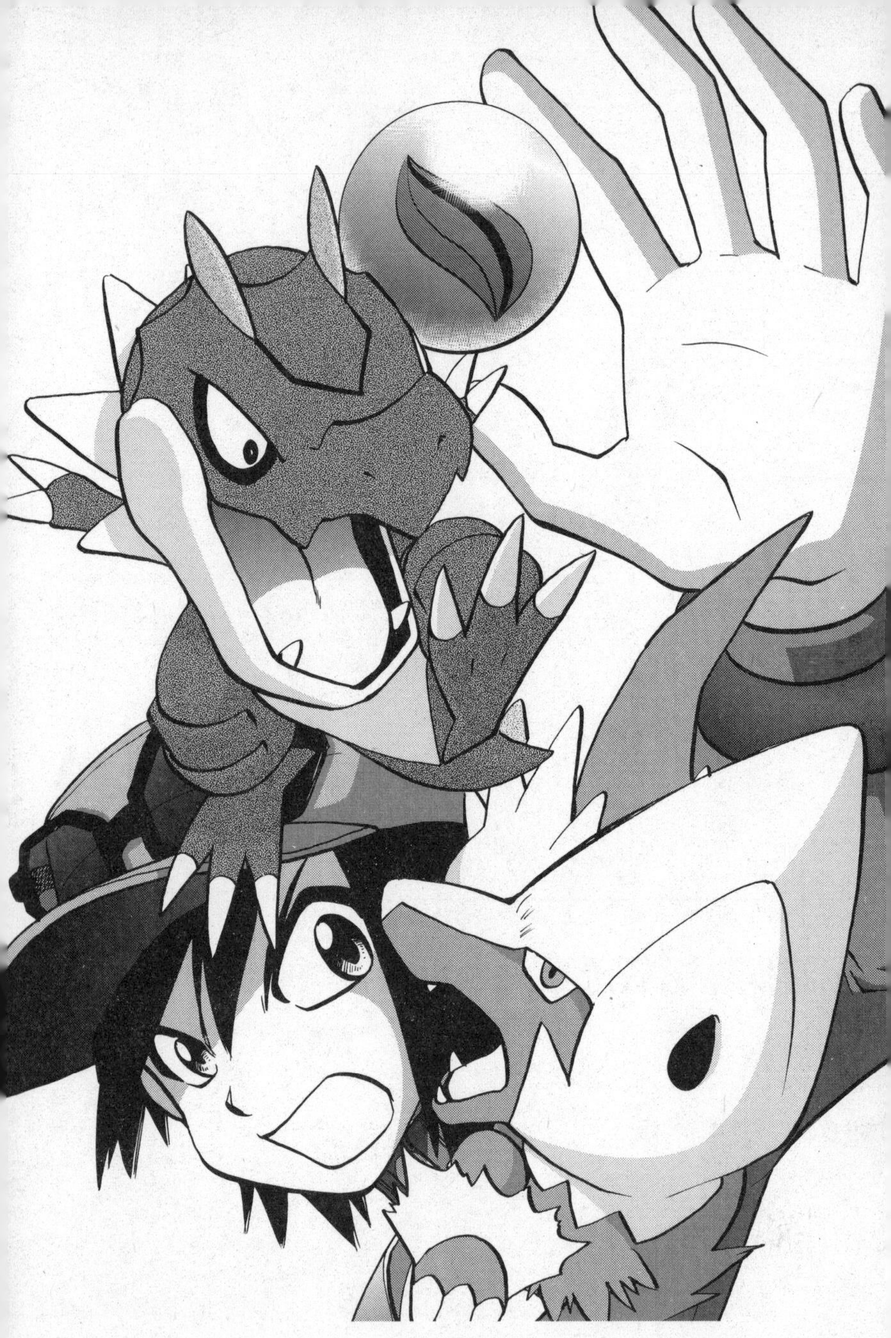

Adventure 18, *Coro Coro Ichiban!*, November 2014 Issue

# Trevor's Notes

◆ **Current Data** ◆

We met a man who was ordered to gather the Mega Stones near Camphrier Town and discovered two things.

Man gathering the Mega Stones

## 1

There is more than one type of Mega Stone. There are as many Mega Stones as the number of Pokémon who can Mega Evolve.

◆ ◆ ◆ ◆

The first thing we discovered were the types of the Mega Stones. "Mega Stone" is a generic term and each stone had a name of their own!

● Mega Stone for Kangaskhan

Kangaskhanite

▲ Yellow with a red and blue pattern inside. Élec sensed its presence and searched for it.

◆ ◆ ◆ ◆ ◆ ◆ ◆ ◆

● Mega Stone for Manectric

Manectite

▲ Discovered in Kanga's pouch. It is yellow with a purple pattern inside.

◆ ◆ ◆ ◆

## 2

The enemy has a list of Pokémon that can Mega Evolve.

◆ ◆ ◆ ◆

Secondly, we discovered that Team Flare has a clear idea on how many Pokémon can Mega Evolve.

| | |
|---|---|
| Manectric | ⑤ Kangaskh |
| Kangaskhan | ⑤ Gyaradosit |
| Gyarados | ⑤ Gardevoir |
| Gardevoir | ⑤ Banettite |
| Banette | ⑤ Medicha |
| Medicham | ⑤ Scizori |
| Scizor | ⑤ Alaka |
| Alakazam | ⑤ Aero |
| Aerodactyl | ⑤ Hou |

▲ The enemy has accurate information at their disposal. This is a frightful situation.

---

## 【 Parfum Palace 】 ✕／✕ ◆ ◆ ◆ ◆

A fierce battle for the Mega Stone. The battle against Tyrunt is still ongoing. Let's hope for Élec to awaken to its power.

## 【 Prism Tower Incident 】 ✕／□ ◆ ◆ ◆ ◆

Viola's elder sister, Alexa, was attacked by the Editor-in-Chief. It was terrible to discover that even the media was under the influence of the Red Suits. What will happen next...?

# 12th Arc – Pokédex Holder Pokémon Data (As of Adventure 18)

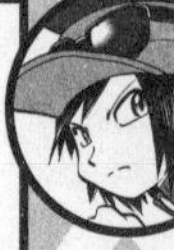

## X's Pokémon

X is a Trainer with the Mega Ring. He has a powerful team centered around Kanga.

### Kanga & Li'l Kanga
(Kangaskhan ♀)

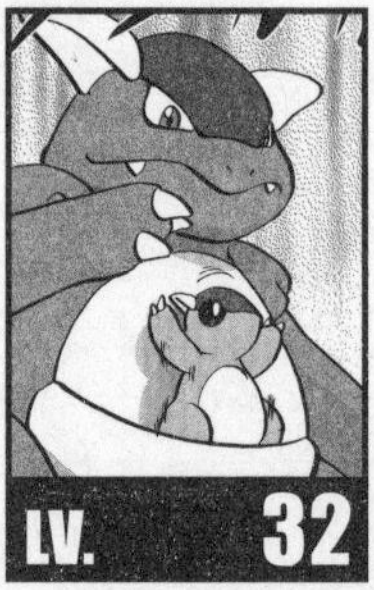
LV. 32

- Coastal Kalos Pokédex: No. 062
- Type: Normal
- Height: 7'03"
- Weight: 176.4 lbs
- Ability: Scrappy
- Nature: Bold
- Characteristic: Very finicky

A Pokémon that X has been together with since childhood. Li'l Kanga will jump out to fight together when it Mega Evolves!

### Marisso
(Chespin ♂)

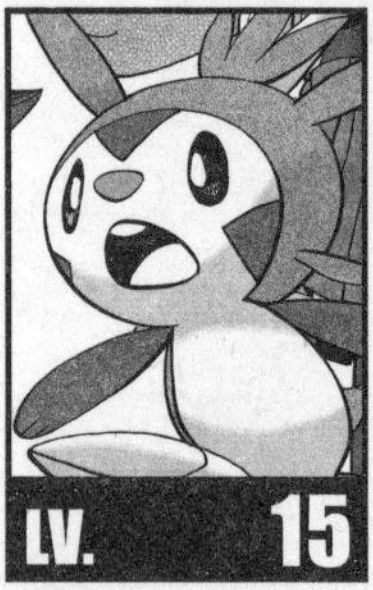
LV. 15

- Coastal Kalos Pokédex: No. 002
- Type: Grass
- Height: 1'04"
- Weight: 19.8 lbs
- Ability: Overgrow
- Nature: Hardy
- Characteristic: Somewhat stubborn

The Spiny Nut Pokémon that was sent over from Professor Sycamore. It fights using the spikes on its head.

### Salamè
(Charmander ♀)

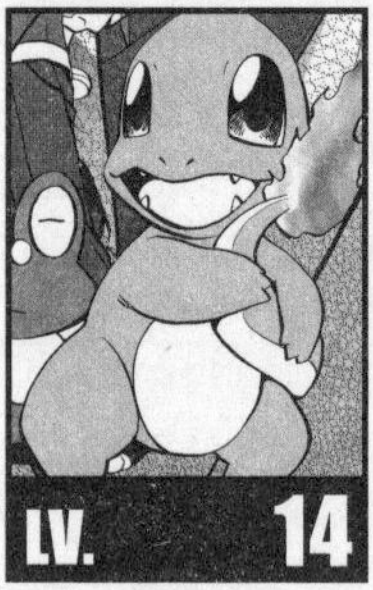
LV. 14

- Coastal Kalos Pokédex: No. 083
- Type: Fire
- Height: 2'00"
- Weight: 18.7 lbs
- Ability: Blaze
- Nature: Lonely
- Characteristic: Nods off a lot

Met X and the others after escaping from the research lab. Is there a reason it is always holding onto its tail?

### Élec
(Manectric ♂)

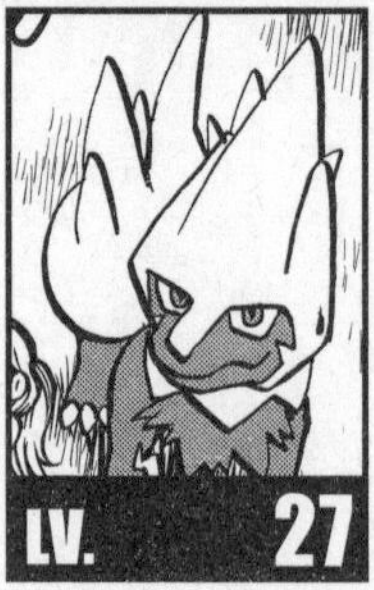
LV. 27

- Coastal Kalos Pokédex: No. 074
- Type: Electric
- Height: 4'11"
- Weight: 88.6 lbs
- Ability: Lightning Rod
- Nature: Naughty
- Characteristic: Mischievous

It followed X and his friends from Prism Tower in search of Manectite. It is currently in the midst of a fierce battle. Who will win?!

## Y's Pokémon

Y soars through the sky in her sky suit. Reliable allies are starting to gather near her as she continues her journey.

**Fletchy**
(Fletchling ♀)

- Central Kalos Pokédex: No. 014
- Type: Normal, Flying
- Height: 1'00"
- Weight: 3.7 lbs
- Ability: Big Pecks
- Nature: Brave
- Characteristic: Highly curious

A Tiny Robin Pokémon that has been training together with Y for a long time. It attacks with its sharp beak but it has a beautiful voice when it sings!

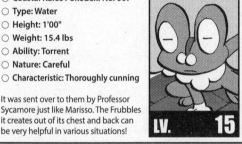

**Croaky**
(Froakie ♂)

- Coastal Kalos Pokédex: No. 007
- Type: Water
- Height: 1'00"
- Weight: 15.4 lbs
- Ability: Torrent
- Nature: Careful
- Characteristic: Thoroughly cunning

It was sent over to them by Professor Sycamore just like Marisso. The Frubbles it creates out of its chest and back can be very helpful in various situations!

**Veevee**
(Sylveon ♀)

- Coastal Kalos Pokédex: No. 085
- Type: Fairy
- Height: 3'03"
- Weight: 51.8 lbs
- Ability: Cute Charm
- Nature: Gentle
- Characteristic: Likes to relax

Y and Veevee grew a lot closer to each other after playing the mini-games and it evolved into Sylveon during the battle against a Team Flare grunt. A super cute Pokémon!!

**Rhyrhy**
(Rhyhorn ♂)

- Coastal Kalos Pokédex: No. 050
- Type: Ground, Rock
- Height: 3'03"
- Weight: 253.5 lbs
- Ability: Rock Head
- Nature: Bashful
- Characteristic: Good endurance

A Rhyhorn race Pokémon. A traveling companion...or compartment for X who keeps the five friends together on their journey!!

# Message from
## Hidenori Kusaka

When I was in elementary school, my mother wanted me to become a public employee. Or if not a public employee, she told me to at least "get a job where you go to work at a fixed time and come back home at a fixed time." She must have basically been thinking of a typical nine-to-five job. But the reality is, my job is quite the opposite. I became a manga artist who pulls all-nighters a lot...! Sorry, Mom. My mother is now in heaven. And I am recalling my memories of her as I work on the story of Y and her mother.

# Message from
## Satoshi Yamamoto

The preceding edition of the X·Y arc was published starting in 2014 and came to somewhat of a conclusion after 12 volumes. Starting in *X·Y* volume 1, we have included the chapters from *Pokémon Fan* that were not included in the earlier edition of the *X·Y* graphic novels with hopes of creating the definitive edition. Also, to differentiate from the preceding edition, the cover illustration I drew is meant to be a re-creation of a scene from the story. I hope the people who have read the preceding edition will enjoy this as well.

**Hidenori Kusaka** is the writer for *Pokémon Adventures*. Running continuously for over 20 years, *Pokémon Adventures* is the only manga series to completely cover all the Pokémon games and has become one of the most popular series of all time. In addition to writing manga, he also edits children's books and plans mixed-media projects for Shogakukan's children's magazines. He uses the Pokémon Electrode as his author portrait.

---

**Satoshi Yamamoto** is the artist for *Pokémon Adventures*, which he began working on in 2001, starting with volume 10. Yamamoto launched his manga career in 1993 with the horror-action title *Kimen Senshi*, which ran in Shogakukan's *Weekly Shonen Sunday* magazine, followed by the series *Kaze no Denshosha*. Yamamoto's favorite manga creators/artists include FUJIKO F FUJIO (*Doraemon*), Yukinobu Hoshino (*2001 Nights*), and Katsuhiro Otomo (*Akira*). He loves films, monsters, detective novels, and punk rock music. He uses the Pokémon Swalot as his artist portrait.

**Pokémon ADVENTURES: X · Y**
Volume 2
VIZ Media Edition

**Story by HIDENORI KUSAKA**
**Art by SATOSHI YAMAMOTO**

©2022 Pokémon.
©1995–2020 Nintendo / Creatures Inc. / GAME FREAK inc.
TM, ®, and character names are trademarks of Nintendo.
POCKET MONSTERS SPECIAL Vol. 57
by Hidenori KUSAKA, Satoshi YAMAMOTO
© 1997 Hidenori KUSAKA, Satoshi YAMAMOTO
All rights reserved.
Original Japanese edition published by SHOGAKUKAN.
English translation rights in the United States of America,
Canada, the United Kingdom, Ireland, Australia and New Zealand
arranged with SHOGAKUKAN.

Translation/Tetsuichiro Miyaki
English Adaptation/Bryant Turnage
Touch-Up & Lettering/Annaliese "Ace" Christman, Susan Daigle-Leach
Original Series Design/Shawn Carrico
Original Series Editor/Annette Roman
Graphic Novel Design/Alice Lewis
Graphic Novel Editor/Joel Enos

Printed in the U.S.A.

Published by VIZ Media, LLC
P.O. Box 77010
San Francisco, CA 94107

10 9 8 7 6 5 4 3 2 1
First printing, May 2022

viz.com

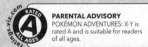

**PARENTAL ADVISORY**
POKÉMON ADVENTURES: X·Y is
rated A and is suitable for readers
of all ages.